Game of Queens

ALSO BY INDIA EDGHILL

Delilah

Wisdom's Daughter

Queenmaker

File M for Murder

India Edghill

GAME OF QUEENS

A NOVEL OF VASHTI AND ESTHER

St. Martin's Press
New York

www.stmartins.com

Designed by Kathryn Parise

The Library of Congress Cataloging-in-Publication Data
is available upon request.

ISBN 978-0-312-33893-0 (hardcover)
ISBN 978-1-4668-8366-6 (e-book)

First Edition: September 2015

10 9 8 7 6 5 4 3 2 1

Dedicated to my own beautiful Persian
who would not come when she was called

Vashti
1972–1990

One hell of a damn fine cat.

AUTHOR'S NOTE

When I read a historical novel, I always like to know what an author altered in the interest of telling a story. But when I started writing this author's note for *Game of Queens,* I realized there's so much background, and so many things I played with to create my own version of the Esther story that the explanations would be as long as the novel. So I'll just hit the highlights here, and if you have any questions about *Game of Queens,* email me at indiaedghill@gmail.com and I'll do my best to remember what I was thinking at the time I came up with My Brilliant Idea.

The perceptive reader (i.e., anyone who reads past page one) will notice the author has taken wild liberties with the original text. Among the more obvious alterations: handing the condemning of the Jews to someone other than the king, eliminating Esther's three-day fast, and cutting the number of banquets Esther gives to one.

The Bible happily conflates Cyrus the Great, who *actually* conquered Babylon, with Darius the Great, and gaily tosses in a Darius the Mede, just to drive writers nuts. I had to pick one, and went with Darius the Great. The Bible also makes Belshazzar Nebuchadnezzar's son, although he was really his grandson. Unless he's not related to him at all. (You're all clear on that? Good, because it confused the expletive-deleted out of me.)

And I had to pick a king because I happily combined Daniel's story with Vashti's and Esther's. I also combined Bel and the dragon, creating a dragon named Bel.

Okay, here we go, short notes first:

Note 1: All spellings are those from the King James version of the Bible. For example, Shushan, not Susa.
Note 2: The number of provinces in the Persian Empire is taken from the Book of Esther, which gives the number as 127. According to Herodotus, there were twenty, and modern estimates vary wildly.
Note 3: The name Bagoas may be the shortened form of names like Bagadata. Or it may mean "gift." Or it may mean "eunuch." Or it may not. I used a meaning that fit my story.
Note 4: Tradition says Vashti was Belshazzar's daughter. I made her his granddaughter.
Note 5: Marmoset—at this time, a name for any small monkey.
Note 6: Mordecai's refusal to bow to Haman is clearly Haman-specific, as Mordecai must be at least bowing to the king!
Note 7: Persians practically revered dogs, regarding them as almost sacred. I was absolutely delighted to discover this fact and promptly put as many dogs as I could justify to my editor into the story.
Note 8: Important Safety Tip: Unless you're a queen in a semifantastical, semihistorical novel, *wolves make absolutely dreadful pets*! Trust me on this.

And now the longer remarks:

Vashti, or, No Crown Is Worth This!

Traditionally, Vashti was considered something of a villainess—a disobedient wife who, in Jewish folklore, forced her Jewish slaves to work on the Sabbath. Naked. Fortunately, opinion has changed on Vashti; she is now often regarded as a woman of strong character who refused to obey a drunken summons to appear before men, in public, in a society in which decent women were strictly secluded. Ahasuerus ordered her to appear at his banquet wearing her royal crown; in some versions, Vashti was ordered to appear at the king's banquet wearing *only* her crown. When she refused to come at the king's bidding, Vashti was either divorced, exiled, or executed, depending on who's telling the story. The Bible doesn't say what happened to her, which gives novelists free rein to decide her fate.

For her refusal to obey an outrageous command, Vashti is now often lauded as a heroine. Works for me!

Esther, or, "Orphan" Is Not a Job Description

All the Bible says is that Esther is an orphan raised by her cousin. However, as time's gone by, she's become poorer and more simple with each iteration of the story; possibly to enhance its Cinderella-esque qualities. (Come to think of it, Esther's really the Perfect Disney Princess.) Nor does the Bible say girls were forcibly acquired for the world's most famous beauty contest, but many novels and all movie versions have soldiers dragging screaming girls off to the palace. I'm not sure why, as being Queen of Persia probably looked pretty desirable to the average Ancient Persian girl.

In the original, Mordecai tells Esther not to reveal that she's a Jew, and she successfully hides her origins—which I've always found implausible. Seriously, unless she was raised in a rain barrel on Mars, lots of people in Shushan must know that Mordecai—who *works in the palace*—has a cousin who's now in the women's palace. And surely there was *some* background checking of the contestants! (Perhaps when the story was originally told, people complained that Esther couldn't keep her origin secret because the palace gossip network would have the info about her all over Shushan in two seconds!)

The Royal Rascal: The Ahasuerus Problem

Ahasuerus, King of Kings, always presents a problem to the novelist: in the Bible he's mercurial, drunk, careless, and takes the advice of anyone who can make him stop drinking long enough to listen. The man doesn't even ask, "Which people need exterminating?," he just hands his royal seal to Haman, saying, "Do whatever you want"! Turning Ahasuerus into a desirable door prize is a major undertaking—which is how and why the ambitious and manipulative Queen Mother Amestris entered my story.

Was I Wazir?: The Haman Problem

Okay, I admit the Haman/Hitler parallels are eerie. A number of authors carry this equation to the extreme of (in one novel from about fifty years ago) giving Haman the swastika as his symbol and a personal army dressed in black. This ignores the fact that until the Nazis literally and figuratively reversed it, the swastika was a symbol of light and good for several thousand years. Tradition says Haman hated the Jews because Haman was descended from King Agag, who was killed by the Jewish prophet Samuel about five hundred years before. Eternal feuds have been carried on for less, but Haman really seems far more interested in personal power than avenging his ancestor. And he'll happily exterminate an entire race of people to get his own way. Frankly, the man's just plain evil.

Bigthan & Teresh: How Not to Carry Out a Murder

The eunuchs Bigthan and Teresh plan to kill King Ahasuerus, a plot point that sounds like something the original writer of Esther came up with because he (or she) needed Mordecai to save the king so later Haman has to honor Mordecai—because really, what good would killing the king do the two eunuchs? So I came up with a plausible scenario—plausible, anyway, if you assume both Bigthan and Teresh are idiots with seriously hurt feelings. Since they were discussing their Cunning Plan where they could be overheard, they don't seem to have been any too bright.

Oh, Susannah! or, Get Your Stories Straight Before Accusing the Innocent

There's a lot of argument about the actual creation and placement of the Susannah and the Elders story in the Daniel canon. (See the Anchor Bible, volume 44: *Daniel, Esther, and Jeremiah: the Additions* by Carey A. Moore.) Because it suited my plot, I set Susannah's peril just before Daniel leaves Babylon for Shushan. Note: There's no evidence Daniel was in Shushan during the Esther story. But there's no evidence that he *wasn't,* either.

Poppies Are For Lovers: The Story of Zariadres and Odatis

A very popular tale in the Persian Empire. (Warning! Spoilers!) Princess Odatis, the most beautiful girl in all Asia, sees Zariadres in a dream and falls in love with him. Zariadres sees Odatis in a dream and falls in love with her. Odatis's father wants her to marry one of his relatives, and invites the candidates for her hand to his palace. Odatis secretly invited Zariadres, who strides in, introduces himself to Odatis, and the two dream lovers flee to Zariadres' kingdom. How Odatis knew where to send the invitation isn't explained.

For readers who'd like still more about Queen Esther, there are plenty of sources to go to:

Novels about Queen Esther

Esther is understandably a hugely popular subject for novelists, so there are far too many to list here (and I'm pretty sure I've read most of them). Search for "Esther, Queen of Persia—Fiction" to track them down in your library system. I will, however, put in a shameless plug for one of my favorite books of all time: *Behold Your Queen!* by Gladys Malvern. This is the best novel about Esther ever written (I own two copies of the original 1958 edition) and it's at long, long last been reprinted and is once more available. Buy it and read it as soon as possible!

Movies about Queen Esther

Esther and the King (1960) starring Joan Collins attempting to be a Simple Jewish Orphan. This is the movie in which Queen Vashti is divorced for doing a strip-tease in front of the king; she also has an affair with Haman. (Trivia note: The actor playing Xerxes in *Esther and the King* played Leonidas in *The 300 Spartans*.)

Esther (1999) (a made-for-TV movie)

A Historia de Ester (Brazilian miniseries; eight hours of colorful enjoyment)

One Night with the King (lively, extravagant, and lots of fun to watch)

A Few of the Books I Read While Writing *Game of Queens*

The Anchor Bible: *The Book of Daniel* by Louis F. Hartman & Alexander A. Di Lella

The Anchor Bible: *The Book of Esther* by Carey A. Moore

The Anchor Bible: *Daniel, Esther, and Jeremiah: The Additions* by Carey A. Moore

Beauty Secrets of the Bible by Ginger Garrett
Biblical Women Unbound: Counter Tales by Norma Rosen
Dictionary of Ancient Deities by Patricia Turner & Charles Russell Coulter
The Holy Bible: King James Version
The Keeper of the Bed: The Story of the Eunuch by Charles Humana
The New Penguin Atlas of Ancient History
The Persian Empire by J. M. Cook
The Persians by Jim Hicks & Time-Life Books (The Emergence of Man Series)
Persians: Masters of Empire by Time-Life Books (Lost Civilizations Series)
Smith's Bible Dictionary
Vashti's Victory: And Other Biblical Women Resisting Injustice by LaVerne McCain Gill

Writing this book was a huge amount of fun. Not only did retelling Vashti's and Esther's stories give me the chance to wallow in research and to reread every Esther novel I could get my hands on (thank you, Adriance Memorial Library, Amazon, and ABEbooks.com), *Game of Queens* allowed me to fulfill a longtime dream: to write the kind of story in which the heroine has a pet wolf.

Happy reading!
India
www.indiaedghill.com

GAME OF QUEENS

PROLOGUE

Stars

HEGAI

Where does this tale truly begin? Does it start in the jeweled garden of the harem of the King of Kings, master of half the world? Shall I begin it there?

Or shall I begin it at an extravagant banquet on the night that a woman defied the King of Kings before all the nobles of the empire?

Shall I begin when the Queen Mother and the Grand Vizier plotted slaughter and treason—or with the extraordinary contest arranged to choose a new queen for a humiliated king?

Or perhaps I should first tell you of a battle fought over five hundred years ago, when one king surrendered to another, only to be beheaded by an outraged prophet—an act that created a feud between the descendants of King Agag and those of King Saul. Yes, that is a place I could begin, with the eternal hatred of the Agagites for the Jews.

But although that long-ago murder played its part in what follows, even that is not the true beginning.

Oh, you know a part of it already, but you only know what all the world knows. You have heard how Vashti, Queen of Queens, the most beautiful woman in all the empire, defied the king her husband and so lost her crown. You have heard how Ahasuerus, King of Kings, commanded the most beautiful maidens in his lands sent to him that he might chose a new queen. You have heard how he set the queen's crown upon the head of the virtuous and beautiful Jewess, Esther.

And you have heard how Queen Esther herself defied both king and law to save her people from the fate the evil Prince Haman had prepared for them.

But beyond that, you do not know what truly happened, for you were not there. I was. I am Hegai, who once ruled the imperial harem. I was there. Oh, yes, I was there when this great and deadly game began. When a beautiful woman deceived her cruel husband, and he plotted his revenge—and so set in motion his own destruction.

For from that commonplace tragedy—a wife's unfaithfulness and its discovery by a furious husband—all the rest flowed, unstoppable as a river in full flood, relentless as time. Its force altered forever the lives of everyone trapped within its current.

But the game we all played began long before any of its players were born. It began in the decadent court of old Babylon. It began when a man I would not meet for many years saved the life of a woman I would never know. . . .

BOOK ONE

The Lion's Den

DANIEL

Somehow, Daniel was not surprised when Mordecai the Scribe came to his small courtyard asking advice and counsel. Having sent his cousin into the snake pit of the King's Palace to become queen or concubine—or nothing, Mordecai now tormented himself.

"You wish to know if you have acted rightly," Daniel said, before Mordecai could speak more than a few words of petition.

Mordecai stared; behind him, Daniel heard a muffled laugh from Samamat. Mordecai's mouth thinned, but he said nothing. To ease Mordecai's mind, Daniel motioned to Samamat, who obligingly vanished into the house. Among the many things Mordecai the pious disliked was Daniel's Gentile wife.

"You are wise indeed," Mordecai said when Samamat had left the two men alone, and Daniel smiled.

"It takes no wisdom to know that a man who's made a fateful decision is troubled in his mind."

"Then tell me—did I act rightly? My cousin . . ." Mordecai hesitated, finally said, "She was not willing. I ordered her to put her name into the contest. We parted ill."

"Did you beat her?" Daniel asked, and Mordecai stiffened, affronted.

"No, of course not."

"Did you force her to drink wine until she no longer knew what she was doing?"

"No!"

"Did you yourself drop her name into the basket?"

"No. The rules—"

"The rules decree that each maiden place her own name in the basket with her own hand." Daniel sighed. "Mordecai, you may have ordered Hadassah to do so—but she herself chose to let her name fall into that basket. I don't suppose you told her why you demanded she enter the contest for queen?"

Mordecai's cheeks burned a dull red; it didn't take any particular talent to interpret that sign. Daniel sighed, and said, with calm certainty, "Well perhaps that was wise. But telling a dream may change a future." Of course, so could not telling a dream. But that was something Mordecai did not need to hear from him now. "Done is done," Daniel added.

"Yes, done is done. But did I act rightly? Did I place too much faith in a dream, and not enough in the Lord our God?"

Daniel sighed. "Mordecai, I am a very old man, and one of the privileges of being very old is that I can afford to tell the truth. And the truth is that no matter what gods we worship, we all cling to dreams and omens and portents to give us hope. And who can say in what form God sends us messages? Are you going to rebuke the Lord for sending a dream, rather than a messenger with a proclamation written in the Lord's own hand?"

For a moment, Daniel thought Mordecai would melt in outrage. "That—that is—"

"Blasphemy? No, Mordecai, it is not. Or do you think the Lord so powerless He cannot chastise me if I displease Him?"

Daniel watched with interest as Mordecai struggled to remain calm. He didn't doubt Mordecai would triumph over his anger; he also doubted Mordecai would choose to truly listen. Daniel's views were too far removed from those of a conventionally pious man like Mordecai.

"You talk like a Persian," Mordecai said at last. "You live like a Persian. And yet—you are right. If what you do is displeasing in the Lord's eyes, it is for Him to punish you, not I."

"You don't approve," Daniel said, and smiled. "Oh, I take no offense—sometimes I don't approve either."

"Then why do you live as you do?"

"Because I can do nothing else and live with a happy heart. And the older I grow, the more I value happiness and kindness over the crueler virtues."

Mordecai shook his head. "Happiness is not a virtue, Daniel."

"No? Perhaps I lived too long in Babylon—or too long here in Shushan, where the gods love lovers."

"That is no way for a good Jew to talk."

"Perhaps I am no longer a good Jew, then. We dwell in Ishtar's city, Mordecai. Sometimes I do not think the Most High rules here."

"Our Lord rules all the heavens and all the earth. How can you—you, who foretold His judgments, whom He saved from savage death—how can you, of all men living, speak so?"

Daniel stared into the dancing blue flames. At last he said, "As I have said, I can speak so because I am old now, and speak my own truth. No one else's—not even God's. If you do not like what I have to say, you are free to leave and seek counsel elsewhere."

Daniel remained sitting by the brazier long after Mordecai left. He did not often let himself dream, for he dreamed now only of the long-dead past. The past, and those who had gone before him into whatever waited after a man finished with this world. Golden days, when he had been young, and been loved. . . .

Too well loved, sometimes. King Nebuchadnezzar's love had nearly killed him.

But that was not truly love. That was fear and despair and madness. It is hard for kings to love.

More fortunate than kings, Daniel had known true love and true friendship; cherished both beyond pearls.

Arioch. Arioch and Samamat . . .

So many years, yet even now the memory of Arioch's wry comments brought a smile to Daniel's lips. The famed night Daniel had spent imprisoned with the king's lions, fierce beasts that had slept peacefully beside Daniel all that long night, so that he had walked out of the cage whole and free at the next dawn.

"You see, Arioch? Faith kept me safe."

"What kept you safe was me feeding those lions enough poppy syrup to keep a dragon snoring for a week. Do you have any idea how much that amount of poppy cost?*"*

"I had faith in you," Daniel had answered, and Arioch smiled. . . .

Daniel never had been able to resist Arioch's smile. Always Arioch seemed to mock himself more than he did others.

It was hard, now, to remember why he had fought so hard against—not Arioch, but himself. What he felt for Arioch was forbidden twice over. Abomination; unclean; if his forefathers knew the pit Daniel had fallen into, they would stone him. Yes, that was the punishment. *In Israel, I would be damned for both my power and my love. Fortunately, I dwell in Persia. . . .*

It had been the third and last year of King Jehoiakim's reign; the year Nebuchadnezzar of Babylon had swept through Israel and its land and cities had fallen into his hands. Even Jerusalem the Bride had opened her wide bronze gates to King Nebuchadnezzar. The conqueror had returned in triumph to Babylon, taking Israel's treasure with him, including the best-born youths and maidens of the Twelve Tribes. Among that living treasure had been Daniel.

I was so young then. And so self-righteous!

Daniel had barely been fourteen when he had walked behind King Nebuchadnezzar's chariot down Babylon's Sacred Way, between sky-blue walls that led to the Ishtar Gate. Fourteen, and convinced of the utter righteousness of the way of the Lord, and of his own ability to follow the Lord's covenants. If he'd been less stiff-necked, he might not have fallen so hard when faced with temptation—oh, not the obvious lures of unclean food and pagan idolatry. Avoiding those had been easy, and his piety had impressed even the Babylonians.

The temptations of the heart... Those were invisible snares, catching him unaware.

At first life at Nebuchadnezzar's court dazzled him; a life rich and strange, redolent of sin and power. Daniel had been a beautiful boy, and had found instant favor in the sight of the prince over the eunuchs who had charge of training the new arrivals from Jerusalem in the behavior expected in the court of a great king. He had permitted Daniel and his equally stiff-necked friends Hananiah, Mishael, and Azariah to choose their own food, to say their own prayers. He had even permitted them to choose their own Babylonian names. The other three had searched long and hard to find names that would convey they were still good pious servants of the Most High God. Hananiah became Shadrach, under the "protection of the Lord." Mishael decided on Meshach, "drawing with the Lord's power," while Azariah now was Abednego, "servant of light."

And Daniel had chosen Belteshazzar.

One who lays up treasures in secret. Daniel kept secrets, both his own and those of others. Daniel had grown up at the Babylonian court; learned that a shy smile and a soft word about his duty to his own God won him approbation, where Mishael, Hananiah, and Azariah's flat insistence on their own ways in everything but serving the king gained nothing. Since influence ruled in the Babylonian court, Daniel thought it better to garner goodwill.

"Someday we'll need friends and favors," he told his three friends, a truth they hotly denied.

"We do our tasks well. We serve Nebuchadnezzar in the proper fashion. Nothing more can be asked of us," Mishael said. Daniel could not agree, but he did not argue.

At least I avoided the sin of pride. But he had enjoyed the luxury and power that came with being a court favorite. And had remained convinced of his purity of heart, mind, and body.

Until I met Arioch.

It had been one of King Nebuchadnezzar's increasingly-rare calm days, and the king had decided to visit the Temple of Ishtar and ordered everyone in the court to accompany him. Daniel had been swept up in the crowd jostling for position, trying to gain a spot close to the king. After a few useless attempts to drop out of the impromptu procession, Daniel had concentrated on not stumbling. He suspected that if he fell, the courtiers would simply trample him in their rush to convince King Nebuchadnezzar of their loyalty and piety.

Despite the fact that a tunnel led directly from the palace to Ishtar's temple, King Nebuchadnezzar led his followers out the main palace gate, through the Northern Fortress, and swung around to re-enter Babylon by the Processional Avenue. The king strode between the brilliantly blue-tiled walls, ignoring the strikingly lifelike images of bulls, sirrush, and lions set into the blue tile. After this long detour, the king and his followers at last entered the Temple of Ishtar.

As the courtiers filed into the temple, Daniel struggled to free himself from the current forcing him to follow Ishtar's worshippers. Up steps inlaid with white marble doves, between tall crimson pillars—in a moment he'd be swept into the temple itself—

A strong hand clamped onto his arm, hauled him sideways. In the shelter of one of the pillars, Daniel gasped out his thanks.

"Well, you didn't look as if you were passionately devoted to Our Lady of Stars."

Daniel found himself staring into eyes steady and golden as a lion's. "Thank you," he said again. "I can't enter Ishtar's temple. Any Babylonian god's temple."

"Why not?" his rescuer asked.

After a moment, Daniel settled for, "Because my god wouldn't like it." Daniel studied the man who had saved him from angering the Lord. Taller and older than Daniel; the strong planes of his face hardened by wind and sun. Daniel needed no special wisdom to know this man was no courtier, for he wore the dark blue tunic and gold trousers of the king's guard.

"Who's your god, and why is he quarreling with Ishtar?"

"He isn't quarreling with Ishtar—well, I suppose in a sense He is, but—" Daniel looked at his rescuer; saw laughter in his eyes. "It doesn't matter," Daniel said. "Thank you. I'm Daniel, but in the palace they call me Belteshazzar."

"Arioch. Captain in the king's guard." Arioch studied Daniel for a moment. "You're the fortune-teller, aren't you?"

"Not really." Daniel had no idea how interpreting a few simple dreams for some of the palace servants had transmuted into an ability to predict the future. "I can explain what dreams mean. Sometimes, that is. If the Lord grants me that wisdom."

Arioch glanced at the temple doorway and sighed. "Well, your Lord must just have granted me wisdom, because I predict we'll be waiting here for hours. Fortunately, I happen to have brought along these." Arioch pulled a set of gambling pieces out of his belt pouch. "Care for a game?"

"Yes," Daniel said, and held out his hand for the *pur.*

By the time King Nebuchadnezzar finally left the Temple of Ishtar, Daniel and Arioch had each won and lost great, if illusory, fortunes. In the process, Daniel saw his own future, saw his life entwined with Arioch's.

Impossible. But to the end of his days, Daniel remembered his first sight of Arioch's eyes. A lion's eyes . . .

Proud as a lion, too. And as lazy, sometimes. Arioch never saw the point of doing well what didn't need doing at all—"Or at least not by me, Daniel. Not by me."

And then there had been Samamat. Samamat with her brilliant mind and her wide blue eyes, her sun-gold hair and loving heart. Impossible to think of Arioch and not of Samamat as well.

She was a Chaldean, brought from the ancient city of Ur when Babylon's king collected boys and girls as if they were gems. Samamat's skill was astrology. As Daniel knew dreams, she knew the stars. She could read the heavens as easily as she could a scroll, and see futures written there.

One of King Nebuchadnezzar's ill-fated hunting trips bound the three of them together. Arioch was there because he was captain of the king's guard. Samamat was there because the king needed someone to read the stars. Daniel—Daniel wasn't sure why he'd been there, but he'd been ordered to come along, and so there he was, trying to stay on the back of a horse.

The king's hunting parties tended to resemble a rather eclectic army on the march. A mix of warriors, courtiers, courtesans, concubines, and even a few of the king's huntsmen, the assemblage moved at the languid pace of the palanquins carrying the women and eunuchs. Except, of course, when Nebuchadnezzar lost what little patience he had and whipped his horse into a gallop, an action that caused the king's guard to bolt after him and the rest of the horde to mill around aimlessly.

Eventually the entire crowd came to the campsite, and after several hours of chaos, during which the Chief Eunuch announced no less than three times that he would fling himself under the feet of the king's elephants if the women's pavilion was not raised *this instant* and the Chief Huntsman complained that any animal that wasn't deaf had long since fled, Daniel was able to find the tent assigned to him and collapse onto the bed. The next morning he rose early—the noise from the animals and the guards made that easy—and walked through the tents until he reached the edge of the camp. He stared at the vast forest that lay waiting, indifferent to the fate awaiting it and its inhabitants.

"I wish I hadn't come," he muttered, and whipped around when a soft voice said,

"I wish I hadn't come either."

Daniel found himself staring into very blue eyes. She was nearly as tall as he, and wore a long vest over a tunic and trousers. Glittering silver stars were so thickly embroidered over the vest they almost hid its midnight-blue color. Her hair was cut unnaturally short; it was the color of sunlight and honey.

"You're a woman." Daniel realized it was an idiotic comment the moment the words left his mouth.

"Yes, I am." Clearly she was used to such idiotic comments. "I'm Samamat. I'm an astrologer."

That explained the starred vest and her oddly shorn hair; Daniel supposed she'd left the astrologer's elaborate headdress back in her tent. "I'm Daniel. I—well, I'm in attendance on the court. And the king. When he remembers who I am."

She glanced around. "Be careful. Words carry."

"No one else is awake yet."

"The guards are, and the grooms. It only takes one word, Daniel."

Daniel understood. King Nebuchadnezzar was half-mad at least half the time, and the other half he was over-conciliatory and morose. The court trembled, never knowing which king would summon them: the mad or the sane. A noise behind him—Daniel turned and watched a groom lead a pair of horses past.

"Beautiful sunrise," Samamat said.

"Yes, very."

They stood watching the sun climb higher into the sky. Vivid blue seemed to arch to forever. "I wonder what the sun is, really," Daniel said. "It looks like a ball of fire, doesn't it?"

"I have a theory about that." Samamat put her hand up to her forehead, shading her eyes against the sun's burning brightness. "I think the sun is just like the stars. I think somewhere someone is watching the sun as a star in his night sky." She turned to Daniel. "I suppose you think that sounds completely mad."

It did sound completely mad, but Daniel managed to not say so. "Well, you're the one who knows the stars. Do you read the sun, too, then?"

"I haven't been able to do that yet. Maybe I'm too close to it." She shrugged; silver stars glinted. "Are you going hunting, Daniel?"

"I'm doing whatever King Nebuchadnezzar commands," Daniel said.

The hunting party could have been a disaster—it was one of what Daniel thought of as the king's furious days, and even on the briefest of acquaintances he already knew that Samamat might be a brilliant astrologer, but she made a poor courtier—but Arioch had joined Daniel and Samamat once the hunting party raised enough dust to obscure clear vision. And then, somehow, the three of them had become separated from the king's party.

"I don't know how that happened," Arioch said blandly, when Daniel looked around and pointed out they were out of sight of the main band of hunters. "Well, come on. I'm sure we'll find them soon."

"Yes," Samamat agreed. "How can you hide two hundred men and two dozen chariots?"

The answer seemed to be "easily enough." Arioch led Daniel and Samamat on a long, rambling walk through underbrush and scrub. Eventually Daniel stopped worrying about the king, and concentrated on following

Arioch. He'd thought he'd need to assist Samamat, but the woman seemed as lithe and energetic as a cheetah.

"Slow down," Daniel finally begged her, as she disappeared around another clump of wild lilac. Apparently she listened, for Daniel nearly bumped into her; she'd stopped and now stood idol-still, staring at a mass of broken stone.

Ruins. No surprise; the plains of Babylon were littered with the bones of shattered empires.

"I saw something like that in Egypt once." Arioch regarded the curve of broken stone as if he disapproved of it. And when Daniel and Samamat moved closer, and put their hands out to the relic, Arioch snapped, "Don't touch it!"

Daniel stopped, his hand almost to the stone. "Why not?"

"Oh, I don't know. Because it's bad luck to meddle with other people's gods? Just leave it."

"I think this is the constellation of the Hunter," Samamat began, reaching toward one of the raised symbols on the arch, and Arioch grabbed her hand.

"What is it about *do not touch that thing* that you do not understand?" Arioch demanded. He and Samamat stared into each other's eyes for what seemed to Daniel an unseemly length of time. At last Arioch let go of Samamat, and she stepped back.

"We're going back to the king's camp. Now," Arioch said. He strode off, leaving Samamat and Daniel to follow or not, as they choose.

"I guess we'd better do as he says," Samamat said. "After all, he's captain of the king's guard."

And that makes him always right, I suppose. But Daniel didn't say the words. He merely nodded, and walked beside Samamat after Arioch. When at last they returned to the king's camp, no one seemed to notice they had ever been gone—for which Daniel gave grateful thanks to the Lord. King Nebuchadnezzar's notice could be a dangerous thing.

That evening the three of them ate together and talked; since Arioch was almost as unwilling as Daniel to talk about himself, it didn't take long to learn each other's stories. Daniel had explained he was one of the Judean captives and worked in the palace.

"And—?" Samamat said, raising her eyebrows.

"And what?" Daniel stared at the bowl in his hands. Was the meat in the stew lawful to eat? It was lamb, after all. . . .

Samamat sighed and leaned forward. "And what do you do in the palace? How long have you lived there?"

"Well, there's not really much to tell. Really. I'm just one of the king's servants at court."

Samamat sighed dramatically and shook her head.

"What?" Daniel looked at Samamat, her hair gleaming in the firelight. "What else is there to tell?"

"You know, Daniel. Only everything," Arioch said.

"I'm really a very dull person," Daniel told them, and Samamat laughed ruefully and shook her head. She slanted a glance at Arioch.

"What about you, Arioch?" Daniel asked, trying to turn the conversation away from himself.

Arioch shrugged. "I'm a soldier. What else is there to tell?"

"Only everything." Daniel looked at Arioch's firmly shut mouth and realized he wasn't going to hear "everything"—at least not tonight. Apparently Samamat understood that too, because when Daniel turned to her, she smiled.

"Do you really want to hear *everything,* Daniel? Because I must warn you it's amazingly dull." Samamat's gaze flashed to Arioch, who merely stared up at the night sky.

Why do I suspect that "everything" includes a great deal of Arioch? Daniel decided not to voice that suspicion; statements of fact based firmly on common sense and observation had led to his undeserved reputation for unearthly wisdom. "I want to hear whatever you want to tell, Sama."

Samamat laughed. "Now that's not truth. You certainly don't want to hear about the conjugations of the stars and how the gods use them to influence men."

"Even that. It's still better than listening to Ari *not* telling us about his life."

"Not what you'd say if I did tell you about it," Arioch said. "March and wait and fight. Oh, and sometimes we wait and march and then fight. That's about it."

"Of course," said Daniel. "So . . . Sama?"

She regarded Arioch with exasperated fondness. "Just remember, Commander-of-a-Thousand Arioch, this is your own fault."

"Oh, absolutely. Go ahead, tell us all about the conjugations of the stars." Arioch leaned back against the tent pole and closed his eyes.

"Very well, but remember I'm an astrologer, not a storyteller." Samamat drew in a deep breath and began, "I was born in Ur, and my family supplied astrologers to priests and kings as far back as—as—"

"—as they could make it up," Arioch said without opening his eyes.

"At least as far as that." Samamat smiled at Daniel, who smiled back. "The stars are in our blood, a gift from the gods. I grew up hearing my father and my uncles and my brothers talk about the stars and how to read them, and how to interpret their meanings. At night I slipped out of bed and went up to the rooftop to see the stars for myself. I even coaxed my father into taking me to the observatory to watch as he worked.

"I had the gift too. I listened, and learned to chart the night sky, and to understand what the stars told me. But when I told my father—" She looked up into the brilliant river of stars flowing across the heavens. "Well, he—"

"He didn't believe you," said Daniel, when Samamat seemed unable to continue.

"What a surprise." Without opening his eyes, Arioch reached over and touched Samamat's hand. Samamat lowered her eyes from the river of stars pouring across the midnight sky, seemed to return from far away.

"No, he didn't believe me. And he wouldn't even give me a chance to prove myself. When I asked why, all he would say was that girls couldn't be astrologers. And when I asked why not, all he would say was there weren't any women astrologers."

"Perfectly circular logic." Daniel thought you didn't have to be a Master of Dreams to know that Samamat had paid a high price for hers.

"And perfectly ridiculous," Arioch added, and Samamat laughed a bit unsteadily.

"I thought so," she said. "So I ran away to the most famous astrologer in all Chaldea. He tested me and learned I spoke the truth when I said I could read the stars. And he cared more about what I could do than about how I looked."

"Dead, was he?" Arioch asked, and Samamat threw a cherry at him.

"No, blind," she said, and laughed, rather shakily. "Neither, but he was"—she frowned, as if seeking an elusive word—"otherworldly," she finished at last. "As if he saw even more than—well, than Daniel here does."

"Me?" said Daniel. "I don't see anything special."

"Of course not." Arioch raised his eyebrows at Samamat, who merely shook her head.

"Do you realize we've been talking since sunset and you two have barely said a dozen words each? *Men,*" Samamat said disgustedly.

"I'd rather listen than talk." Daniel would certainly rather look at Samamat as she spoke. He supposed she was beautiful; but it wasn't her sun-gold hair and sky-blue eyes that drew his gaze to her face. *She's good and wise and strong. She's not a Jew, but she's a woman of valor. Above rubies.*

"What are you thinking about so intently?" Samamat asked, pulling Daniel abruptly back from his contemplation of her virtues. Unable to think of an unrevealing answer, he fumbled with the bowl he held, as if the lamb stew sought to escape.

"Stop asking questions you already know the answer to," Arioch told Samamat, who laughed. She took the bowl from Daniel's hands and set it on the ground.

"Look up," she said. "Look up, Daniel, and I'll read the stars for you."

Unlike as they were, the three still became close friends. Daniel had not known, before, that men and women could be friends. But Samamat *was* his friend; he hoped, wistfully, that someday she might be more. Just as Arioch was his friend, and must never be more than that. Daniel had violated many commandments; had savored pleasures his stern God would not approve of—although Daniel had never been struck down for any of them, so perhaps God wasn't nearly as strict as Shadrach.

But in this—No, never more than friends.

And Arioch's heart belonged to Samamat, although neither Arioch nor Samamat seemed willing to admit that truth. Still, some of Arioch's love belonged to Daniel. It would be easy to claim more—so easy—Daniel knew that, and knew that he should not surrender to the urgings of his heart. No, that he *must* not. He wasn't a boy now, but a man.

Youth and innocence would no longer serve as an excuse.

"Daniel? *Daniel!*"

Violent pounding on his door; shouting that pulled him out of dreamless sleep. *It's deep night. What—?*

"Daniel!"

The pounding continued; awake now, Daniel recognized Arioch's voice. Fumbling for his robe, Daniel rolled out of bed, wondering vaguely where the servants were. *Oh, well, if Arioch wanted to come in, the servants wouldn't be much use in keeping him out. But this isn't a very discreet visit—*

Daniel flung the robe over his head and groped for the door. He set his hand on the latch and drew the bolt. "Arioch, are you drunk? It's the middle of the night."

Arioch stopped his fist just as he was about to pound on Daniel's chest. "It's whatever time the king may-he-live-forever says it is. And he says it's time to play guessing games."

"What?" Daniel stared at Arioch, who looked neither drunk nor amused. In fact, if Daniel didn't know Arioch couldn't be frightened by dragons or lions, he'd say Arioch was afraid. "Arioch, what's wrong?" Daniel grabbed Arioch's arm and hauled him into the bedchamber.

"Good idea," Arioch said, and slammed the door shut and threw the bolt home. "That ought to keep the servants out. Where's the lamp? Forget it, we don't need one. Listen, Daniel—the king's gone mad. Truly mad."

"What?" Of course, Nebuchadnezzar had always been high-strung, even erratic, but mad? *It's Arioch who sounds mad.* Daniel spoke calmly, striving to soothe his friend. "Arioch, calm yourself. Now tell me what's sent you here at this hour—and in this state. Slowly, please."

"Right." Arioch drew a deep breath. "Well, the king woke up at midnight screaming loud enough to wake the dead in the lowest level of hell. All the guards *in* his chamber ran out and all the ones in the hall ran in and by the time they got sorted out, someone had had the sense to wake me up."

As Arioch paused for breath, Daniel said, "Shall I call a servant to bring you some wine? Beer? Anything?"

"We don't want a servant hearing this, and if I never smell wine again it'll be too soon after tonight. But you need to hear the whole story before you talk to the king. So I run through the palace and get to the king's bedchamber—"

And there had stood Nebuchadnezzar, stark naked except for his crown and with his body dripping red liquid.

"It was wine," Arioch explained.

Nebuchadnezzar glared at Arioch—"As if I'd woken him up, instead of the other way around"—and howled. The only word understandable was "dream."

"So I got the idea that the king had suffered a bad dream. Which was better than my first thought, which was someone had slipped past his guards with a poisoned dagger."

Nebuchadnezzar had dreamed. He had dreamed vividly, disturbingly, fearfully. The dream had troubled him so he had woken shouting and trembling and soaked with sweat. Fearful he'd find it gone, he had reached for his crown and set it upon his head. He had demanded wine, and more wine, and instead of drinking, he ordered the guards to pour it over his body. He stared at Arioch and issued an order—

"Bring all the magicians and wise men and sorcerers and astrologers—"

Somehow Daniel had known the word "astrologers" would follow "sorcerers." *I don't like this. I have a bad feeling about this. I'm so glad I have no special talent—*

"—to him *right then.* In his bedchamber."

"In his *bedchamber?*"

"That's right." Arioch leaned against the door. "I got out of that by pointing out—with great and dutiful subservience—that they wouldn't all fit in his bedchamber. And that it would be much more in keeping with the glory of the King of Kings for the mages and sorcerers and astrologers to be brought before him in his throne room. When he was dressed."

"Arioch, you didn't say that?"

"Oh, but I did. Not quite in those words. You'd be surprised how tactful I can be when my head's on the line. So the King of Kings calmed down and agreed that it would be much more proper for the mages and so on to see him as the King of Kings should be seen. So his servants started wiping wine off him and I went off to carry out my orders."

Interpreting the king's order to mean only those who dwelt within the palaces and directly served the king's court, Arioch sent men to wake the required magi, sorcerers, and astrologers. They were told to gather in the throne room, and not to waste time getting dressed. Arioch had woken Samamat himself, and explained the crisis to her, and personally escorted her to the throne room.

"I told her to be tactful, Daniel. No matter what the king did."

Of course you did, Arioch. I'm sure she listened as well as she always does.

The hastily assembled experts in magic, spells, charms, incantations, and stars confronted the King of Kings in all his jeweled splendor. Nebuchadnezzar glared down from his high gold throne and announced that they had been summoned because he had dreamed a dream and his spirit was deeply troubled. The King of Kings wished to know what his dream meant. The most exalted in rank of the experts bowed deeply and most humbly asked the King of Kings to retell his dream, that it might be interpreted for him.

I have a very *bad feeling about this—*

"And that's when Nebuchadnezzar said he couldn't remember what the dream was."

"What?"

"And . . . that's . . . when . . ." Arioch began to repeat very slowly.

"All right, I understand. The king couldn't remember his dream. Then why did—"

"He call in all the magi and the rest? Because he wants this dream that he doesn't remember interpreted. And if they can't do it, Daniel, he's ordered them all executed. Them and every other dealer in magic and science in the whole city—or maybe in the whole kingdom. I'm not quite clear on that one yet."

Daniel stood very still and reminded himself that invoking the name of the Lord in vain broke one of the Commandments. For a few moments neither man spoke. At last Daniel said, "And I suppose Samamat—"

"Couldn't keep her mouth shut? Of course not, Daniel. Why would she do a sensible thing like that? No, she bowed and *most* respectfully beseeched the King of Kings to wrack his royal brains and see if maybe he could remember just a little bit of the dream, which would really help his loyal and obedient subjects interpret it for him. So then he ordered Samamat to tell him his dream."

Oh, no. "And she said—?"

Arioch sighed. "She said the stars don't tell things like that. They—oh, you know what she talks like. I can't understand half of it. What it boiled down to is another *I don't know.* And the king doesn't like that answer."

"But it's the truth."

"Of course it's the truth. The king's *mad,* Daniel. He doesn't even remember the damned dream. Assuming he had a dream in the first place, and not just a hangover."

"And you want me to talk to him?" Daniel's mind always clung to details; he hadn't forgotten Arioch's statement when the story began. "If he's mad, what am *I* going to be able to do?"

"I don't know, Daniel. Think of something? Because if you don't Samamat and the rest of the astrologers are going to be lion food. And that's if they're *lucky.* Come on." Arioch grabbed Daniel's arm and Daniel heard the bolt slide back.

"Wait, Arioch."

"Daniel, there's no *time.* He could be sending for lions right now."

Arioch's fear beat against him; Daniel forced himself to summon calm. Nothing, absolutely nothing, would be gained by unruly haste. "Arioch, I have to think. And I have to dress."

"Think while you dress then. And think hard."

✦

Daniel barely noticed what his servants chose for him to wear. He was trying to think hard, and failing. At last he abandoned the attempt; ordered his panic-stricken servants to leave him. When he and Arioch once more stood alone in the bedchamber, Daniel held up his hands. As Arioch began to speak, Daniel said, "Give me silence, for a little time. Your patience will help, too."

"We haven't *got* a little time, Daniel."

"I know. I know. Just—wait. Please."

Arioch shook his head, but stepped back and folded his arms. Daniel cupped his hands before his face and closed his eyes. *O my Lord God, You who are king over all the world and the stars, help me. I know I have fallen from grace in Your eyes, but I ask your aid.* A warm certainty filled him; yes, this was right. Ask and it shall be granted. *Give me the wisdom to*—To what? The certainty faded. No one knew better than Daniel how vital it was to make the proper petition. To ask for the right thing. Should he lay the whole burden upon his God?

No. This is my task—*I know this task has been set for me, but I need Your help. Give me the wisdom to calm the raging king, and to bring peace back to his life.*

Slowly, Daniel lowered his hands. How odd; he'd intended to ask help to save Samamat. And the others, of course. But he had asked what he had asked, and it was too late to change his words. . . .

"Are you ready *now,* Daniel?" Arioch asked, shifting restlessly, and Daniel nodded.

"Yes, Arioch. I'm ready. Take me before the king."

"O great king, I have found a man who will tell you your dream. Live forever." Arioch bowed and nudged Daniel with his elbow. Daniel bowed and began the long walk between the rows of terrified mages, sorcerers, and astrologers to the steps leading up to the king's throne.

He walked slowly, making each pace deliberate, measured. At the steps of the throne, he bowed again. He hoped his slow, steady movements would calm the king, that he would seem no threat to whatever raged within Nebuchadnezzar.

"O king, live forever. How may I serve the king?" Daniel's voice soothed, coaxed. King Nebuchadnezzar's glare softened.

"I have dreamed a dream," the king said. "And I would know its meaning. And none of these useless creatures"—Nebuchadnezzar swept his scepter in a wide arc, aiming it at his fearful audience—"will tell it to me. If you can tell me, I will raise you high above all other men, and if you cannot, you and all these worthless mages will be cut into a thousand pieces and fed to the royal lions. Now what dream troubles me?"

Daniel glanced over at Samamat. She smiled encouragingly, nodded very slightly; Daniel hoped he would prove worthy of her faith in him. He drew a deep breath, and began.

"O great king, I myself am nothing, but God in heaven is great, and He reveals secrets. He makes known your dream to you."

Nebuchadnezzar's eyes narrowed. "You don't know. You're trying to gain time, just as the others did. Arioch, you've deceived me!"

Daniel took a step forward. "No! This is your dream, O king—" Certainty filled him; gave his voice strength. "You saw a huge image, the image of a king. His head was of gold and his chest and arms were silver. His thighs were brass and his legs iron, and his feet were made of clay."

The king was leaning forward, intent on Daniel's words. His rapt silence gave Daniel new strength. Apparently this hastily spun dream appealed to the king.

"And then—then a stone hit the image and it fell to pieces and was carried away upon the winds. The stone became a mountain, filling all the earth." *I have no idea what I'm saying. But whatever it is, Nebuchadnezzar seems to like it. Thank you, God of my fathers.*

"Yes. Yes, that is it. That is my dream!" Nebuchadnezzar clapped his hands together in childish delight. "And its meaning? Tell me that! Tell me!"

Daniel bowed again, and took a moment to stare at the inlaid tiles beneath his feet. "You are the gold head, O king. You are a king of kings, and your kingdom is precious as gold. And after you shall come a lesser kingdom, and then a lesser still, and after them a kingdom strong as iron." Then Daniel heard himself saying unplanned words. "And after all of these, a kingdom of iron and clay, strong as iron and weak as clay. And the God of heaven shall create a kingdom which will never be destroyed, but hold all the other kingdoms within it. And it will endure forever."

Daniel stopped talking. There was a long silence. *I failed. It didn't work. I'm sorry, Samamat. I'm sorry Arioch—*

"How did you know my dream? And what it meant? How? How?" Nebuchadnezzar demanded. He stared almost blankly at Daniel.

"I asked my God, who is great, and He showed me the dream." *Why did none of the others have the sense to create the king's dream for him?* Perhaps they had feared the king's wrath too greatly. Samamat, of course, had taken the king at his word, and told only truth, disastrous though truth might be. *I must thank God with all my heart, for He truly aided me.*

Nebuchadnezzar smiled—an oddly ominous expression on his ravaged face. Abruptly, he stood, and half-flung himself down the steps. He threw himself at Daniel's feet. "You are great. You are greater than the gods. You are greater than I. Bless me. Lend me your favor. I will worship you and raise you above all men."

As Daniel stared down at the king, horrified, Nebuchadnezzar kissed his feet. Then the king sat back on his heels and called loudly, "Bring incense, bring sweet oils. Bring them now! We will all bow down before Daniel and worship him!" Nebuchadnezzar glared around the throne room. "Bow. Bow before Daniel, Master of Dreams!"

"No, O king—" Daniel tried to lift Nebuchadnezzar up, but the king flung himself at Daniel's feet again. And all around Daniel, men and women were kneeling, bowing—Daniel looked across a sea of heads to where Arioch stood. Arioch shrugged, then bowed. Daniel stared down at the king, who was once again kissing Daniel's feet.

Me. They're worshipping me. Daniel hadn't realized blood really could run cold until this moment. *This is not by my will or wish, Lord!* But Daniel knew he must stop this, and at once. After the great favor the Lord had granted Daniel, to repay Him by violating the first and greatest commandment—Daniel shuddered, and hastily tried again to raise King Nebuchadnezzar up. "O king, I did nothing but speak the words the Lord my God put into my mouth. Please do not do this. I am no god, nor am I worthy of worship."

The ranks of dutifully bowing and kneeling courtiers opened to allow half a dozen priests to pace solemnly in, carrying golden bowls full of incense. Smoke drifted upward, thin silver cords of fragrance. Daniel knew he must not permit the priests to offer him incense. And he could think of no way of stopping them, for every man and woman in this vast chamber was far more afraid of King Nebuchadnezzar's wrath than of the wrath of Daniel's God.

Daniel searched for Arioch, seeking aid. At last he saw Arioch, half-hidden by one of the winged Beings. Samamat had wrapped her arms around Arioch, and the two were kissing as fervently as if they were Ishtar and her Consort.

Of course. Why should I be surprised? But he was, and as he gazed wistfully upon the two dearest to his heart, Daniel sensed the presence of the Lord again. And the Lord seemed to be laughing. . . .

"Bow down to Daniel!" King Nebuchadnezzar glared at the assembled courtiers as if they might actually argue with him—and Daniel dragged his attention away from his friends and back to his own danger. He held his hands out in supplication.

"Please, O king, if I have pleased you and found favor in your sight—"

"You have," Nebuchadnezzar roared, "which is more than these useless vermin have. They will bow to you and worship you and—"

"—and the Lord my God will strike me down for blasphemy." Daniel only hoped the king would believe this. *It's true, after all.* "If the king would grant my petition and request, let my service to him be reward enough."

To Daniel's intense relief, this pleased King Nebuchadnezzar. The king promptly began berating the courtiers for bowing to a mere man, and the incense-bearing priests swiftly began chanting the king's praises. And a strong hand gripped Daniel's arm and drew him backward until a stone wing hid him from Nebuchadnezzar's eyes.

"Hug Daniel *later,* Sama—we're not out of sight, out of the king's mind yet. Now *come on.*"

Daniel had never been quite sure what happened after Arioch dragged him and Samamat back to his chambers. When he was being honest with himself, Daniel admitted he didn't *want* to know. They had gotten very drunk on a jug of highly spiced wine—*That I remember, and the headache the next day*—but for the rest of it—well, both the Lord and Daniel's memories had remained silent.

The events of the next few years convinced Daniel that the Most High God surely enjoyed watching mere mortals make fools of themselves. Daniel named himself as first among the fools.

The affair of the King's Dream was the beginning of Nebuchadnezzar's fall into total madness. Oh, for a time the king seemed to become once more the ruler who once had laughed and loved enough to create the incredible beauty of the Hanging Gardens for his favorite wife. And perhaps, had Queen Amytis still lived, she might have anchored the king in sanity. Without her . . .

With no one ruling his heart, King Nebuchadnezzar had no reason to remain sane any longer. As Daniel said one night to Arioch, "I think the king looks forward to his bouts of madness. He can forget his sorrows when he forgets himself."

"Yes, and he causes a lot of sorrow for a lot of other people." Arioch shook his head. "I don't know, Daniel. I think something seriously bad is about to happen. Remember the king's dream?"

Who didn't? No one who had been in the throne room that night could possibly forget standing before Death, knowing no one could answer the king's impossible question. Daniel still thanked God daily for the inspiration that had saved them all—

—and had raised Daniel high in King Nebuchadnezzar's favor. The king had created Daniel ruler of the province of Babylon, governor over all other governors. It hadn't taken Arioch's warning to make Daniel see the danger in this promotion to a rank only one step lower than that of the king himself. Taking advantage of Nebuchadnezzar's embarrassingly great gratitude, Daniel begged that the position be given to three of the most talented of the young men who had been brought from Israel and trained up in the king's court. Shadrach, Meshach, and Abednego made better governors than Daniel ever would—

"Not nearly as concerned as you are with morality, just with appearances," Arioch said. "Good idea, Daniel. Let those three be targets for the evil eye. Better them than you."

"I don't see why so many resent me, Arioch." Daniel knew himself to be the target of much malice and envy now that King Nebuchadnezzar had proclaimed him little less than a god.

"They don't resent you, Daniel, they *hate* you. And they hate you because you've got the king's ear and at the moment he'll do whatever you say."

"So they're afraid of me."

"It took the Great Daniel, Master of Dreams, this long to figure that out? Yes, Daniel, they're afraid of you. So since you won't remember to watch your back, I've got men watching it for you. Oh, and Samamat says be careful what you eat and drink."

"Does she read danger for me in the stars?"

"She reads danger for you because she's not stupid. But yes, I think she did mention something about the stars and poison in the same sentence. Maybe you should buy a food taster."

"I won't put another's life at risk just to save mine."

"It isn't that much of a risk, assuming you buy a good food-taster. Haven't you ever wondered why they cost so much?"

"Because they don't live long?"

"Daniel, King Nebuchadnezzar's food-tasters are both older than my grandfather'd be if he were still alive. Good food-tasters spend years becoming immune to most poisons. All that time and training costs money."

"So . . . you think I should—"

"Take some of that treasure the king keeps handing over to you and buy the best food-taster in the market. Yes, I think that's a good plan, Daniel."

The combination of Arioch's firm insistence and Samamat's worried pleading convinced Daniel. Reluctantly, he paid an exorbitant amount for a rotund, middle-aged Greek who swore not a morsel of food or sip of drink would get to Daniel untested.

Wonderful. Now I, too, can live like a king. Paranoid and hungry.

⁂

The Greek turned out to be a sound investment; within a month, the man fell ill after tasting wine that had been sent to Daniel—supposedly from the king. Guilt flared as Daniel stood at Pontos's bedside, watching as a doctor laid cool wet cloths upon the man's swollen lips.

"I'm sorry," Daniel said, and to his surprise, Pontos managed to whisper,

"You see? I'm worth it."

"Your man's a treasure," the doctor said. "Most would be dead, even of such a small dose."

"You mean he'll live?" Daniel could hardly believe that, but the doctor nodded.

"Trust a Greek for poisons. And Pontos here has a great reputation, you know."

"No," said Daniel. "I didn't know." He supposed the doctor thought him a fool, and was now ruefully certain that Pontos considered him so. *And I suppose Arioch will say "I told you so." Well, and so he did.*

Daniel told Arioch and Samamat of the poisoned wine, but refused to complain of it to King Nebuchadnezzar. Not that everyone in the palace didn't already know—but Daniel thought it better if the king could pretend ignorance.

"After all, Arioch, the poisoned wine allegedly came as his gift."

"And?"

"And Daniel's right, Arioch." Samamat reached out and clasped Daniel's hand in hers, a rare intimacy.

"He is?" Arioch regarded Daniel doubtfully.

"Suppose the wine really was sent by the king?" Daniel asked. "I don't think I want to remind him of something like that, do you?"

For once, Arioch agreed with Daniel. When dealing with a mad king, discretion became survival.

Nebuchadnezzar's next venture into the kingdom of madness was on so vast a scale it became impossible to conceal. The king ordered a statue cast in gold, a huge image of the goddess Ishtar. Reasonable enough, in Ishtar's own city. But the golden idol had not been intended for a temple, or to crown the Ishtar Gate, or to adorn the throne room of the palace.

King Nebuchadnezzar commanded this exquisite example of the goldsmith's art to be conveyed to the plain of Dura, a dozen miles from Babylon. There the precious idol was set in the middle of an open field, as if it were nothing more than a clay figure for a roadside shrine.

And all the great men of the kingdom—the princes, the governors, the generals, the priests, the treasure-masters—were commanded to attend the king there at Dura.

All except Daniel. For no reason Daniel could ever determine, the king ordered him to remain in Babylon.

"And fortunately, the king has commanded no women be permitted at his great assembly, so I don't have to trek out to Dura. In this weather, too." Samamat shook her head. Summer was no time to hold a gathering on the plains bordering the Tigris River.

"Well, you can help me rule in the king's name." Daniel still couldn't believe Nebuchadnezzar's orders, and couldn't decide if it would be wiser to obey and put the crown on his head, or to disobey—humbly. He put the question to Samamat, who shrugged.

"I don't know, Daniel. Who knows what the king will choose to do these days? I just hope . . ."

"Hope what, Sama?"

"Well, the stars indicate a change coming."

"What kind of a change? A new king?"

Samamat frowned. "I can't tell. Maybe. Something different. I'll keep studying them, of course. Perhaps they'll reveal more after the full moon."

Something different certainly summed up what happened on the plain of Dura. Once the hundreds who had been commanded to travel there arrived, they found not only the statue of Ishtar blazing like fire under the summer sun, but King Nebuchadnezzar holding court there. All the musicians in Babylon had also been commanded to Dura; they ringed the idol, waiting with their harps and lyres, their flutes and timbrels and drums. Arioch sent Daniel a long letter, scrawled on new papyrus in Arioch's own slashing hand, warning him of what happened then—a forewarning for which Daniel was deeply thankful.

*First, there wasn't enough water. Or food. The king, may he live forever, told everyone they could turn right around and go home—*after *they all prostrated themselves in front of the idol. Which they were supposed to do when they heard music start. And whoever didn't prostrate himself would be thrown into a fiery furnace. As if the sun wasn't hot enough to melt a helmet. So once the heralds had managed to shout this to everyone on the field, the king raised his hand and the musicians started playing, and I don't think anyone told them what to play, because I never heard such an uproar in my life. Harps and drums don't mix that well anyway.*

So everyone fell over himself to be the first man flat on his face. Except, of course, for those three friends of yours. Which the Chaldean mages helpfully pointed out to the king, because there were so many people there the king really couldn't see past the first dozen or so rows, not with that sun glare and the dust. So the king, may he live forever, ordered everyone to stand up again, and ordered the music to start again, and everyone fell flat on his face again.

Except Abednego, Shadrach, and Meshach, of course. The three of them waited around, standing, until I and the guard got through the rows of prostrated worshippers—I hope Ishtar appreciates what the king's doing for Her Glory here—to arrest them and haul them before Nebuchadnezzar. Who demanded to know why they weren't worshipping as ordered. They said it wasn't permitted by their own god, so the king ordered them thrown in a fiery furnace.

Of course, there wasn't a fiery furnace out there on Dura plain, so I had to take the three of them and find one, and who has a furnace burning at this season? Or one big enough to hold three men, come to that? But I had to do something, friends of yours or not. So I told the king, may he live forever, that his will would be carried out, which seemed to please him enough to order everyone to stand up and go home again. I brought the prisoners to the nearest blacksmith's and had him get the forge going. We nailed up blankets around the forge and we all waited while Abednego, Shadrach, and Meshach stood in the forge, and why they didn't all three drop dead of the heat in there I don't know.

Finally I figured they'd been in a fiery furnace long enough to satisfy the king's command and ordered my men to haul down the blankets. Frankly, Daniel, I expected to find at least one of them dead of the smoke if nothing else, but all three of them were fine. Sweaty and sooty, but not dead. I suppose they had the sense to lie down on the ground and stay as cool as possible. They said the Lord Their God had saved them, and maybe He had, because it must have been hell in there. And of course once they'd said that, *half my men were convinced they'd seen a mysterious fourth person in the smoke when we took down the blankets. And then they decided this mysterious fourth person looked like a god. Which is what they told everyone when we got back to the plain of Dura* with *Shadrach, Meshach, and Abednego alive and pretty well, considering everything.*

And that's when Nebuchadnezzar ordered that anyone in his kingdom who spoke one evil word about this Great God of yours would be cut up in little pieces and thrown to the crocodiles in the Tigris.

All I can say is that I hope the king, may he live forever, doesn't want to hold any more mass religious rituals. Especially on Dura plain. In the middle of summer.

Better burn this even if it is *a waste of papyrus.*

Your friend, Arioch.

King Nebuchadnezzar never again emerged from the madness that devoured him. After months of nerve-shattering dreams—dreams Daniel interpreted as soothingly as possible for the raging king—Nebuchadnezzar abandoned humanity entirely, living naked in the palace gardens, eating grass, and snarling at anyone who came near him. Nebuchadnezzar's death, caused by his insistence on consuming nightshade leaves, came as a relief to almost everyone.

His heir, Prince Belshazzar, ordered a splendid tomb erected to hold his father's body, and then began his reign as he meant to finish it: drunk. Better than madness, Daniel thought, but not by much.

I hope the wine at least drowns Belshazzar's dreams. I hope King Belshazzar forgets I'm alive. I'm tired of interpreting dreams for kings.

Darius the Mede, Darius the Great, Darius the Lord of Half the World, marched upon Babylon, followed by an army so vast no man could count its soldiers—although they numbered at least ten thousand, for that was the size of Darius's elite corps, the Immortals. Darius had already conquered vast lands in Asia and Africa. There was little chance for Babylon to stand against him, and King Belshazzar apparently didn't even intend to try.

At a moment of ultimate crisis, Belshazzar ordered up another feast.

Rumor had it that all that was served was the strongest wine. What was not rumor, but truth, was that Belshazzar had dragged out the plunder his father Nebuchadnezzar had looted from the Temple in Jerusalem, and was using the Temple's sacred vessels as wine cups. No one had been able to dissuade Belshazzar from this sacrilege.

Daniel hadn't even bothered to try.

Darius's army marched ever closer to Babylon, and Belshazzar and his guests grew ever drunker. Arioch rode out with the king's guard to watch the approaching host, leaving Samamat in Daniel's care. The two of them waited through three long tense days and nights. On the third night, someone knocked softly at Daniel's door.

Daniel and Samamat looked at the door, and then each other.

"I don't think Darius's soldiers would bother to knock," Samamat said, and Daniel answered, "Probably not." And Arioch would simply have entered without knocking. Another glance passed between them, and then Daniel opened the door.

A veiled woman stood there. "Daniel Dream-Master? The king has need of you. Will it please you to come to him?"

"King Belshazzar asked for me?" Daniel found it hard to believe that King Belshazzar could remember his own name by now, let alone Daniel's.

"No. I asked for you." The woman lifted the veil, revealing her somber face and her ivory hair. Belshazzar's wife.

"Queen Ishvari, I am honored. How may I be of service to you?"

"Come to the banquet hall," she said, "and read for the king the writing that he sees upon the wall."

"The king sees writing upon the wall?" Daniel asked, cautious. "What sort of writing, my lady queen?"

"The sort of writing that only a king's eyes may see." Queen Ishvari chose her words carefully; Daniel understood exactly what awaited him in the king's banquet hall. A drunken, delusional king and—

And writing upon the wall that he alone sees. O Lord, what is wrong with these kings of Babylon? Daniel vividly recalled the night that King Nebuchadnezzar demanded a dream interpreted—a dream the king didn't even remember. Now Nebuchadnezzar's son needed invisible writing read to him. . . .

"O queen, if only a king's eyes see the words, what can I do? I am no king."

Ishvari regarded him with calm, steady eyes. "You are the Dream Master. You tell the meaning of dreams, and what is this writing the king sees upon the wall but another form of dream? The king will believe what you read to him. I could tell him what the words tell him, but he will not listen to me."

"King Belshazzar may not listen to me either," Daniel said, and Ishvari's crimson-tinted lips curved in a bitter smile.

"Perhaps he will not—but you and I will have done our duty."

Daniel had sighed, and gone to tell Belshazzar what anyone sober could have said to him: that with Darius's army at the gates of Babylon, Belshazzar was doomed—

—news Belshazzar was too drunk to understand.

Darius proved an enlightened conqueror. Once Belshazzar was dead, Darius granted clemency to Queen Ishvari and her infant daughter. And Darius, seeing no reason to execute good servants merely because they had served their king well, left the palace hierarchy in place. More, Darius sought out those whom Belshazzar had forgotten; Daniel found himself once more in a king's favor and raised to high rank.

"What is it with you and kings?" Arioch asked. "Do *I* wind up made a general? No, I'm still just captain of the king's guard."

"In other words, you have one of the most important posts there is. And I suppose Darius thinks I may be useful," Daniel offered.

"Right. That's why you're set up over all the other princes and governors. Be careful, Daniel. *Try* to remember you have a food-taster."

Arioch was proven right—although it wasn't poison Daniel's enemies used, but law.

⁂

It was the king's custom to hold court and receive petitioners, and to grant requests honoring his favorites. And when that request was that Darius decree that for a month any man who prayed to any god or man save Darius should be thrown to lions, at first Darius smiled, thinking this a jest. But it was no jest, and upon the petition being repeated, Darius agreed.

"I hate to say this, Arioch," Samamat said, when the new law had been read out and posted at every city gate, "but I don't think Darius is any better than the Babylonian kings. What kind of mad law is that?"

"The kind of law that gets Daniel thrown to lions," Arioch answered grimly. "Look, Daniel, I want you to promise you won't pray to anyone or anything but King Darius for the next month. Better yet, don't pray at all."

Daniel knew he couldn't swear that. "I will pray only in private, silently."

"It won't help," Arioch said.

"Which is why I won't promise, Arioch."

"Daniel's right." Samamat touched his hand, lightly. "All someone has to do is swear they saw or heard him praying to his god and not to Darius."

"You mean *lie*? To the great king himself? Yes, you're probably right." Arioch turned to Daniel. "Well, try to stay out of trouble and close to the king."

But even that tactic couldn't save Daniel for long. Sooner or later, he had to go aside, and once he was out of the king's sight, he was doomed.

King Darius did his best to mitigate Daniel's fate: offered the accusers gifts to change their testimony, attempted to alter the penalty. But he had sealed the decree into Median and Persian law, and such a law could not be changed—even by the king himself.

All the king could do for Daniel was furnish his cell with a comfortable bed and provide good food and wine. And allow him visitors. Daniel always suspected King Darius had conspired with Arioch to arrange Daniel's deliverance; even Arioch's resourcefulness had some limits. . . .

"Daniel," said Arioch, "is it absolutely impossible for you to stay out of trouble with kings?"

"It wasn't my fault."

"It never is. So—lions."

"Yes," Daniel said. "Lions. Maybe if I sit quietly, they'll leave me alone."

"Maybe if you sit quietly, they'll have an easier time eating you. No—don't say anything. Let me think." Arioch always liked to pretend thinking was a difficult task that he undertook as infrequently as possible.

"Arioch—don't tell Sama. She'll just worry."

"You think so? And by the way, do you really think the entire city—including Samamat—doesn't already know? The men stalking you made sure the whole thing was bellowed in the marketplace and from the top of the Hanging Gardens to the bottom. Darius isn't getting out of carrying out the penalty."

Daniel sighed. "I know. I'm sorry."

"You're sorry? You're about to be devoured by lions, and all you can say is 'I'm sorry'?"

Daniel thought about it; shrugged. "What else can I say? King Darius can't flout his own law."

"Does the law actually say you have to be thrown into a den of *live* lions?" Arioch suddenly stopped talking, and when Daniel began to answer, Arioch held up his hand. Daniel obediently waited; clearly Arioch had just thought of something.

One of those clever ideas he always swears he's too dull-witted to think of—Daniel only hoped Arioch's idea wouldn't cause even more trouble. You never knew where one of Arioch's ideas would lead you.

"All right," Arioch said at last. "Here's what we're going to do. Do you know if Samamat uses poppy syrup?"

"To read the stars? I doubt it."

"Well, how would I know what astrologers use? I'll ask her—she may know where I can get the stuff."

"Arioch, you can get poppy syrup from half the merchants in the Street of Spices."

"Not as much as we're going to need."

"And how much *are* we going to need?" Daniel asked.

"As much as it takes to send half a dozen lions to the Land of Dreams. Oh, and we'll need meat to put the poppy in. I don't think lions will just drink it."

"Probably not," Daniel said. "Do you actually think this is going to work?"

"It'll work better than *not* feeding the lions meat and poppy. With any luck, they'll be too full and too sleepy to bother with you. And trust me, Daniel, King Darius will be a lot happier if you *aren't* devoured by lions. I *like* kings to be happy."

"But how will I explain—"

"Still being alive? Let's see—you pulled a thorn out of the lions' paws when they were cubs and they're so grateful they didn't eat you. You're a Jew, and lions don't eat Jews. You're a smart man, Daniel—you'll think of something."

Even knowing that Arioch had personally watched the lions devour the drugged meat, Daniel found it hard to attain the calm he knew would help him survive the night. He managed to walk into the lions' den outwardly serene; to remain still as the iron-barred gate shut behind him and the bolt slid home.

The lions—three full-maned males—looked up as Daniel entered. No lioness; good. The males were more impressive but less dangerous than the faster, smarter females. One lion heaved himself to his feet and took an unsteady pace forward. Daniel didn't move. The lion apparently decided the effort was too great, and collapsed back onto the stone floor.

Well, this is going to be boring. I hope. Daniel carefully moved until his back was against the wall; slowly lowered himself until he was sitting. The floor was cold and hard, but Daniel didn't care. His entire attention was on the three lions. The beasts weren't asleep, but they weren't alert either. With luck—*And with Your help, Lord*—the lions would leave him alone. Arioch had ensured they weren't hungry, so as long as Daniel didn't do anything to engage their attention, the lions probably would lapse into slumber.

The largest lion turned his head and stared at Daniel, then yawned. The lion had a fine set of teeth, with fangs that looked as long as Daniel's hand. The rank odor of a meat-eater's breath filled the damp air.

Daniel sighed. It was going to be a long night.

Yes, that was a very long night. Sometimes Daniel missed Babylon, but he rarely missed its mad kings—and merely sitting on the throne in Babylon seemed to drive kings mad. At least Daniel had survived everything Babylon had hurled at him, just as Arioch and Samamat had survived.

Lions, idols, dragons . . .

Daniel always swore the dragon had not been his fault. He had merely pointed out to King Darius that just because food offerings disappeared from a temple every night, it didn't mean the idol worshipped there was a god.

"No?" King Darius had said. "Then who eats the food, if it is not the god?"

"Probably the priests and their families," Daniel said. "That's what ate the food offered at our temple in Jerusalem—except nobody there pretended the Lord our God ate the temple offerings."

Irritated, Darius had been intent on executing the priests and their families for cheating worshippers, and Daniel had only talked the king out of such a massacre by offering to prove that no one seriously believed the stone idol ate the food.

"Well, you're probably right. Now I suppose you'll say the dragon in the Temple of Bel isn't a god either," Darius said.

"The king is wise," Daniel had told him, and Darius laughed. Daniel then spoke seven words too many. "I'll also say it isn't a dragon."

King Darius conveniently forgot the matter of the vanishing temple offerings. "Of course it's a dragon. It may even be a god, although it's not one I worship myself. Go prove it's not a god, Daniel. But I defy even you to prove it's not a dragon."

⁂

"Daniel," said Arioch, "how do you get yourself *into* these things?"

"Never mind that now. The important thing is for Daniel not to be eaten by the dragon." Samamat began dropping dried figs into a leather pouch. "Should I put in some of the roast lamb as well?"

"Why give the dragon any ideas about eating meat?" Arioch regarded Daniel sadly. "Daniel, when will you learn to leave well enough alone? Or to *agree* with a king once in a while?"

"I *did* agree with the king. He said I'd say the dragon wasn't a god, and I agreed with him."

"Oh, Daniel—" Samamat shook her head ruefully and handed him the bag of dried figs. Daniel looked at his two friends and sighed. "I'm sorry—"

"You always are." Samamat kissed his cheek. "Try not to argue with the dragon, Daniel."

Daniel tucked the bag of figs into his belt. "Do either of you know anything about this dragon? Have either of you ever been to the Temple of Bel?"

"Me? Set foot in a temple? You know me better than that. I don't supposed you'd condescend to take a weapon with you?"

"And my gods aren't earthbound," Samamat added.

"No weapon," Daniel told Arioch.

The Dragon Temple crouched, old and squat, in the heart of the temple district. Small, almost overwhelmed by the brilliant new buildings surrounding it, it hardly seemed an appropriate place for any god, let alone one in the form of a dragon. Not that Daniel believed what lay within any of the temples was a god at all, but the Babylonians believed temple idols to be their gods—*And you'd think they'd treat a live dragon god especially well.* Dragons decorated the Ishtar Gate, after all.

In honor of Daniel's inspection, the Dragon Temple was empty, for which favor Daniel was duly grateful. Talking to priests who knew he'd come to judge their temple on behalf of the king meant both priests and Daniel were ill at ease. However, he wished the temple were better lit; the sanctuary lay in deep shadow. A low basalt altar that reminded Daniel of a feeding trough stood between him and whatever moved restlessly in that shadow.

"I come on behalf of King Darius," Daniel said. "I mean no disrespect."

"Truly?" A woman's voice. Doubtful, suspicious; Daniel couldn't blame her.

Trapped in a place like this—"Truly. Will you speak with me?"

A pause. "We will." A moment later a creature padded out of the darkness behind the altar.

I was wrong. It is a dragon—

A living image of those decorating the Ishtar Gate, the dragon was large as a pony. Its neck snaked long and sinuous; its golden eyes gazed at Daniel, intent. Hungry . . .

"She thinks you have an offering for her." The woman who spoke moved supple as the dragon, as if she danced through the temple's heavy air. She stopped and looked at Daniel with the same intent gaze. "Did you bring her an offering, my lord Daniel?"

"You know my name?"

"All Babylon knows your name."

Daniel studied her: small, honey-colored, head shaved smooth; mouth red as poppies and eyelids painted green as the dragon's scales. A gold chain hung with scarabs circled her hips. Tattoos swirled over her body. Since she wore only air, Daniel had no trouble studying the tattoos. Lotus flowers. Winged serpents. The heavy outline of an Eye of Ra just below her throat. The Eye gazed at Daniel accusingly.

"Egypt," Daniel said, and she smiled.

"Egypt," she agreed. She laid her hand on the dragon's neck. "Did you bring her an offering?" Her tone hinted that Daniel had better have brought the dragon an offering.

Daniel pulled out the dried figs. "I brought these. Can she eat these?"

The dragon answered his question by gulping up the figs. It had a very long tongue and once the figs vanished down its gullet, the dragon licked Daniel's hand hopefully.

"Yes," said the dragon's keeper.

Daniel ignored the mockery. "Does she have a name?"

"Of course. But why does my lord Daniel need that knowledge?"

"I'm not going to hurt her—look, you must have a name as well."

The dragon's priestess stared at him. "You're not here to harm her?"

"No, of course not."

"Then why are you here?"

How do I get into these conversations? Daniel sighed. "To prove the dragon's not a god."

"And if she is not?"

"Well . . ." Daniel was no dragon expert, but the creature looked—unhappy. Both dragon and priestess showed bone pressing through skin; the beast's scales seemed dull. *Thin and forlorn, both of them. Dragon it may be, but it's still just a big lizard*—a very big lizard—*and this is no place to keep the poor thing.* Lizards liked sunlight. So did Egyptians.

"If she's not a god," Daniel said, "she needs to live someplace better for her than this temple."

The dragon-priestess smiled. "Then I will swear that she is not a god upon any holy object you choose."

Lying through your teeth, to get your dragon out of this hole. Well, it is only a lizard. Certainly it's not a god! "I'm sure that will convince the king—"

"My name is Amunet-Nefer-Setmut-Elu-ki," said the priestess. "You may call me Elu-ki, if it pleases you." She curved her arm over the dragon's neck. "And this is—" she hesitated, then looked straight into Daniel's eyes as she said, "—my pet. You may call her Bel."

Whether it pleases me or not.

"Now may we return home?"

Daniel sighed. "To Egypt? I'll ask King Darius." He regarded the dragon with interest. "I was expecting something bigger."

"She will grow as the years grow. And she is quite big enough to bite. Hard." Elu-ki smiled sweetly at Daniel. She had very white teeth. "When will you ask King Darius if we may go home?"

Daniel wasn't surprised when King Darius refused his request that priestess and dragon be returned to Egypt. The king did grant Daniel's next request, and Daniel returned to the Temple of Bel to explain.

"I'm sorry, Elu-ki, but King Darius won't let you return to Egypt—not right now, at any rate. But—" *And I don't believe I actually begged the king for this, and what Arioch will have to say I don't want even to think about!* "—the king will let you both stay with me. And I'll try to get you home to Egypt. Someday."

"Someday. Someday is like tomorrow. It never comes." Elu-ki shrugged. "Still, 'someday' is better than 'never.' We thank you, Daniel Dream-Master. Now may we leave this place?"

To Daniel's surprise, Arioch merely regarded Elu-ki and her dragon and sighed. "Don't tell me," Arioch begged. "Just—don't."

Samamat laughed. "Welcome, priestess. I'm—"

"The lady Samamat, reader of stars." Elu-ki tugged on the plaited leather rope attached to Bel's wide collar as the creature attempted to shove its nose into a basket full of apricots Samamat held. Samamat smiled and offered Bel a handful of apricots; the dragon gulped down the fruit and licked Samamat's hand.

"All right, Arioch. Say it." Daniel waited, resigned.

Arioch raised his eyebrows. "Me? I'm not going to say a word, Daniel. Not one word."

"It wasn't my . . ." Unable to truthfully say bringing them here hadn't been his idea, Daniel settled for, "fault. Really."

"Oh, I can't wait to hear this," said Arioch, conveniently forgetting his plea that Daniel not tell him a word about the matter.

"Well, you see . . ." Keeping an eye on the dragon, Daniel explained precisely how he wound up bringing home an Egyptian priestess and a dragon-god. "I didn't think the king would let me, but when I told him the dragon would probably die if left in the temple, he—"

"—was so delighted the Great Daniel had actually been *wrong* for a change he'd have granted whatever you asked for," Arioch finished.

"But I wasn't wrong," Daniel said.

"You told the king it *was* a dragon," Samamat pointed out.

Daniel thought about this for a moment. "Oh," he said at last.

Elu-ki turned and pressed her face against her dragon's neck. A sun-scarab adorned the base of her spine. Arioch stared at the tattoo as if memorizing it.

"Come with me, Elu-ki, and I'll find you something to wear," Samamat said firmly. "And you men go find a place for the dragon, and something for it to eat."

"Bel," the dragon's priestess said. "Her name is Bel."

Smiling sweetly, Elu-ki handed the dragon's leash to Arioch and followed Samamat.

Arioch stared at the dragon; the dragon stepped delicately over to Arioch and with one swift movement of her snakelike tongue, licked his neck. "Ahriman's hells!" Arioch said. "Here, *you* take it." Since Daniel was bent over laughing, Arioch dropped the leash over Daniel's neck. "And stop that stupid laughing," Arioch added.

Samamat had managed to find a garment to cover Elu-ki; Daniel thought he recognized one of his own tunics. Since the priestess was small-boned and delicate as a child, the linen tunic more than covered her. Samamat tried, vainly, to belt in the tunic. Too much fabric; the cloth bunched up, and the little priestess looked like a badly packed bundle.

"I'm sorry, Elu-ki," Samamat said, "but there's nothing here to fit you. We can go to the marketplace tomorrow and buy cloth. My maid can make you something to wear."

"I know I'm going to regret asking this," Arioch said, "but why can't your maid alter what our pet priestess has on right now?"

"I gave her the day off to watch the parade of the guilds." Samamat regarded Elu-ki critically, and sighed. "Elu-ki," Samamat began.

"No." Elu-ki spoke gently but Daniel heard the iron beneath the soft voice.

"You don't even know what I'm going to say," Samamat protested, and Elu-ki smiled.

"No, I will not cover my head with a wig or veil. I will not hide the marks of my office as priestess."

Samamat sighed; Arioch laughed, and said, "She reminds me of *you*, Daniel."

"Me? Why?"

"Oh, I don't know—because she answers questions no one's asked? Because she's got a dragon as a pet? Because she's just plain strange? Because she's—"

"Egyptian?" Samamat finished sweetly.

"Absolutely. Egyptian."

"Arioch, that's ridiculous. We're nothing alike."

"Of course not. You're not . . . Egyptian," Arioch said.

Samamat stared at the priestess as if seeing her for the first time. *"You're Egyptian!"* Samamat ran off; they heard her dashing up the stairs to the roof. Elu-ki raised her eyebrows.

"I've learned not to ask," Arioch told her.

A few moments later Samamat dashed back carrying a piece of papyrus and a reed pen. "Elu-ki, have you ever seen something like this?" With swift strokes of the reed, Samamat drew the curves of the broken stone arch they had stumbled upon the day of King Nebuchadnezzar's hunt.

Elu-ki stared, then smiled—or at least she showed her teeth. "Oh yes. The gods come through such gates, when they deign to speak with mortals. It is good that you did not touch it."

"I told you," Arioch said.

"Never touch that which belongs to the gods," Elu-ki agreed.

"Always good advice," said Arioch. "Now if Daniel here could only manage to keep out of matters that belong to kings—"

"The dragon wasn't my fault," Daniel insisted plaintively.

"It never is, Daniel," Arioch said. "But somehow we're now saddled with a dragon. I'm just pointing this out before the next time you decide to bring home a little something from a temple."

Daniel glared at Arioch. "There isn't going to be a next time."

Silence. Skeptical silence. Priestess Amunet-Nefer-Setmut-Elu-ki smiled very sweetly and stroked Bel's long supple neck.

"And Bel's a very small dragon," Samamat pointed out.

"Somehow that's not a very great comfort to me," Arioch said. "I just hope that King Darius, may he live forever, won't give Daniel any more gifts."

But it wasn't any royal whim that had carved Daniel's reputation for wisdom in stone.

It had been a desperate husband's plea. And for once, Arioch's accusation that Daniel sought out trouble was right, for Daniel had deliberately involved himself in the affair. Oh, it was the woman's husband who had begged Daniel's help, but it was Daniel himself who had sought the man out. Even now, Daniel hesitated to speak of what had sent him, unbidden, to judge between lies and truth—not because Arioch and Samamat would scoff, but because they would believe. And Daniel wasn't sure he wanted to carry the burden of that belief.

All Daniel knew was that God had sent him to save Susannah. And that was all he needed to know.

He could no longer remember the words that had commanded him, nor the sound of the voice—if voice there had been. Once that troubled him. How could he not recall what the Most High had said to him, or how? Later he realized that wasn't important. What mattered was that the Lord had intervened to save a virtuous woman . . .

. . . and if Daniel had not proven Susannah's innocence, thousands of lives would have been lost many years later. Daniel tried very hard never to think of the future that would have come if Susannah had perished.

The three of them had been peaceably occupied at home when Daniel heard the summons. Between one breath and the next, time ceased, and Daniel became the still center of a silent world. He waited, while beyond him, Arioch and Samamat moved slowly, as if through clear honey instead of air. He saw Samamat's lips move as she spoke, but he could hear nothing but the beating of his own heart.

A voice echoed within him, commanding, pressing him to act. **Act now. Act against falsehood. Against evil. Seek it and destroy it.** *Where?* Daniel asked the silent voice. **You will know. Go. Go *now*.**

The force released him as suddenly as it had seized him. Daniel stumbled and Samamat steadied him; for a breath he clung to her arms, drew in the scent of her hair. "Daniel?" she said. "Are you all right?"

He pushed himself away from her. "I have to go."

"Where?" Samamat looked at him as intently as if he were a new star in the night sky.

"I'll explain when I get back."

"Oh, no, Daniel." Arioch moved to block the doorway. "You'll explain now."

"There isn't time. Stand aside, Arioch—I have to go *now.*"

For once Arioch hadn't argued. He'd stepped aside, and Daniel had fled into the street, following the Lord's command.

The voice had been right: Daniel knew at once which way to run. As he hurried through the gate into the Jewish Quarter, a man ran hard into him, and only luck kept them both upright. Daniel found himself gazing at a man whose youthful good looks were marred by ashes rubbed over his skin and hair, and the long tears through his fine linen tunic.

"I'm Daniel. You must be why I'm here."

The man stared at him, then clutched at his arms. "Daniel? You're Daniel, the wise man? Praise the Lord!"

"Yes. And you?"

"Come, come quickly!" The man grasped Daniel's garment, pulled as if to lead him in the direction Daniel already knew he must go. He went with the frantic man, moving swiftly through the streets as he heard why he had been sent here so suddenly.

The desperate man was Joakim, a wealthy Jewish merchant whose most precious jewel was his wife. "My beloved wife—you must save her, Daniel, you *must,* these are lies, foul lies—never, never would she do such a thing—my perfect wife—"

Susannah.

Susannah, prized for her absolute virtue—and her absolute beauty. Noted for her piety and modesty, by her husband's order she did not wear the all-concealing veil she herself would have chosen, but one that covered only her hair. A wife's duty is to obey her husband, and Susannah's husband enjoyed displaying his most valued possession: his beautiful and untouchable wife. . . .

"Now that's *a really bad idea."* Daniel heard Arioch's acid comment as clearly as if he stood beside him listening to Joakim's tale. *And Arioch would be right. Joakim's a fool.*

Susannah, beauteous and perfectly formed as a pagan goddess. Hair black as deep midnight, skin as smooth and pale as cream, lips red as roses. Eyes violet as the sky at twilight. Susannah, full-breasted and slim-waisted, hips swelling in a perfect arch. Neither too tall nor too short: her hands slender and her feet small and high-arched . . .

"Please, Joakim, I don't need to know all that," Daniel said hastily. "Tell me what *happened.*"

"I'm sorry. I'm sorry. I just—you must help! The Lord put it into my mind to come to you, surely you can right this wrong and save my wife!"

"I will try. We must have faith in the Lord, Joakim."

"I do. I do. This is my fault, mine—I was too proud. But Susannah—she is so beautiful, so pure, so devout. I gloried in that. Whenever a man asked, 'Who can find a virtuous woman?' I always thought, *I can. Yes, I can.*" Joakim bowed his head and buried his face in his hands.

Daniel sighed. "Now, tell me what has happened that your wife must be saved. What has she done?"

"Nothing! She has done *nothing!*"

"Someone did *something,* Joakim, or I would not have been sent here. What?"

The story Joakim told didn't exactly surprise Daniel, although it did disgust him. How could men do such things and live with themselves after? Two older men, respected elders, judges, of the Jewish community, had watched Susannah in the marketplace and coveted her.

"They spied upon her in her mikvah. I built one for her in our garden, so that she might purify herself in private. How could she know they would watch her in her most private moments? Unclothed, innocent of their vile gaze?"

Daniel didn't bother to ask how the two men had gained such a view of the virtuous wife. *They probably climbed the wall, or even drilled a hole through it. What matters is that they can describe every mark on her body.*

Watching Susannah bathe incited even more lust in the two men. Knowing they had no chance of gaining her by any other means, one day they entered the garden while she was bathing and demanded she lie with them—or they would accuse her of adultery.

"She refused, placing her faith in God, and cried out for help."

But when the servants ran into the garden, her would-be rapists shouted that they had caught Susannah in the arms of a young man. The young man had fled, but they had prevented Susannah from doing so. And as they had threatened that if she denied them, they would accuse her of adultery. Jewish law called for death by stoning.

But stoning was more than merely a sentence of death. Stoning was death by slow torture. The stones were chosen carefully; stones the size of a man's fist. Men would hurl those unyielding stones at her until she died. Unless a man took pity upon her, and threw his stone hard and true and smashed the thin bone at her temple, it would take a long, long time for Susannah to die.

And they will make her husband watch. They will make him hold a stone in his hand. They will make him throw it at his wife. And if he does not . . . Daniel knew what happened when a crowd transmuted into a mob. Joakim, too, would die. *And those so-called judges will claim his wealth.*

Daniel grabbed Joakim's arm, making the other man stop. "So, Joakim, these two men accuse your wife of adultery and you did nothing? You let them take her away?"

"I did not! They dragged her to the synagogue and told their lying story again there. When I came home, my servants and slaves were weeping so hard it was hard to draw from them what had happened. As soon as I knew, I ran to claim her back, but they would not release Susannah to me. I swore I did not believe the accusation, I swore there is no more chaste and faithful wife in all the empire than my Susannah. It was no use. All I gained was half an hour alone with my wife. And she asked—she asked me to . . ." Joakim's voice faltered.

"I can guess what she asked of you. Did you agree?"

"I told her I would not let her die. I swore I would reveal her accusers for the false, evil men they are, and bring her safely home."

"That is a great deal to promise, and she asked only one thing of you. Did you agree to do as she asked?" Daniel waited, and at last Joakim said in a voice so low Daniel barely heard him,

"I promised I would not let her suffer."

Daniel looked deep into Joakim's eyes. "Tell me, Joakim, do you believe your wife with all your heart? Does any doubt, however small, trouble your mind?"

"*No!* No, I do not doubt her. Never would Susannah be unchaste in heart or mind or body. And even if I doubted, even if I thought she had done what they accuse her of—" Joakim drew in a deep breath. Suddenly he looked old and weary. "Even if she had, I would never give her into the hands of men who seek only to kill by slow torture."

Daniel stared down at the dusty bricks under their feet. "What would you do? If she truly had played the whore?"

Joakim sighed. "I would beat her, I suppose. No one would blame me for that, least of all Susannah."

At last Daniel lifted his head. "Come, then. I will—"

"Speak to Susannah?"

"To Susannah?" Daniel smiled and shook his head. "No. No, Joakim, I am going to talk to those two pious, virtuous, God-fearing men who uncovered an adulterous wife by spying upon her in her bath."

"Do you realize how fatally easy it is to gain a reputation for great wisdom?" Daniel asked when he returned home to find Arioch and Samamat rather grimly waiting for him.

"Yes," Arioch said.

"Daniel, you look exhausted." Samamat put her arms around him. "When did you eat last?"

"I—don't remember," Daniel said apologetically. "What do you mean, 'yes'?"

"I mean, yes, I do know how easy it is to get a reputation for great wisdom, Daniel. Why? Was I unclear?"

"Oh, stop taunting him. He's tired." Samamat put a cup of wine into Daniel's hands. "Drink this. Now. Then you can have some lamb stew."

"The word was clear enough," said Daniel, "but what did you mean?"

"I meant all you need is common sense, which is anything but common. The average man has less sense than the average sheep," Arioch said.

"And the average woman?" Samamat asked, smiling.

"Has twice the sense of either," Arioch said. "Except in this case, in which *none* of them have the brains the Wise God gave a new-hatched minnow."

Although Daniel expected Samamat to object, she nodded agreement. "I hate to admit it, but you're right. It's as if Susannah was gifted with so much beauty there wasn't room for brains as well."

"I didn't know you knew Susannah," Daniel said, and Samamat smiled rather grimly.

"I saw her in the marketplace once. I think she's the most beautiful creature I ever saw. And of course everyone knows about her now. The story flew through the city like—like—"

"Like scandalous gossip?" Arioch suggested.

"Oh. Well, then you know all about it already," Daniel said. "Sama, may I please have some more wine?"

"Later. We don't know *all* about it." Samamat smiled and patted the bench. "Come, Daniel, tell us how you knew those men were lying about the most beautiful and most virtuous lady in all the Jewish Quarter—"

"Aside from the fact that their lips were moving," Arioch said, and Daniel laughed.

"Aside from that? It wasn't difficult, really."

No, not difficult, only pathetically ridiculous. And if Susannah's foolish husband hadn't been fond enough of her to seek Daniel's advice, she would now be dead, victim of two men's rejected lust and her iron virtue.

The most beautiful and most virtuous lady in all Babylon . . . Susannah held her beauty cheap compared to her faith, her virtue, and her husband's honor. *It would have been better had she prided herself on her perfect face and figure . . .*

"Daniel? You're thinking again." Arioch waved his hand in front of Daniel's eyes. "Men? Lying? Remember?"

"Oh, yes. Well, you heard about the accusation?"

"All Babylon heard about it." Samamat frowned. "As if the Most Virtuous would actually lie with a man not her husband—and in her own garden."

"Yes, that did sound odd, didn't it?" Arioch said.

"Especially since her husband's young and handsome and utterly besotted with her," Samamat finished, and Daniel nodded.

"Very odd." But with two venerable elders both swearing that they had seen Susannah seduce a young man into her garden and then into her arms; two men able to describe every beauty mark upon her body, Susannah was doomed. Of course they could describe her in loving detail; the two men had spied upon the lady as she bathed. "Clearly more than once," Daniel added.

Susannah's only defense was to state that she had not sinned and to call upon God to witness to the truth of her words and the purity of her body. Against her two accusers, her words weighed nothing. But at least Susannah's husband possessed some sense, for he had urgently sought out Daniel.

"So I went, of course. First I spoke to the Most Vir—to Susannah, and I took each of Susannah's accusers aside and spoke to him alone."

"By the way, could these reputable elders of yours describe the young man our virtuous lady supposedly risked her life to embrace?" Arioch asked.

"Actually, they could. Of course, one said he was tall and dark, and the other that he was fair like a Greek."

"A *Greek*? Daniel, what would a Greek be doing in the Jewish Quarter?" Samamat demanded.

"Having an affair with Susannah, obviously." Daniel shook his head. "Clearly the two men hadn't bothered to come up with a consistent story."

"Of course not. Accusation constitutes proof, against a woman." The bitterness in Samamat's voice made Daniel wince.

After a moment, he continued, "It was simple, really. The two men claimed Susannah and her lover lay together under a tree in her garden. So I asked Susannah's accusers what kind of tree she and her lover lay under. One said it was a mastic tree and the other said it was an oak."

"Just as her lover was both dark and fair. So *that's* how you knew they were both lying," Samamat said earnestly, and Daniel looked at Arioch and saw that Arioch, too, was trying not to laugh.

"Sama, it didn't matter *what* kind of tree they said it was. These two men supposedly watched a beautiful naked woman in the arms of—"

"An equally beautiful naked man," Arioch added helpfully.

"—so it is extremely unlikely that they paid the least attention to the tree," Daniel finished. "But yes, their stories didn't fit together at all."

"And?" Samamat prompted.

Daniel sighed. "And then, since they had borne false witness against an innocent woman, the two men who accused her were sentenced to death. I came away as soon as I gave Joakim some advice."

"What did you tell him?" Samamat asked.

"To let his wife wear whatever veil she wished."

"Preferably one made of very, very thick cloth," Arioch added, and Samamat slanted a glance at him.

"Because all the gods forefend that men act like civilized creatures." It might have been a jest; her tone made that possible.

But Daniel didn't think Samamat jested. "I think you're right. A man acts like a rabid beast, and claims it the woman's fault—that can't be either just or righteous."

"And you?" Samamat turned to Arioch. "What do you think?"

"What I think," Arioch said, "is that Susannah's husband needs to build a much higher wall around his wife's garden."

The Susannah affair sealed Daniel's reputation as a truly wise man for all time—and sent Daniel from Babylon to Shushan. For saving Susannah, Daniel had been repaid with open hostility from much of Babylon's Jewish community, a fact that baffled Daniel. Arioch seemed unsurprised. "You made them realize they're so stupid they'd stone a woman first and look at the facts later."

"Now, Arioch, that's not completely fair—" Daniel began.

"Just *how* many of those commandments of yours did they all break? Two? Three? Do you think they *like* you for pointing out their stupidity and hypocrisy?"

"And you deprived them of their fun," Samamat added. "Those men looked forward to stoning a beautiful woman to death. You stopped them. Arioch's right. Now the Jews here hate you too."

Daniel sighed. "I don't know what I can do about it. I had no choice. Susannah was innocent."

Arioch smiled. "I've done something about it. King Darius is finished with Babylon. He's going back to Shushan and we're going with him."

The king had appointed a governor to rule the city and ensure Babylon would be reminded it now existed as a satrapy of the great empire Darius had carved out of dozens of bickering kingdoms. The king and his court were to return to the ancient city of Shushan, and Arioch had—"Tactfully," Arioch claimed—suggested the king take Daniel Dream-Master with him. "The king wanted to take you along anyway, but you know how considerate he is. He hesitated to offend the Jews here by stealing away their famous and pious—don't forget how pious you are—Daniel Dream-Master. So the fact that the Jews here hate you is an excuse for King Darius to do what he wanted to do in the first place. A really *good* excuse."

"Don't look so tragic," Arioch said, as Daniel stared at him. "Sama and I are going too. And I suppose your priestess and her dragon—"

"Elu-ki isn't *my* priestess," Daniel began, and then abandoned the effort. The news that they were all moving to Shushan stunned him. Daniel had lived in Babylon since he had arrived at the Gateway of the Gods when he was a fourteen-year-old captive from conquered Israel. "But Arioch, I've never been to Shushan. And I'm no good at traveling . . ."

"Oh, Daniel, you are so!" Samamat put her arm around him. "You traveled with King Nebuchadnezzar on hunting trips and—"

"And I didn't like it."

"—it's not as if you have to walk to Shushan, you know."

"And good luck never lasts forever. I'm amazed you're still alive. So this move is a *good* thing," Arioch told him. "I don't know about you, Daniel, but I'm very, very tired of mad kings. At least King Darius has the sense to get out before he's worshipping alien gods and eating grass."

"Well . . . I hear Shushan's a fascinating city," Daniel had said hopefully.

"And I hear Shushan's hot as Ahriman's hells and dusty as Nineveh's archives," Arioch said. "But at least it's not Babylon."

Samamat had pointed out that Shushan's merits and drawbacks were irrelevant. "Since we go by the king's command."

"There's one other good thing about Shushan . . ." Arioch came over to stand beside Samamat and draped his arm around her shoulders. "Those three bigoted friends of yours won't be there."

"They haven't really been friends of mine in years." Daniel tried to be sorry, but as the years passed Shadrach, Meshach, and Abednego had grown so intolerant, so rigidly pious, that they could hardly bear to acknowledge Daniel at all. Not seeing them was the simplest way to avoid endless argument.

Somewhere, somehow, along the road to Shushan, the priestess Amunet-Nefer-Setmut-Elu-ki and the dragon Bel had vanished. Daniel assumed the priestess and her pet god had seen a chance to return home to Egypt and taken it. Daniel suspected Arioch knew more about their disappearance than he would ever admit.

And since Samamat would happily recount her own intervention on their behalf, Daniel knew better than to ever ask her.

Sometimes, in his dreams, Daniel saw Elu-ki leading Bel over pale hot sand, girl and dragon walking steadily into the west.

Toward Egypt.

Toward home.

At last the day came when the three of them stared across the flat plain at the city that was to be their new home. There was a long silence no one seemed in a hurry to end. At last Daniel said,

"That's Shushan?"

"Yes, Daniel," Samamat said, "I'm very much afraid it is."

"Why does everyone call it 'Shushan the Beautiful'?" Daniel asked plaintively.

"Because, Daniel, if everyone called it 'Shushan the Flat and Ugly,' no one would ever come here," Arioch said.

"The palace is very—very grand," Samamat added, after gazing at it for several long, silent moments. "And the Great Staircase is supposed to be a wonder."

"I'm sure it is." Arioch studied the citadel and sighed. "I wonder where—or *if*—the architects of that palace studied their craft?"

"Well, at least it isn't Babylon," Daniel offered up hopefully.

"I *liked* Babylon."

"Arioch, you were the one who insisted we had to leave even before King Darius ordered us to come with him!"

"That's because I like being alive more than I like Babylon. Come on, let's get this over with."

Distance deceived under the steady blazing of the sun. Shushan had seemed to be only a few miles away—but it took hours for the king's caravan to reach the city. Shushan seemed to hover just above the burning plain, a shimmering illusion forever beyond their reach.

At last they drew close enough to see past illusion to the Choaspes River, and past the river to the city walls on its eastern bank. *Sand.* Daniel stared at the city that would now be their home. High walls built of mud brick; the harsh sun had dried the bricks to the gold of sand. The city walls veiled most of Shushan.

But you couldn't miss the palace. It stood at the north end of Shushan—and in a land flat as a mirror, the palace loomed above the city walls.

"A man-made hill. A good idea, for a citadel." Samamat stared at the palace; Daniel suspected she was calculating how many men, buckets, and hours of grinding labor it had taken to create such a huge mound.

"At least the river doesn't run through the city," Arioch said, his voice flat.

Daniel knew Arioch was remembering how King Darius had taken Babylon, and with Babylon, what was left of a once glorious empire. The Euphrates ran through Babylon, dividing the city in half. King Darius ordered his engineers to divert the river and open the water gates.

And then Darius's army had simply marched into the heart of Babylon. . . .

"Arioch. Done is done." Daniel gently touched Arioch's hand.

"The Choaspes is said to have the sweetest water in all the world."

Samamat, gentle but firm, changed the subject. "It's said to be the oldest city in all the world, too."

"That doesn't surprise me. Mud is cheap," Arioch said. "What in the name of the Seven Hells is *that?*"

The Great Staircase, newly gilded in honor of King Darius's return, burned bright under the midday sun. Daniel studied the wide sweep of steeps and terraces. Shushan could not compare with Babylon in beauty—but it was impossible not to admire Shushan's hard-won magnificence.

"Who do you suppose sweeps the steps?" Samamat asked, staring.

"The royal step sweepers, of course." But even Arioch sounded impressed.

King Darius entered Shushan to an enthusiastic welcome. Daniel hadn't realized there were so many rose petals in the world, and all of them seemed to have been gathered to fling joyously at King Darius and his attendants. Arioch had been assigned by Darius to ensure neither Daniel nor Samamat absentmindedly wandered off to investigate Shushan; as a result, they managed to arrive at the foot of the Great Staircase with the rest of the procession.

They looked up a long hill of stairs wide enough for a dozen horsemen to ride up abreast. In honor of King Darius's return home, the entire stairway waited, golden and empty, for him to ride up from the city to the palace citadel. Once the king and his advisors, followed by the king's guard, the famed Immortals led the way, everyone else was at last free to climb up to the palace citadel.

It took them almost an hour to make their way up the Great Staircase. When they reached the top, Daniel looked back across the smooth plain. Babylon lay far away. Shushan was home now.

I hope Shushan proves more peaceful than Babylon. I'm tired of solving problems for kings and queens.

Daniel arrived in Shushan to discover that his part in Susannah's deliverance had transformed him from a man who could spin meaning out of puzzling dreams into a sage as wise as Ahura Mazda Himself. Or, to the empire's Jews, into a man wise as Solomon in all his glory. Daniel tried to live a quiet life, and hoped he would no longer be called upon to meddle in the affairs of kings.

He twice over hoped and prayed there would be no more need for him to intervene to save any more lives. Sometimes he dreamed that the two elders had concocted all the details of their accusation beforehand, that Susannah had been doomed, and he had to watch as she died . . . .

Samamat and Arioch helped him past those nights, all of them staying awake together until the sun rose and shadows flew west into the dark.

Yes, we survived, we three. By then Daniel could not remember what life had been like before he met Arioch and Samamat. They were part of him; he could not give either up. He had learned that when the king decreed that all captive peoples might return freely to their homelands.

Daniel spent long troubled hours trying to persuade himself to return to Jerusalem, a city he hadn't seen in twenty years. Could he give up Arioch and Samamat? Was Jerusalem a fair exchange for abandoning his heart?

The answer, for Daniel, was no.

How could I have left Arioch and Samamat? Not been there to watch them marry, to see their son born? A boy whose parents named him Dariel, to honor King Darius and to honor Daniel . . .

". . . because he wouldn't have been born without the king, and you, bringing us together." Samamat held the baby to her breast; she glowed with happiness.

"By that reasoning, we should have named the boy Nebuchadnezzar," Arioch had said.

How could I not have been with them to watch Dariel grow up? And if I had returned to Jerusalem—

If he had returned to Jerusalem, he would not have been there when Arioch died.

If he had returned to Jerusalem, he would not have been there when Samamat needed him. He would not have been there to ask her to marry him. To his eternal wonder and delight, Samamat had said yes. . . .

Now we are old together, and should be at peace. Instead, I see another den being built, and lions gathering to fill it.

Daniel tried to convince himself that the contest for queen, the struggle for power in the palace, would pass by him. *Perhaps Samamat and I will be left in peace.*

But it didn't take a Dream-Master to see the future they faced: a long-sleeping dragon waking.

Or to see that this time Daniel would not escape the dragon's coils.

BOOK TWO

The Court of Miracles

HEGAI

I was seven when my father killed my mother, and fourteen when he gelded me. Seven years passed between my mother's death and my death as a man—seven years during which I struggled to elude my fate; to run away, escape to the faraway mountains guarding the eastern horizon, or to the ever-changing sea far to the west. Yes, I tried, desperately, but my father kept me well guarded, and each time I thought myself free, his guards caught me before I reached the end of our street.

And even if I had succeeded in gaining any of the city's seven gates, my father had paid all the guardians of all the gates well. None of the guards would have permitted me to pass; my father's money had ensured that.

Why? Why had my father slain his beautiful highborn wife? Cut off his lineage by gelding his son?

Questions simply answered: his wife proved unfaithful, and her beautiful clever son was sired not by her husband, but by an Abyssinian slave. But that I did not learn until the day the man I called my father slit my mother's slender throat.

The day I turned seven, my father called for my mother and me to come to him in the harem garden. My mother closed her eyes when she heard the summons, but said nothing. She took my hand and led me in silence until we stood before him. When I saw my father, I bowed to him as I had been taught. He thrust me away so hard I staggered and fell on the cool tiles.

"Father? What is wrong? What have I done?" I could think of no mischief I had done, no sin I had committed. I stood up and stared at him, puzzled. But not fearful. Not yet.

He looked past me, to where my mother stood rigid and silent. "Tell him," he said. "Tell him the great wrong you have done. Tell him who and what he is. Speak the truth and earn a quick death."

His words seemed to echo in my ears. I ran over and threw my arms around my mother. "What does he mean? Mother, tell me!"

"Yes, tell him." My father smiled, and for a moment I saw, not my father, but a demon, one who served Ahriman the Dark. "Take as long as you wish. I can wait."

My mother looked down at me; bent and kissed my forehead. "I will tell you the truth—the truth, so neither I nor your true father will be forgotten. Remember us, my son. Promise me that you will always remember."

"Yes," I said, even though I did not understand, and my voice trembled as I gave her the vow she wanted from me, "I promise."

"Listen then." Her voice took on the cadence of song; slow and mournful. "I was married very young—far too young. I was not even a woman when I wed, and I was afraid. But my mother swore to me that my husband would wait to claim his right to use my body. She told me I must be married at once, for my husband was an ambitious man, and I brought to him as dowry both my pure Persian blood—"

Here my father laughed; a harsh, cruel sound. My mother flinched, but she continued to speak, her voice soft and her words clear.

"—and my father's influence in the king's court. So my new husband thought the gold he paid for me money well spent." She stared past me, as if her eyes sought to see that frightened young bride.

She fell silent; my father stalked up and stood close. There was a knife in his hand now, and he pressed the blade against the blue vein throbbing beneath her skin. "Go on," he said. "The boy must hear the whole story, and from your lips. Tell him all the lies, all the false promises—tell him. *Tell him!*"

Trapped between them, I felt the man I had always called my father shake with the force of his long-banked anger; felt my mother tremble with cold fear. But while he gave his hatred free rein, she struggled to remain calm, to control her terror—and I knew she did so for my sake.

"It is a long story," my mother said. "May I sit, while I speak?"

For long moments, he stared at her, slowly pressed the knife harder against her soft neck. I held my breath, dared neither speak nor move. At last he laughed—it was not a joyous sound—and lifted the knife away from her throat.

"Why not?" he said, and wound a handful of her dark hair around his fist. He used her hair as a leash, dragged her to her favorite spot in the garden: the bench beneath the lemon tree. There he released her hair and shoved her down onto the smooth marble bench. She suffered all this silently; once seated, she held her arms out to me, and I fled into her embrace. She settled me beside her on the bench, her arm tightly around me. She stroked my hair, and began.

"First you must understand, my son, that the world goes as the Good God Ahura Mazda desires, and not as mortals wish. If I had understood that, I would have saved myself, and you, and my husband much suffering. But I did not, for when I was given in marriage, I was still only a girl . . .

. . . a girl too young to realize that her new husband was also young. Too young to understand her husband was ambitious—and he had a cruel heart. Then the only things he had wed her for melted away like snow in summer. Her father died before he could gain a royal appointment for his son-by-marriage, and her mother returned to her own people, who refused to acknowledge her husband. For their blood could be traced back into the mists of time, while his—

"Was good enough to mingle with yours when your lying father needed money."

My mother ignored him, and spoke on, as softly as if telling me a bedtime tale. She told of her loneliness and sadness, and how she did not even have a child to console her, and so her husband accused her of being barren as well as useless.

Then came the day her husband purchased a new slave, a young man from far-off Abyssinia. Tall and dark and handsome—

"And I? Do you dare say I am ugly?" He looked ugly, as I stared at him, and I had always before this thought him as fine-looking as a king.

—but it would not have mattered had the Abyssinian been short and ugly. For he was kind. And the girl and the slave took comfort from each other, and the fruit of their love was a beautiful boy. But one day her husband learned of her betrayal. And he killed the slave . . .

"—and sentenced his unfaithful wife to death." My mother bent and kissed my forehead as I stared, barely comprehending her words. And then she said, "Remember that I am guilty. My husband could have slain me the moment he found me with your father. But he let me live to bear you, and to nurse you, and to see you grow. Seven years. He gave me seven years with you, my son. He let you live. He promised he would not kill you. For that, I will bless his name in—"

"In Hell," my father said. "Now set the boy aside and come to me."

My mother bent to kiss me once more, then gently pried my hands from her skirts. "Good-bye, my son. Live well. Be happy." Then, to my horror, she walked over to him, her head high and her steps steady.

He grasped her arm and made her turn so that she faced me, pulled her close so that her back pressed against him. She stood there quietly, made no move to escape, or to resist. He pulled his knife from the sash around his waist and lifted it slowly to her throat. He laid the long blade against her slender neck, the keen edge just touching her smooth skin.

And just before he slit her throat, the man I had called my father displayed the cruel heart my mother had spoken of. "Yes, he will live, and he may even be happy as a eunuch." He pressed the knife's blade harder against her skin. "Your son will be a eunuch and a slave. Think of that, as you beg Daena the Lady Guardian for mercy in the afterlife."

My mother did not answer him, either to beg mercy or to curse him. She looked straight at me. "Close your eyes," she said.

Those were the last words she spoke to me. I did not even have time to obey her command before the man I had always called "father" yanked the blade across her throat. He let her body fall into the blood pooling scarlet at their feet and dropped the knife upon her body. Then he looked at me and I no longer saw my father. I saw a man who hated, who hated so greatly that even slaying his unfaithful wife did not ease that hatred. Now he would try to slake his anger by tormenting me.

And there was no one and nothing to stand between me and Lord Haman's thirst for vengeance.

But Haman did not make a eunuch of me then. No, with true cruelty, he waited another seven years to fulfill his last vow to my mother. Seven years during which I was treated in all ways as if I were Haman's true son.

Seven years in which I was in fact a prisoner in the most opulent and gilded of cages.

I thought of nothing but escape. I tried, and I failed, and with each failure Haman's grasp upon me tightened. By the time I turned fourteen, I had been confined to my rooms—rooms with barred windows and barred doors—for two years. Even the gardens had been forbidden to me.

The day I turned fourteen, Haman hired the most expensive, most sought-after prostitute in the city. "She will be yours—for one night. One night, so that you will know what you have lost," my father said. Mad hatred glittered in his eyes. "Your life will be my revenge on that whore, your mother."

He took me to the room he had prepared for this occasion. A feast had been spread over a low mirrored table, and the smell of honeyed wine lay heavy upon the air. Beyond the table I saw a bed covered in extravagantly embroidered coverings. A woman sat upon the bed. She smiled when she saw me and rose to her feet, graceful as a willow in the wind. Slowly, she walked across the room until she stood before me. Her skin gleamed like old ivory and a perfume of cinnamon and roses hung upon the air around her.

"This is the boy? But he is lovely, my lord Haman. You led me to expect a monster." She put her fingertips under my chin, turned my head from side to side as if judging my value.

Haman ignored her jest. "You have one last night as a man," he told me. "What you do with this night is up to you. But one last bit of fatherly advice, Jasper—if I were you, I would not waste these hours. Remember, dawn follows night."

And you have another room prepared, one in which a man and a knife wait for me . . . Strangely cold, I did not move as Haman laughed and strode out. I heard the bar drop into place, imprisoning me in this lush chamber.

—and then the gleaming, perfumed woman set her hand upon my arm. Her skin burned against mine; suddenly my whole body trembled. Then she gently made me turn until I faced her. After one swift glance, I stared at the floor as my face burned with shame and my stomach seemed to rise into my throat. I thought I would vomit.

"I—I am sorry," I managed to say.

"Look at me." Her voice was soft; I found myself obeying her command. When I did, she touched her fingers to my lips.

"Hush. There is nothing to fear, and I tell you now that you are not acting foolishly, my young lord." She stroked my hair; my body trembled at her touch. "My name is Zebbani."

I managed to say, "Yes, I know." For Zebbani was the most famed, most desired, most expensive courtesan in all Shushan. I had seen her once, as her palanquin was being carried past the courtyard gate of Haman's house.

She smiled, and somehow gave me the impression that it pleased her that I knew of her—when I considered that night later, I realized how fine an actress a courtesan must be. "Now, tell me your name."

"Jasper," I said. "My name is Jasper."

"Jasper." She made my name into a caress. "You are well-named, a treasure indeed." She slid her hands down my arms, entwined her fingers with mine. She pretended not to notice how my hands trembled. "Now come, for the night is long, but not endless."

She drew me over to the waiting bed, made it easy for me to follow her down onto the silks and furs. By the time she had me half-undressed, I was more than half in love with her. My first woman.

My *only* woman. Ever.

Or so I thought on that one precious night. *Now, and never again.*

But as in so many other things, I was wrong, although I did not learn that for many years, in yet another life.

I lay there beside her and wondered if she could see how hard my heart beat. To me, each throb seemed to shake my whole body. *This one night will be all I will ever have. This is the only woman I shall ever touch . . .*

Then, as despair lay heavy in my bones, something spoke to me. *Do not abandon hope. A task awaits you. Will you let evil thrive?*

I do not know which god or goddess chose to speak to me that night. If I did, I would build a temple of gold in that deity's honor. Those few words strengthened me, gave me purpose.

I will survive. I will live, and I will pay back to Haman every pain he has ever caused. I looked at Zebbani, who possessed everything that makes a woman desirable to men. My life, if I survived the knife, would be spent as less than a man—I would be seen as a safe servant and guardian of women. If I were strong and clever, I could rise high in such service. . . .

"Teach me what pleases a woman," I said to the finest courtesan in all Shushan. "Teach me how to make a woman happy."

She did—and more, Zebbani taught me what I had not even thought to ask: how to please a man. I barely listened to what she said, but my body remembered, later. Sometimes I wondered just how much Zebbani knew of Haman's plans for me, for that knowledge proved very, very useful. Men have more interest in young pretty eunuchs than women do.

And the last words she spoke to me as the lamps guttered out at dawn remained, echoing through the long years until I gained happiness. On very dark nights, when I counted hours and could not sleep, I would hear that faint echo, and wonder if Zebbani had been a woman at all. Surely only a *peri* or a *fravashi* could have repeated my own thoughts back to me; only a goddess could have given me such a blessing. Perhaps she had been Daena Herself, Judge of the Dead.

"You think to escape Fate, but you cannot. If I could procure escape, do you think *I* would be here?" She laid her hand upon my cheek; her palm smelled of musk. "My chains are very pretty, O Master of Treasures, but gold imprisons as surely as iron. All I can do for you is tell you what I tell myself, when I cannot sleep."

"And what is that?" I asked.

"Make your enemies pay." She leaned forward and pressed her lips to my forehead, softly, as if she were my mother. "And make yourself prosper."

⁂

I remember horror and I remember pain—but I survived the knife, and my body healed. And I was fortunate, for already I had become enough of a man that no one would ever think me a woman. But neither would I ever be mistaken for a whole man. My beauty fell into the realm between the two . . . and I knew that beauty, too, was as much a weapon as knowledge and courage. I would need all the weapons I could attain to achieve my goal:

Haman's downfall.

I wanted him to suffer as my mother had suffered. I wanted him to know the Three Pains: of body, of mind, of heart. All I did would aim, like a poisoned arrow, at that target. Not an easy task, nor a swiftly achieved one. Even at the age of fourteen, I knew my vengeance lay long years away. But I was young.

I could wait.

Zebbani had advised me to weigh my own worth, to gauge my appearance as if it were a weapon. *"Which it is. Never forget that." Zebbani had smiled. "Always make sure you own a very, very good mirror. Silver, if you can get it. Bronze, if you cannot. Failing either, find an honest critic." I had asked her for her judgment, and she told me coolly, "You are very beautiful, Jasper. But never think that beauty alone is enough."*

By the time I healed, I had studied myself carefully, trying to prepare for whatever would come next. In my room was a silver mirror only as large as my hand—but it was highly polished, and I had ample time to stare into it. Small as it was, I tilted and angled the shining disk, gazing upon myself intently. Zebbani had told me I was beautiful—but my true father's dark Abyssinian blood had mingled with the pure Persian of my mother's to create a strange, exotic creature.

I was tall, far taller than most boys of fourteen, supple and slender as the hunting cheetahs kept in the royal stables. My skin was far darker than amber; my eyes slanted long over high cheekbones. My hair curled without aid from me, and it had not been cut since the day Haman killed my mother. Flowing night I could gather into my hands. *Long enough to braid into a rope to wrap around Haman's neck. Long enough to choke out Haman's life.*

If I had possessed anything at all with which to cut that braided hair from my head, I would have killed Haman even if I died myself for it. But I did not. Haman had ensured there was no blade of any kind for me to take up in my hand.

I wasted many hours wishing for that blade—of course, with a blade, I would not need to cut my hair, for instead I could have cut Haman's throat, as he had my mother's. I always ended by chanting silently, *Wait. Not now. But someday. Wait.*

Words I used as a shield every time Haman came to threaten and bully, for he could not resist gloating over his next scheme for my life. He had not yet divulged this, but clearly he expected me to await it with terror. Having survived gelding, I found it hard to worry over his brutal mocking hints. But I feigned fear, and refused to meet Haman's eyes. I convinced him I was terrified. Helpless. Why should he not believe that? As I learned much later, Haman fed on fear.

Haman had gloated for so many months over how he would sell me that I had almost given up hoping for it—you may think it odd that I longed to be sold, but I knew only that would free me from Haman. So the day Haman had me brought into his courtyard to be inspected by the dealer's keen eyes, I was anxious to make a good impression on the man. I did not want him shaking his head and walking away without me.

Summoned, I followed my guard down to the shadowed archway. In the courtyard beyond, I saw Haman talking with a bored-looking man with the sleek, well-fed look of a successful merchant. Clearly Haman extolled my virtues; equally clearly, the man discounted at least half of what Haman said. But then Haman came over to where I stood and grabbed my arm.

"See for yourself—here is the boy." Haman yanked me into the full light, and I saw the man's eyes widen.

But the slave dealer was canny; did not admire me too openly. "Yes, he is pretty enough—but what is wrong with him?" the trader asked. "I have no time to waste haggling over a boy suffering from the falling sickness or so bad-tempered even beating will not cure the fault."

Haman smiled and shook his head. "His fault is that I cannot endure the sight of him since his mother died."

I saw understanding in the trader's face, and a certain sympathy. I almost admired Haman's cunning; he told truth—in part. I listened as they haggled over my future, and I wondered if my calm obedience surprised Haman. If it did, he made a virtue of my tameness.

"You'll have no trouble with him," Haman said, as he and the slave dealer agreed upon my price. "The boy is a coward, like all eunuchs."

"Truly, they are all so, and sly as cats." There was no real interest in the dealer's voice as he agreed with Haman.

Even as hate burned through my veins, I listened, and learned what I was expected to be now. *A cunning coward. I can play that part. And I can wait. And someday, Haman, I will avenge my mother, and my own life.*

The trader touched my arm. "Come along, boy." Haman smiled like a wolf, expecting me to protest, to struggle, to watch me dragged away. *Oh, no, 'Father.' I will never give you what you crave.*

At that moment, I desired only one thing: to destroy Haman's fierce triumph. I reached out and took the trader's hand and let him lead me away. I looked back only once, when we paused for the gatekeeper to open the heavy door to the street beyond.

And when I looked back, I smiled. For long years afterward, I cherished the swift baffled anger on Haman's face.

I had won that small prize, at least.

Because I let tears fill my eyes and let timid-seeming smiles tremble on my lips, and because I was beautiful and slender and only a boy still, the trader thought me cowed and biddable. I did not disillusion him; I hoped even now to escape the fate Haman had condemned me to. I would always be a eunuch—but I vowed on my mother's blood that I would not remain a slave.

To my surprise and relief, I was not forced to endure the humiliation of the public auction block. The trader to whom Haman had sold me regarded me as a valuable asset. As such, my sale would be as carefully calculated as that of a rare gemstone. Nor was the man unkind to me—why should he be? I gave him no trouble, and he wished to get as large a price for me as possible. I, too, wished that. The more I cost, the more I would be valued and the better I would be treated.

Or so I thought then. I was too inexperienced to know that while it was true for most owners, for some a high price served as goad.

Just before the sale, the slave trader presented me with a gift to ease my path through this new life. "Here, boy—" He handed me a small ivory box. "This is for you. Open it." I did and found myself looking at a dozen gilded pills. Puzzled, I tilted the box and let one of the gold spheres slide into my hand.

"Go on," he urged. "Take it."

I hesitated, then did as he had ordered. I was, after all, known to be both meek and obedient.

The poppy's gift eased tension I had not realized I suffered, and let me enjoy being readied for display to potential bidders. By the time I had been bathed and massaged with sweet oil so that my skin gleamed, and my hair combed so that it waved down my back like a dark cloud, I found myself smiling at everything and nothing.

The slave merchant inspected me carefully and nodded his approval to the servants who had tended me. I smiled again; he said, "Good boy," and patted my shoulder as if I were a pet dog. He led me into a large room lit by dozens of lamps. The little flames sent light dancing over my oiled skin, and that, too, seemed worthy of amusement. But I did not laugh, for the lamplight glinted on watching eyes.

Men stared, studying me, assessing my face and body. The opium seemed to withdraw, abandoning me to the gaze of avid eyes.

In later years, I would have known how to react in such circumstances. I would have made it my business to discover who might attend the sale merely to watch, and who to buy, if he could. And I would have known how to convey my interest to the buyer I wished to win the bidding. A glance at the proper moment could persuade another hundred darics from the right man.

But I was only fourteen, and required all my strength of mind merely to stand calm. I refused to offer up even one tear for the amusement of these men. I kept my eyes downcast as the slave merchant extolled my virtues; I must have seemed modest, or shy. Better they think that of me than see the anger burning in my eyes.

I heard voices calmly offering coin upon coin. Sometimes there would be a pause—I slanted a glance up through my lashes to see why, and discovered that some men merely lifted a finger to indicate a bid. More and still more was offered as I stood there. Words flowed into a babble of noise. Time slowed, became meaningless.

And then suddenly it was over. I belonged to a new owner, and I could only hope he would be kind.

My new owner treated me as if I were a dog he had just gained: with soothing words and gentle care. Still clouded from poppy, I must have seemed as soft and yielding as a puppy, and as eager to please. I remember being bundled into a cushion-filled litter and carried through the streets while the man who had purchased me stroked my hair and promised me I had nothing to fear. Once we reached his dwelling, I was taken to the bathhouse and left there with all I needed to prepare myself.

Clearly my master had good taste as well as wealth: the bath was open to the sky and lapis dragons coiled over the tiled walls. The tubs were formed of pale stone, and the soaps and ointments laid out were new, untouched. And there was a choice of scents.

So. I have some choices left. Not many. But some.

I lingered in the bath as long as I dared as the water cooled and the poppy withdrew, leaving my mind all too clear. I prolonged the ritual of combing out my hair and oiling my skin. Every minute I delayed was a small victory, but in the end I must submit. I could only hope what I must endure would not be too degrading, but I knew that whatever happened, I must conceal my disgust. *"Smile,"* Zebbani had told me, *"Smile." "And if I cannot?"* I had said. *"Shed a few tears—and then smile. Always smile."*

I survived the cutting. This cannot be worse. I wrapped the thin robe around me and tied the gold-spangled sash tight—as if a silken knot would protect me. Then I pulled the small ivory box from its hiding place and opened it. The gilded pills promised sweet oblivion, turning painful reality into soft dreams. I tipped two of the pills into my hand, lifted my hand to my mouth . . .

. . . and hesitated with the opium already upon my tongue. Yes, opium softened life, but it also weakened body and mind, leaving a man vulnerable.

And I am a man. I am. Yes, a few bits of flesh had been cut away from my body. But I still had my mind and my will.

I spat out the gilded pills into my hand. *No. I will not let Haman win. I will not succumb to despair. I will live, and I will prosper, and someday I will make Haman suffer as he has made me suffer. As he made my mother suffer. No matter how long it takes, or what I have to do, I will see Haman groveling in the dirt at my feet. And then I will kill him with my own hands.*

And I could not achieve that goal if the Lady of Poppies ruled me. I set the ivory box down and picked up the polished silver mirror. I studied my reflection in the shining metal. Smiles I could manage, but I did not know how to banish the cold anger from my eyes. That, I must learn. But for tonight, lowered lashes would have to hide that unsuitable emotion. With any luck at all, my owner would merely think me shy.

A slave silently led me to the master's bedchamber, and there I waited until he chose to join me. I had thought myself prepared, but his entrance still startled me. At last I took a sober look at my future: a man in late middle age, fleshy of body and face, with nothing to create beauty in his appearance but his eyes. While all else about him at best could be called plain, oddly enough his eyes were perfect, long and soft and dark as ebony. To my surprise, he looked as nervous as I felt.

"I am Orodes. Lord Orodes." He fidgeted with his sash and those lovely eyes of his refused to look at me. "I know I am neither young nor handsome. But you will find me a kind master. I am neither quick to anger nor impatient."

Why is he telling me this? I am his, bought and paid for. I lowered my lashes as if shy, thinking hard. I could not escape what he wanted of me. Now, what did he truly desire? I remembered Zebbani's words:

A woman must study the man who owns her, even if only for an hour. She must seek out what will please him, what he yearns for. Sometimes he himself does not know what it is he craves. Learn that, and the slave becomes the master . . . in the bedchamber, if nowhere else.

Now, in this bedchamber, I studied my new master carefully. He regarded me hopefully, like a dog longing for a soft hand and a gentle word. *He desires love. I cannot give him that.*

But I remembered what Zebbani had taught me: find out what a woman wants, she had said, and give her what she desires. This was no different. I drew a deep breath and walked across the room to stand beside him. When he looked up at me, I smiled, and held out my hand. Lord Orodes took my hand and kissed it, which astonished me.

"You will not be sorry," he began. "I will be generous, give you jewels and—"

"No," I said. "Not now." And before he had a chance to ask anything of me, I leaned forward and kissed his mouth.

When I pulled back, he took his hands from me at once. Clearly he feared to frighten me. "Why do we not sit and talk, and drink some wine?"

"We will do whatever you wish, lord. I am yours."

He laughed as if I had made the wittiest of jests. "Why, so you are—what is your name?"

"I call myself Bagoas, lord. But of course you may call me whatever pleases you." I had swiftly learned when the slave trader had renamed me that Bagoas—"beautiful boy"—was a common name among good-looking young eunuchs. That knowledge made me cherish the name instead of despising it—for how could Haman find one Bagoas among a city full of them?

"You are beautiful enough for a Bagoas. Beautiful enough for any name you please." Again I saw wistful longing in his eyes.

I reached out and took his hand. I was not sure what to do next, but guessed that he was no novice at this game. And I did not want to sit, and to talk, and to drink wine, and to pretend we were friends. I wanted the act over and done with, at least for tonight. So I said,

"You are my first." That was truth, if I did not count Zebbani—who was a woman. The words sounded unsteady, trembling between us.

He raised his eyebrows. "Truly?" I nodded, and he laughed. I stared at him, baffled, until he said, "I assumed the auctioneer told less than absolute truth when he described your virtues. Well, Bagoas, I am sorry—"

It took no great wisdom to know what he was about to say, and that I should not let him say it. "Well, I am not. How could I be sorry that I have come to a man who is gentle, and kind, and . . . and . . ."

I could think of nothing else to say, but he had already gathered me into his arms and was stroking my hair. I was glad, for my face was hidden from him, and while he truly was kind and gentle—and as he had said, generous—that did not mean I found him desirable. But he must think me, if not eager, at least willing. So I pushed back from him, and before he could speak, I put my hands on his cheeks.

"I know nothing, so you must teach me, my lord." Then I kissed him again, and whispered, "You have such beautiful eyes. . . ."

After that, Lord Orodes was mine to do as I liked with. I was too canny to pretend an instant, overwhelming passion for him. Lord Orodes was soft-hearted, but that did not mean he was a fool; he would never believe that I had fallen in love with him on sight. But that I grew to love him—*that* he believed, because he wished to believe. I feigned love, granting his unspoken hope. And he had desired me at first sight; I do not know if he truly loved me, or merely confused love and craving.

I did not really love him, of course—but I gave him no reason to suspect that. And I did become fond of him. Why would I not? Lord Orodes treated me generously and kindly.

In addition to fine garments and costly trinkets, he permitted me great freedom, and granted any request I made of him. Since I had the sense to ask only what he could easily give, he happily gave me that and more. He even allowed me to learn how to ride—an activity I found uncomfortable at first, but one that I deemed it necessary to learn. A man on horseback was a man only a swift ride away from freedom. No matter how kind my current owner, I never for one heartbeat forgot that I was only a slave.

A slave could never avenge his mother's murder.

Somehow I must set my feet upon a road that led to Haman, and to revenge—a vow I swore anew the day I learned Haman had married again. His new wife proved extremely fertile; Haman already had one new son and another on the way. By the time Zeresh ceased providing heirs to Haman, he possessed ten sons.

The three daughters Haman sired did not survive more than an hour after their birth. Haman did not value girls.

Two years. So long a time, when one is young. So brief a time, when one loses something precious.

I lived with Lord Orodes for two years, and I learned a great deal from him, for he was truly a gentle man, with excellent, exquisite taste. I learned to appreciate good food, good wines, good art. Lord Orodes taught me elegance and style, and I was grateful.

Always my owner seemed to look to the future, and to its hazards. One night, as we lay together on the linen sheets that covered his wide silver-chased bed, he clasped my hands and made me be still.

"Bagoas, my dear boy, there is something you should know." Lord Orodes smiled as I stared at him, oddly uneasy. "Oh, do not fear, nothing is wrong." He caressed my cheek; sighed. "You are so young, so beautiful—and I am neither. No, do not deny it, Bagoas." He looked at me intently. "So I have settled my affairs in such a way that when I die, you will be freed, and a sum of money settled upon you so that you may live as you please."

I had not expected this—nor did I expect the grief that sent tears pressing hot behind my eyes. I flung myself into his arms, and for once my wet eyes and my caresses were not calculated. I managed to control my unruly emotions long enough to say, "But you will not die for a long time—you must not!" As I said the words, even I believed I meant them; baffled, I pressed my face into his neck.

Although we never again spoke of what would be mine when he died, it was not necessary. My unfeigned affection, gratitude, and tears had pleased Lord Orodes. When I think of him, I am always glad I gave him that honest pleasure, and I still feel sorrow that I could not love him as he deserved. But we are formed as it pleases the gods to make us, and how and who we love is not ours to choose.

I learned that lesson hard, and even now, long years later, as I look upon my beloved wife, I sometimes hear silent laughter ripple through the air.

⁂

Lord Orodes lived only another half a year; that summer he slipped while descending the Great Staircase and broke the bones in his wrist as he tried to save himself. But broken bones did not kill him—that injury was easily splinted and bound, and would have healed. The small rents in his skin destroyed him, wounds so insignificant the physician barely noted them, and they scabbed over and were forgotten.

All I can think is that sealed some unclean matter into Lord Orodes's body, for within a few days, his hand swelled, that pressure opened the scratches, and pus oozed from them. The physician forced vile-smelling concoctions down Orodes's throat, and bound the contaminated hand with black ointment, but none of his remedies eased my master's pain.

I sat with him all day and all night, wiping his fire-hot skin with cool cloths, coaxing lemon-water through his dry lips. Nothing helped. The infection blazed through him, inexorable and deadly.

At least he knew I was there. I held his hand as life burned out of him, and when his skin slowly cooled until his hand lay cold and heavy in mine, all I could be was glad he no longer suffered. I bent and kissed his hand, and then I slowly rose and went quietly to my own room.

I did not think of what Lord Orodes's death meant to me, nor did I weep. I was too weary. All I did was curl onto my bed and fall instantly to sleep. Nor did I dream. A small gift from the gods.

What happened next should not have surprised me, but I was still young. I received another lesson, iron-hard and as valuable as gold. Lord Orodes's heirs—two nephews and a married daughter, all three greedy and grasping, which I suppose is why I had never seen any of them until their wealthy relative lay dead—produced his will, which allocated all his fortune to them. Of my manumission and bequest, nothing, and I swiftly realized why.

I, too, was part of Lord Orodes's wealth, and his heirs had no intention of losing so valuable an asset. By the time I learned this, I was locked in my room while they sought a purchaser who would offer the outrageous sum the heirs had set upon my youth, my beauty, and my many exquisite skills.

I shook with anger and did as much damage as possible to my room and its contents—but I did not make the mistake of deciding that all men were cruel and all women treacherous.

I did decide that if ever I had the chance to repay those two men and that woman, I would do so. They not only had consigned me to more years as a slave, they had thrown Lord Orodes's good name down into the mud. Perhaps they thought I did not know he had promised me freedom when he died, and I did not waste time and breath contesting their treachery.

The Phoenix Garden offered the most for me, and so I became the property of one of the most exclusive brothels in Shushan. That was also the year Great Darius's death shattered the world. All Shushan watched as the Immortals escorted the royal body of the King of Kings through the main streets on its final journey. Since the Phoenix Garden stood three stories high, its rooftop permitted us a view over the lower buildings; although not close, still we could stare upon the royal funeral procession's steady progress.

Even I stared, just as did the rest of the Garden's elegant whores. I had never seen such a spectacle before—well, few had.

First came the king's favorite horse, a stallion black as midnight; the horse wore a saddle and bridle so gilded and studded with gems the leather could not be seen; peacock feathers crowned his head. His coat gleamed, oiled with frankincense, myrrh, and cinnamon. An Immortal led the stallion, which paced calmly; so smoothly and serenely that I suspected it had been fed opium in its morning grain.

More Immortals followed, rank on rank, marching as solemnly as the black stallion. To look upon these elite soldiers, each in a blue-and-yellow uniform, each carrying a ceremonial lance tipped with a silver pomegranate, was to look upon a marvel, not upon men. In the noonday sun the Immortals were bright shadows, impossible to count. After the Immortals walked the Magi in dark blue robes: astrologers who summoned the future by reading the stars in the heavens; alchemists who dealt in the elixirs of life and death.

And then Darius, King of Kings, passed through the streets of Shushan for the last time.

Six white oxen with gilded horns pulled the huge chariot that carried all that remained of Great Darius, Ruler of the World. He left Shushan immured in a sarcophagus of sandalwood from Hind; so much gold and so many gems adorned the coffin that the costly sandalwood was hidden.

I would happily have watched in silence, but the other girls and boys chattered away like Egyptian monkeys. "Oooh, look at the jewels!" "They say spices—including saffron!—fill the coffin around the king's body." "And frankincense, too. Look, there are the Seven Princes!" "The royal harem will be desolate. The new king is so very young!" "Oh, look. Oh, isn't it all wonderful? Sad, of course, but . . ."

Isn't it all wasteful? But I said only, "Even in death, the King of Kings must have only the best." Who could argue with so true a statement?

Behind the sarcophagus rode the Seven Princes of the Face, and following them uncounted nobles; court favorites; personal household slaves; regular army; more horses with golden bridles and braided manes and tails; snow-white oxen with gilded horns.

Then the last doomed oxen plodded past, and the procession vanished. And the mistress of the Phoenix Garden clapped her hands sharply and ordered us all to go downstairs. She anticipated many lucrative hours ahead.

I walked down the smooth brick stairs. The gaudy spectacle, the brief hour of amusement, was over. It was time to go back to work.

I did not remain more than half a year at the Phoenix Garden, for one patron desired me for his own—not so much for my fine eyes, but for my connection with Lord Orodes. The man seemed to believe I could imbue him with Lord Orodes's virtues. I had prayed he would tire of me, but he did not, and at last offered so much gold that the Phoenix Garden consented to let him purchase me outright. I would far rather have remained in the brothel.

The man to whom I now belonged owned a fortune so new almost all of it was in coin rather than land and livestock. His name was Isqanqur, and he was everything Lord Orodes had not been: sleek, well-built, handsome.

Lowborn, hard-hearted, crude.

Isqanqur displayed his wealth lavishly in his dress and in his dwelling. Too lavishly.

He had paid an extravagant sum to obtain me, and he treated me as he treated any other expensive creature he purchased. As something without a mind, without feelings. Something to be used.

I despised Isqanqur, and he knew it. He knew I thought him crude, untutored. Oh, not because I ever said a word against him—no, I was more subtle than that. More cruel; only later did I realize how cruel and how foolish I had been. I merely let my distaste lurk in my tone of voice, in the tilt of my head, the slant of my eyes. I had thought I feigned all my affection with Lord Orodes. Now I realized how much true fondness I had for him, and how far I still had to travel to be even half as successful as the courtesan Zebbani, for I could not pretend even to like Isqanqur, let alone to offer up to him a passionate desire. No, not even to save myself from a whipping. I learned that the hard way, when Isqanqur made a sneering remark about Lord Orodes and I could not keep the scornful curve from my lips, conveying all too clearly that I thought Isqanqur less than the dust on Orodes's grave.

That was my first whipping, and after it Isqanqur made me crawl over to him and kiss his feet.

I did as he ordered, and as I set my lips to his feet, I learned an invaluable lesson—although it was not the lesson Isqanqur wished to teach me. I learned that he could not shame me, because I did not care. Yes, I despised him. But I did not *care.* I did not even care enough to hate him. He could abuse my body; he could not touch my soul.

I learned another lesson from Isqanqur as well—I discovered what Haman truly was. For Isqanqur was hot-tempered and unkind, but he was still a man. Not a good man, perhaps—but he was no less and no more than man.

Now I understood what Haman truly was: a monster. Oh, not because he killed an unfaithful wife—any man might do as much. Isqanqur would not hesitate in the same circumstance. Had Haman caught his wife with her lover and slain her in hot rage, or had he learned of her betrayal and executed her in cold anger, he would have done no more than was his right.

But to tell her the day and time of her execution was to be in seven years?

To let her live, and raise her bastard child; to treat her to all outward appearances as a pampered wife, and only then draw the blade across her throat? That was cruelty of no mean order.

And then, as she knew she drew her last breath, to tell her that my fate would be far worse than a clean death . . .

Yes, Haman was a monster.

Even if I could have forgiven all the rest, to tell her that, to send her into the afterlife knowing what awaited her cherished son—that I could never forgive. If only for that cruelty alone, Haman must pay. Someday and somehow, I would find a way to make him suffer as my mother had suffered.

But understanding that Isqanqur's wickedness fell far short of Haman's did not endear him to me. As I have said, Isqanqur regarded me as nothing more than an expensive pet, of less worth than his dogs and his horses. He had purchased me because I had belonged to Lord Orodes, and Isqanqur longed to be as highly regarded. Isqanqur could not grasp the truth—that he could not buy what Lord Orodes had possessed. For a man whose god was wealth, this failure baffled and angered him.

Sometimes I wondered why he had bothered to buy me at all, for after the first month or so he seldom called me to his bed. When he did, I knew I would spend the days afterward nursing bruises and trying to forget what I had been forced to do. It was not so bad after Isqanqur bought himself another gift: twin sisters.

Padmavarna and Padmavati. Girls from the easternmost, the richest, province of the empire. Hindush, where rivers ran bright with gold. I had never seen anything as lovely as those two girls. Small, light-boned as doves, but full-curved at breast and hip; skin the pale gold of ripe wheat and hair that rippled like black water to their knees. Green glass bangles glinted on their wrists and silver bells chimed on their ankles, and I lusted after both girls.

I see you shake your head, disbelieving—for after all, am I not a eunuch? How can I ache to caress a woman? Well, I was not cut until I was nearly grown, and Haman's final poisoned gift to me was a night that taught my body what it was for. And I remembered. Oh, yes, I looked upon Padmavarna and Padmavati and I burned to possess them as any man might.

And I had them, too. At first I saw them only at a distance. Isqanqur amused himself with his new toys, and then grew bored with them. He had long since grown weary of pretending he wanted me.

One night he summoned all three of us to his bedchamber. I remember standing at the door into that room, the two sisters beside me. They held hands, their fingers so tightly laced the skin paled. And in their night-black eyes I saw the same hopeless contempt that I felt.

"Endure. He cannot enter here." I pressed my hand over my heart, hesitated, and then reached out and brushed my fingertips across the swell of their left breasts. "Not here," I said as I felt the hard beat of their hearts. I learned later they barely understood Persian, but that did not matter, for they grasped my meaning well enough.

We needed endurance that night, for Isqanqur demanded services from all three of us, and when that palled, he ordered us to perform with each other. We obeyed, of course. We touched what he told us to touch, kissed and caressed and fondled as he ordered. I locked myself away; I felt nothing, not even shame. Padmavarna and Padmavati later told me they had done the same. A vital skill for those whose bodies belong to whoever pays. I wondered if Isqanqur even noticed that none of us displayed any sign of passion. No smiles, no sighs, no gasps or moans. We followed his commands in silence; our faces as unrevealing as painted masks.

When at last Isqanqur tired of watching his toys at play, he sent us away brusquely. Perhaps he had noticed after all; I did not care. The twins and I fled his bedchamber, and without a word spoken among us, hastened to the bathhouse. None of us cared that it was late in the night. We stripped off the gaudy ornaments Isqanqur had us wear and helped each other bathe, scrubbing and rinsing until at least our bodies were clean.

Then I began the task of combing out Padmavarna's thick black hair, while she did the same for Padmavati. The silence began to oppress me; I dipped the sandalwood comb in oil, and as I coaxed the comb through a tangle, I said, "I am sorry."

"Is not your fault." Although the bathhouse was warm, Padmavarna shivered.

I put my arms around her and she curved around and buried her face against my chest. I felt her tears hot and wet on my skin. I pressed my cheek against the top of her head as I held out one hand to her sister. Padmavati too came into my embrace. How long we sat curled into each other, offering silent comfort, I do not know. I do know that night was the turning point, as if the gods decided I had learned enough, suffered enough, to be ready for the next move in their eternal game.

Isqanqur had pushed us past fear. Now Padmavarna and Padmavati and I became, not friends, but allies. I taught them more Persian and they taught me the language of Hindush. That was not all they taught me. The twin lotuses—for they both were named for that flower—were supple as serpents, and knew erotic tricks that would have made the famed courtesan Zebbani blush.

The pleasure we gave each other's bodies was enhanced by the knowledge that each honey-sweet kiss, each shuddering delight, each smile and soft laugh, we stole from Isqanqur.

The precarious balance of life in Isqanqur's house could not last. My contempt for him became too obvious; reveling in deception, I became careless. If I angered Isqanqur, he would whip me. I had suffered that before; the threat of it no longer troubled me. I did not realize how deeply Isqanqur's anger ran, and I was not nearly as clever as I thought I was.

Of course, it was my contempt, and my failure to conceal my scorn, that opened the gate to the future I needed. First, however, I received one last lesson. Much later I realized the value of that beating; I needed to rein in my pride and to curb my tongue.

On my last day as Isqanqur's slave, he decided to have me accompany him as he paraded through the streets to the slave market. For such a sober task, Isqanqur had donned garments more suitable to a royal banquet, while I had been weighed down with half a dozen gaudy necklaces, earrings so long they brushed my shoulders, and bracelets so heavy I could scarcely raise my hands. As I followed Isqanqur through the streets toward the market district, I wondered if he truly thought flaunting his wealth in this fashion impressed anyone. Lord Orodes would have despised such a tasteless display.

My thoughts showed plain on my face, which was a mistake. Isqanqur glanced back at me; turned and grabbed my arm. "Stop that," he snarled. "You don't belong to that soft, overbred idiot Orodes now. I won't permit—"

I never learned what he wouldn't permit, for words seemed to come out of my mouth of their own will. "At least Lord Orodes knew what to do with a boy, or even a girl. Of course, his slaves were willing to go to *his* bed—"

Even as I said the words, I knew I had gone too far. So swiftly I had no chance even to turn away and run, Isqanqur grabbed me by my hair and hauled me to my knees before him. Then he began to beat me. His fist hit fast and hard as a stone, and all I could do was try to protect my face from his furious blows. I tried to withdraw into myself, distance myself from what my body suffered, but there was no rhythm to Isqanqur's wild attack. He struck in maddened rage, and I was unable to separate myself from the harsh pain. I could only endure, and pray he stopped before he killed me.

I barely noticed when my prayers were answered. Isqanqur slammed his fist into my cheek; pulled back, readying to strike again. I waited for the next blow, wondering how many more he would slam into my body before he tired, how many more I could endure before he damaged me beyond repair. I raised my hands to protect my face, and waited—and slowly realized Isqanqur's next blow would never land. A man grasped Isqanqur's wrist and Isqanqur had released my hair and rounded upon him.

"There's no need to kill the boy." My savior spoke in the mildest of voices; he opened his hand, freeing Isqanqur's wrist. That, I thought dazedly, was a mistake.

"I'll do as I please with what I own," Isqanqur told him, and turned back to me.

"If you do kill him, it will be murder, you know."

This time Isqanqur lifted his fist to add emphasis to his anger. "And if you don't pull your nose out of what does not concern you, I'll—"

"I really wouldn't advise doing that," the man said. He did not move, and no fear showed either on his face or in his voice.

"Oh you wouldn't?" Isqanqur stared at the man, who was plainly dressed and wore little jewelry. I could see Isqanqur dismiss him as someone of no importance, with nothing about him to impress or fear. "Who are you to give *me* orders? Be off before I teach *you* manners as well!"

But where Isqanqur saw only an interfering passerby, I saw a man whose plain garments were made of the most finely woven linen—linen dyed a pure sky blue, a color difficult to achieve and costly to acquire. As jewels, he wore only earrings and a bracelet—the earrings exquisite silver doves, and the bracelet a wide band of hammered gold. I judged his garb at least twice as costly as Isqanqur's flashy robes and gaudy jewels.

All this I swiftly noted even as Isqanqur ordered the man away, and I acted even faster. Ignoring the pain throbbing through my body, I flung myself at my rescuer's feet. "Please, my lord . . ."

The man bent, grasped my arms. "Can you stand?" Although I didn't know whether I could or not, I nodded, and gasped as the pain lanced sharper as he helped me to my feet. I clung to his hands, trying desperately to find the words that would snare him, make him claim me from Isqanqur.

But all I could manage to say was, "Help me. Please."

The man looked at me intently. Very gently, he touched my battered cheek. "Yes," he said, "Of course." Then, to Isqanqur, "What is the price?"

"Oh, he's not for sale." Isqanqur grabbed my arm hard; I flinched and bit my lip to keep from yelping as his fingers clenched over bruises. "I have plans for him."

"I see. I have plans for him, too, so shall we say . . . one hundred darics?"

Isqanqur's expression changed, for of all things under the sky, he most loved money. One hundred darics was a huge sum, and I was only a slave, after all. Replaceable. "One hundred darics? You carry such a sum with you?" Isqanqur sneered.

The man's tranquil expression didn't change. "Of course not. You can collect it at the palace." He waited, and then, as Isqanqur gaped at him, sighed and said, "All right, two hundred darics."

Apparently struck dumb, Isqanqur nodded. The man gently set me aside, and I leaned against the nearest wall for support as he pulled off his seal ring and held it out to Isqanqur. "Take this to the office of the king's treasurer and tell him to give you two hundred darics, and that my ring proves the request true and valid. Leave the ring with the treasurer and I will claim it back from him. Oh, and have him write out a receipt for the sale for you to sign."

As if entranced, Isqanqur accepted the seal ring. "The king's treasurer. Two hundred darics. A receipt." He didn't even glance at me as he left, hastening to claim the money before the man changed his mind.

Once Isqanqur had gone, I pushed myself away from the support of the wall. Forcing myself to ignore the varied pains as I moved, I bowed low before my rescuer.

"You do not know what horrors you saved me from, my lord. But I do, and in gratitude for your intercession I would be your willing slave—even had you not purchased me." I noted that my new owner flushed, and shifted as if embarrassed. Was he shy, then? Well, I knew how to deal with shyness. "You paid too much for me," I added. "A few minutes' bargaining, and you could have had me for a quarter of that." Bold, you will say—but boldness is a virtue, with a certain type of man.

"Perhaps," my new owner said. "But it doesn't matter." He seemed about to say something more, but fell silent as he studied me. I could do nothing about the vivid whip marks, or the many-hued bruises, but I could smile at him. Even that hurt. "What's your name?" he asked.

I slanted my eyes at him. "I call myself Bagoas."

He sighed. "Of course you do. But you're free now, so you may call yourself whatever you wish—even your own name."

His steady eyes compelled, and I found myself telling him the truth, or at least some of it. "My owners have called me Bagoas."

"And is that what you wish to call yourself?"

"No." I thought for a moment. "I will be Hegai now."

He tilted his head, regarding me with interest, as if I were a scroll he wished to read. "Hegai? You want to call yourself 'eunuch'?"

"I am a eunuch. And I must be called something."

"Why not still call yourself Bagoas, then?"

"Something . . . suitable," I said.

"Oh, I see." He did not ask any more questions about my name, for which I was thankful. I did not need Haman learning where I was now, or with whom. I let a few moments pass before I asked, "May I know my lord's name?"

"Oh. Daniel. I'm Daniel. Now come along, Hegai, we need to get you to someone who can treat those injuries."

My luck had changed again, this time for the better—no, for the best. For the first time, I mounted the Great Staircase to the palace. All the world seemed to be on those stairs—merchants with wares garnered from Cathay at the eastern end of the Silk Road to Damascus at the western; princes who had traveled a thousand miles on the Royal Road to come before the King of Kings; Immortals riding oil-sleek horses; messengers running up and down upon palace business.

Bazaars lined the sides of great flat terraces between the long wide flights of stairs. Booths sold everything from turquoises to crimson leather boots to golden fish in crystal bowls. Scribes and booksellers and tailors; jewelers, swordsmiths, perfumers; a dozen dozen booths selling flowers. There seemed no rule to what was sold where that I could see—just a vast brilliant confusion of bright-hued tents and treasures of every sort in every color the gods had ever spread upon the earth.

When at last we had climbed the Great Staircase, I paused for a moment at the top of the vast expanse of smooth-polished marble and gazed out across the bright city to the mountains far to the east. I smiled, and followed Daniel through the King's Gate into the palace.

Or, more truthfully, into the citadel that crowned Shushan. Many palaces had been built within the citadel's shielding walls. Oddly, I had not been surprised to discover that Daniel lived within the palace or that he ranked so highly he had been granted his own house and a small walled garden.

As he led me through the gate into his garden, a woman came out of the blue-tiled house. She had fair hair and blue eyes, and carried a copper bowl full of figs. She stopped when she saw us and regarded Daniel reproachfully. "Oh, Daniel, what have you done now?"

"I bought a eunuch," Daniel said.

"You bought a *what*?" A tall, lean man strode out of the house; stopped and glared at Daniel.

The woman set down the copper bowl. "Arioch, you're frightening the boy."

Arioch's gaze shifted to me. After a moment, he said, "I doubt it. All right, Daniel, what happened *this* time?"

"He can tell us later. The boy needs his injuries looked after." The woman came over and gently put her arm around my shoulders. "Come with me." Her voice was kind and her touch soft; I let myself relax into her support.

Behind me I heard Daniel say, "His owner was trying to beat him to death, so—"

"So you bought him," Arioch finished. "How much, Daniel?"

There was a long pause before Daniel answered. "Two hundred darics."

"Two hundred darics?" Arioch said. "Daniel, are you out of your *mind*?"

I drew myself up and turned, looked straight into Arioch's lion-gold eyes. "I'm worth it," I told him.

"Oh, I'll just bet you are." Arioch went over to Daniel and flung his arm around Daniel's shoulders. "Come on, Daniel, tell me what trouble I'm going to have to haul you out of this time."

"None. No, really, Arioch—"

I heard no more, for the woman guided me into the house. "I'm Samamat," she told me. "Sit here, and tell me how and where you're injured . . ." I knew what silent question hung in the air, so I said, "Hegai. My name is Hegai."

"Hegai." Samamat sounded as if what she really wanted to say was, "It is not!" Instead, she said, "Very well, *Hegai*. Now tell me what happened to you and what hurts."

She listened as I explained, and examined me carefully. I had been fortunate; although badly bruised, no bones seemed broken, and my face had not been marred beyond mending. Samamat wiped my skin with vinegar and wine; the liquid stung like fire in the small cuts it found. Then she handed me a cup. "Drink this. It's honey and poppy syrup. It will stop the pain."

I drank, and she was right; the mixture stopped the pain. I felt nothing until I awoke the next morning.

That is how I came to the palace of the King of Kings: brought there by Daniel Dream-Master, a Jew long famed for his wisdom and judgment, and for telling the truth of dreams. He possessed another gift as well. Daniel saw the future. Much later, when all plots had been spun and all debts paid, I asked Daniel what he had seen, that day he saved me from death and brought me into the life of the imperial palace.

"I saw a boy being beaten to death," Daniel said, and when I asked if that was all, if there had been nothing more, Daniel merely smiled and said,

"Isn't that enough?"

It was a pleasant life, living as Daniel's servant. Yes, servant, for the first thing Daniel did was manumit me. After three years, I was no longer a slave. I was free. *Free.* No one owned my body but me, and if I chose to walk out of Daniel's garden and out of the palace and go anywhere the wind took me, I could do so.

I did not choose to leave, for I now dwelt in the best place possible: the palace. Power coiled itself within palace walls; I needed power if I were to destroy Haman. I would have stayed with Daniel in any case, once I discovered who he truly was. For he was a man of such importance that King Darius had brought him from Babylon. Daniel was far-famed as a master of dreams. Kings had bowed down before him.

So I willingly remained with Daniel and the two who lived with him, Arioch and Samamat. Unlike most, I did not find it odd that one of Daniel's dearest friends was a woman; the life I had been forced to lead had taught me not to despise women. Arioch had served King Darius as captain of the palace guard. Samamat was Arioch's wife. An astrologer from Chaldea, and very learned, I soon realized that she softened Arioch's keen mistrust and anchored Daniel's absentminded tolerance. Both men loved Samamat—that I saw at once.

Just as I saw that Daniel also loved Arioch. I wondered if either man knew it.

Naturally my first scheme to gain Daniel's goodwill was seduction, but he seemed oblivious to my advances.

I tried to flirt with him, indicate I found him desirable despite his age. But I soon realized that Daniel didn't care how exquisite my eyes were, how flawless my skin. I didn't know whether to be grateful or angered—everyone I had yet met, man or woman, had at least acknowledged my beauty. Daniel ignored it.

So I turned my efforts to making myself indispensable in other ways, flatly telling Daniel I wished to learn all I could.

"About what?" Daniel asked, and when I said, "Anything," he laughed, and said he would teach me what little he knew. To hear him tell it, he knew nothing more than any man with common sense might. "You would learn more from Arioch, and far more from Samamat."

"I would learn from all three of you," I said, and that was how I became Samamat's student, learning mathematics and the science of stars, as well as the ancient tongue of Chaldea. Captain Arioch occasionally would trouble himself to give me a lesson in using a sword, or a dagger—but most of what I learned from him, I learned by watching, and listening. He had a keen sense for danger, even when the threat was still barely a thought in a man's mind, an excellent skill to acquire.

The three of them had survived the reigns of the last kings of Babylon, and that was no easy feat. Then they had been swept up by all-conquering Darius and carried here to ancient, royal Shushan. Kings seemed to find Daniel irresistible, as I once overheard Commander Arioch say.

Even though Commander Arioch and the lady Samamat had married, and she had borne him a son—who was now a man grown, a warrior as his father had been—they shared Daniel's dwelling. The most valuable lessons I learned from them, they did not even guess they taught. For as I studied them, stalking every advantage I could gain, I slowly began to comprehend the emotions that bound the three together. Friendship, love, trust—and in the depths below, yearning, hunger, guilt. I saw the bright passion burning between Arioch and Samamat, and Daniel's dark craving for them both. Samamat knew. Arioch did not.

And Daniel refused to know.

Once my eyes were opened to the invisible currents flowing between Daniel, Samamat, and Arioch, I practiced my new skill any time I encountered two or more people gathered together. Tongues lie; bodies reveal truth.

So do our dreams. To my dismay, the lotus twins, Padmavarna and Padmavati, haunted my sleep. I tried to ignore them, told myself to forget. I refused to care. *I will not risk the ruin of all my plans. No.*

But one morning I found myself asking Daniel if he would be willing to purchase two more slaves from Isqanqur. Once the words had flown free, I stood and stared at Daniel in silent horror. Now he would question me, demand to know why, and I knew I would have to answer . . .

Daniel apparently found nothing odd in my request. "Friends of yours, I suppose? I am sorry, Hegai—I should have asked if there was anyone . . ."

At first his words seemed to echo oddly in my ears; sounds that made no sense. I stared at the floor so he could not see the tears burning my eyes. The only questions Daniel asked were those needful to ensure he acquired the right girls.

"I don't know if we really need two girls here, but I'm sure you'd like to see them again, so I'll ask Samamat. She'll think of something—"

"No," I said hastily. "No. Not here."

"That may be for the best," Daniel said, after a moment's thought. "I don't think I want to explain to Arioch that I've just bought twin Hindush slave girls."

I kissed Daniel's hands, not caring that the homage embarrassed him. He promised he would tell me when the twins were free of Isqanqur, but I never wanted to see or hear about Padmavarna and Padmavati again. When I said that, Daniel merely nodded and said, "All right, Hegai. It shall be done as you wish."

Those were the last words Daniel ever said to me about the matter. He never needed to tell me anything more. I knew the lotus twins were safe, because they no longer danced soft-footed into my dreams.

✢

The day I turned eighteen, I asked Daniel if he would grant me a boon—"If it pleases you, of course." After all, I had acted as chamberlain, scribe, and messenger to Daniel Dream-Master for over a year, and in that time I had learned the palace ways and ingratiated myself with court officials, high-ranking servants, and even with slaves. Since I was a eunuch, I could enter any portion—men's or women's—of the vast complex of palaces, courts, and gardens that formed the royal citadel—and I had charmed a number of the harem women. Most of them were delighted with a flirtation even with a eunuch, as the king who owned them was only seven years old.

"You want me to grant you a favor? Of course," Daniel said. "You want to leave, I suppose? I have to admit I'll miss you, Hegai."

"Oh, no, I have no wish to leave." *Leave the palace? Why would anyone want to do that?*

"Oh." Daniel looked faintly baffled. "What *do* you want, Hegai?"

"If I have pleased you, my lord, and found favor in your sight—"

"Just ask," Daniel said.

"Yes, just ask, Hegai." Arioch wandered into the room from the garden; even at his venerable age, he had a knack for untimely—and very silent—entrances. "You know Daniel hates it when people grovel."

I bowed my head. "Very well. My lord Daniel, my petition and request is that you recommend me to the Chief Eunuch of the Women's Palace."

"You want to work in the Women's Palace? But why?"

Only Daniel would ask such a question. "It will provide me with greater scope in my livelihood."

"Scope?" Arioch said with blatant disbelief.

"Yes, my lord Arioch." I kept my voice bland, my face smooth. "Scope." Few people held as much power as the Chief Eunuch of the imperial harem. I lusted after that power, but to grasp it, I must first gain a place in the palace hierarchy.

"Very well, Hegai," Daniel said. "If that's what you really want, I'll arrange a meeting for you with the Chief Eunuch."

In those days, the Chief Eunuch of the Women's Palace was an amiable, indolent creature called Giti, who had held his office more years than I had lived. To become the Chief Eunuch was the height of ambition for my kind, so once Giti must have been capable and cunning. But now . . . now the king was a small child, the harem's women had belonged to the last king, and the Women's Palace languished, useless. Giti's skills languished as well, and he became content to grow old in comfort.

All Giti wished to do now was bask in sunlight and admiration, and indulge in sweet food and wine. I intended to ensure that Giti's simple wishes were granted.

That Daniel Dream-Master offered me to him pleased the Chief Eunuch a great deal. I was a visible sign that Daniel held Giti in high regard—and Giti knew how well I cared for Daniel's affairs. On the occasions I had encountered the Chief Eunuch, I had carefully flattered him and offered him admiration that was not entirely feigned. Giti had, after all, managed to grow old as Chief Eunuch; he had much of value to teach—survival is a valuable skill to learn.

So to the satisfaction of all parties involved, I became the Chief Eunuch's servant. I intended to become as indispensable to Giti as I had tried to be to Daniel. I knew I had never truly become necessary to Daniel—but Giti was a much simpler master to manipulate. I intended to become Chief Eunuch someday. Becoming essential to the current Chief Eunuch, to the smooth running of the Women's Palace, was a vital first step to that goal.

I thought at first that I would have to offer the coin of my body to obtain advancement—but although Giti openly admired my beautiful body, his true desire was to be granted the respect due his rank and age. I granted him both, as well as the added pleasure of instructing me as I listened with avid interest. By the time I was twenty, I acted as Chief Eunuch in all but name.

I intended to have the title as well, in time. The Chief Eunuch held nearly as much power as a king, or as a queen mother. Now I began an unhurried campaign to persuade Giti he wished to retire and to recommend me as his successor. Giti began to speak wistfully of rest after his long years of service, of the joy of simple living in a small palace in the cool mountains, fantasies I happily encouraged. Then Giti died by sheer mischance; between one bite of honey-cake and the next he lay dead, a look of faint surprise on his round face. I had been Giti's creature; I had acted as Chief Eunuch with

Giti's goodwill, but I did not possess the title. All my careful plans lay in ruins.

Or so I thought. For even as I arranged ostentatious funeral rites I knew would have pleased Giti, I received a summons that nearly stopped my breath. Queen Mother Amestris commanded me to appear before her.

Of course I had seen the Queen Mother, but I had never been permitted near enough even to hear what her voice sounded like. Palace gossip slid around the subject of Amestris; unwary words too easily reached her ears, for she had spies everywhere—or so it was whispered. Daniel had mentioned her rarely, and Samamat cautiously. Arioch never spoke of her at all.

I had emulated Captain Arioch; I listened when others spoke of the Queen Mother. For Great Darius's death had bestowed upon the empire a new King of Kings barely five years old, and Queen Mother Amestris seized the reins of power and ruled in her son Ahasuerus's name.

Even the council of the Seven Princes bowed to Amestris's will. In the Women's Palace, rumor had it that Amestris controlled the Seven with fear and lust. No one would dare say the Queen Mother ordered death, or that she welcomed men, or women, into her bed. But somehow she knew everything—or so it seemed.

I cared only for the fact that the all-powerful Queen Mother had sent for me.

Giti must have spoken of me to her. Can she possibly wish me to replace him? A hope I dared not indulge when I needed to prepare myself for the most important encounter of my life.

At last I would meet the true ruler of the empire, for until the king was no longer a child, power lay in Amestris's lap.

Of course I wore my finest garments and gems; nothing less would do for this occasion. At the appointed time, I walked through the harem gardens to the Queen's Palace, which Amestris still inhabited even though protocol demanded the Queen Mother remove herself to the Queen Mother's Palace once the king her husband died. But Amestris created her own rules.

She did not receive me in her reception hall with its queen's throne, but in a private chamber as brilliant as a jewel-box. Amestris formed its most precious gem. When I was ushered into her presence, she sat on a couch, playing cup-and-ball. As I bowed low, she flipped the ivory ball into the cinnabar cup with great precision. Her garments of blue and silver shimmered in the lamplight.

"Oh, rise," she said. "I cannot judge you without seeing your face." Her voice should have been a delight to the ear, soft and sweetly modulated. But I used my own voice as a weapon and as a mask, so I recognized the tactic.

I straightened and then, when I saw that I towered over her, I sank gracefully to one knee. "Thank you, O great queen. May you live forever."

Amestris looked upon me, smiling; I knew she studied me as intently as I did her. "Did you know that Giti spoke of you to me?"

"No, O queen." Truth: I did not *know*—but I had guessed, for Giti had hinted of it to me often enough. "That was kind of him."

"He spoke very well of you. Now that he is dead, a new Chief Eunuch must be appointed."

"As my queen says," I murmured; behind my bland words and smooth face, my heart beat fast and hard. I could not let her see how very much I desired that appointment. The Chief Eunuch of the Women's Palace held more power in his hands than many kings.

Amestris sent the ivory ball into the air again, caught it neatly in the cinnabar cup. "Do you think yourself fit for the position?"

And here I had thought it would take hours to come to this point! I smiled. "Yes, O queen."

"You are very direct." She did not sound offended.

I took a risk. "So are you, O queen."

She laughed softly. "Why, so I am. So you think yourself fit to replace our dear Giti? Well, he seemed to think so. I believe you call yourself Hegai?"

"I do, O queen."

"Well, I suppose it is appropriate. And you are loyal, are you not?" Amestris stared at me, assessing, her eyes cold and flat as a snake's.

I bowed, so I did not have to face those serpent eyes—and so that she could not look into mine. "I am loyal to my queen," I said, and by the time I straightened, I was smiling. To my intense relief, the Queen Mother also smiled.

"I am a generous mistress," she said. "And I have women who can make you forget you are no longer a man."

"Thank you, my queen. But I would rather have women who can make me remember that I am not a woman."

"So, Hegai . . ." Amestris seemed to taste the name, savor it upon her tongue. She smiled, an expression I did not trust.

I kept my face smooth and bland as milk. Let Amestris speak, and so reveal her thoughts. I would keep silent, and reveal nothing.

But she surprised even me; as I stood and watched her, the Queen Mother rose gracefully to her feet and walked, slow and deliberate, down the steps from her couch. She reminded me forcibly of a panther, sleek and dark and deadly. She stood before me and regarded me with bland malice.

"So you wish to serve as ruler of the Women's Palace? You wish to command the women of the King of Kings?" To hear Amestris speak, one never would guess that the King of Kings had not yet attained the age of fourteen. "Very well, show me your skill. Undress me."

Panther indeed; I dare not hesitate. I neither startled nor smiled. I merely said, "As my queen commands," and unpinned the brooches at her shoulder. Nor did I pause when all that still covered her body was a shift of silk so finely woven her skin gleamed through the cloth. Since she did not countermand her order, I unlaced the gilded cords closing the shift, and then Queen Mother Amestris stood before me clad only in her jewels and her sandals of crimson leather.

"Well?" Amestris said. "What do you think, when you look upon me?"

I studied her calmly. "I think that you are very beautiful." Small and lush and perfect, her beauty was that of a flawless sculpture. "But of course you know that. Do you wish me to remove your jewels and unbraid your hair, O queen?"

She laughed softly, and put her jeweled hand upon my chest. "No, Hegai. That is not what I wish. What I wish to know is just how great is your desire to serve me." Her hand slid lower; I could feel the heat of her skin even through my clothing. "Are you a true eunuch, Hegai? Did the knife cut away ambition?"

So the Queen Mother wishes to test my resolve, does she? Well, let us see if I can surprise her. I regarded her steadily. "Ambition is not what I lack, O queen. Nor do I lack skill."

Amestris raised her slim, elegantly arched brows. "Ambition and skill both?" Words almost whispered, gentle and tender—but I heard a cruel purr beneath the softness. She stepped back, as self-possessed as if she wore royal robes rather than nothing but the perfumed air. "Well, let us see—and let us see what lies beneath those splendid robes." Now her words cracked whip-sharp.

But if she thought to see me blush or flinch, I disappointed her. "As my queen commands." No emotion disturbed my voice or troubled my features. I neither frowned nor smiled as I obeyed Amestris's command. I did not smile even as I, too, stood naked to the lavishly scented air, and she gestured in wordless demand. I merely set my hands and then my mouth upon her, and learned her sharp harsh needs.

And as I tasted the bitterness of her perfume and felt her gilded nails etch my skin, I silently thanked the courtesan Zebbani. Of all the truths Zebbani had taught me during that one fierce night, the one that saved me was this:

The body is nothing. Never give more than your body, Jasper. If your body is all they possess, they have no power over you.

Afterward, Amestris ordered me to dress her again; she stood silent as I performed that task. When I had finished, I bowed, and waited—waited, calm and patient, until Amestris indicated that I might dress as well. Then I waited again. At last Amestris said, "Do you not wish to know my decision, Hegai?"

"Of course, O queen. But you will reveal it when it pleases you to do so." I knew I dared greatly, but I could do nothing if I did not know Amestris better than she knew herself—and if she did not respect me.

Her eyes narrowed—if I had not been studying her face, I would not have seen that revealing movement. But that was all; she smiled, and said lightly, "Wise as well as beautiful and skilled. Now run along, Hegai—and think upon how you will order things now that you are Chief Eunuch over all the women in the palace."

Over all *the women?* I doubted my authority covered Amestris herself; Amestris intended the palace to have but one mistress—and no master.

"Whatever you wish, you have only to ask for and it will be granted." Amestris sounded bored; she twisted a gold bracelet around her wrist, seemed intent upon the gleam of emeralds and gold.

"Anything, O queen?" *She lies. She would not grant me half the kingdom—or tell me the truth, even if I asked it from her. So this is a test.*

Amestris said nothing as meaningless as "anything within reason." Instead, she said merely, "You are clever and ambitious. Spend whatever you will upon whatever you please. And remember that with the blessing of the Lord of Light, you may be Chief Eunuch for many, many years."

Nor did she ask if I understood her. She knew I did—and if I did not, whatever I commanded would warn her that I was either foolish, or greedy, or both. And a greedy fool would not reign over the Women's Palace for long.

"Now go." Amestris never took her eyes from the bracelet she toyed with.

What came next seemed, when I pondered upon it later, inevitable. Destined. I bowed and backed away from the Queen Mother—and as I straightened and turned to leave, I found myself face-to-face with Haman.

Ice and fire roared through my body; I froze, incapable of movement or speech. I had awaited this moment since I was fourteen—and now that it had come, I was unprepared. All I could do was wait for Haman to—

"Welcome, Lord Haman." Amestris sounded more bored than welcoming. "Allow me to introduce to you the new ruler of the Women's Palace. And you, Hegai, behold Lord Haman, a man of many uses."

Her voice steadied me; I bowed. "Greetings, Lord Haman." When I straightened, I looked into his eyes, and saw nothing there but indifference. In all my imagining and planning for just such a moment, never had it occurred to me that Haman would not know me instantly. But he did not. The last time he had looked upon my face, I had been a maddened, grief-stricken boy of fourteen. Now I was a head taller than he. Now my hair curled oiled and sleek down my back to below my waist, and malachite and kohl, gold dust and carmine, masked my face.

Haman inclined his head very slightly, but said nothing in response to my polite words. He clearly saw no reason he should bother to feign interest in me.

He does not know me. Jubilant, I bowed again, and swept past Haman. As soon as Haman could see me no longer, I stopped and leaned against the wall. Smooth stone pressed cool against my burning skin and steadied me.

Haman. Haman and Amestris. Now that was a pretty pairing; I wondered just how much the Queen Mother knew about her favored courtier. *They are well matched. I must tread carefully. Very, very carefully.*

But Haman at last had entered my world again, and I possessed weapons he did not. *I am Chief Eunuch now; I am a person of high rank and great importance. I have power, and I have learned how to wield it.*

And I can wait. I already have waited half my life. I can wait until Haman overreaches himself and I can bring him down to despair and pain. For I did not simply wish Haman dead.

I wanted him to suffer. Nothing less would satisfy me.

My new dwelling within the Women's Palace was two stories high and larger than Haman's fine house had been. Bedchamber, dressing chamber, servants' rooms. A reception hall many kings would have been pleased to claim. My own bath. A courtyard open to the sky. A garden. All of it had been Giti's. And now all of it was mine.

Mine, to do with as pleases me—for so long as I please Amestris. I could not rely on the Queen Mother's goodwill; someday she might decide I was no longer useful, and then she would discard me. *Or at least she will try to do so. Before that day dawns, I must ensure that she cannot.*

But that problem I would face in a different hour. For this span of time, I would permit myself to take pleasure in what I had achieved. I walked slowly back through the rooms and passageways, pondering what I must do to make the Chief Eunuch's apartments truly mine. Already I had noted a lack I wished to remedy. I beckoned to the nearest young eunuch.

"I wish to meet with the best silversmith in Shushan."

He bowed. "As my lord desires. When does my lord wish to speak with him?"

"At once; when else?" I smiled, to show I jested—a small thing, but fearful servants are useless. I wanted those who served me to do so contentedly; I knew all too well the damage an unhappy servant could cause. Amestris might have elevated me to this high position to reward me, or to punish another; as a jest, or on a whim. Whatever her true reason, I intended to grasp and hold what she had so casually bestowed. There was no better place in all the empire for me.

Chief Eunuch. Master of the king's women. Ruler of the Women's Palace. Only Queen Mother Amestris herself possessed more power than I.

For now. What had been bestowed upon me could be withdrawn. I needed to become so strong that even the Queen Mother would think thrice before challenging me. That would take time, and cunning.

But I had both.

I was still daydreaming my way through the Chief Eunuch's apartments when the best silversmith in Shushan arrived. The messenger I sent had been swift and diligent; I must remember to reward him.

"What is my lord's desire?" the silversmith asked.

"A mirror. I desire you to create a mirror as tall and wide as I am, and to burnish it until it shines bright as the full moon."

Delighted by such a lucrative commission, the silversmith promised me a wonder indeed. "Such a mirror has never been seen before," he declared. "Why, you will be able to see your entire body all at once." Then he began asking me questions, and taking notes upon his wax tablet. At last, satisfied he knew precisely what was required, he praised my wisdom and good taste, bowed low, and went away smiling.

As well he might. Such a mirror would cost the royal treasury dear; cost as much as a king's crown. I did not care—and if Amestris did, at least I would learn swiftly how to rate her promises.

The silversmith proved a true artist. He set the sheet of polished silver within a frame of ebony; silver stars adorned the midnight wood. My mirror shone bright as the full moon and reflected images clear and unwavering. I had the mirror placed in my reception hall, a tangible reminder that the Queen Mother favored me—and what that favor meant. I pretended not to notice when my servants and slaves paused to gaze into its brilliant depths. Even I found it hard to ignore such a matchless treasure—and the cost was indeed enough to buy at least one royal crown. . . .

Queen Mother Amestris never once mentioned my silver mirror.

Nor, to my great relief, did Amestris ever again demand my erotic skills. Although I had pleased her body, pleasure had not been her goal. She had learned what she needed to know: that I would do anything to gain what I desired. And I had learned the same of her.

Now we each knew the most important thing about the other.

Neither of us needed to repeat the experience.

Of course my sudden ascension to Chief Eunuch caused great disturbance throughout the vast maze of gardens, courtyards, gates, and palaces that constituted the palace of the King of Kings. All the women and eunuchs hastened to congratulate me and to bestow gifts upon me. I thanked them for their good wishes and their gifts, smiling upon them all equally.

And while no man might enter the Women's Palace unless the king himself granted that honor, courtiers sent me rich gifts and good wishes. Most of the gifts I set aside. But one offering, a pretty eunuch of twelve, I kept—a singular honor for the man who had sent him to me.

Haman.

I told myself I kept the boy because he would be a useful weapon against Haman, but I knew this was nonsense. I kept Hatach because he had clearly been terrified when he thought I would refuse to accept him, and I could not send anyone back into Haman's claws. It did not turn out as badly as it might, for Hatach proved industrious and good-natured, although he always had a nervous temperament, seeing threats in every shadow. Of course Haman prided himself on having obtained my favor, which might someday prove useful.

What I learned from Haman's gift proved even more useful, for it displayed Haman's contempt. He had made no attempt to discover what might truly please me; he had merely sent what he thought any eunuch must desire. Haman had sent the Chief Eunuch the gift of a pretty young eunuch just as he sent the Queen Mother the gift of a gaudy gold-and-lapis necklace.

What else could a eunuch desire but a younger eunuch to play with? What else could a woman yearn for but jewels?

The Queen Mother, being far more clever than Haman, had troubled herself to discover what might delight me. On the day that I had been Chief Eunuch for a year, she sent me a pair of Salukis brought from Arabia, one pale as clear moonstone, the other dark as moonless night. She had taken heed of the hints I had dropped within the harem that in me, the Persian's love of dogs doubled.

Not so pleasing was the gift of a fine horse, a Nisean stallion with a coat as gold as a new-minted daric and big enough to carry me easily, along with a saddle and bridle with phoenixes tooled into the crimson leather. Amestris had also troubled herself to hunt me back from Daniel to Isqanqur, from Isqanqur to the Phoenix Garden to Lord Orodes, who had permitted a pretty eunuch to learn to ride a horse . . .

Queen Mother Amestris knew all this, and wished me to know that she knew. I thanked her for the stallion with bland face and utmost politeness. I only hoped she had not traced me back as far as Haman. If she had . . .

"A thousand thousand thanks, O queen." I knelt and kissed her myrrh-scented feet. "Who else but you, Queen of Queens, would think of such a gift? Who else would know what it means to me?"

"Who else indeed." Amestris's voice was smooth as cream.

I rose to my feet. "With my queen's permission, I will name the horse Phoenix."

"If it pleases you . . . Hegai. What do I care what name you choose for your stallion?" That was all she said, but it was more than enough.

So I knew my enemy's blindness, and my ally's shrewdness. They knew of me only what I wished them to know—at least this was true for Haman. As for Amestris, I never for a moment forgot that she was far older than I, and had not become King Darius's most favored wife because her heart dripped honey. Amestris could play the sweet, gentle woman to great effect, but that was only one of many masks she donned at need.

She also played the game of favorites with great skill; I allowed myself to be a pawn in this game. But I refused to play it within my own realm. Within the Women's Palace, to the surprise of all and the consternation of many, I had no favorites. I treated all the women and eunuchs under my charge kindly, but none more so than another. Nor did I create quarrels and hard feelings by preferring one servant over another. The inmates of the Women's Palace did not know what to think of me.

They called me cold, ice-hearted—not to my face, of course, but my spies dutifully reported such unwary words to me. Because I did not blame them for reporting unflattering words or punish them for bringing unwelcome news, my spies gave me honest reports. Agents afraid of their employer's anger would offer any tale they thought would please.

What I demanded from my people and rewarded them for was the truth. Nothing less would serve my purposes.

Under my rule, the Women's Palace ran as smoothly as any place can when its very reason for being scarcely exists. Ahasuerus, King of Kings, was a child—a child who needed a loving mother, not a haremful of concubines.

Ahasuerus ran wild, spoiled by the palace servants and permitted every childish whim and folly by his mother. I knew someday I would need Ahasuerus's favor, when he became a man, and king in fact as well as name, so I tried to gain his liking. But Amestris had already taught him to be wary of fondness; that affection came with a price. So I settled for trying to engage his mind, which was in a fair way to being ruined by total indulgence.

I taught Ahasuerus to play chess. Once he realized I would not simply let him win, he set himself the task of learning. *At least,* I thought, as I watched the boy struggle to remember the rules before he moved a pawn, *at least he will have this.*

Remembering all they had taught me, I took Ahasuerus to visit Daniel and his two companions. Once.

For I returned to my own rooms to find a message waiting from Queen Mother Amestris. It consisted of only one word.

No.

I never took Ahasuerus to Daniel's house again.

⁂

The day King Ahasuerus turned fourteen, Amestris summoned me. She wasted no time on pleasantries. "The king is to marry. Ready the Queen's Palace for his wife."

I bowed. "Of course, O queen. May I ask what the royal lady favors?"

"The royal lady is Princess Vashti of Babylon, and as she is barely ten years old, I doubt she has any taste at all as yet. Do as seems good to you."

I hesitated, then asked, "And for the Queen Mother? Where—"

"Shall I reside?" Amestris smiled, never a reassuring sight. "I shall move to the Red Palace. You need not concern yourself, for I shall arrange matters there myself. You will have quite enough to keep you busy, for at the beginning of Tevet I go to Babylon to fetch the princess. You will have, I think, three months to make the Queen's Palace ready for her."

Thinking hard, I bowed myself out of her presence. *Vashti of Babylon—why her? Of course*—Princess Vashti's grandfather had been the last king of Babylon; marriage to her would link King Ahasuerus to an ancient royal lineage. And since the princess was only ten years old—*Amestris can mold her into a toy queen, just as she has shaped Ahasuerus into a toy king.*

Now all I need do is completely re-create the Queen's Palace to suit the taste of a girl I know nothing about. In three months.

I sometimes went to sit with Daniel and Samamat just to bask in their tranquility. Now I desperately needed that soothing atmosphere.

Only Daniel and Samamat lived in the blue-tiled house now, for Arioch had died three years ago. To no one's surprise, Daniel had married Samamat. What surprised me was how much I missed him; when I sat in Daniel's garden, I still expected Arioch to wander out of the house and make one of his mocking comments. Sometimes I even thought I heard him. Today was one of those times.

"The harem is full of discontent." I turned the cup I held in my hands, wondering if an answer lay in the wine. I had been Chief Eunuch for five years the day I went seeking solace in Daniel's garden. I did not know my world was about to change utterly.

"The harem is full of discontented women. Sell all the women and buy the king a fast horse. At least he'd ride that."

Yes, that is what Arioch would have said. Oddly, his ghost always said what I wished to say but could not utter.

"Well of course it is," Samamat said. "Don't spill that, Hegai, the stain will never come out of that silk."

"Yes, of course it is, and it's only going to get worse." I took a deep breath, and then a long swallow of the wine. I had come here today knowing I would reveal this, and I didn't bother asking Samamat and Daniel to swear not to repeat my words. I knew they would not.

"Hegai? Going to get worse?" Daniel prompted, and Samamat added, "Why?"

I set the wine cup down. "Because the king is to be married. Amestris has chosen a wife for him."

"But—the king is barely fourteen!" Samamat said. "How old is this wife?"

"And more to the point, who is she?" Daniel asked.

"She's Princess Vashti of Babylon," I said, "and she's ten years old."

None of us spoke for long minutes. I heard birds chattering in the garden's trees and the soft hum of insects in the flowers. And again I seemed to hear Arioch's mocking voice: *"Oh, that's going to work out well. I'd move to Memphis if I were you. I hear there's great scope for eunuchs in Egypt."*

The silence weighed heavy; Samamat took my hand, laced her fingers through mine in silent comfort. I looked at our entwined hands and saw hers had the thickened joints and fragile skin of old age.

"You're right," Daniel said at last. "It's going to get worse."

A certain tension vanished when Amestris left for Babylon. My days were full, as I had to banish all signs of Amestris's tenancy from the Queen's Palace and create instead a royal bower for its new occupant. Not knowing any of her tastes, I worked half-blind, but I did my best to create a domain such a very young lady might enjoy. Anything she disliked could easily be altered to please her.

The day a messenger came to tell us that the Queen Mother and Princess Vashti would arrive in Shushan the following day, Ahasuerus came to me and demanded I play chess with him. "Of course, O king," I said, and set out the pieces while he sat and scowled. I waited, and at last he spoke.

"I'm not sure I want a wife," Ahasuerus said, frowning at the game board.

"You need not see her often," I pointed out. "But remember, O king, that Princess Vashti is a very young girl, and will be overawed by your—"

"Magnificence?" Ahasuerus hesitated, then moved a pawn forward. "She'll like my mother best. Everyone does."

He sounded resigned to this fact. I studied the pattern of the chess pieces. "Not everyone," I said at last, and slid my tower aside.

"Then they like me because I'm the king." Ahasuerus stared at the board so long I thought he had forgotten the game. At last he touched his vizier, and looked up. "If I move this, it's checkmate, isn't it?"

I looked at the paths his vizier might travel, and then smiled at him. "Yes, O king," I said, and tipped my king over in defeat. "I believe you've won the game."

Unlike the rest of those eagerly awaiting the new queen's arrival, I did not spend all the morning hours staring at the harem gate and sending to ask if anyone had yet spotted the queen's entourage. I knew Queen Mother Amestris far too well to think she planned her entrance for any hour other than full noon. Amestris would arrive at the city's Western Gate when the sun was high enough that all Shushan would be awake and watching. Her progress through the city would be slow, deliberate. Royal. She would take care that everyone had plenty of time to gaze upon the palanquin containing two queens.

My time that morning was spent in a last inspection to ensure all was prepared to welcome the new little queen, from her attendants to the coverings upon her bed. I walked through the rooms and courtyards of the Queen's Palace, regarding everything critically. Servants followed me, anxious lest I utter a word of criticism. But I had no complaint to make. "Beautiful," I announced. "Fit for a queen." I smiled—and watched my audience relax. Some laughed at my small jest; I took note of them, for it is always wise to glean clever servants for one's self.

Once I had satisfied myself that everything in the Queen's Palace was as

I desired it to be, I went to my own apartments and changed into my finest robes. Only then did I leave the harem and climb the stairs to stand on the top of the King's Gate and look down into the crowded streets of Shushan.

I had timed my day well; the procession had just reached the broad square at the foot of the Great Staircase. A bodyguard of the Immortals escorted the massive royal palanquin. A gratifyingly large crowd pressed into the square, striving to catch even a glimpse of the palanquin, or even of the curtains shielding the women within. The first rank of Immortals began to climb the Great Staircase, and I turned away without haste. The palanquin would not reach even the outer gates of the harem for another hour; I would be waiting in my proper place to greet it long before Amestris and her chosen daughter-in-law arrived.

Just before the sun reached its zenith, the harem eunuchs who had carried the palanquin on this last stretch of its long journey set it down gently on the velvet-smooth grass. I smiled—yes, I had indeed paced the time well; if only I had wagered upon it!—and bowed, reached my hand in past the opened curtains. "O queen, may you live forever. Welcome home."

The Queen Mother set her deceptively soft hand in mine and seemed to float up out of the litter. "Thank you, Hegai." She gestured to the litter, a movement graceful as a dancer's. "And here is—"

"Princess Vashti." I smiled, and once more held out my hand. I bowed very low. "O little queen, live forever. Welcome home."

Then I was staring at a face that seemed all eyes and amazement. After a moment, she smiled back at me and clutched my hand with both of her small ones. With my aid, she scrambled out of the litter and stared around her with eyes wide as full moons. Then she remembered to thank me.

I knew she was only a child, but I did not expect her to be so very young!

I looked over Vashti's head and saw Amestris regarding the awestruck child and smiling. Something in that smile made me uneasy; Amestris looked too amused, too self-satisfied, for her expression to seem either fond or kind.

As we headed into the labyrinth that was the Women's Palace, I held out my hand again to Vashti. She clung to it gratefully, and I thought of a forlorn kitten—why, I do not know, as this little girl was destined to be the new Queen of Queens. A life of the utmost luxury and ease awaited her.

But still, there was Amestris's odd smile . . .

Never mind, my little queen. I will make sure you are not only Queen of Queens, but happy. I do not care what Amestris wishes.

I shook my head to banish this treacherous thought. Why should Amestris choose Vashti from all the girls in an empire that spanned half the world and then be unkind to her?

All will be well, I told myself firmly, and then heard those disloyal words whispering again, *It no longer matters what Amestris wishes, for Vashti is your queen now.*

Now a ten-year-old girl was Queen of Queens: whatsoever she asked for became hers; she had only to utter a whim to have it granted. And she was surrounded by flatterers who seemed to care about only one of her attributes.

Such as Simin, a eunuch who had last smiled before the little queen had been born. He stopped me as I was on my way to inspect the harem kitchens. Before I could even ask what he wanted of me, Simin launched into a paean to Queen Vashti—or, more accurately, to Queen Vashti's appearance.

"I saw her in the bath," Simin said, almost breathless, "I would not have believed it had I not seen her with my own eyes. So perfect! Skin like pearl—"

"Yes, she is very pale," I said. "We must take care the sun does not burn her." I might as well have remained silent.

"And that hair!" Simin enthused. "Have you ever seen such hair before?"

I sighed inwardly; already tired of hearing endless tributes to Queen Vashti's hair. "Oh, yes, her hair. Lovely," I added after a pause, as Simin seemed to expect more.

"Lovely? Such hair is fit for a goddess, let alone a queen!"

She is a little girl—who one day will have power over all of us. Do you want to spoil her utterly?

"Very true," I said. "The King of Kings is a fortunate man indeed."

"Or will be—in time. When that green peach is ripe." Simin laughed and made a vulgar gesture, hiding the crude movement of his hand in the folds of his cloak.

And that displayed all most people saw when they looked upon Queen Vashti. Her glittering hair.

Fortune favored me; spoiled and petted though she was, Vashti possessed a kind heart. Someday she might even possess a clever mind as well. But I soon realized that Amestris did not seek a clever queen for her son. Amestris did not want a rival. If Amestris had her way, Vashti would remain a beautiful ignorant child; another pretty plaything for Ahasuerus.

And why should she ever desire to become more than that?

BOOK THREE

Queen of Beauty

VASHTI

Had I not been beautiful—fair as summer stars—I would never have worn a jeweled crown.

And had I not been as proud as the Daughter of the Morning, I would never have lifted the weight of that crown from my head, and said no.

No, I will not display myself like a common harlot.

No, I will not permit you to exhibit me as your most prized possession.

No, I will not demean myself.

"No," I said to the servants sent to fetch me, as if I were no more than a gem, than a statue, than an object. "No. Tell the king that I will not come."

Until the day Queen Mother Amestris took me to the palace at Shushan to be wife to her son the king, I never passed beyond the walls of my father's house in Babylon. A timeworn city palace and the courtyards hidden within its walls—that was all my world until I was ten years old. My father was a prince, and my mother a king's daughter—and a woman so virtuous that even her maidservants went veiled from our gate. Not that even her servants often walked out into the city; when my mother wished to purchase something, merchants sent their wares to our house.

My mother needed to be both virtuous and cautious, for her father had been Belshazzar, the last king of Babylon. Belshazzar had been both reckless and extravagant, and no warrior. He had been so enamored of lavish feasts that he was drinking deep of Shirian wine when the army of Darius the Great swept into Babylon. Darius had let Belshazzar's bloodline live—since the only one of that line who survived the battle for Babylon was a mere girl—but she had been swiftly married to one of Darius's most loyal men. My mother knew she lived only at Darius's pleasure, and that safety lay in modesty and seclusion.

And in her hope for the future: me.

I was the last child my mother bore, and the only one who lived past infancy. My mother guarded me closely, for I was a jewel of great price. Not only was I the last princess of the royal line of Babylon, but even as a child I was oddly, exotically beautiful. I was born with hair pale as ivory, and that rare color never darkened. My eyes, too, gleamed with extraordinary color; infancy's smoky blue transmuted into a myriad shades of silver and green, opalescent.

Nor did I become awkward as I grew. My body and limbs remained in perfect equipoise; I was neither too plump nor too slender. My skin stayed smooth as cream. And as I have said, there was my hair.

Not content to rely on my beauty alone to guarantee my future, my mother taught me most carefully how I must act at all times. She ensured I learned how to sit very still, to speak very softly. Always she impressed upon me my absolute duty to behave as befit a virtuous daughter of royal Babylon.

She charted each moment of my day. I was never alone, guarded always not only by high walls and locked gates, but by the constant vigilance of my mother and her trusted servants. I was a valuable commodity and no chance was taken that might jeopardize that value.

Modesty was a woman's greatest prize in my mother's world. Once my mother married, only her husband saw her unveiled face. And she reared me far more strictly than she, herself, had been raised. The path I would walk had been laid out for me from the moment of my birth, and my mother would not chance the slightest deviation, lest my glittering future vanish like a dream.

No one told me what had been planned for me; what need had I to know? What I wished—might dare to desire for myself—did not matter.

What did matter was that I was a princess, and beautiful, and that was all I learned to be. Highborn maidens need know only how to be chaste, modest, and obedient. My mother ensured I was the first; to reach my bedchamber, it was necessary to walk through my mother's room. And two maidservants attended her always, by day and by night. The night-maids remained awake while she slept.

Night or day, eyes always watched me. I did not know what it was like to be alone.

Nor did I know how it felt to walk through the streets of Babylon. Only when I climbed to the rooftop of the women's quarters could I gaze upon the city beyond my father's gate. If I looked to the north, I could see the Hanging Gardens, a marvel built by King Nebuchadnezzar for his wife Amytis, a queen homesick for the mountains in which she had grown up. If I stood upon a bench, I could see a flash of vivid blue; the Ishtar Gate. I longed to look upon that great gateway, to feast my eyes upon the lions and dragons marching evenly across turquoise-glazed tiles. I had no hope that I ever would.

My mother's laws for me were clear as winter air: I was King Belshazzar's granddaughter. Never, never must I forget that, even for a breath.

Sometimes, as I stared longingly out at the city forbidden to me, I wished I could forget my lineage. If only my mother's father had been a merchant, I would have journeyed the Silk Road with his caravans. Or a scribe, who would teach me to read and to write. Or even a farmer. Then I would live uncaged beneath the wide sky, and raise doves and poppies.

But my mother's father had been the last king of Babylon, and so all those things, and many more, were forbidden to me.

I dwelt as a princess in Babylon, the world's wonder, and yet saw less of the glorious city than did the poorest beggar.

⁂

On a day no different at first from any other, my life changed utterly. My mother received as a guest a lady of such high rank my mother would not even speak either the lady's name or her title to me.

I spent a whole day in our bathhouse, enduring the longest, most thorough purification I had ever undergone. I sat in hot water until my skin softened. Then the bath-maids scrubbed me with a paste of crushed almonds and honey, a paste it took many ewers of lemon-water to rinse away. At last they deemed my skin clean enough to be massaged with perfumed oil. When that was done, I gleamed like a pearl and smelled of roses.

My mother's most favored handmaiden painted my eyelids a brilliant green and my mouth a deep crimson. She painted thick lines of kohl around my eyes. The darkness surrounding them made my eyes shine pale as full moons. She combed my hair until it lay smooth, and then deftly wove it into three braids, twining strings of pearls into the strands. She pulled the three braids together and bound them into one. The pearl-woven braid lay heavy down my back to my waist; a tassel of pearls dangled from the end of the braid to the backs of my knees. My neck ached from the weight, but I knew better than to complain, or to let my head droop.

I was dressed in garments I had never seen before: a gown of thick silk the color of new cream, and over that a vest of cloth woven with gold and silver threads in a pattern of suns and moons. I set my feet into slippers of crimson leather, and then stood while my mother circled me, examining each twist of my braids, each stitch in the shining vest. She touched the emerald and pearl earrings dangling to my shoulders.

"Now, Vashti, come with me and do exactly as you are told."

As I always did as I was told, this order seemed odd, and for the first time in my life, I heard worry in my mother's voice. This was so unusual that I, too, became anxious.

I followed my mother into the chamber in which she received honored guests. In my mother's chair sat a small dark woman whose garments glowed with the fire of true Tyrian purple, and whose eyes gleamed bright and keen as a cat's. My mother bowed, and said, "Here is King Belshazzar's granddaughter, O queen." She did not tell me to bow, so I remained still, awaiting her command.

"I see a painted and gilded doll," the dark queen said. "Take those clothes off her and wash her face. And unbind the poor child's hair. Then I will look at her."

A day's effort on the part of my mother and her servants, and of obedient patience on mine, was undone within an hour. I returned with my body covered only by a shawl, my face bare of paint and my hair rippling down my back. My mother gazed upon me and I saw her mouth tighten; she was not pleased.

"O queen," my mother began again, "here is Belshazzar's granddaughter—"

"You may leave us," said the queen, and my mother hesitated. Never before had I seen my mother uncertain, or humble. The queen ignored her as if my mother had vanished like a djinn. "Come here to me, Vashti."

The queen held out her hand and smiled at me. As I walked forward, I heard a fading whisper of silk that meant my mother had obeyed; that she had left me alone with this unknown queen.

"There, that is better." The queen put her hand under my chin, tilted my face, examining me as if I were a jewel she might—perhaps—wish to buy. "Do you know who I am, child?"

"You are a queen," I said, and she smiled again.

"I was Queen of Queens once. Now I am mother to the King of Kings. Now do you know my name?"

I did; my mother had deemed it proper for me to learn the House of Darius by heart.

"You are the Great Queen Amestris."

"And do you know why I am here, Vashti?"

I shook my head.

"I am here because of you."

"Me?" The Great Queen Amestris had come to see *me*? But why?

"Yes. Now let me look at you properly. Let go of that ridiculous shawl."

I knew my mother would expect me to obey Queen Amestris, however immodest her command. I opened my hands and the shawl fell to the floor.

Then I waited, too bewildered by the day's events to suffer shame under the queen's keen gaze.

She said nothing as she studied me, until at last she said, "Turn around, slowly." I obeyed, waiting for her to speak again. I felt her lift my hair, testing it as if it were a skein of silk. Still I remained silent; Queen Amestris let my hair fall and laughed, softly.

"Your mother may have taught you nothing else, but at least you know that silence is a virtue." She took my hand and made me face her again. "But so are words well-chosen and well-spoken. Tell me about yourself."

She might as well have asked me to tell her how the stars came to be in the sky. I had no idea what I should say. Seeing my confusion, the queen tried another question.

"What do you like to do?" Queen Amestris waited, but I could think of nothing. At last I said, "I don't know, O queen."

"You don't know?" Oddly, this answer seemed to please her; she laughed, softly. "Well, then, we must teach you. Would you like to come with me and live in the great palace in Shushan, Vashti?"

I thought carefully. "I would like it if the queen wishes it, and if my mother commands it."

"The queen wishes it very much." Amestris held out her arms and since she clearly expected it, I walked into her embrace. She hugged me with a warmth my mother had never displayed. "And your mother no longer commands you, Vashti. From this hour forward, you may command her."

That was how I was chosen to be queen. Because I was King Belshazzar's granddaughter, and because my hair glowed like ivory silk—and because I had been so very carefully brought up that I knew nothing.

Not even what I liked.

Queen Mother Amestris wasted nothing, least of all time. I left my mother's house with Amestris that very day. My mother ordered me to remember all she had taught me, and kissed my forehead. My father did not bid me farewell; he was, I think, away from Babylon at that time. I had only seen him rarely, in any case, and did not miss him. Queen Mother

Amestris took me with her in a great gilded palanquin carried by a dozen men dressed all alike in blue-and-yellow garments.

I stared, for of course I had never seen anything like either the palanquin or the men. The queen laughed, softly, and told me to climb in. I stepped into the palanquin, marveling at the carved and gilded wood, the brilliant silk curtains, the cushions soft as cloud. Amestris settled beside me, graceful as a cat, and took my hand. I was glad of that a moment later, as the palanquin rose and moved; I clutched her hand hard.

"Don't worry, Vashti. The bearers will not let us fall." Amestris seemed to know my every thought, although I suppose it was not hard to guess what I was thinking. "Would you like to look out?" she asked, and I nodded, still astounded at my good fortune in being chosen by Queen Mother Amestris. For what I had been chosen, I did not know. My mother had taught me not to ask questions.

Amestris lifted her hand and pulled back one of the curtains. The bearers carried us smoothly at a swift, sure pace; the tiled walls lining the street seemed to flow past, rivers of bright color. The sight made me dizzy. And suddenly fear touched me, turned my skin cold.

Again Amestris understood me without words; she let the curtain fall, closing out the frightening wonders I had wished to see for so long. "Too much, too suddenly," she said. "You have never traveled in a litter before, Vashti?"

"I have never left our house before, O queen." For one horrible moment I wished myself back in that house, where I knew each step I must take, each word I must speak. My eyes burned; I squeezed my lids shut against tears.

"Never? Well, that changes now, little one." Amestris stroked my cheek. "Soon you will be accustomed to living as a princess should. And that does not mean dwelling like a frog at the bottom of a well."

I opened my eyes and stared at her. *Yes, that is what I was. A frog in a well.* Until that moment, no such thought would even have touched my mind. Greatly daring, I asked my first question of her. "What does it mean, to live as a princess should?"

Queen Mother Amestris smiled and smoothed back my hair. "It means to learn whatever you wish to learn and to do whatever pleases your heart. What do you think would please your heart, Vashti?"

"I . . ." I nearly said I did not know. Then, as I looked into the queen's dark eyes, I found the courage to answer truthfully. "I would like to see the Ishtar Gate, O queen. I want to see the dragons and the bulls."

So at last I saw the Ishtar Gate. I stood beside the blazing blue walls and set my hands upon the gold dragons and red bulls. I counted them, all the one hundred and fifty-two guardians of the gate. And I saw the dry moat beneath the gate in which the royal lions had once been housed. The lion's den was empty now; the beasts had been taken by King Darius as part of Babylon's tribute.

I saw the Hanging Gardens, too—the queen took me there after I had marveled at the Ishtar Gate. We walked up the long ramps to the highest level of the gardens, the queen holding my hand as I gaped at the trees rising on terraces above us. When we reached the top, all Babylon lay spread below us like a richly woven carpet. Walls forty feet high bounded the city; nine gates permitted entrance. Tiles brilliant as summer sky covered the walls; gilded bronze gleamed at the gates. To the north soared the shining blue towers of the Ishtar Gate. That men had built so marvelous a creation as Babylon amazed me. I had never before seen anything so beautiful.

"Are these gardens not magnificent, Vashti? They were created for a princess whose husband indulged her every desire." Queen Mother Amestris smiled down at me. "Just as your husband will indulge you, my dear. Yes, I think I chose wisely when I chose you."

Already I felt more at ease with her than I ever had with my own mother. So I dared ask more questions. "What have you chosen me for? To be your daughter?" I thought I would like to be Amestris's daughter.

"Is that your highest ambition, Vashti? I'm flattered. And in a way, you are right, for I have chosen you to be my son's wife. You will be Queen of Queens, Vashti."

"I will?"

"Yes," Amestris said, "you will."

We walked slowly back down the long ramps until at last we reached the true ground once more. The Queen Mother's palanquin waited there, and Amestris's eunuchs handed her in. With far less grace, I followed. As the palanquin carried us away, I stared back at the Hanging Gardens.

"I will be a queen?" I asked, and she smiled.

"Yes, my dear. You will be a queen."

"If a princess does whatever pleases her, what does a queen do?"

Instead of answering, Amestris pulled an ivory ball from behind one of the blue-and-yellow-striped cushions and set it upon my lap. I stared down at the ball. My hands barely fit around it; small dragons coiled about the ball, carven into the new ivory.

"A puzzle for you," Amestris said. "If you can find your way past the dragons and open the ball, you will find a treasure within."

I had never owned a puzzle before. I stared at the carved ivory dragons as if they might speak and reveal the secret. Amestris put her hands over mine and moved my fingers over the curves and ridges.

"Feel this line, Vashti. Twist here. I will tell you no more—see if you can find what I have hidden for you inside the ball."

Encouraged by the slight movement beneath my fingers, I spent the rest of our ride to the palace in Babylon engaged in a struggle with the puzzle-ball. The task so engrossed me that I forgot to wonder about a queen's life. And when at last the ivory sphere opened, a gold lion, small and perfect, fell into my lap.

I was so delighted that it never even occurred to me to wonder about my king and whether he would like me—and I, him.

I had my heart set on being carried out of Babylon through the Ishtar Gate, between the white and yellow lions adorning the walls along the Procession Way. When I learned we were to leave Babylon by the Uras Gate instead, my disappointment was so great I could have wept. But never in all my life had weeping gained me the least favor from my mother or father, and so I did not weep now.

Nor did I need to, for Queen Amestris easily read my moods. Now she explained why the Uras Gate had been chosen—

"Because this gate opens to the south, Vashti. Unless you wish us to add nearly a day to our journey, the Uras is a better choice. Do you truly wish to cross half Babylon to the Ishtar Gate, and then circle around the city back almost to the Uras Gate, only for the pleasure of leaving by the north?"

Amestris paused, as if she would alter her commands if I wished it so. But I knew the answer she wished me to make. Under her amused, tolerant gaze, I shook my head.

"A wise choice, Vashti. And once we pass through the Uras Gate, you will be able to look upon the river. You will like that."

As always, Amestris was right. I did like seeing the Euphrates. A broad, flat ribbon of water, its smooth surface reflected the sky's clouds. I knew a bridge crossed the river, linking the western and the eastern halves of Babylon, but I did not see it. The bridge lay behind us, hidden by the city walls.

My eyes opened so wide, so often, during the journey from Babylon to Shushan that Amestris told me I would soon be round-eyed as an owl—

"And never again will you be able to close your eyes to sleep at night." Amestris touched her fingertips to my lashes, making me blink; she laughed. "There, you see? You can still shut your eyes. Not an owl yet."

I laughed too, rather uncertainly. Then, since the Queen Mother merely smiled upon me, I returned to staring at the world beyond. The land lay flat between the Euphrates and the Tigris. Flat and golden-green with crops; irrigation ditches crossed and recrossed the even earth, river water bringing life to desert. Men and oxen labored in the fields. I asked Queen Mother Amestris what they did there.

"Plow and plant and reap, I suppose," she said, and then, when I ventured more questions, she shook her head. "If you wish to know more, you must wait until I can summon a farmer to teach you. But my dear child, you will never need to know such boring things."

I accepted this as I accepted all that I was told: I believed what she said was truth. And I must admit that I already dearly loved this new world in which I was petted and adored. How could I not enjoy such warm affection, such indulgence? Amestris seemed to know all I desired before I uttered a word, and nothing I wanted was withheld.

By day, I was permitted to gaze out freely—Amestris drew back one of the carven shutters so that not even the impediment of curtains sheer as morning mist came between me and the slow-changing land. When that diversion palled, as it did after an hour or two, Amestris ordered one of her eunuchs to tell me stories. He was very old, and knew so many songs and tales it would have taken a far longer journey than ours was to be to hear even the half of them. He told a tale of a prince who abandoned all his riches and rank to travel the world as a holy man; another of a queen so lovely two great nations warred over her for ten long years; still another of a boy raised by a pack of wolves.

And when I missed my mother—for I did, especially at night—Amestris swiftly changed my mood, dazzling me with a new bauble, a toy, a bright gem. The journey from Babylon to Shushan took twenty days. Even though we traveled the Royal Road, which messengers could ride from Sardis to Shushan in a week, an entourage as large and cumbersome as the Queen Mother's moved with regal deliberation. At last, despite Amestris's efforts to prevent it, I grew bored riding in the extravagant litter, as spacious and opulent as a palace chamber, and demanded to be allowed to walk—

"Or to ride. I wish to ride with one of the guards." Already I began to demand, rather than to plead, and such waywardness always made Amestris smile. As yet, my imagination had not stretched far: it did not occur to me to demand to ride a horse myself.

Instead of correcting me when I insisted I must ride, Amestris seemed to consider this a reasonable request. "Poor Vashti—this journey is very tedious for you." Amestris nodded to her attendant, who leaned out and ordered the riders to halt.

And then, to my astonished delight, I was handed from the Queen Mother's litter into the care of the captain of the guard, who swooped me up to sit before him on his horse. My joy vanished as the horse danced sideways and I stared down at hard ground as far below me as Ahriman's pit.

"Hold tight, princess. And don't worry, I won't let you fall." The captain spoke in a matter-of-fact tone that somehow convinced me.

Already I began to believe that whatsoever I wished would be granted me. Queen Mother Amestris ordered my life now—and she seemed to delight in my newfound boldness.

"You will be Queen of Queens, Vashti," Amestris told me, whenever I acted with the meekness my mother had taught me to display. "Queens do what pleases them. Hold your head high—it must bear the weight of a crown soon."

After that day, whenever I grew bored with riding in the litter, I demanded that the captain of the Queen Mother's guard take me up upon his horse with him. He was very old—silver gleamed through his hair and beard, and long years in the sun had darkened his skin and scored lines around his eyes and mouth. But old or not, he smiled and talked with me; like Queen Mother Amestris, Dariel of the guard spoke to me as if I were his equal. An odd thought, for I, soon to be Queen of Queens, was far above him in birth and station.

Dariel, too, regaled me with stories, but his were less fantastic than those of Amestris's song-master. Long journeys he had taken to Egypt and to the Spice Lands; battles he had fought; intrigues he had avoided. Later I realized that all he had truly told me of himself could be written on a tablet smaller than my palm. I did learn that his father had been a soldier too. A famous one, Dariel told me.

"My father captained your grandfather's father's guard, and when King Nebuchadnezzar died, my father captained your grandfather's guard. His name was Arioch, who was Daniel Dream-Master's friend."

I learned that Arioch had been summoned from Babylon to Shushan when Great Darius had overthrown my grandfather King Belshazzar and gathered up the kingdom of Babylon to adorn his empire. "That is why I have so odd a name: I was named for Daniel and for Darius both." I learned that Dariel had been born in Shushan, and his father had died there. And I learned that Dariel missed his wife.

Most of what Dariel told me I forgot by day's end. Dariel's words were merely another diversion. All the Queen Mother's staff and servants devoted themselves to amusing me; Dariel no less than any of the others.

⁂

Half of our journey lay behind us when we reached the western bank of the Tigris. The river spread wide, its waters smooth and heavy with golden-brown silt.

"How do we cross over the river?" I asked. Our caravan had halted where the river stretched widest. The far bank seemed miles away.

"We don't. We cross through it." Dariel turned his horse so that we faced Queen Amestris's palanquin, behind us on the road. "Does my lady princess wish to cross in the Queen Mother's litter, or trust herself to me and my horse?"

I hesitated, questions crowding my mind. The river loomed, broad and imposing, and I could not imagine how we could cross without a bridge. I tilted my head, looking up at Dariel's face. He waited, smiling slightly, for my answer.

I wanted him to tell me which would be safer: to ride across on a horse, or in a litter. But even as I opened my mouth to question him, I found myself thinking: *Why, it is a—a trick. Neither carries a greater risk than the other. Dariel would not offer a choice if either held peril.*

For a breath I glared at him, indignant. I was a princess of Babylon, soon to be a great queen. How dare he mock me? "You may carry me across." I tried to make my tone one of cold command; my mother's weapon. I failed, of course.

"So my lady princess would rather ride? Good choice." Dariel raised his voice and called to one of the guards. "Tell the Queen Mother that the princess and I will cross first." And to me, "Hold on to me, princess."

Dariel spurred his horse forward to the river's edge, and as I clung tightly to Dariel, the horse walked unhesitatingly into the water—which never rose above the beast's knees. Halfway across, I eased my clasp on Dariel's arm. "You deceived me," I accused.

"I? A mere captain of the Imperial Guard? Deceive a princess of Babylon?" Dariel commanded his voice far better than I did mine; not even a whisper of laughter tinged his words.

"You didn't tell me the water was so shallow I could have walked across myself." A startling notion—that I could cross a river unaided.

"Very few people tell everything they know," Dariel said. "There's a bridge ten miles downstream, and a ferry ten miles upstream. But the Sirrush Ford is the most direct route—at least at this time of year. In the spring, the water runs higher than a camel's head." A pause. "Does my lady princess wish to walk the rest of the way across by herself?"

Something made me consider my words with care. "If I said yes, would you set me down?"

"Does my lady princess think I would?"

I looked up at him. "No," I said, and Dariel smiled. He did not look half so old when he smiled.

"Good answer," Dariel said. "My lady princess is as clever as she is beautiful."

Delighted, I smiled back. I had spent my life hearing that I was beautiful. No one had ever before called me clever.

By the time the palace of Shushan loomed at the end of the Royal Road, I had learned to hold a vastly high opinion of myself. And if I felt any guilt at abandoning the harsh rules a highborn maiden should obey, it vanished under the weight of Amestris's praise and flattery.

The ancient city of Shushan lay on a plain by the river Choaspes. The Choaspes was not a great river such as the Euphrates or the Tigris, but it served Shushan well enough. If I looked past the lazy river, the plain stretched far into the east. On the eastern horizon the Zagros Mountains climbed the sky; silver flashed on the highest peaks.

Snow. I had heard of mountains and of snow, but this was the first time I had seen either. Both mountains and snow were far away, and that day I did not dream I ever would dwell among either. I knew my life would be within Shushan's walls now.

Although it had become the dazzling capital of empire, Shushan had no soaring towers, no vast gardens. At first I thought Shushan possessed nothing to match the glories of the Ishtar Gate or the Hanging Gardens. Then I lifted my eyes to the palace of the King of Kings.

The hill supporting the palace rose high above the flat land. Even as far away as I was when I first set eyes upon the great palace at Shushan, I looked up at its shining walls. I could not see past them.

I entered the great palace of Shushan through the King's Gate. The Queen Mother's litter was carried up the Great Staircase, past stone lamassu taller than ten men. I did not see much of all this, for indulgent as Amestris was, she did not permit me to open the curtains and stare out. But what I saw through the narrow gap she allowed enthralled me. I had plenty of time to stare, for it took the bearers an hour just to climb the Great Staircase.

At last we were carried through a long courtyard open to the sky and ringed with columns tall as cedars. "The Men's Palace is ahead of us," Amestris told me, "and the King's Palace lies beyond that. The Women's Palace is to the left of the men's, and the Queen's Palace beyond that. From the Queen's Palace, you can look out and see the city, and the mountains. You'll like that, Vashti."

Of course I would. How could I not? To look out on all the world, after my confined views of Babylon? Having grown greatly daring, I flung my arms around Amestris. "O queen, I love you more than—than anything!"

My mother would have scolded me for such forward, uncontrolled behavior. Queen Mother Amestris smiled. "Than anything, Vashti? Well, we shall see." She patted my cheek. "Patience, sweet child; you are nearly home."

The Immortals left us at that first courtyard, and the bearers left us, too. Eunuchs came to take their place; the changeover was made so swiftly and skillfully I felt no lowering of the litter at all. That exchange made, the litter was carried through a gate guarded by four tall soldiers armed with two swords each.

"The gate into the Women's Palace," Amestris said. "And now you may pull the curtains open, if you like." Amestris smiled again as I yanked back the heavy silk.

I leaned out to stare at the gate behind us. On this side, too, the gate was guarded. Half a dozen richly garbed eunuchs had posts at the gate. Two stood in front of the gate itself, and the others sat nearby.

I gazed avidly at all we passed. A long narrow garden planted with lemon trees and roses. An open courtyard bounded by a colonnade of pillars carved with flowers painted red and yellow and white. Women stared back at me; women dressed in vests and gowns so fine I wondered if this might be some great feast day. Gold chains draped about their necks, gems glowed in their ears and on their hands. Their cheeks glittered gold and lips gleamed crimson.

"Vashti, I must ask you not to stare so." Amestris's rebuke was soft, but I flushed and ceased gaping at the palace women.

Then the bearers stopped and lowered the litter to the ground. A hand—large, soft-skinned, heavily weighted with rings—reached in. "O queen, may you live forever. Welcome home." A kind voice; a strong voice. Amestris laid her hand in his and gracefully rose from the litter.

"Thank you, Hegai. And here is—"

"Princess Vashti," Hegai said, and even though I could not yet see his face, I knew he smiled. Then Hegai bent and held out his hand to me. "O little queen, live forever. Welcome home."

Now I could see him, as he bowed low so that I could reach his outstretched hand. A man with dark, kind eyes and a smooth face; a eunuch, of course. He was richly garbed and most kings would be pleased to own the jewels he wore. And I had been right: he smiled.

I liked his face, and his smile. I held out my hands to him and he lifted me out easily. At last I stood within the palace at Shushan. "Thank you," I said.

"Vashti, this is Hegai, who is very dear to me—and I know he will be just as dear to you. You may regard him as head of your household now. Listen to him, and learn. Now follow me."

As Amestris walked forward, Hegai held out his hand to me again. I took it, and we followed Amestris through another garden—this one was round, with a round pond at its center in which I saw golden fish swirl about—and a hall whose walls were painted with scenes of cats and dogs and monkeys. That led to a corridor, and another gate. This gate's bandings of bronze were gilded, and the cedar was inlaid with gold and silver suns and moons. Two eunuchs guarded this gate, although it was far within the Women's Palace.

Beyond that gate we entered into a garden so beautiful it truly seemed the paradise it was named. "This is the Queen's Palace, Vashti. Now it is yours."

"Isn't it yours?" I asked. "I do not want to take away your palace."

"You are not. I dwell in my own palace, on the other side of the House of Women. I will leave you here with Hegai and your maidservants. They will take good care of you—and Hegai can tell you anything you need to know."

I was about to say that I would do as Hegai bid me when I remembered that now everyone was to do *my* bidding. So I merely nodded. I wanted to ask when I would meet King Ahasuerus, but even as I began to speak, Amestris walked away, leaving me staring after her.

"Princess Vashti?" Hegai's voice was gentle, soft; he put a hand upon my shoulder. "You must be tired. Come and let us bathe you, and then perhaps you will wish to eat, and to rest. I know all here is strange to you, but this is your home now. And I will help you. You have only to ask, and whatever you wish will be granted."

His voice soothed, his hand on my shoulder comforted. I looked up at him. "Can you tell me when I will see the king?" I asked, and Hegai smiled.

"Soon, little queen."

"And will he like me?"

Hegai seemed to weigh his words before he said, "His mother chose you for him out of all the maidens in the empire. Now come and let us make you happy here."

The court astrologers studied their charts and the stars and agreed upon the most auspicious day, and so the ceremony that made me Ahasuerus's wife and queen took place three days after I entered the great palace. The stars were the only thing Amestris waited for, since everything a royal bride required lay ready for me in chests of cedar and sandalwood.

I spent all the day before the wedding being bathed and massaged with oil perfumed with myrrh. My hair was washed and dried over a brazier in which frankincense burned. My hands and feet were tinted with henna.

The morning of the wedding day Hegai and seven maids spent all morning garbing me in heavy robes of cloth of silver, clasping jewels about my arms and throat and ankles. They braided and gemmed my hair, painted my face—as my mother had done. I now knew that my mother had dressed me as a king's bride the day I had been shown to Queen Amestris. But today I also wore a veil that covered me to my knees, a veil so sheer the gems shone through it, bright as stars.

When Hegai pronounced me ready, Queen Amestris came to examine me. She said nothing, merely smiled upon me and held out her hand. She led me through the corridors of the House of Women and through a bronze gate into a courtyard set with azure tiles that shone like summer sky. In the center of the court stood a priest beside a brightly burning fire. Across the court was another gate. That second gate led to the great palace itself.

As Amestris led me forward, a golden flame seemed to advance from the second gate. My bridegroom. The cloth-of-gold robes he wore burned like the fire itself. Behind the king came the Seven Princes. One of my mother's lessons had been to memorize the names and virtues of each of the Seven Princes; now that I was to marry the King of Kings, that knowledge at last became useful. But today all the Seven looked alike: clad in elaborate robes banded in white and blue, fringed in silver and gold. Today they were not important. Only the king, only my bridegroom, captured my eyes.

Amestris stopped, and I stood before the Sacred Flame and looked upon Ahasuerus's face for the first time. He had dark eyes and dark hair and he stared at me as doubtfully as I stared at him. Then Amestris reached out and took his hand, and set my hand into it.

His hand was cold. I wondered if he were as nervous as I.

A great feast was held to celebrate our wedding and our wedding night. Banners of white and blue and green silk draped the great banqueting hall; gold and silver ropes twined about the tall pillars. Hundreds of tiny lamps hung on bronze chains transformed the ceiling to a sky of bright flickering stars. From dusk until dawn the palace glowed in the light of a thousand torches and echoed the sounds of laughter and easy talk, for a royal wedding did not end until the sun rose upon the new-made husband and wife in their marriage bed. In the best of weddings, a prince followed nine months after that first sunrise.

Our bedding was a farce, of course—or say, rather, a ceremony so old that it held more force than mere law: it was the custom. Custom did not care that neither of the two most involved could act out the parts custom dictated for them.

"Now you must not worry yourself over this bedding, child," Queen Mother Amestris told me as seven handmaidens prepared me for the king's bed. "You will simply sleep beside Ahasuerus tonight, and tomorrow your union will be proclaimed to the empire." She smiled at me, and stroked my pale hair.

"And then what?" I asked.

"Don't you remember what I promised you, my dear child? Then you may do whatever pleases you. You have all the Queen's Palace to play in, and you have only to ask for whatsoever you desire."

Whatsoever I desired! I still shivered with pleasure at the mere thought. No more days spent in quiet obedience. *Ever.* Queen Mother Amestris had said so, and her words made wishes truth.

She laughed, softly. "Yes, I see you will be happy here—that is all I want for you, Vashti. Happiness."

Since I wanted to be happy, I had no fault to find with this. Then, as I began to dance with joy, Amestris ordered me to stand still. "For if you fidget so, you will never be ready for the king's bed. Now stand still, my beautiful new daughter, and let your handmaidens make you more lovely than you already are."

I obeyed her honey-voiced command, reveling in her praise. I was beautiful. I was queen. I was to do whatsoever I wished, and I was to be happy. Easy commands to follow!

When the seven handmaidens finished their work, I wore a gown so sheer I might have been clad in water. All the gems and ribbons had been unwoven from my hair, and the braids that had taken so many hours to create had been undone. My hair had been combed out with sandalwood combs until it shone like moonlight down my back.

My face had been washed clean of all the bright paint. All my jewelry—the earrings, the necklaces, the armbands and bracelets, the bangles about my ankles, the pearl-strung chains about my feet—had been stripped away. My bare feet had been freshly tinted; I looked as if I stood in blood.

After all the finery, the rich garments, the ornate creation I had been during the wedding ceremony, this seemed drab. "Am I still beautiful?" I asked, and Queen Amestris laughed.

"Of course you are, child. Now take the fire to your husband's bed." She handed me a shallow bowl; a small flame danced upon the oil within the vessel's curve.

I cradled the bowl carefully in my hands, and followed as the Queen Mother led me from the robing chamber into the corridor that ran between the queen's rooms and the king's. Hegai awaited us there, to lead us to the king's bedchamber. The sight of Hegai gave me courage. *We all fear change. This is change again. That is all.*

The palace eunuchs lined the corridor and watched as I walked past. Amestris stopped before the door to the king's bedchamber. She nodded to the eunuch standing beside the doorway, and he lifted the bar and pulled the door open. The eunuch bowed low and Amestris said:

"May you find happiness with your husband. May you be the mother of many sons." More words that must be spoken to me because they were spoken to all brides. Amestris spoke them solemnly—but she smiled and patted my shoulder. "Now go in, and sleep well."

At the last moment, I looked back at Hegai. He smiled at me, and nodded, and I wished he could come with me into the king's bedchamber—

"Go in, Vashti." Amestris did not like to repeat an order; I heard impatience in her voice.

Hastily, I stepped through the doorway, and as the door closed behind me the flame I carried flickered wildly. For a breath I feared the fire would go out, but then the small flame once again burned steady and bright. I looked past it into the room. At first I saw nothing but shadows, for I carried the only light, and it dazzled my eyes.

"You're supposed to bring the flame over here to the bed, you know." Ahasuerus's voice startled me; I looked past the fire I carried and saw the darker shadow in the center of the room. The king's bed. Beside it, Ahasuerus stood waiting.

I walked forward, and as my eyes became accustomed, I saw that the room was not truly in darkness. The full moon's light poured through the tall windows, turned shadow to silver. I reached the bed, and there I stopped. I knew I must set the bowl in my husband's hands, that I must let him lead me around the bed, and that I must then lie down on that bed with him. But my body refused to obey me.

I stared mutely at Ahasuerus. He seemed no more able to move than I.

But at least he had command of his voice. "I'm tired. Are you?" he asked, and suddenly I realized that I had been awake since before dawn. I nodded. "You must be cold, too," he said.

Still silent, I held out the flame to him. He took the bowl from my hands and set it on the floor. As I stared, surprised by this casual dismissal of ritual, Ahasuerus flung himself onto the vast bed.

"Come on," he said, "get into bed."

He was both king and husband; his words my law. And I was weary and chilled, and wanted nothing so much as warmth and rest. I scrambled into the bed after him. Ahasuerus shoved some pillows toward me, and handed me a thick soft shawl. I wrapped the shawl around me and regarded Ahasuerus with awed gratitude.

"Why are you staring at me like that?" he said. "I'm the King of Kings. I can do whatever I want. My mother says so."

The first words I spoke to him were, "I love your mother." Then we both stared, silent, at each other. Beside the bed, the flame guttered and went out. The small fire had eaten all the oil in the bowl. The only light we had now was the moon's gift.

"You can do whatever you want, too," Ahasuerus added kindly. "Because you're queen now. Let's go to sleep. We can talk in the morning."

Rather awkwardly, we lay down beside each other. After a few moments, Ahasuerus put his arm over me, and I curled up against him. We fell asleep that way. Peacefully, like tired kittens.

Weary though I had been, I still awoke early. Pale gold light fell across the bed; dawn light. I sat up and looked at Ahasuerus, who seemed to be still asleep. I was wrong, for as I began to crawl over to the edge of the wide bed, he sat up.

"Where are you going?"

I sat back on my heels. "I don't know. Where should I go?" Until Queen Mother Amestris had transported me to Shushan, my days had been strictly ruled. The freedom offered me now often baffled me.

Ahasuerus yawned and stretched, and then jumped out of bed. He wore a robe as sheer as mine. It was the first time we had looked upon each other in full light—and as I said later to the woman who became his true wife, we saw too much, and were too young to wish to see more. Ahasuerus grabbed up one of the silk-and-gold shawls draped across the bed and tossed it toward me. I hastily wrapped the shawl around me, and when I turned back to Ahasuerus, I saw that he had taken another of the shawls to cover himself.

"Where are the servants?" he demanded. "I'm hungry. Are you hungry?"

I nodded, grateful for a question I could answer. Then I dared ask a question of my own. "When are the servants supposed to come to you, my lord king?" I was sure there were rules governing every hour of the king's wedding and wedding night and the morning following.

"I don't care. I need them now and they aren't here. Come on."

He strode off, shawl trailing behind him. Obedient—and curious—I followed, taking care not to trip over the voluminous shawl covering me. Ahasuerus led me into another room, its entrance hidden by a curtain woven in a design of running lions. The room had no windows, and was lined with chests of cedar and of sandalwood. Ahasuerus knelt by one and lifted the lid. As I watched, he pulled out tunics and tossed them onto the floor.

"Choose one and get dressed." Ahasuerus caught up a tunic for himself as I stared.

"But those are your clothes. I can't wear the king's clothes. I can't wear a boy's tunic." I thought even Queen Mother Amestris might be shocked by such an idea.

"I'm your husband and your king, and I order you to wear it." Ahasuerus sounded impatient now.

Husband and king—of course he owned the right to command my obedience. I stared down at the tunics he had scattered before me, and grabbed the closest. Then I retreated to the other side of the lion-curtain and pulled the tunic on over the sheer gown. Ahasuerus, wearing a dark blue garment sewn with gold lion heads, came to join me and studied me critically. Since he was larger than I, the crimson tunic I had chosen fell about me in heavy folds and covered me to my ankles. Boy's garb or not, I was still modestly clad.

"Come on." He strode off and I hastily followed.

Ahasuerus guided me swiftly through palace corridors until we reached a kitchen that stretched so far into the distance I could not see where the room ended. The kitchen staff paused in their tasks as Ahasuerus walked in. I expected them to kneel, to greet him as King of Kings, to wait in humble silence to hear his pleasure. They did none of those things. Most of them bowed their heads briefly, and then returned to their tasks. One of the cooks came forward, smiling; Ahasuerus greeted the woman with easy affection.

"Kassa, is the morning bread ready yet? I am *so* hungry I could eat a *stone!*"

"You're always hungry, my lord king." The woman's voice held only amused affection. "And what of you, my lady queen? Are you hungry, too?"

"Oh, yes," I said, so fervently that I heard muffled laughter from some of the other kitchen servants.

"You entered hungry, but I vow you won't leave hungry. Sit down, my little king and queen, and let me see what I can set before you on this fine morning."

What Kassa the cook set before us was a bowl of amber-ripe apricots and a platter of flat bread hot and golden from the oven. Beside those she placed a cup of honey and another bowl filled with cheese cut into neat cubes. Ahasuerus ate with steady efficiency, while I dipped apricots in honey and then licked the honey off the plump fruit. Smiling, Kassa watched us devour the food; the more we ate, the more broadly she smiled.

To my surprise, the other servants and slaves seemed equally pleased to see Ahasuerus. It seemed odd to me that the King of Kings should be so familiar with the kitchens; puzzled, I looked at him and he grinned. "Don't tell my mother," he said.

He was my king and my husband, and older than I, and I was bound to obey him. "I won't," I said, and hoped Queen Mother Amestris would not ask me if her son ever spent time in the palace kitchens.

Of course she did not; she didn't need to ask. Amestris knew everything that happened in the palace.

We spent that whole day together, Ahasuerus and I. He showed me more of the palace than I should have been permitted to see. But he was king: who was to stop him, if he chose to bring his queen to the king's great hall, to the throne room, the treasury, the stables?

That day set the tone of our marriage: he carelessly daring, I admiringly copying him.

In the evening, Queen Mother Amestris came into my bedchamber to bid me good night. She smiled at me, and touched my hair. "So you have now been queen for one whole day, Vashti. Are you pleased?"

"Oh, yes," I assured her fervently. "I love being queen! I love being married! I love Ahasuerus!"

Amestris laughed. "I am so glad. Now go to sleep. You have many days ahead of you, each as pleasant as this one has been." She bent and kissed my forehead, and then she left. I watched her go, and I saw Hegai, too, gazing after her. For a breath, I thought he frowned. Then I realized it must have been a shadow cast by the flickering lamplight.

At first marriage was unending joy to me. With my marriage to Ahasuerus, I had gone from being Belshazzar's granddaughter, a girl expected to keep her voice soft and her face smooth, to being the Queen of Queens. I was petted, indulged, pampered as if I were one of Queen Amestris's prized long-haired cats.

Anything I desired was mine for the asking. I had a dozen dozen gowns, gems beyond counting, servants and slaves to do everything for me from combing out my hair to tying my silver sandals upon my feet.

Within a month I was utterly spoilt—or would have been, had not Ahasuerus treated me with a sort of dutiful indifference. Since I admired him greatly, I longed to gain his attention, and that was one of the three gifts that saved me.

I followed Ahasuerus about and obeyed his commands, however ridiculous. And unlike his slaves and servants, I was not obliged to attend upon him; there was no need for me to enter his presence if I did not wish to—or if he did not command me to come to him. Ahasuerus knew this, and so my constancy engendered affection. Soon he treated me with the careless fondness of a brother for an importunate younger sister.

So I had a playfellow and a friend who never told me, "You must not, Vashti. It is not proper for girls to—"

To run. To ride. To read. To laugh loudly.

Ahasuerus permitted me to do all these things, and more. I spent many hours of my day with him, learning everything he already knew, and that he was delighted to teach. I think, now, that already he had grown a little bored with his endless liberty. In me, he had an apprentice, a follower, an admirer who never told him to run along and play and *"Leave this matter in the hands of those who know best how it should be managed."*

So we both were pleased with our marriage. Ahasuerus treated me as if I were his beloved little sister, and I followed him about the palace like his shadow. We were joyous friends, permitted a closeness few royal spouses ever knew. We were not yet lovers. The true consummation of our marriage was another event Amestris wished to put off as long as possible. One of my charms, for her, was my extreme youth. My mind was that of a child; my child's body did not even hint at what it would someday become.

The second gift that kept me from becoming a spoilt, demanding tyrant was Hegai. He treated me not only as the queen I was called, but as the child I still was. It was Hegai who ordered toys brought for me, knowing I found more joy in a gilded leather ball than in a gold necklace, that a game board of amber and ivory entranced me more than bolts of Cathay silk.

It was Hegai who understood my tastes when I myself had not yet learned to recognize them. Hegai saw that I liked roses better than lilies, preferred cinnamon to coriander. He noticed what colors pleased my eyes, what stories made me laugh. He found songs I liked to sing. It was Hegai who discovered I had never owned a pet, and who remedied that lack by presenting me with a puppy—a small, plump creature with a coat soft as brown velvet and a fondness for chewing my jeweled slippers.

And it was Hegai who comforted me when night's dark hours freed a strange misery to torment me. When I woke and wept, Hegai sat beside me on my bed—a bed so large I sometimes feared demons lurked in its vast empty corners—and gathered me into his arms. I did not understand why I was unhappy, but Hegai knew that, too.

"Yes, of course you love your palace and your gardens. And yes, everyone is kind to you." Hegai stroked my hair. "But wonderful as your new life is, still it is new and different, and if there is one thing our minds and hearts fear above all else, it is change. There will be many nights when that fear will waken you, but with time it will pass. And I will always be here, Vashti."

"Always?" I said, clinging to his tunic.

"Yes, little queen. Always."

By day, I had no such qualms; I delighted in possession of my own palace, my own gardens, my own handmaidens and slaves. Even in such matters as my servants, Hegai's wisdom enhanced my happiness, for he selected a dozen girls of my own age for my household. For the first time in my life, I had playfellows—although they never forgot that I was queen and they were not.

In the fabulous, outrageously opulent life that I now led, Hegai remained constant, a rock to cling to as the court swirled about me. I could not imagine a life without Hegai close by to scold me and hug me, and ensure I did not gorge on honeyed rose petals, and that I looked for myself to see that my pets were being properly cared for. I thanked the Good God each morning in my prayers for the gift of Hegai.

For the first time in my life, I had freedom to explore my world—and so found the third gift that kept my character true. I ran down garden paths and no one ordered me to walk slowly, meekly. My world now was the great palace complex that rose above Shushan, and it seemed so vast I would never find its end.

I roamed the palaces—closely attended by a fussy eunuch named Hatach, a half-dozen years older than I, who ensured I did not lose myself—and at the far end of one of the many gardens, I came upon a gate, and behind that gate, a small house set into the deep wall between the women's world and the men's. The walls of the house were tiled in a deep rich blue that made me think of the Ishtar Gate in Babylon. Two lemon trees in yellow-and-white pots stood beside a door banded with copper. Crescent moons and seven-pointed stars were etched into the copper bands.

"Whose house is this?" I asked Hatach, but before he could answer, I heard a voice say,

"It's the king's house. But he lets me live in it."

An old man rose from a blue bench set against the wall. A very old man; I thought he must be older than the stars above the world. As I stared, he smiled. "Welcome, Queen Vashti."

"How did you know who I am?"

"I know many things." He smiled. "And everyone knows who you are. Few are graced with such hair. Who else could you be?"

I was not accustomed to such unanswerable questions. At a loss, I fell back upon the only thing that had made me of any value in the world until Queen Mother Amestris had plucked me out of Babylon and brought me here. "I am Belshazzar's granddaughter."

"Yes, I know. Your grandmother had hair like yours. Hair pale as sweet cream."

"My grandmother?" I had heard a great deal about my grandfather Belshazzar, the last king of Babylon. Of his queen, my grandmother, I had been taught only her name—Ishvari. No one had ever said that she, too, had bone-white hair.

"Yes. A very wise woman. I was fond of her."

My mind stretched to a question. "Did she have eyes like mine?"

He shook his head. "No. Her eyes were brown, like spring earth. But she had the same questioning look that you do. Don't look so startled—questions are good things. How else will you learn?"

Another question I had no idea how to answer. Fortunately, he didn't seem to expect me to say anything. He sat down again, and patted the bench beside him. "Come and sit with me, Vashti. Tell me your dreams, if you like."

I heard my servant gasp, and turned. Hatach bowed low, and said, "You do the queen honor, my lord Daniel." Clearly this Daniel was a man of great importance. Therefore I should do as he asked of me. I glanced at Hatach, whose eyes were wide; clearly impressed, Hatach nodded. So I walked over and bowed to Daniel, then sat beside him as he had asked.

"So—does my lady queen wish her dreams unbound for her?" The man called Daniel regarded me as if I were a riddle he must solve. "You don't know who I am, do you?"

"You are Daniel." Since I had just heard him named so by my servant, I felt this safe enough to say.

"But that name means nothing to you, does it, Ishvari's granddaughter?"

Never before had I been named as the granddaughter of any save Belshazzar. *Ishvari's granddaughter.* I savored the words.

"No, I see you've never heard of me. So much for my undying fame."

"Daniel, stop teasing the child." A woman as old as Daniel stepped out of the house into the sunlight. "Greetings, little one. So you're our new queen?"

I nodded, and she smiled at me. Then she glanced at Daniel and raised her eyebrows. "What have you been telling her, Daniel?"

"Oh, just that she looks very much like her mother's mother. Queen Ishvari. You remember Ishvari, don't you, Sama?"

"Of course. A very clever woman, and a very brave one. And very beautiful."

I noticed that for the woman Daniel had called Sama, my grandmother Ishvari's beauty came a poor third to her wit and courage. "What did she do that was so clever, and so brave?" Between one breath and the next, my grandmother Ishvari had become important to me.

"Ask Daniel," Sama said, and my gaze turned back to Daniel.

"Now who's teasing the child?" Daniel shook his head, ruefully accepting that he could not escape my new-roused interest in Queen Ishvari.

"Will you tell me about Queen Ishvari? If it please you?" Although it had been impressed upon me that almost everyone in the empire must now bow very low to me, I somehow sensed that if it did not please Daniel to reveal a thing, haughty command would not bring the words to his lips.

Daniel smiled. "Yes, O queen. Since you ask it of me, I will tell you the tale of Ishvari, the last queen of Babylon the Great."

She came from far away, from the far shores of the Black Sea, where wolves ran swift beneath the moon and women gazed upon the future in mirrors of polished jet. She was beautiful beyond dreams and wise beyond words, and when Belshazzar of Babylon heard of her beauty, he ordered her sent to him as tribute.

"And of her wisdom?" I prompted, as Daniel fell silent.

"What, child? Oh, Belshazzar cared nothing for that."

"Why not?"

"Because men see far better than they can think." This from the old woman, Sama. To my surprise, Daniel merely laughed.

"As you say, Sama. As you say. Where was I?"

"Belshazzar the Sot had ordered Ishvari of the Black Horse People sent to him like a bolt of silk or a bag of pearls." Sama's voice cut sharp, but again, Daniel only agreed. At least this time he remembered to continue the tale.

Now, Ishvari of the Black Horse People was a lady high-born and high-bred, and she had grown up riding the wild horses that were her people's wealth. Horses and gold. And horses and gold and Ishvari were sent to Babylon, to King Belshazzar.

No one in Babylon had ever set eyes upon a woman like Ishvari. She rode her own horse, a mare white as Ishvari's own hair, down the great Street of Processions, between the walls of sky-blue tiles and painted lions, through the towers of the Ishtar Gate. She sat her horse straight and tall as a warrior. And any who chose to look might gaze upon her unveiled face. She rode her horse up the palace steps and into King Belshazzar's throne room, and at the foot of his throne, she reined in her mare.

"King Belshazzar sent for Ishvari of the Black Horse People. Well, I am here."

Belshazzar stared at her, moonstruck. And then, as his guards—

"Dithered," Sama muttered, and Daniel shot her a reproving glance.

—waited upon his command, and his courtiers gasped in astonishment, the king rose and

came down the steps from his throne. He reached up and lifted her down from the moon-white mare, and then he took Ishvari's hand and led her back up the steps to stand with him before the throne of Babylon.

"This is my queen," Belshazzar declared. "She will reign over my heart, and all men will bow before her as if she were the king himself."

I sighed, enthralled by the images Daniel's words summoned.

"*That* didn't last very long."

"Sama, please."

But greatly as Belshazzar loved Ishvari, he loved wine better. Against such a rival, Ishvari could not win. Being wise, she abandoned a hopeless battle. She knew that beauty fades and wisdom grows, and she became the true ruler of Babylon. Her work consoled her, as did her child. For at last she conceived, and bore a daughter.

"My mother?" I asked, and Daniel smiled at me. "Your mother," he said.

But now Darius the Mede had turned his eyes upon Babylon. Yes, and marched his all-conquering army toward Belshazzar's kingdom. As Darius marched, Belshazzar held a great feast at which wine flowed freely as a spring river. Belshazzar ordered all the nobles and all the princes and all the lords of Babylon to attend. And he ordered the Master of Treasures to open the treasure vaults, and to bring forth the vessels of gold that King Nebuchadnezzar had plundered from the great temple of the Lord God in Jerusalem. It was Belshazzar's delight to use those sacred vessels as wine-cups for his great feast—

"Queen Ishvari told him that was a bad idea. Arioch told him that was a bad idea. *You*—"

"*I* had the sense to keep my mouth shut on that occasion, and if you wish to finish this story, Samamat, certainly you may. No? I may continue? My humble thanks."

So Belshazzar ordered sacred objects used for carnal purpose. And he ordered Queen Ishvari to attend this feast wearing all her most precious jewels, and to drink from the golden bowls of the Lord's temple in Jerusalem, but she refused.

"My most precious jewels are my daughter and my honor," she said, "and I will not display either for the pleasure of drunken, impious fools."

Well, Belshazzar was not pleased to receive such a message, but what could he do? He had surrendered his power as a man to wine, and as a king to his queen. So he drank ever more deeply, and said nothing, until he looked up and saw a ghostly hand dip itself into his wine cup. And then the hand wrote across the wall of the banquet hall in the king's wine these words: ***Mene, mene, tekel, upharsin.***

Daniel paused, watching Samamat, but she pressed her lips tightly together and shook her head very slightly. Daniel smiled, and continued.

Now, Belshazzar could not tell the meaning of these words, nor could any other there in the banquet hall with him. And the king was much distressed, and confused, and being greatly troubled, he sent again for his queen—for at last he remembered that she was not only beautiful, but wise as well. And this time, being humbly petitioned, Ishvari came into the hall and up to the king her husband, and set her hands upon his. And Belshazzar showed her the writing on the wall and told how greatly it troubled him that none could interpret its meaning. And Queen Ishvari said:

"My lord king, there is a man in your kingdom who is master of dreams, a man whom the king your father made ruler over all the astrologers and magicians and soothsayers. My lord king, ask Daniel."

Now, King Belshazzar thought Queen Ishvari's advice good, and he bade her summon Daniel to him. Ishvari went herself to Daniel and asked him if he would come to the king and ease his mind concerning the writing on the wall.

"Which he alone can see, Daniel. There is nothing on the wall. Nothing save splashes of wine. They are all drunk beyond telling."

Daniel looked into Ishvari's earth-brown eyes and saw that she knew all he must say. That Darius the Mede's army surrounded the city, that Belshazzar was doomed. That Ishvari and her daughter were doomed—for no one knew that Darius had a great heart, and would spare them. "Very well," said Daniel. "I will come and tell the king what I can."

"Tell him what he must hear," Ishvari told him, and they went together to the banquet hall. And there Daniel told Belshazzar that the words the king saw upon the wall read thusly: that the kingdom of Babylon is ended, for its king has been tested and found wanting, and his kingdom has been given into the hands of the Medes and Persians.

But Belshazzar was too drunk to care any longer, and returned to his depravity. So Queen Ishvari took her daughter, and her royal crown, and asked Arioch, the commander of the king's guard, to escort her to the tent of Darius the Mede, whose camp lay outside Babylon's mighty walls. Ishvari knelt before Darius and submitted herself and her daughter to his rule. Darius accepted her homage and granted her petition that her daughter's life be spared. And Darius spared Ishvari's life as well, that she might raise her daughter in the ways of honor.

And Ishvari praised Darius for his mercy.

But Ishvari wept for Belshazzar, whom no one could save, for he had doomed himself. For she had loved him once, and he had once loved her. . . .

"And so you, her daughter's daughter, were born to be—well, queen, I suppose. I hope I have not bored you, Queen Vashti."

My name startled me, brought me back into myself. Daniel's words had bound me to a past long dead, as if I had seen for a time with Ishvari's eyes. I stared at him. "Are you a sorcerer?"

"No. Just a man with a gift for words, and dreams."

Samamat laughed softly at that. But while I somehow did not hesitate to demand answers of Daniel Dream-Master, I did not have the courage to question Samamat. Not that day.

Just before I stood up to leave, Daniel asked again a question I had forgotten. "No dreams to read for you, my queen?"

Dreams linked us to the gods; to our pasts, our present, our futures. Each morning my mother had demanded to know my dreams. I dreamed, of course—everyone dreamed. But I rarely remembered my dreams at all, and when I did, their images fled me as soon as the sun burned its way into the sky.

My mother had not liked my truthful answer, so I had learned to create dreams to tell her that she liked to hear. Now I told Daniel what I had so often told my mother.

"Crowns," I told him, obedient. "I dream of crowns."

Silence in the small garden. Daniel stared at me; I do not think he saw me, though. He looked through me, into my cold, banked dreams.

"That's not what you dream of, Ishvari's granddaughter," Daniel said. "You do not dream of crowns. Not of crowns at all."

But he would not tell me what I did dream of. He merely smiled, and told me I might come and visit him whenever it pleased me to do so. I soon learned this was a great honor; even Queen Mother Amestris walked in awe of Daniel, a man who had survived the reigns of five sovereigns and who guarded memories of ancient glories.

I bowed to Daniel, and thanked him. I think he knew I cherished the gift he had given me: knowledge of my grandmother. From that time onward, I thought of myself, not as Belshazzar's granddaughter, but as Ishvari's.

Some nights I dreamed of her. She walked out of the night sky, clad in clouds and moonlight, a circle of stars crowning her shining hair. She bent and kissed my forehead, and smiled. She lifted the crown of stars from her own head and held it out to me. The stars burned so bright I could not look upon them. I reached out—for the crown, for my grandmother—which? And then, as the stars flared, Queen Ishvari faded, slipping like moonlight through my outstretched hands. . . .

I did not tell anyone that Queen Ishvari visited me as I slept, not even Daniel Dream-Master. I did not even tell him I now dreamed of a crown; a crown of stars. I entrusted my dreams to no one.

My dreams were a secret treasure; mine alone to cherish.

"I have spoken with Daniel the Dream Master," I told Hegai proudly. "Did you know he once lived in my grandfather's court? He says I look like my grandmother!"

"Yes," Hegai said, "I knew that. He has lived a long time, and served many kings. And Daniel is now very old." Hegai studied my face, and added, "Yes, little queen, older than I. Far, far older." Hegai did not laugh, but I saw him smile. "Now come see what the Queen Mother has sent you today."

Today Amestris had sent me a butterfly in a silver cage. Within the silver wire, the butterfly sat motionless, wings trembling. I carried the silver cage into the Queen's Garden. *My* garden. There I opened the cage door and watched the beautiful creature fly, its wings flashing blue as lapis among the flowers.

Unlike Queen Mother Amestris, the lady Samamat expected more of me than my beauty; she expected me to use my mind. Samamat was the only person I knew who seemed not to care at all what I looked like. Even Ahasuerus had been pleased to see that his wife was beautiful. Samamat did not regard beauty as an achievement.

"But isn't it better to be beautiful?" I asked her, and Samamat sighed.

"Yes, Queen Vashti, it is. Why? Because that's the way it is. But remember that beauty can vanish in a breath. And beauty's not much good if you don't know how to analyze it and use it."

When I demanded to know how to use beauty, Samamat smiled and said, "Oh, child, I'm not the woman who can teach you that."

"Who is?"

Samamat never brushed any of my questions aside. Now she said, "I'll think about that one, Vashti. Now would you like to help me sort and soak the beans?"

Despite her great age and high learning, Samamat performed many of her small household's common needs herself. When I had asked her why—for she could have afforded as many slaves as she chose to buy—Samamat had said that it was always wise to know how to achieve things without aid. "Suppose someday you have no slaves, no handmaidens, to attend you. Will you die of hunger because you cannot cook even the simplest dish, or of thirst because you are too proud to lift a pitcher for yourself?"

Since I wished Samamat to think very well of me, I shook my head. And I allowed her to teach me what she thought I needed to know. I learned, although I could not imagine a life in which I had no servants rushing to care for me.

It is to Samamat that I owe such womanly skills as I possess. She also took me up to the palace roof at night and taught me to know the stars. I learned their names, and how to tell what hour of the night it was by their placement in the sky. And I learned the stars would guide me, if I were lost. One pale bright star stood in the north.

"It never moves," Samamat told me. "The sky wheels around it—see that arc of stars, there? Follow that arc to its end, and there you find a trustworthy guide."

Only one other person—so I thought then—required more of me than my beautiful eyes and my exotic hair. Daniel Dream-Master spoke to me as if I were his own age; it was my task to follow his words, if I could.

It was in Daniel's courtyard that I first learned how others truly thought of me. One afternoon I had just run into the small courtyard when I saw Captain Dariel enter through a door in the eastern wall. A woman ran to him, hands outstretched, and Dariel had her in his arms before either saw me standing there watching. Then the woman pulled away from him, and her honey-hued skin paled to a sickly white, as if she had been stricken gravely ill.

I knew of course that Captain Dariel was the lady Samamat's son, sired by her first husband Arioch. And I remembered one of the things Dariel had told me on my journey here to Shushan. I smiled in delight. "You must be Captain Dariel's wife!"

Dariel sighed. "Yes," he began, and the woman grasped his arm. "No!" Her denial cut sharp. "Say nothing. She will run and tell it all to Queen Amestris before nightfall."

"Will you do that, Queen Vashti?" said a soft voice, and Samamat walked slowly out of the blue-tiled house and stood beside me.

I studied the woman who stood clutching Dariel's arm. She was far older than I, perhaps thirty, but she was still very beautiful, with long eyes dark as a moonless night and hair that rippled like black water to her knees.

"Of course she will. She tells Amestris everything." The woman sounded . . . afraid. Bewildered, I looked up at Samamat.

"You do," Samamat told me. "Have you never wondered why no one says anything of importance in your hearing?"

"Of course she hasn't." Daniel had come out to join us, and now Dariel sighed. "Yes," Daniel added, "it is getting crowded. Now, Sama, why should the child have noticed any such thing?"

Samamat liked me to puzzle things out for myself; now I looked up at her, and then at Dariel, and then at the beautiful woman. Why would she be afraid of me, or that I would tell Amestris?

"You are not supposed to be here!" I said, delighted that I had found the answer. No one said anything, not even Samamat. The silence stretched uneasy between us, and I thought over what else had been said. That no one would speak freely before me because I ran and told the Queen Mother everything—*But this is a secret, and it is not mine to tell. Is that what Samamat means? But why would Dariel's wife be a secret?*

"But you are Captain Dariel's wife," I said, "Why shouldn't you be here with him? And with his mother?"

"You see?" said Dariel's beautiful wife. Dariel sighed. "This is my doing, Cassandane; I mentioned—once—that I missed my wife, when I was telling the little queen stories to pass time on the road."

Samamat smiled at me. "You have a good memory, Queen Vashti."

"Too good." Cassandane buried her face in her hands, and Dariel put his arm around her.

"We will leave Shushan," he said, and Cassandane shook her head.

"And go where?" She lifted her head and stared at me; the bitterness in her face startled me. "It is hopeless, my love. We knew that from the start."

Again no one spoke, waiting. At last I said, "Why?"

Samamat stared hard at her son, who sighed again but obeyed that silent command. "Because, my queen, Cassandane belonged to King Ahasuerus's father," Dariel said.

I thought hard about this. A king's women always belonged to him, or to his successor—but I cold not imagine Ahasuerus desiring to have a woman as old as Cassandane, even if she was still beautiful. So why should she not marry Dariel? My silence was not easy for Cassandane to endure—later, when I was older and we were friends, she told me she had used that span of silence to practice the words she would use to ask Dariel to kill her swiftly, before the royal executioners could carry out whatever grisly death the Queen Mother would decree for her.

"Surely Ahasuerus will let you marry if I ask him to," I said, and Cassandane made a choking sound and pressed her hand over her lips.

"You see?" Cassandane's voice trembled. "She is a child; she will not be silent."

"She is the queen, too. Ask her," Daniel said.

Cassandane stared at me, doubtful. Then she sank to her knees before me. "O queen, if it pleases you, grant my petition and my request. Give me my life, and Captain Dariel's life. Tell no one what you have seen here today. Do not tell Queen Mother Amestris that you saw me with Dariel. Do not tell the king. I beg of you."

Kneeling, her warm brown eyes gazed into mine. I saw fear there, and hope. This was the first time someone had asked a boon of me as queen. I looked over to Daniel and Samamat, but their faces revealed nothing. I was to make this decision myself.

I drew a deep breath. "It pleases me to grant your petition and your request, Cassandane. I will tell no one that I saw you with Captain Dariel. No one."

"Even Queen Mother Amestris?" Captain Dariel asked, and Samamat laughed; it was not a pretty sound.

"My son, you're assuming Amestris doesn't already know," Samamat said. "She's quite capable of keeping that knowledge to herself until it's useful to her."

"Perhaps she does," said Captain Dariel. He reached down and took Cassandane's hand and helped her to her feet. "But the word of Queen Vashti that she will say nothing is the best we can do now."

The word of Queen Vashti is the best we can do now. Captain Dariel's words echoed in my mind, and the weary hopelessness they carried made my cheeks burn.

. . . the best we can do . . .

Seeking comfort, I ran straight to Hegai, who took one look at me and caught me up in his arms. "What troubles my queen?"

About to spill the entire tale into his ears, I suddenly remembered I had sworn to grant Cassandane's petition and request. To tell no one that she was married to Dariel. To tell no one I saw her with Dariel. Did that also mean I could tell no one I had met Cassandane at all?

"Vashti? What has upset you so? Or who?" Hegai's voice calmed, coaxed. I decided I could at least speak of seeing so beautiful a lady. If I could not trust Hegai, who swore he belonged to me utterly, then I could trust no one.

"Hegai, do you know a lady in the palace named Cassandane? She is old, but very beautiful."

"Yes, I know of her." Laughter warmed Hegai's voice. "And she is not so very old."

"Not as old as Queen Mother Amestris?" I asked.

"No, not so old as that. Where did you meet her, my queen? Was she unkind to you?"

Faintly baffled by the question, I shook my head. No one in all the palace had ever been unkind to me. I could not imagine such a thing. But still *"The word of Queen Vashti is the best we can do"* whispered behind my ears. Not unkind words—not meant unkindly, at any rate.

But were they true? Was my word worth so little?

No. I am Queen Ishvari's granddaughter. I will do as I have promised.

Hegai hugged me and set me down. "No, I did not think the lady Cassandane would be unkind. Did you like her, my queen?"

"Oh, yes." I saw again Cassandane's face lit with joy as she ran to Captain Dariel, and then the sickly white beneath her skin when her eyes saw me watching them. "Hegai—may I have the lady Cassandane to serve in my household?"

I thought this ploy very clever, and it did not once occur to me that my wish would be denied.

Nor was it. The lady Cassandane joined my household, and soon it seemed she had always been a part of my life. Too clever to attempt to act as a mother to me—that role belonged to Amestris—Cassandane claimed the position of elder sister for herself. She taught me the value of silence, and how to listen. Men, Cassandane told me solemnly, wished to be entertained.

"And nothing amuses a man quite so much as talking about himself," Cassandane said. "If you remember only one thing about men, my queen, remember that."

I did not always listen to Cassandane's wise words; why should I? Cassandane, too, indulged me and bowed to my will. I was the queen, and she only one of the last king's concubines. And I knew a secret about her that would be her death if I breathed so much as one word of it. So Cassandane did her best to teach me what I was willing to learn, but fear and caution kept her from denying me anything I chose to demand.

It was Queen Mother Amestris who still ruled my days. Only later did I understand how thoroughly I was her creation. And although a few tried to mitigate her influence on me, they could only hope I would heed them, and that their tending would someday bear sweet fruit. And they had to work subtly, and in shadow.

No one dared openly defy Amestris.

It never occurred to me even to try. All Amestris ever desired of me was that I amuse myself and please her son. I did not realize then that she had no intention of ever surrendering the reins of power; she strove to create two beautiful, frivolous puppets. Amestris wished me to put my own pleasure above all else; I did not have many duties as queen, and those few formed the only dull spots in my bright butterfly life.

One of my duties I found not only dull, but unpleasant: I disliked choosing new girls for the king's harem. I silently scolded myself for this, calling myself selfish and unkind—for why should Ahasuerus not enjoy pleasures I could not yet offer him?

At first, when told I must learn to choose girls for my husband's harem, I was shocked. Then, as Amestris explained to me why I must learn to do this, my shock and embarrassment faded, replaced by a desire to prove to the Queen Mother that I *could* behave in a proper manner; I *did* possess the skills a queen must have. Something in Amestris's tone of voice always had that effect: irritating and inspiring.

"A king must have more and better than any other man. A king must possess only the best. His women are gems upon his robes, and they must be gems of flawless quality. Someday I will not stand here beside you, Vashti. You must learn to choose the king's jewels. Remember, only the best, the most beautiful. The King of Kings must possess nothing that is not perfect."

So simply as that, Amestris reminded me again that I was the most beautiful, the most perfect, of Ahasuerus's possessions.

I still remember the first time it was my duty to gaze upon beautiful girls and decide which would pass into the king's harem and which would leave weeping and rejected. I was sitting in the queen's courtyard, trailing peacock feathers for my Chin puppy to chase, when Hegai came to me. I smiled and ran to him, but stopped when he bowed low to me.

"O queen, will it please you to look upon the maidens that have been brought to the palace, and choose those that will remain for the pleasure of the King of Kings?"

Queen Mother Amestris had told me I must do this; still I was taken by surprise. *Choose concubines for Ahasuerus? Now?* I stared at Hegai, too dismayed to speak.

Hegai put his arm around me. "The sooner it pleases the queen to come, the sooner the task will be completed."

I followed Hegai to a vast room in the Women's Palace. The walls were hung with crimson and yellow curtains embroidered with scenes from the tales of the Loves of Ishtar, and rugs woven bright with flowers covered the smooth stone floor. In the middle of the room half a dozen maidens stood. Their faces were painted so heavily and they were so richly garbed I could not tell what they truly looked like—or one from the other.

I looked up at Hegai, hoping he would indicate which girls he thought I should select for the king's harem, but he did not meet my eyes. So I knew I had to make my own choices.

I stared at the waiting girls, hoping the Good God Ahura Mazda would send a sign telling me which to favor. Then I realized Ishtar, goddess of love, was more likely to be of help in this matter and swiftly and silently petitioned Her for aid. But Ishtar sent no sign either.

I was only ten years old—what did I know of what would please a man? At last I pointed at random.

"That one," I said, "and that one. And that one." I stopped, having no real idea of how many new concubines the King of Kings needed. And as I hesitated, I looked again at the girls and saw that one of the three I had not pointed to had tears glinting in her eyes. The second stared at the rug beneath her feet; the third bit her lip hard.

Their sadness spoke to my heart; I could not send them away. Whatever happened to a girl I rejected, that fate drew tears. I drew in a deep breath, and said swiftly,

"And that one and that one and that one too." I looked up at Hegai, who smiled.

"Good choices, all," Hegai told me.

But if Hegai was pleased by my kindness, Amestris was not. "Vashti, you are the most foolish child! If you will not listen to me, you should at least listen to Hegai. You must at least make a pretense of judging the girls!"

I stared at the floor between us. I did not say that Hegai had smiled at me, approved my generosity in choosing all the girls. Nor did I say that I remembered each of Amestris's rulings perfectly, but that I had simply found myself unable to carry them out. "I am sorry. But the ones who thought themselves unchosen wept, and—"

"And found the right weapon to make you surrender." Amestris sighed. "Well, there is nothing to do about it now. But next time, Vashti, at least ask to look upon them unclothed. Or make them wash the makeup from their faces!"

I raised my head and saw an indulgent smile on Amestris's red lips.

But all childhood ends. Mine lasted longer than that of many girls, for Amestris saw no need to rush me into her son's bed. "Yes, you are a woman now," she told me the year I turned fourteen, and began to bleed with the moon. "But you are still not a woman grown. Trust me, there is no need for haste."

I did trust her; how should I not? She had been nothing but kind and indulgent since the hour she had come to take me out of my old life and into this one. So I happily continued as Ahasuerus's friend and companion—and continued to pick pretty concubines for his bed—for another two years. I did not understand how my unnaturally prolonged childhood affected my husband's feelings for me, or how gravely it damaged our marriage.

HEGAI

There never seemed enough hours to accomplish all I must; the position of Chief Eunuch to the harem of the King of Kings is no sinecure. Sometimes, as I gravely allotted garments to the king's women, or tallied up the nights they had spent in the king's bed, I would stop and stare and suddenly realize that after all the days and nights that had passed, I was no closer to my goal of destroying Haman than I had been the day he killed my mother. Had his death been all I desired, I could have sunk a knife into him a dozen times over, not caring if I escaped punishment for the deed. But I wanted more than just Haman's death.

I wanted him ruined. I wanted him to know that I had triumphed and he failed utterly.

I wanted him to suffer.

So I waited.

That was what I told myself, and I thought it truth. I told myself I dreamed only of vengeance, never realizing another dream waited for me.

It is never wise to tempt the gods, especially Ishtar. What could be more enticing to the Lady of Love and War than my serene belief in my iron control over my passions and my heart?

Fifteen years lay between us; I was old enough to have fathered her, had I been a whole man. I counted far too heavily on those fifteen years to safeguard me.

But time is mutable; years melt away like sugar in the rain.

When we first laid eyes upon each other, she was ten years old, and I was twenty-five. She was a child and I full-grown. But as she grew, the gulf between our years altered, as if time itself flowed differently for her than it did for me.

When Vashti was fifteen and I thirty, I had changed very little since the day I lifted her out of the royal palanquin and ushered her into the Women's Palace. But those five years had wrought magic on Vashti. The little girl had vanished; in her place stood a woman. And although I did not yet know it, my heart no longer belonged to me. It was hers. Forever.

All that remained was for Ishtar to blow the dust from my blind eyes at the time and place of Her choosing.

How odd to think that two yelping wolf cubs changed the course of the Persian Empire. But they did.

The king wished to hunt, and so the court hunted. The queen wished to do whatever the king did, and so I and a dozen miserable eunuchs attended her. As we galloped after the king, I again gave silent thanks to Lord Orodes, who had let me learn to ride a horse properly.

Ahasuerus hoped for lion, but he hunted only an hour's ride from Shushan; too close to the city for lions. After a long morning of seeking and backtracking, he at last flushed quarry. A wolf ran almost under his stallion's hooves; Ahasuerus shouted in delight and spurred him after the fleeing wolf. Of course all the rest of us sent our own mounts charging after him—and Vashti, who was more daring than skillful on horseback, raced past everyone save the king.

The wolf led us through brush and into rising hills. By now the beast tired, and at last, in a narrow ravine, it turned at bay, sides heaving. In the time it took me to draw a few breaths, Ahasuerus sent half-a-dozen arrows into the exhausted animal and claimed the kill. As the courtiers acclaimed him as the son of Nimrod himself, Vashti urged her fretting horse closer to the dead beast.

"Look, Ahasuerus—it's a bitch. See, she is nursing cubs." Vashti stared down at the fallen wolf.

Ahasuerus glanced at his prey. "So she was." He then gazed around at the sides of the ravine. "I wonder if she led us to her whelps? You"—he gestured to the nearest Immortal—"search the area for the wolf's lair."

I sighed inwardly. I doubted the lair could be found, and the hunt had led us far from Shushan. Even if we turned back now, we would not ride back into the palace until nightfall. However, what the King of Kings wanted, he got, and so I edged my horse closer to Vashti's, prepared to wait patiently. When I was beside her, I saw at once that something troubled her. Her crystal eyes were clouded, her tender mouth set in a tight line. I reached out and gently touched her hand.

"What perturbs my queen?"

Vashti stared past me, watching as a dozen Immortals searched about the ravine for the she-wolf's lair. "I wish she had escaped."

"You have a tender heart, my queen."

"Do I?" Vashti twisted in her saddle so that she could face me squarely. "She ran so long and so hard, but in vain." Her eyes glittered with unshed tears. "Oh, Hegai, I wish—"

At that moment shouts from the searching Immortals drew all attention to them. Ahasuerus whooped with triumph. "They've found the den!"

Even as he drew breath to speak again, an Immortal ran up to him and went down on one knee beside his horse.

"It is even as the king says. We have the cubs—two only, O king." The Immortal spoke as if the lack of more wolf cubs were a fault of the searchers.

"Bring them here." Ahasuerus beckoned, and two more Immortals approached, each holding a wolf cub by the scruff of its neck.

The cubs were small as yet; I judged them to be perhaps two months old. Dangling from the Immortals' iron grasp, the cubs squirmed and whimpered. Ahasuerus regarded the frightened little creatures with satisfaction.

"Excellent," he said, and smiled at the Immortals, who bowed their heads in acknowledgment of his praise. "Easier to take the evil beasts now, before they've ravaged a farmer's flock."

Beside me, I sensed Vashti tense, her hands tightening on the reins. Her horse danced sideways in protest and I reached out and caught the reins just below its chin. Beside Ahasuerus's horse, the two Immortals held the wolf cubs high, so that all might see them. One cub hung limp, whimpering faintly. The other cub still struggled against its captor and uttered outraged yelps.

"What is the king's will?" one of the immortals asked.

Ahasuerus said, "Cut their throats."

And Vashti cried "No!" and flung herself off her horse so fast she landed on her hands and knees in the dust.

Before even I could move to stop her, she scrambled to her feet and snatched one dangling cub out of the Immortal's grasp. She pressed the whimpering wolf-cub to her breast.

"You won't kill them. I won't let you."

Ahasuerus frowned. "They're evil. Wolves belong to Ahriman the Dark, you know that. Now give that creature back to my guard and"—he looked around, indicated me—"let Hegai put you back up on your horse."

He didn't add "where you belong," but that was so clearly what he meant I was not surprised to see Vashti's eyes narrow. I knew Vashti could be stubborn as a dozen mules—but her will was so rarely crossed. She was denied almost nothing.

Almost. Now I watched this careless license change before my eyes. *The king is no longer a child. He is nearly twenty; a man, and men do not like to be gainsaid. Especially before so many witnesses.*

Obeying the king's command, I dismounted; I bowed and dutifully murmured, "O king, live"—Vashti pivoted and shoved her wolf cub at me; involuntarily, I enfolded the cub in my arms—"forever," I finished, and stared down into the cub's blue eyes. The cub stared back and bit my thumb. It had teeth like new needles, and only years of learning to control every emotion let me endure the sharp pain without crying out.

Now Vashti grasped the second cub and the Immortals who had held the cubs looked to Ahasuerus for guidance. He merely scowled at Vashti. Before either king or queen could speak, I swiftly stepped in front of Vashti.

"Give that cub to me as well, O queen."

"No, you give me back that one. I'll carry them myself." Her chin lifted and she glared past me at Ahasuerus.

The glint in her eyes might only have been reflected sunlight, but it still made me uneasy. Queen Mother Amestris might think the king still a boy, but the anger in his face had been a man's, not a boy's. As for the young queen—I looked down into Vashti's face and saw, not petulance, but determination.

"I will not have them hurt, Hegai." The cub Vashti held squirmed and nuzzled her neck.

"Then let me hold both so you do not drop them while mounting your horse." I held out my hand.

Vashti hesitated, but permitted me to take the second cub from her. The little creatures squirmed and squeaked; I looked at them and sighed inwardly. Dirt covered the cubs, a fact Ahasuerus pointed out crossly. I agreed—

"And doubtless they are infested with fleas," I added.

Exasperated by this levity, Vashti stamped her foot. "Then I shall bathe them—"

"Which means you, O queen, will have fleas crawling upon you as well." As I spoke, I saw Ahasuerus shake his head and turn his horse away. And I saw that Vashti did not notice his displeasure.

Vashti put her hand on one of the wolf cubs and smiled up at me. "Then you, O Chief Eunuch, shall bathe *me*." Even then, as she slanted her opal eyes up at me and she smiled, her words seemed only a young girl's jest.

"As the queen says. Now mount your horse and go ride at the king's side."

"Must I? I'd rather go back with you and help you with my wolves."

"And the King of Kings would rather you hunted with him."

"Oh, Ahasuerus won't care, and besides, I don't wish to hunt any longer today. I'd rather go with you."

"My queen, you begged to hunt with the king and he agreed to permit it—so it would be wise for you to accompany him now. He is not pleased about the wolf cubs."

Vashti shrugged, but to my surprise, she then nodded. "Oh, very well. But mind, I expect to see my wolves waiting for me when I return."

"Of course, my queen." Already I was considering how to carry the cubs back to the palace and safely accommodate them in Vashti's palace once they had been bathed and fed. Doubtless I would think of something. For the moment, I simply thanked the Wise God for Vashti's unexpected obedience.

Once we returned to the palace, I thrust the wolf cubs into the hands of the eunuch in charge of the queen's pets, and instructed him to clean them, feed them, and ensure they did not bite their royal owner when she next saw them even if he had to drug them to ensure their docility—

"Oh, they won't bite *her*." He held the cubs by the scruff of their necks, regarding them with appalled resignation. "Nothing ever bites *her*."

"If you mean the most royal lady Vashti, Queen of Queens, say so." But I spoke mildly, for expecting him to deal with wolves truly was outrageous. "Pretend they're dogs," I advised him, and hastily left to seek out Vashti.

For once she was where she ought to be, waiting for me in the Queen's Bath. I walked through the rippling light and saw Vashti reclining on one of the marble slabs. No one else was in the room; I sighed, wondering what mischief she had plotted now.

"O queen," I said, "where are your bath-servants?"

"O chief of my servants," she said, "you promised to bathe me yourself."

For long slow heartbeats, I looked through the hot moist air that lay between us. Vashti smiled and sat up. She stretched, and her pale hair cascaded over her shoulders and back and thighs; her skin glistened, spangled with sunlight. She looked like a *peri* damp with morning dew, like a flawless pearl, like the most beautiful creature ever created.

She looked nothing like the fierce girl who had wrested a wolf cub from an Immortal's hands and defied the King of Kings. She didn't look like a young girl at all—

She looked like a woman.

I had seen her naked body many times. I had seen the pretty, overawed child. I had seen the exuberant, overindulged girl. Never before had my blood burned beneath my skin when I looked upon her. I felt ill-at-ease; embarrassed by what should have been a commonplace to me.

She beckoned to me, laughed and stretched again. In the dim shadows of the Queen's Bath, her hair was only another shadow; paler than most, but still a shadow. I walked slowly across the warm damp floor until I stood beside her, and for the first time since the day I had welcomed her to the palace of the King of Kings, I did not dare lay my hands upon her body.

"You needn't stare so." Vashti added, "I am not so dirty as you clearly fear."

"Dirty? You?" My voice sounded strange and forced as it echoed against the bright golden walls.

She tilted her head and regarded me curiously. "Hegai, what's wrong? What are you staring at?"

I am staring at a woman I desire. I am looking at you. Not at her ivory hair, or her pearl skin, or her opal eyes. At *her.* I desired *her.* Any man who tells you a eunuch cannot know desire . . . well, let him be cut after he has even once known a woman, and then let him say that.

"Hegai? What are you thinking?"

I am thinking you are a woman now, a woman I may touch but never possess. I am thinking of your sweetness and your laughter. I am thinking of the way you defied the King of Kings to save some filthy wolf pups.

I managed to smile and offer a diversion, hoping she would forget whatever she saw in my eyes. "I am thinking, it is time and past time, O brave one, that the Queen's Bath reflected Queen Vashti and not Queen Amestris."

My offering worked—yes, Vashti was a woman now, but still a very young one, and she delighted in creating her own world. She did not yet realize how small that world was; how high and thick the palace walls that bound her.

And my hasty misdirection held much truth, for the old Queen's Bath had never truly suited Queen Vashti. Heavily gilded walls and gaudy tile murals overwhelmed her moonlight beauty.

"Oh, yes, Hegai! What changes shall we make?" Vibrant with eagerness, she bounced off the marble slab on which she'd been sitting. She padded over to me and put her arms around my waist, and tilted her head to look up into my face. "I'm so glad you thought of it, for I really don't like all those sea monsters staring at me as if they wished to eat me!"

As her body pressed against mine; the scent of her favorite perfume drifted to me on the humid air. I inhaled the warm bite of amber, the rich sweetness of roses. I looked down into Vashti's opal eyes and silently thanked Ishtar that at least one layer of cloth lay between us—I wore only a sleeveless tunic of thin linen that covered me only from throat to knee, but it was better than nothing—

Which was all that Vashti wore. Nothing. *Nothing but the scent of amber and roses . . .*

"Hegai? Hegai, where are my wolves?" Her words broke whatever spell and kept me staring. I shook myself free of visions of Vashti dancing before me, that scent of amber and roses swirling about her in the hot moist air.

"O queen, did you think I would bring them in here?"

"Well, no, but I wish to see them after you bathe me. Do *you* think they're evil and cunning?" Vashti regarded me hopefully.

Cunning and cowardly . . . The words echoed in my memory. *Cunning and cowardly, like all eunuchs.* I knew those words were false.

"No, my queen," I said, "I don't." Another question to draw Vashti's attention occurred to me. "What do you intend to do with the cubs?" I knew the answer before she spoke, of course; Vashti possessed an ever-growing menagerie of pets.

"Why, keep them, of course." She looked baffled, clearly wondering why

I even asked so foolish-evident a question. "I've chosen names for them—can you guess what they are?"

I shook my head. "No, my queen. I cannot. And no, I do not wish to guess what they are. I wish you to tell me."

"Oh, very well. I have named the smaller Vayu and the larger Atar. *That* will show Ahasuerus what I think of his silly notion that they're evil."

Wind and Fire. Vayu, the wind, chases away evil and Atar, son of the Good God Ahura Mazda, is fire. Fire burns evil to ash. Vashti had indeed chosen names that would reveal her thoughts to Ahasuerus. Clever, yes. But wise?

"What do you think? Do you like the names?" Vashti regarded me so hopefully I could not chide her.

"They are most clever." They were too clever, but I would try to persuade Vashti of this at another time, in another place in which Vashti did not sit naked smiling at me. "Now come, my queen—let me see how much work I must do to make you as clean as your pet wolves."

After a week in which I could find no peace in either my thoughts or my dreams, I awoke to the fact that I was acting like a fool. I went to stand before my famed silver mirror and stared at my reflection.

Behold the Chief Eunuch of King Ahasuerus's palace, third most powerful official in the empire. The respected and well-liked Chief Eunuch. Why are you throwing all this into the midden? And for what? For a desire I could not slake? Always, always I had kept my temper curbed, displayed a serene face to the world. Now my mood poisoned the whole Women's Palace.

Very well, you are so out of temper even your dogs will not approach you. And what are you going to do about it?

Ah, I see. I silently thanked the Good God, and I did what I should have done a week ago. I went to Daniel and Samamat, who could always be relied upon for a clear-eyed examination of problems. And at the moment, *I* was a problem.

First, however, I devoted an hour to persuading Moon and Night, my beautiful Salukis, that I was myself again. I knew I had succeeded in calming my mind when the two dogs padded happily beside me to Daniel's house.

There they lay content in the sunlight as I unfolded my troubles to Daniel and Samamat. I began with the king's hunt, and the wolf, and Queen Vashti's defiance—

"Oh, yes, her pet wolves. I must go and see them. I wonder if they will grow to be just like dogs or will pine for the wild when they are grown." Samamat, who loved dogs like a Persian, had settled herself on the ground beside Moon and Night and was stroking their silken ears.

"They seem content to remain with whoever feeds them at the moment." I hesitated, then told of my unease upon seeing Vashti in her bath, swiftly, as if it were of little import. I did not miss the glance Samamat exchanged with Daniel as I hurried to explain I was designing a new bath for Vashti. "Of course it's a great deal of work . . ."

"Well, it's not as if you have to lay the tiles yourself, Hegai." Samamat leaned her cheek on Moon's sleek head. As if seeing her with new eyes, I realized her fair hair had silvered enough to match the Saluki's moon-white coat.

Daniel regarded the Salukis speculatively, as if the dogs could provide him answers. "Tell me, Hegai, what do you think really troubles your mind and heart?"

"Truly, Daniel, I—well, of course Vashti is beautiful as a goddess, but I've always known that. Who would not admire her beauty?"

Daniel regarded me with that odd steady gaze that I found so impossible to decipher. "Hegai, what would you say to someone who came to you with the same story you just told me?"

I had to struggle to conceal my emotion. Anger. I wished that Commander Arioch were still alive to reprove Daniel for such exasperating serenity. Then Arioch's voice seemed to echo in my mind, giving me words to speak aloud.

"I don't know what I would say to someone who came to me with such a tale—but I know what I would say to someone who kept answering my questions with other questions." Even my voice seemed to echo Commander Arioch's. "I would say 'Daniel, *learn how to answer a question.*'"

Lady Samamat stared at me, clearly startled by my tone, but Daniel regarded me calmly. "Would you really?"

That was when the lady Samamat laid her hand on my arm and said, "Walk with me, Hegai? I need your opinion on a matter of some importance."

I helped her rise, and after we had walked around the garden twice, I unbent enough to ask what troubled her. Samamat smiled. "Hegai, I just cannot decide which of the two of you to hold under the fountain until you see sense."

"Daniel Dream-Master," I told her, and she raised her eyebrows.

"A swift answer. Upon what do you base that conclusion?"

"It is simple, my lady. I can be made to see sense. My lord Daniel, on the other hand—"

"Will never learn common sense. I see." The lady Samamat paused beside a rosebush—a wayward, untamed plant, unlike the tidy rosebushes in the other palace gardens. She cupped one hand about a rose dark as blood and bent to inhale its perfume. Then she said, apparently to the small red rose, "Do you really want an answer to your question?"

I did not pretend to misunderstand. "Yes, my lady, I do."

She sighed. "Do you know the true trap of palace life?" She looked straight into my eyes. "Sooner or later, it becomes impossible to tell the truth—even to one's self. I'm no dream-master, but even I can know that you can answer your own question . . . if it's not too late for you."

As I walked back through the corridors and courtyards to my own apartments, I considered the lady Samamat's words. Was it too late for me?

Or could I still tell the truth—even if only to myself?

By night a *peri* danced through my dreams, her hair trailing over my skin like clouds. By day I found myself gazing upon the queen and imagining her without the royal blood that made her untouchable. No crown, no palace—only a joyous, loving creature delighting in the world and all it contained. Oh, I knew the truth, but too late, as the lady Samamat had feared.

The truth is that I love her. I did not merely desire her lovely body; that was harmless enough. Desire faded. But love—love endured.

I love her. I love Vashti. I could not afford love; that, too, was truth. And love could prove fatal to us both.

⁜

For Vashti, I created an underwater grotto. Now, the Queen's Bath glowed with a soft greenish light. Tile green as glass lined the walls, lay glass-smooth under my feet. Above me the ceiling arched; little stars had been cut into that arching sky. The sun's rays streamed through those stars, golden ribbons of light.

There were two small pools and a large one, and wide marble slabs to lie upon. Water poured down the far wall into the large pool. Watersong echoed against the green tile walls. The work took months, but when all had been done as I commanded, not a sea monster remained.

Within this tranquil world, Vashti glowed like a pearl. Simply to look upon her there delighted the eye.

And she had been delighted with my gift—although I think she enjoyed the anticipation of waiting to see her refurbished bath, and the novelty of using the bath in the Women's Palace, as much as she did the new Queen's Bath. She was still dashing about like a mongoose, examining each change and running back to fling her arms around me and kiss my cheek and tell me how enchanted she was by all she saw, when the message came from the Queen Mother.

Oddly, Amestris had sent a written message, rather than an oral one. Vashti could not stop whirling about long enough to read it. "You read it to me, Hegai. Oh, look how beautiful the sunlight is on the waterfall! What does the note say?"

"It's sealed." What could be so private that Amestris sent a sealed written message, yet not private enough to summon Vashti to tell it face-to-face? I slid my fingernail under the Queen Mother's seal, unfolded the small sheet of papyrus.

"Well?" Vashti had stopped dancing about and clung to me, tilting her head to see what Amestris had written.

"Amestris the Queen Mother, may she live forever, sends all the proper greetings to Vashti the Queen of Queens, wife to King Ahasuerus, Lord of Half the World—"

Vashti plucked the papyrus from my hand. "Oh, never mind all that." She began to read, and as she did her eyes widened. She stared at me, seemingly struck mute.

"My queen? What is it?" I snatched the note back, read it silently, as Vashti had. My hands trembled, and there was a great echoing in my ears. The world stopped as I fought to breathe steadily.

Since Queen Vashti has attained the age of sixteen, it is time she became King Ahasuerus's wife in body as well as in name. Chief Eunuch Hegai is to prepare Queen Vashti to go to the king's bed tonight.

We stared at each other over the Queen Mother's message. The air still clamored in my ears. "Vashti," I began at last, and as if her name freed her to move, Vashti flung herself into my arms. I was not dead; I pulled her close to me, held her fiercely tight. After a moment, I realized she was crying.

I forced myself to loosen my grasp on her, ease her away from me. "My queen, you must not weep upon receiving such a summons."

She nodded, her hands curled into fists, knuckles showing white. "No, of course not. I don't even know why I'm crying."

"You cry for happiness, as women do," I suggested.

She lifted her chin, nodded. "Yes. Yes, that must be why. That *is* why. I have waited so long for this day." Bravely said. Only the slightest quiver in her voice betrayed her.

I longed desperately to take her into my arms again, to comfort her. I longed with equal desperation to know what Amestris knew, or guessed. Sending that message in such a fashion carried a second message, hidden, like a serpent coiled beneath a rock.

Who is the true message for? Vashti? Me? Or for us both?

So at last it would be my privilege to prepare the queen for her wedding night. *I would rather kill myself,* I thought, and heard a mocking ghost say, *"Oh, that will* really *help the woman you love."*

I drew a deep breath, and reached out and took Vashti's hands. "Come, my queen. It is time to make you even more beautiful than you are, so you may delight your husband's eyes."

You have known for years that this night must come. If you love Vashti at all, you will make this easy for her. She is Ahasuerus's wife, after all.

Not yours.

VASHTI

I think now that the true turning point in our lives came on the night I turned sixteen. By then, I had been Ahasuerus's queen for six years, and I should have already gone to his bed. I should already be carrying his child. Girls younger than I became mothers every day. Amestris had insisted that there was no need for haste, that I was too young—but now the Seven Princes petitioned Ahasuerus, begging him to consider the welfare of the empire. The King of Kings needed an heir.

And when Ahasuerus told this to his mother, Amestris knew she could delay our coupling no longer. She called for me and told me, "This is what you need to know, when you go to your husband's bed." Amestris gave concise, cold instructions, then dismissed me without giving me a chance to ask even one question.

Uncertain whether to be unhappy or angry, I ran to my garden, where I sat and watched my half-grown wolf cubs chase each other's tails. The thought of performing the acts Amestris had so grimly described revolted me. How horrible—

—*but it can't be.* All the love songs, all the poems—could they all be nothing but beautiful lies? I could ask Hegai—no. I did not know why, but the thought made me uncomfortable.

The wolves ran over my feet, spun around in a scrabble of paws to dash in the other direction. And my thoughts found another direction as well. I clapped my hands, and when one of my maids came to me and bowed, I smiled and told her to ask the lady Cassandane to come to me.

Cassandane bowed low, supple as water. "O queen, live forever. How may I serve you?"

"Oh, rise," I said, "and come sit beside me." When she hesitated, I patted the cushion beside me. "Sit," I said again. "There is something I wish to ask you."

Cautious as a wary cat, Cassandane sat as I had bidden her. Once she had done so, I offered her fruit, and sherbet, and sweet cakes, and wine, until at last Cassandane interrupted the flow of my words.

"What is it the queen wishes to ask of me?"

I began twining the fringe on my sash into tiny braids. "Cassandane, you have spent nights with a man—" I took care not to name him; any listener would think I meant Ahasuerus's father.

"Yes, O queen, I have," Cassandane said, filling the silence. Laughter rippled beneath her respectful words.

I drew a deep breath and spoke quickly. "What is it like?"

Cassandane looked surprised. "Surely someone has instructed you?"

"Yes, of course. I know what happens. But what is it *like*?"

"Ah—that. When it is good, it is wondrous." Cassandane's red lips curved into the same smile I had seen on images of Ishtar. "It is like fire and roses, like stars shouting joy."

"And when it is not good?"

Cassandane smiled again. "That is something you need never worry about, Queen Vashti."

Just before I went to my husband, I stood before Hegai's huge silver mirror and studied myself as carefully as if I were choosing a concubine for the king's harem. I had chosen many women for my husband's pleasure; would he now find me less desirable than they?

Reflected upon the shining metal was a tall slender figure; riding and hunting and swimming had created a thing of strength and grace out of a round, soft little girl. My skin was clear and smooth, but perhaps more sun-gilded than it should be. My hair still fell smooth as ivory silk down my back.

Perhaps I should darken it. Henna, or oak-galls—No, that was folly. My husband knew perfectly well what color my hair was, and as for my skin, it was his own doing that had led me into the sun's light.

In any case, it was too late now to do more than look upon myself, and remember that whether or not there were a dozen lovelier women within the King's Palace, I was still the only one who was the king's wife.

⁂

As on the first wedding night when we were children, I was escorted with all ceremony to the king's door. As on that first night, I carried a small flame in an alabaster bowl and Hegai escorted me. I thought he looked sad; I did not know why.

"Will you wish me good fortune?" I asked him, and oddly, it took a long moment before he smiled at me. But he said, "You need no wishes from me, my queen. You have everything the world desires. What more could you need?"

For some reason his words made tears press hard against my eyes. I managed to remain dry-eyed, but I did not look at Hegai again until we reached the door to the king's room. There I did gaze up at Hegai, longing for comfort. But Hegai said only,

"O queen, may the Good God bless you. May this night bring you joy." His voice seemed unsteady, but I was too nervous to say anything in answer.

As on our first wedding night, the room was darkened. But this time, small lamps lit part of the vast room, cast shadows across the floor. This time, Ahasuerus sat upon the bed waiting for me. And this time, he said nothing as I walked across his room and held out the little bowl of fire to him.

Ahasuerus took the alabaster bowl, stared into the flame. After a moment, he set the bowl carefully on a small table beside the bed. Then we stared at each other. Neither of us spoke. My face burned; for the first time, Ahasuerus's gaze embarrassed me. I wished desperately that he would make one of his careless jests. . . .

The silence stretched into something strange and heavy. I knew if one of us did not soon speak, the silence would endure between us forever. I clutched desperately for words, and found myself saying,

"This reminds me of our first wedding night."

Ahasuerus stared at me, and I realized he, too, labored under the weight of awkwardness and embarrassment. We had been playfellows too long for this change to seem—right. I tried to smile, and added, "I'm sorry, Ahasuerus. But one of us had to say *something.*"

"I suppose you are right." He shifted, clearly uneasy, then patted the bed beside him. "Come, sit by me."

I turned and sat beside him on the broad bed. "At least this time we have been given lamps."

"Yes."

Again we both fell silent. I rested my hands on the bed; my left hand brushed Ahasuerus's right. A pause. Then, slowly, as if trying to catch a wary quarry, his fingers touched mine, slid over mine. It took all my strength to remain still.

"Vashti—"

"What?" I knew I should say sweet words to him, but every word I knew had fled, leaving me baffled and half-mute.

"Vashti, you know we must—it is time . . ."

Don't be a fool. Remember all Hegai told you. Remember the Queen Mother's advice. Remember how Cassandane smiled. Remember you are Queen Ishvari's granddaughter. I slanted a glance at Ahasuerus, and another thought flashed into my mind. *And remember that he is at least as fearful, and must do all the work!*

"Are you laughing at me?" Ahasuerus demanded, and I realized I had smiled at that last, bawdy image.

"No. No, of course not. It's only that I—well, I am so nervous! And then I thought—" Greatly daring, I leaned over and whispered into his ear the words that had brought the ill-timed smile to my face.

Or perhaps it had been a well-timed smile—for as I spoke softly into his ear, Ahasuerus turned and put his hands on my shoulders, holding me still as his mouth sought mine.

Later, far later, I would kiss another, and learn at last how a man kisses the woman he loves and desires. But that night, our true wedding night, my husband kissed me for the first time as if I were his wife, rather than his friend, or his sister. On that night, such a kiss seemed—

Wrong.

As if I had spoken that thought aloud, Ahasuerus sat back. For long moments we stared at each other. My heart beat so hard I thought Ahasuerus must hear it.

"Do you want to kiss me again?" I asked, dutifully recalling Amestris's cold instructions. Ahasuerus nodded.

"I suppose I'd better," he said.

But our second kiss summoned no fire in me—or, I think, in him. Queen Mother Amestris had raised us up as if we were brother and sister. It was hard, now, to become more than that.

And when Ahasuerus kissed me, I found myself thinking of the concubines I had chosen for his harem. Had he kissed them so dispassionately? *I am the most beautiful woman in all the empire. Everyone says so. Why doesn't Ahasuerus want me?*

And why didn't I want him? He was handsome, and kind, and generous, and I did love him. But I loved him fondly; nothing about him kindled desire's fire within me. I stared down at my hands, and wished desperately that I were in my own palace, in my own bed. I wished it were Hegai's arm around me. Hegai always knew what to say, what I should do—

"Don't cry, Vashti!" Ahasuerus's voice sounded unsteady, panic beneath his hasty words. "Please don't cry!"

"I'm not." I hastily wiped my eyes, not caring that I smeared the kohl and malachite weighing down my eyelids. "Truly, I'm not."

"Yes you are. Don't worry, I swear there is nothing to fear." Ahasuerus patted my shoulder, cautiously, as if worried I might bite. Even more cautiously, he leaned forward and kissed my mouth again.

Reminding myself once more of everything I had been taught, I kissed him in return. Encouragement enough, it seemed, for after that I need only follow where Ahasuerus led, until at last I was Ahasuerus's wife in body as well as in name. To me, the act hardly seemed worth the time and trouble; Ahasuerus seemed to derive far more pleasure from it than I. Doubtless because he was a man, and men got the best of everything—something I had learned long ago, as I ran after Ahasuerus through the great palace.

The next morning, I woke before Ahasuerus did and stared at him as he slept. *Fire and roses. Stars shouting joy. You were wrong, Cassandane.* I thought of Cassandane's face as she had spoken of love, of the Ishtar smile upon her lips. And then, as if urged by Ishtar Herself, I knew what I would ask of Ahasuerus when he awoke. *Cassandane can be happy, even if I am not—*

No. No, I am happy. I have everything I desire. Of course I am happy. Very happy. . . .

When Ahasuerus opened his eyes, he seemed surprised to find me still there. He managed to smile, and to greet me properly. "It is your right to demand a gift of me, now. What do you want, Vashti? Whatever it is, I shall grant it, even to half my kingdom."

A husband must offer his wife a gift after their wedding night; she may either ask for what pleases her or refuse his offering. I would not insult Ahasuerus by refusing. "Nothing so great as half your kingdom. But—there is a woman in my household whom I wish to give in marriage. May I do so?"

"Is that all? Of course; do what seems good to you in the matter." Ahasuerus clearly could not understand why I asked such a thing, and since it was plain that what he most wished for was me to be gone, he did not question me further.

"A thousand thousand thanks, O great king!" I leaned over and kissed his cheek; as I slid out of the massive bed, Ahasuerus grasped my hand.

"And Vashti—I hope—" He did not meet my eyes, and if he had not been a man, I would have said he blushed.

I freed him from the need to find words. "I hope I pleased you, my lord king," I said hastily. Suddenly I desired only to return to my own rooms, my own servants. "Have I your leave to go?"

"Of course, my queen. Go if you wish."

I hastily thanked him, and ran to the door to the corridor between his rooms and mine. Hegai awaited me there with a shawl to wrap about me. I flung my arms around him. "Oh, Hegai, I am so glad you are here!"

"Are you?" Hegai swiftly kissed my forehead; his lips warm against my cool skin. "That pleases me, my queen."

I managed to stand still long enough for him to tuck the shawl around my body. "Hegai, where is Cassandane? I must speak with her."

"You should come bathe, and rest." Hegai coaxed my hair into a loose braid that I half-undid when I shook my head.

"No. Not until I have spoken with Cassandane—oh, better, have her come join me in the Queen's Bath."

"Of course." Hegai's voice sounded odd, but when I glanced up at him, his face revealed nothing. "May I ask what you must so urgently say to her on this of all mornings?"

"That she is to be married at once!" I envisioned Cassandane's delight—and I found myself able to smile at Hegai, and then to laugh and run off down the corridor, back to my own palace—just as if nothing had changed.

HEGAI

I had known this night must come for years. What had I been hoping for? For the young king to die? Even if Ahasuerus died, what good would his death do me?

It had been my duty to escort the queen to the king's bed. But no rule said the Chief Eunuch must stand outside the royal door all night. So when the great door closed behind Vashti, I left to walk through the corridors and gardens of the Women's Palace. I spent hours trying to flee the image of Vashti naked in Ahasuerus's arms. But the image refused to vanish.

When the moon stood high overhead I walked back to the Queen's Palace, though I knew Vashti would not be there. *She is in the king's bed—no. No, do not think of her there, of him giving her pleasure.*

Do not think of her naked in your arms instead of his. . . .

In morning's clear light, Vashti at first seemed happy enough after her wedding night. But her joy seemed forced, and her gaze slid aside from mine.

The second night, Hatach slid into my apartments long before midnight to tell me that the queen had already left the king's bedchamber. I managed to calmly thank Hatach and send him to his own bed without alarming him. Then I went swiftly along the path to the Queen's Palace, and then to Vashti's private rooms.

I saw no one. The rooms were empty. The lamps had not been lit. Only the full moon's light softened the gloom. I stepped out of my slippers and walked cat-soft into Vashti's bedchamber, through the darkness to her wide silver bed.

Vashti lay with her face pressed into a pillow, clearly hoping to silence her misery. Now I knew why there were no servants in the queen's rooms. The queen had sent them away.

Why was she here alone? What had Ahasuerus done? Surely he had not hurt her? Been unkind? I stroked Vashti's hair. "What's wrong, little queen? Come, tell me. Why are you crying?"

Still she said nothing, and trembled with unspent sobs. I was not even certain she had heard my words. I tried again, hardly realizing I spoke not as Chief Eunuch, calm and commanding, but as worried lover. "Vashti, tell me, please. What happened?"

She rolled away from my caressing hand and sat up. She pushed back her hair and uttered a gasp of unsteady laughter. *"Nothing."*

"Nothing," I repeated. Of all the things I had worried myself into near madness over as I contemplated Vashti's nights with her husband, never had I thought of this.

"Oh, Hegai, you should *see* your *face*!" Then she began to laugh, a harsh, wild sound.

"Stop that or I will pour cold water over you," I told her calmly; enough vases of flowers stood in her room to make this possible. Vashti stopped, laughter ending in a few hiccups; she pressed her hand over her mouth and stared at me round-eyed as an owl.

"Now, my queen, tell me what happened and why I find you here, alone, weeping." I could not stop myself from adding, "You say 'nothing' happened. Do you mean the king did not—"

"Oh." Vashti blushed, her pale face crimson. Her gaze slid away from me; apparently there was something intensely fascinating on the floor to her left. "Of course I did not mean that. I—it was—nothing like I expected, I mean."

Ah. Nothing that pleased you. Ahasuerus did not please you. Unworthy joy flooded me and I let the subject of what had happened in the king's bed fade away. Vashti made it easy to do, as she leaned forward until I could see her breasts beneath her sheer silk gown.

"Hegai, do you think my body beautiful?"

Something in her voice made me understand that my answer was important; that she asked a grave question. I took her hands in mine and looked into her eyes. "*You* are beautiful. You will always be beautiful to my eyes."

"Always?" The word choked on a last sob.

"Always." I wiped her damp face with my sash, silently thanking the Great God that I had worn such unadorned garb. It is difficult to comfort someone and wipe tears from her face with a sash embroidered with gold and silver until it is stiff and heavy as ice.

"How long is always, Hegai?"

"Until we both are old and our hair is gray."

She laughed, rather unsteadily—but she laughed. "But Hegai, how will you know when *my* hair turns gray?

"I will know," I said, reaching out to stroke her hair.

Vashti flung herself into my arms—for comfort, I told myself. Just as she had done since she was a child, she turned to me for comfort and consolation. "You love me, don't you, Hegai?"

For a heartbeat hope flared up, and I put my hands on her cheeks, tilted her head back so I could look into her eyes. Hope faded, for what I saw there was the plea of an unhappy child. *You are not truly a woman yet, Vashti. But at least you turn to me. I will not fail you.*

I bent and kissed her hot damp forehead. "Of course I love you, my queen."

Vashti smiled, and curled herself into my arms. A few minutes later, she was asleep. *Yes, Vashti, I love you.* I settled myself comfortably on her bed, and stroked her back as I watched the full moon's light fading toward morning.

I will love you until the stars burn out.

Not even Vashti must ever know what I felt for her—but I longed to create some visible symbol of my love. *What gift from lover to beloved will be safe to give?*

Late one night, I found my answer in the timeless story of Zariadres and Odatis, two lovers who fell in love in a dream. *Poppies. I will plant a bed of poppies in the Queen's Garden.* No one would see anything odd in an addition to Vashti's garden. And every time she danced past that plot, she would see my gift: the eternal lover's flower.

Yes. I will give my beloved red poppies.

Smiling, I picked up my scroll again. I wished I could thank the poet who had inspired me—but the song was so old no one even knew who had first written down its words. My thanks would have to be silent; as silent as my gift to my beloved.

VASHTI

Cassandane's wedding to Dariel took place despite the Queen Mother's objections—or possibly because of them.

"Ahasuerus, are you mad? The woman belonged to your father King Smerdis! No other man may touch her without the king's permission!" Amestris said, and Ahasuerus looked straight into his mother's eyes and said:

"I am the king, Mother, and I grant the lady Cassandane permission to marry whom she wishes."

I think that was the first time Ahasuerus had ever defied his mother. Amestris seemed to hesitate, and then merely shrugged, as if the matter were too trivial to concern herself about. So I happily watched Cassandane married to her beloved Dariel. I put a silver casket filled with pearls into her hands as a wedding present, and Ahasuerus granted them apartments in the palace.

Amestris presented Ahasuerus with Dariel to be captain of the king's guard instead of the Queen Mother's—which I think was meant to indicate her displeasure with both of them. But I do not think either of them objected to the change.

After that, Ahasuerus unexpectedly announced that the King of Kings and Queen of Queens would spend their marriage month at the old summer palace in Ecbatana, in the high mountains. There we rode out hawking, or walked through fields full of spring flowers, or stood upon the rooftop and watched the summer stars. And there neither of us had to pay any heed to Amestris, who remained in Shushan.

At first I hoped that away from the imperial palace, things might change between Ahasuerus and me; I longed for the passion Cassandane had so lovingly described. But I swiftly realized that hope was vain; I must be content with fondness. Ahasuerus the husband, the man, eluded me.

HEGAI

With Vashti gone, I was lonely. An odd complaint, you may think, from one who barely had an hour go by without someone seeking him out. To be master of the imperial harem is no sinecure; I was the one who ensured all ran smoothly, from the smallest task to the greatest.

But even surrounded by all the slaves and servants, eunuchs and concubines, who inhabited the Women's Palace, I missed my beloved. I missed Vashti.

And I knew that when Vashti returned from Ecbatana, she would return changed. She would return as Ahasuerus's wife.

Mine only in my heart, and in my dreams.

Ever since I was appointed Chief Eunuch, I had made it a habit to go out into the streets of Shushan each week. I admit I took pleasure in going down the Great Staircase, gazing upon the city and the fields beyond its walls—but my true reason for doing so was to keep apace of Shushan's gossip.

That explains how I came to be standing in the market, watching a slave merchant offer his wares. That Vashti had been in Ecbatana on her marriage-month and I missed her deeply explains how I came to commit an act of arrant folly. That disaster did not follow was purest good fortune.

As I stood there, my attendant waving a peacock-feather fan beside me to keep the dust and flies away, assistants led a slave out from the merchant's courtyard and pushed him toward the steps up to the platform. He resisted, a movement that caught my eye. I turned to look—

—and for a heartbeat thought I looked upon Vashti playing the maddest of mad jests. Moonlight hair streaming down—

Then the slave turned, and I breathed again. Of course it was not Vashti.

But I could not rip my gaze from the boy. He was perhaps fifteen, and from the slant of his eyes and the sunburnt amber of his skin, I judged him to be of one of the horse tribes from the north. His long soft hair, his supple young body, entranced me. Had Vashti been born a boy, she would look like this. . . .

"Will it please my noble, gracious lord to see more of the boy? Would you hear him sing, or see him dance?" The slave merchant had noted my interest, scented a rich sale.

I ignored the unctuous queries. "How much?" I asked, and the slave dealer shook his head.

"A thousand apologies, noble lord, but I have promised a dozen men that he will be shown on the auction block. A eunuch of such high quality, a pearl of such perfection, such rarity, will bring—"

That, of course, is why he is being pushed onto the sale platform even as the dealer speaks. I suspected the boy had become too difficult to handle; a rebellious slave is a liability to a slave merchant. I interrupted the dealer's recitation of the boy's virtues by raising my hand.

"Do not waste my time. You know who I am, and whom I serve. I want that boy. Now tell me how much." I should have pretended only a mild interest, begun the bargaining by pointing out the boy's faults. I knew I acted as foolishly as Vashti, but I did not care. I cared only that when I went back to the palace, that boy came with me.

The merchant hesitated, clearly trying to decide just how much he could overcharge me. At last he said, "Two hundred darics."

An outrageous amount for an untrained, unruly boy, and both the slave merchant and I knew it. But I found myself saying, "Very well. Two hundred darics." It was, after all, the price that Daniel had once paid to free me from a cruel fate.

The merchant stared, but managed to say, "Did Your Excellency agree?"

"Yes," I said, "My Excellency did. Is the bargain sealed?"

The slave merchant agreed so swiftly he nearly choked on the words. And that is how I came to return to the palace with a very beautiful and very sullen young eunuch following me.

I sent my new acquisition off to bathe and eat before I talked with him. So it was not until the sun had set that the boy was brought to my bedchamber. His skin glowed with sweet oil, his hair flowed like mountain snow down his back, and his expression radiated defiance. I remembered when I had been that young, and that terrified. . . .

I shoved undesired memories away. "So," I said, "what is your name?"

He stared at his feet, and mumbled something that might have been anything from his name to a curse.

"Look at me," I said calmly, "and try again. Now, what is your name?"

He lifted his head and stared at me. And in his eyes I saw, not Vashti, but myself—a highborn boy whose future had been destroyed by one stroke of the gelding knife.

"Bagoas," he said. "My name is Bagoas."

Of course it is. You should learn to lie more convincingly, child. I smiled at him and held my hand out to him. "I was Bagoas once. Well, be Bagoas if it pleases you. But if it does not—someday you will have your own name. One *you* choose."

He ignored this. He looked from me over to my broad bed; clearly reluctant, he walked over to the bed, sat on it in the most graceless fashion possible, and stared at me, waiting. Drawn by the lamplight dancing over his hair, I went to him and sat beside him. When I put my arm around him, he turned rigid as stone.

"I do not wish anyone unwilling in my bed," I said, and moved my arm, letting him go if he wished. When he did not move, I said, "There are other beds. Find an empty one and go to sleep. You've had a long, hard day and need rest."

"Yes, my lord Hegai." He slid off my bed and bowed, then ran to the door and disappeared through it before I could change my mind.

I lay back against the pillows and stared at the stars painted on the ceiling. *Tell me, Immaculate One, what am I to do with the boy now?* I could give him to Vashti; she always delighted in gifts. *Ah, well—I will think about it tomorrow.* Now I should take my own advice, and go to sleep.

Sleep eluded me for many hours, and when at last I did sleep, I suffered such bad dreams I wished only to wake. It was a relief to rise and begin the day—at least until I remembered I now owned a beautiful young eunuch who called himself Bagoas.

The next night was far worse, for Bagoas came to my bed. Unsummoned, and clearly determined to repay my kindness to him in a fashion he believed acceptable to me.

So. Bagoas slid into my bed, and I ran my fingers through his long pale hair. Bagoas cupped my face in his hands; through that touch, I felt him tremble. He leaned forward and pressed his mouth to mine.

He tried. Skin against hot skin. We both tried. Flesh pressed against flesh. But in the end, we both failed. His touch failed to rouse any emotion in me but revulsion and I wished with all my heart that I had never seen him. *Sheer folly. Callous and revolting. How could I be such a fool?*

Then I noticed that the boy trembled and his eyes shone with tears. He must fear his lack of passion had angered me.

"Don't cry. It doesn't matter."

"I'm sorry," he said. "Let me try again. I can—I know how to give you pleasure, I do. I was taught, well taught. Please, my noble lord—"

Well taught—yes, by pain and fear and force. Not every pretty young eunuch had such a tender, gentle teacher as I had. Not for the first time, I blessed Lord Orodes's name. I put my arm around the boy. "Hush, Bagoas. It is not your fault that neither of us likes to bed with men."

He stared at me with tear-filled eyes. "What does it matter what I like? I shall never have it."

"Never is a very long time, Bagoas."

"At the end of *never,* I will still be a eunuch," he said bitterly. "What woman will ever want me? What woman will want half a man?"

"You will be surprised to learn how many women would rather welcome a eunuch to her bed than a whole man. Come to that, you will be surprised to learn how many women would rather share her bed with her cat or her dog. I even knew a woman who would rather sleep with snakes than with her husband." I had my reward; Bagoas laughed.

"I, too, would rather sleep with serpents than with any man I have yet seen." His muscles relaxed, and he tried to suppress a yawn. The small flames of lamplight sent ripples of shadow over his moon-bright hair, his sun-amber skin.

"Trust me," I said, "women will fling themselves begging at your feet, if that is what you wish."

He looked skeptical, but said only, "Surely it is as you say, lord."

"Surely a boy with your face and your wit can carve his future to his liking. And there is more to life than rolling about in a bed with a woman, or man, or whatever it is that you favor." I stroked his pale hair, so like Vashti's. *But he is not what you desire. He is not Vashti.*

I forced away the image of Vashti on her wedding night. *The thinnest of silks over her skin, skin that gleamed like pearls in the flickering torchlight. Her hair unbound, falling down past her hips, sliding over her thighs with each step she took. Her eyes uncertain at the door to the king's bedchamber, as I opened it and guided her over the threshold into the waiting darkness . . .*

"My lord Hegai? Do you wish me to leave or to stay?"

The image of Vashti's uncertain eyes vanished. "Oh, you may stay. There is room enough. And there is something I wish to ask of you. No, two things."

He stared down and drew in a deep breath. Clearly he believed I was about to ask he perform some unknown but repulsive act. "Of course, my lord. Whatever you desire. I am yours." He managed to speak with only the faintest tremor of fear and anger. Definitely he had great promise.

"The first is that you tell me your name."

After a long silence, he told me, but his name sounded so strange to my ears I could not easily repeat it. Well, many of us came into the palace with one name and remained here with another. After a moment, he offered something freely. "It means wolf."

I smiled. "Then you may keep your name, but it will be said in Persian. You are Varkha now."

He regarded me warily. "Varkha means wolf?"

"Yes, Varkha means wolf."

He considered for a moment, then nodded. "Then I am Varkha now. What is the second thing you wish to ask of me, my lord?"

"That you do not cut your hair."

Since among his own people, as he told me later, when we were friends, neither men nor women ever cut their hair, Varkha gladly accepted this condition.

"Good," I said. "Now go to sleep, young wolf, and soon I will introduce you to a woman who is very fond of wolves."

VASHTI

When at last I returned to Shushan and my own palace, I was so delighted to see Hegai waiting for me I flung myself into his arms. I meant to tell him about Ecbatana, and the mountains, and the journey, and a dozen other unimportant things—anything other than my marriage month—but instead I burst into tears. Hegai announced that the journey had wearied me and carried me to the Queen's Bath.

The familiar, soothing routine of the baths banished tension I had not known I suffered. Hegai asked no questions, and refused to allow any of my servants to trouble me with questions either. They tended me in obedient silence; I nearly fell asleep as Hegai combed my hair.

When at last he set the sandalwood comb aside, I stood and stretched. "Oh, Hegai, I did miss you!"

"Did you, my queen?"

I turned and put my arms around him. "Of course I did—" I stopped; surely I should have been so enthralled by my husband I cared for nothing else. I stared at Hegai's chest as if fascinated by the cinnabar amulet he wore.

Hegai kissed my forehead, his lips cool against my hot skin. "Gifts from the King of Kings await you. Come."

Hegai told me all the gossip that had flowed through the palace while I had been gone, and showed me the gifts Ahasuerus had ensured would be waiting for me. There was a chess set, its pieces made of ivory and ebony, and its board of silver and copper. I picked up a cup-and-ball carved from cedar and adorned with silver stars. I tossed the ball upward and caught it on my first try. I set the cup-and-ball aside; I could play with it later. There were many more games and half a dozen new riding outfits of silk-soft leather. But the gifts that pleased me most were the new pets Ahasuerus had bestowed upon me.

There was a little deer with a collar of scarlet leather hung with golden bells, a long-tailed parrot that could say a dozen words, and a pair of silver fox kits so tame they came prancing up to me as if they were puppies. The gift that delighted me most was a half-grown cheetah, an elegant, regal creature that deigned to sniff my fingers and let me stroke its head. The cheetah wore a wide collar of gold set with emeralds.

There were also silver collars adorned with amber for Vayu and Atar, so I knew Ahasuerus truly wished to please me, for he never did grow to like my wolves.

And to care for these creatures, Ahasuerus had given me two new slaves: a pair of girls with the ebony skin of Nubia and the elegant cheekbones and almond eyes of Egypt. Hegai told me their names were Ajashea and Bolour—

"And we love animals more than anything! We can care for all of your pets, royal lady." Ajashea barely remembered to bow, and her enthusiasm made me laugh.

"Well, I am very glad to have you. Are you sisters?" They looked enough alike to be that close.

Both girls shook their heads, the crystal beads braided in their dark hair flashing. "We're cousins," Bolour said. "My mother is her mother's sister, and her father is my father's brother."

Such close-knit unions indeed made them almost sisters. I thought I might dress them alike; they would look charming—or I could dress them as opposites . . . Hegai touched my arm, and I stopped daydreaming and told the two girls I had many pets for them to care for, and then let them run along to play in the garden. The foxes dashed after them, yipping, while the deer followed more slowly, the bells on its collar chiming. The cheetah watched the deer wistfully, but, well trained, did not bound after it. The parrot remained on its perch; I held out my hand and it stepped delicately onto my wrist.

"It was very kind of the king to send me such gifts." I slanted a glance at Hegai, but his face revealed nothing.

"Very kind," Hegai agreed.

"The king loves me dearly," I said.

"Yes," said Hegai, "he loves you dearly." His voice was soft and low, and his eyes did not meet mine. He reached out and gently stroked the parrot's head.

I longed to fling myself into Hegai's arms again, and ask him why Ahasuerus did not want the most beautiful woman in all the empire. Why he did not want *me.* But when at last Hegai looked at me again, I saw a resigned despair in his eyes. And I realized there was nothing I needed to tell him.

But if Hegai never asked about my marriage month, I knew the Queen Mother would not be so restrained. I created a tale for her rich with fulsome praises of my husband and endless recitations of my delight in his gifts. Later, I found other ways to mislead her. For Ahasuerus had a harem full of lovely women whom I had dutifully chosen for him to enjoy. Now that we had returned to Shushan, Ahasuerus called for them most nights, and not for me. Oddly, now that we were truly married, I saw Ahasuerus less than I had before.

Still, he called for me once each week—a clear sign of favor. His harem was large, as befit the King of Kings, and some of his women were summoned to him only once in a year. Upon my nights with Ahasuerus, we often merely played chess, or read silently, or simply slept. That was one more secret I kept from Amestris.

"If he loves me, would he not call for me more often?" I thought this a clever complaint, implying I lusted for Ahasuerus. Queen Mother Amestris smiled and patted my cheek, as if I were her pet monkey.

"Of course my son loves you, Vashti. But he is king as well as husband. It is most suitable that he put you first—he calls for you every seventh day. And it is also most suitable that he not neglect his concubines. Many of them come from important families, and it would not do to seem to slight them. How wise of you to see this."

Somehow she twisted my childish protest into a virtue, and left me nothing to say but thank you.

HEGAI

I withheld my new gift for Vashti for a week after her return from Ecbatana. By then I saw how unhappy she was, and how puzzled, by the lack of passion in her marriage. She had changed, yes—but she had not changed into Ahasuerus's wife. I tried not to delight in that.

When I brought Varkha to the Queen's Palace and presented him as a gift to Vashti, she took one look at him and twirled about him, looking him up and down and clapping her hands with delight. And when I told her that her new eunuch was Varkha of the Amber-Eyed Wolves tribe, and that he came from the endless plains to the north of the empire, her despondency vanished.

"My mother's mother was Ishvari of the Black Horse People." Once again my queen was all smiles and delight. "Do you know of them? Perhaps we are cousins? Do you think Varkha and I might be cousins, Hegai?"

"You might." It seemed most unlikely to me, but if it pleased Vashti to think so—and who knew? Perhaps it even was true.

"Cousin!" Vashti said, and pulled off a turquoise necklace and clasped it around Varkha's neck.

Varkha cast me a rather nervous glance, but I smiled and nodded at him—and once he became used to Vashti's dragonfly playfulness, they got on very well.

To Vashti's joy, Varkha adored her two wolves. Atar and Vayu took to Varkha at first sniff. Wolves were the totem of Varkha's tribe, and the sight of Vashti fawned upon by wolves convinced Varkha she was worthy of high regard, so both of them were pleased.

Varkha proved an excellent investment and, as I had hoped, a very useful gift. He not only greatly improved Vashti's mood, he kept me apprised of any of Vashti's mischief she wished to keep secret from me. Less useful was his use as Vashti's double; dressed in garb that re-created her favorite costumes and flaunting his moon-pale hair, he easily passed for Vashti at a distance. I discovered Vashti's new amusement only after she had ordered Varkha to put on one of her favorite gowns and play with her wolves in the largest of the queen's gardens—being no fool, he came to me at once.

By the time I tracked down "Varkha," Vashti had managed to spend an hour sitting on the Great Staircase eating apricots and watching the caravans come in through the Western Gate. When I put an end to this delightful pastime and demanded to know why she had done this, Vashti looked at me and said, "But isn't that what you intended, when you gave me Varkha?"

"No, it is *not*—" I stopped, realizing what dangerous footing explanations could lead us to. I settled for saying, "You must never do such a thing again without consulting me first."

Vashti tilted her head, regarding me slantwise through her lashes. "And if I do? What will you do then?"

"What I should do," I said, "is beat you until you behave yourself."

"And how long do you think that would take, *dear* Hegai?" Vashti twined her fingers in my hair and pulled my head down until she could kiss my cheek. Then she ran off laughing while I stood staring after her, my fingers tracing the outline of her lips on my skin.

VASHTI

Nothing changed now that I was Ahasuerus's wife in fact as well as in name—save that now I could ask anything of Ahasuerus and have it granted. He bestowed gifts upon me as if I were a favored child, and I took free advantage of his guilt-driven generosity. My life settled back into its routine of pleasing, amusing days. The only true difference was that now my servants regarded me closely each month, to see if I ripened with the king's child—and each month, they were disappointed. But I was young; the empire would wait.

As one year ended and a new began, I sensed a change in Ahasuerus. Although he still laughed, he seemed less amused by my pranks now. When I complained to Amestris, she assured me I was mistaken.

"Ahasuerus relies on you for diversion, Vashti. Pay no heed to his dark moods."

Taking Amestris's words to heart, I decided to divert Ahasuerus with the greatest prank we had yet played, one I knew would delight him. There was always another long dull banquet being held, a banquet at which the king by law and by custom must drink the king's wine. Ahasuerus hated the king's wine, which had spices and poppy mixed into it; he disliked its sharp strong flavor and its deadening of the senses.

So when I told him I had a suggestion to shorten and enliven the next banquet, Ahasuerus listened to me—and laughed as he used to when we both were children, and agreed that my plan was good. And embellished upon it—*I* had thought only of the mice.

So began the mischief that led to all that came after. At the next banquet—one honoring I forget whom—I stood behind Ahasuerus's chair, dressed in the wine-red tunic and trousers worn by the royal cupbearers. My hair was braided around my head and hidden by a turban, and no one noticed me—or so I thought. At my feet half a dozen large gilded reed baskets waited, seeming to tremble with eagerness.

I eagerly awaited Ahasuerus's signal—but he seemed to pause, to slide a sidelong glance at me, and then at the baskets. He shook his head slightly, and seemed about to speak when Prince Shethar filled the king's gold wine-cup.

"My lord king, will you not lead us in wine?" Shethar asked.

Ahasuerus hesitated; he disliked the traditional king's wine, but no one else could drink if he did not. Prince Shethar lifted the full wine-cup and offered it to Ahasuerus . . . who took the wine-cup and, after staring for a moment into its depths, drank. Deeply. A tremor shuddered through him, but he emptied the wine-cup.

A sigh of relief seemed to sweep the banquet hall as the guests began to drink. Ahasuerus set his wine-cup down and glanced at Prince Shethar, who took this as a command to refill the king's wine-cup. Ahasuerus stood, lifting his wine-cup high. He glanced and me and smiled and nodded, and I bent and flung open the baskets.

A horde of field mice promptly fled through the banquet hall, swiftly followed by half a dozen ferrets. Dozens of mice ran over the guests' feet, swarmed up onto the tables, scurried through the carefully cooked dishes of lamb, rice, and fish. Close on the mice's tails followed the ferrets, intent on their prey. Both prey and predator slipped in the rich sauces, slid across the tables, sometimes into the guests' laps.

Ahasuerus and I laughed so hard we never noticed we were the only ones amused. No, that is wrong. Prince Shethar watched the havoc and smiled rather grimly. Later, when we regaled her with the tale, Queen Mother Amestris laughed and hugged us both, saying we brought joy to a gloomy court.

But later still, when I wrapped my arms around Hegai and told him what Ahasuerus and I had done, he did not laugh. He did not even smile.

"O queen, such a trick is suited to a child, not a woman," was all he said.

"Everyone laughed," I insisted.

"Did they?" Hegai stroked my hair. "Well, perhaps they did. It is wise to laugh when the king laughs. Come, let me ready you for bed, my queen."

I swiftly forgot the mouse banquet. It was only one among many such tricks Ahasuerus and I had often played upon the court, tricks the Queen Mother laughed at and encouraged.

But as Hegai knew, Ahasuerus and I were far too old for such childish games. The night we set mice and ferrets free in the banquet hall, I was almost eighteen years old, and Ahasuerus nearly twenty-three. We were no longer children.

The Queen Mother might laugh, but the Seven Princes did not. The Seven began to meet in secret. They did not speak treason—not yet—but they had been provoked beyond enduring by the childish actions of a king who should long since have been leading the Immortals to war.

The Seven could not rid themselves of Ahasuerus; indeed, the thought of ridding themselves of the King of Kings was too far for their thoughts to stretch. Nor did they dare challenge Queen Mother Amestris's fierce influence over her son.

But there was one person they could free the court from.

Me.

It remained only for the Seven Princes to decide how best to remove me, and then to set a queen of their own choosing in my place. One with womanly virtues; one who would give the king heirs. One who would stay where she belonged: behind the high gilded walls of the Queen's Palace.

Although I knew nothing of their plotting, in the end I made the path smooth and easy for them. Or say, rather, that Queen Mother Amestris did. For what was I but the eternal child she had so carefully created?

After the banquet of the mice, Ahasuerus changed. He still treated me fondly, but I sensed a withdrawal, a subtle difference in the manner in which he regarded me. He no longer wished to hear plans for pranks to play upon the court, nor did he invite me to dress as a boy and ride with him any longer.

"I've ridden out with him hundreds of times. I ride as well as he does! Better! He even said I shouldn't leave the palace at all unless I'm carried in a litter," I complained one evening as Hegai combed out my hair.

"I hope you didn't say that to the King of Kings." Hegai's placid voice irritated me; I twisted and caught his wrist, stopping the steady motion of the sandalwood comb through my hair.

"Well, of course I did. Why shouldn't I? Why is Ahasuerus being so—so *difficult?* Don't you think he's acting very oddly?"

"No, my queen, I don't."

Startled, I waited for him to say more. But although he hesitated, as if about to speak again, Hegai remained silent. For long moments he seemed to study my face, his long dark eyes intent. Then he bent and kissed my forehead, and gently resumed the task of combing out my long pale hair.

HEGAI

The last jest the king and queen ever played together began innocently enough. Even cleverly enough. But by its end, the king was angry and the queen indignant; the disaster to come began because of—what else?—Vashti's ivory hair.

"Hegai!" Vashti's voice rang against the cool tiles of my courtyard. She dashed up to me and spun around before me, her braided hair swinging against the backs of her thighs. "Do you like it?"

Smiling, I studied her as she spun around; layers of bright silk skirts floated about her and golden bells rang from her braids and ankles. She looked like a bazaar dancer. A very, very wealthy bazaar dancer. "I cannot say, O queen, until I know whether you truly mean to toss away your crown and dance in the marketplace for your bread, or—"

Vashti laughed and tucked her hand into the curve of my elbow. "Oh, Hegai, you are a beast," she said cheerfully. "Say you like it, for *this* time Ahasuerus thinks my idea a great jest, and wagers that I will be instantly recognized. What shall I ask of him, when I win?"

"Whatsoever pleases you, of course, even unto half of his kingdom." I reached out to touch her braided and belled hair, halted just before my fingertips touched its ivory silk strands. "Tell me, how did you persuade the king—"

"—to play this trick?" Vashti opened her opal eyes very wide. "Why, I asked him, of course! Truly, Hegai, Ahasuerus thought it clever."

I wondered if King Ahasuerus had been drinking wine before Vashti proposed this prank. The king had no head for wine. I sighed. "How many dancers?"

"Oh, as many as I like. A dozen?"

"All dressed just as you are?" Instantly I saw the flaw in Vashti's plan, a fortunate flaw that would end this scheme before it began. "O queen," I began, but she did not hear as she twirled around me, skirts flying and ankle bells chiming.

"Yes, all dressed just as I am. Isn't it the best of tricks to play upon those stuffy princes?"

You are too old to play such pranks, my love. And Ahasuerus was far too old to be laughing at such behavior, let alone encouraging it. *Dancing before all the world at a formal banquet—*

"You have forgotten something, my queen," I said; Vashti spun to halt in front of me, silk skirts flowing around her like clouds.

"What is it?" she asked.

"Your hair, my queen. You cannot hope to hide it." Half a dozen ways to do so instantly came to my mind—but I had no intention of helping Vashti to such scandalous behavior. "But the king will win unless you hide your hair, my queen."

"I know—and that is why I've come to you. I know you'll think of something. Perhaps henna, to turn it red as fire?"

"And perhaps *not*." What Queen Mother Amestris would do if Vashti dyed her empire-famed hair even I did not wish to contemplate.

Vashti frowned . . . and suddenly twirled around me again, stopped to grasp my hands as she smiled gleefully. "Oh, I know, Hegai! I know! I won't hide *my* hair. All the other dancers will dye *their* hair to match *mine*."

She stared at me expectantly, like a kitten entranced by a butterfly. My heart seemed to fall, a cold stone. There would be no stopping this outrageous trick now—not with the king complicit and Vashti herself checkmating my objections. "It will be difficult, my queen." *But not impossible.*

"You'll find a way to achieve it, I know you will. You are so clever!"

Slowly, I said, "Not so clever as you, my queen."

She was right; her scheme would work. Nothing would turn their hair the pure pale moonlight of Vashti's, but her dancers would perform before men who had been drinking all evening, would move constantly under the shifting light of torches and lamps. Powdered with gold dust and covered with veils of sheer glittering silver, all the dancers would seem to have queen's hair—at least for one night.

Delight shone in Vashti's eyes. "Clever? Do you truly think so?"

I nodded, afraid to do more. Afraid that if I so much as touched my fingertips to her cheek I would not be able to stop with chaste caresses.

She flung her arms around me and kissed my cheek, then danced around me, chanting, "*Wise and clever, Hegai is most wise and clever,*" until I could not resist laughing. Once she had made me laugh, she stopped and grasped my hands.

"And I, too, have a cunning thought, Hegai. Varkha shall be one of my dancers! There, am I not almost as wise and clever as you?" Vashti rubbed my hands against her cheek, then released me and began twirling about me once again. "*Wise and clever, you and I are wise and clever!*" she sang as she danced.

I looked down at my hands, still warm from her touch. *Wise and clever*— But neither wise nor clever enough to rule my mind or my heart. I could only do my best to keep my beloved happy.

And when Vashti won her wager with Ahasuerus, she would be delighted with me again, and hug me and kiss my cheek.

Her arms holding me tight. Her lips warm against my cheek. Only for a moment, but that moment would be enough.

It will have to be enough. It is not only Varkha who desires what he can never have.

The ill-starred jest began well enough. Halfway through King Ahasuerus's banquet for the chiefest princes of the realm, a dozen dancers clad in gauzy gold-and-silver garments whirled in, bells chiming. No, not twelve: thirteen. The thirteenth was Vashti.

One of the dancers swayed forward, bowed deeply before the king. "Great king, one of us is a fit mate for you. Choose, great king. Choose your queen." Without pause, she spun back among the other dancers.

The music rose and fell, the dancers curved and turned—and the guests loudly guessed that each dancer in turn was the queen. I stood close by the king's chair, listening to the bawdy comments of his guests, who were dazzled by the swaying, spinning figures. Ahasuerus himself seemed amazed. He stared intently at the dancers, his gaze darting over the veiled faces. He leaned forward as Varkha curved and twirled before him. For a moment I thought Ahasuerus would raise his scepter, but then he sat back again and I saw him frown.

He does not recognize her. He cannot choose her from the others. I could not imagine how he could not find Vashti among the dancers. But Ahasuerus had watched Vashti swirl past him a dozen times and not known his own wife.

The music slowed; obeying the drumbeat, the dancers swayed before the king like white poppies in a gentle wind. "Very clever," Ahasuerus said, "but I am not deceived by a clever trick." He rose to his feet and pointed the scepter to his choice. The dancer came forward, bowed, and touched the tip of the golden scepter. Then the dancer lifted the silver veil.

It was Varkha.

That was the last banquet that King Ahasuerus permitted Queen Vashti to attend in any guise. "She is the queen," he told me after the dancers had swirled out again, taking Vashti and her laughter with them. "It is not meet or proper that the queen attend men's banquets, or be seen by men's eyes. You are the Chief Eunuch, Hegai—you are in charge of the queen. Tell her she must behave like a queen. Now go."

I bowed very low. "As the King of Kings commands," I said, and went away before he thought of any more commands he wished to add. Telling this one to Vashti was going to be bad enough.

VASHTI

The year that I had been Queen of Queens for half my life, Ahasuerus decided to demonstrate his power and his generosity by giving a feast that would last a full seven days. All the princes would be invited, and the great warriors, and every manner of man in all the empire.

And I did not see why I, too, should not attend. I had spent the last hour first asking, then cajoling, and now begging, Ahasuerus to let me attend his great feast. For once, he had steadfastly denied me, something I was not accustomed to. "No," was not a word I often heard.

"But Ahasuerus, I can borrow some of your royal robes. We'll fool everyone again. I'll be a prince—I'll be the prince of—of Cherkessia!" For a heartbeat I thought I'd won, and then Ahasuerus sighed, and shook his head again.

"Oh, Vashti," he said, "don't be silly."

My husband's refusal to permit me to attend his great feast incensed me. Every time I remembered his rebuke, my irritation grew. How dare he speak to me so? Had he not once been as eager as I to deceive the courtiers, to create jests, to amuse ourselves at their expense? I frowned; tried to remember when Ahasuerus had last laughed with me, eager to fool the court. When he wagered on my ability to deceive him as a dancer—so long ago as that—?

"*Vashti, don't be silly . . .*"

Those few words explain why I decided to hold a feast of my own, for the wives and daughters of the king's guests. If the King of Kings could give a great banquet for his half of the world, the Queen of Queens could do as much for her portion of the empire. Once my anger at Ahasuerus faded, the idea of my own feast became more and more pleasing.

Of course there had been queen's feasts before, but those had been small, intimate gatherings. This feast of mine would be on the same grand scale as the king's. Everything the king's feast had, the queen's would have also. And I would have new garments for the feast—and a new crown. I ordered Hegai to oversee the creation of the crown, telling him I wished it to be the most beautiful adornment ever created. Then I went running down to the kitchens to badger the cooks into producing the newest, most costly, most intriguing dishes ever invented.

When I told Amestris—although of course she knew already, having been informed the moment I spoke the words that set preparations for the feast into motion—she smiled, and approved. And so did Ahasuerus. He ordered that whatsoever I desired for my own banquet should be given me.

Cloth of gold and silver draped my banqueting hall; I ordered the rarest wines and most precious spices to give savor to the delicacies that would be served. And I demanded a fountain whose water would be scented with attar of roses.

Seven outfits were sewn for me, one for each night of the feast. Each night's garment was a different color, adorned with different gems. I was pleased with this notion. But nothing pleased me so much as the new crown that Hegai created for me.

Hegai carried the crown to me upon a cushion of silk the deep blue of a full-moon midnight. "Here is your Star Crown, O Queen of Stars. Does it please you?"

I stared, dazzled by perfection. A broad circlet of ruddy gold, etched with the symbols of the heavens about the band. Pure rock crystal formed tiny stars. That was all—but it was so beautiful my breath caught in my throat and my eyes glistened.

"Oh, *Hegai.*" That was all I could say, but that seemed to be enough. Hegai smiled.

"Put it on, little queen. I wish to see its stars shining against your hair."

Carefully, I took my new crown into my own hands and set it upon my head. It weighed oddly heavy; I ignored the sensation and let Hegai lead me to his own apartments to gaze upon myself in his tall silver mirror. When I looked into my reflection in the shining silver, I saw that I had been right.

The Star Crown was perfect.

Had Amestris been there, matters would have fallen out differently.

But that last night, Amestris lay ill upon her bed. Very ill, so that the word *poison* slipped from some lips. I was sorry she suffered, but wondered if she had indulged too greatly in the rich foods and wines that had been set before her since my feast began. I sent Hegai to tend her, and forgot the matter as my handmaidens dressed me. So neither Queen Mother Amestris nor Chief Eunuch Hegai was by my side that fateful night.

This was not by chance, of course. As I later learned, the Seven Princes had dared greatly, and paid enough in gold darics for one of Amestris's kitchen maids to add a drop of poison to her food. A drop, to make Amestris ill—although had it killed her, I doubt the Seven Princes would have mourned. Without the Queen Mother at my side, the Seven counted on my own folly to aid their plan. And they were right.

For the seventh and last night of my feast, I wore a gown of cloth woven so thick with gold thread I glittered like a new-lit torch. To display what the world considered my greatest glory, my hair, I had ordered it combed out and left free. The command had scandalized my servants, but the widened eyes as my guests gazed upon my hair proved I had chosen rightly. Over the past days, the women had become accustomed to my gowns, my gems, even my new star-bright crown.

Tonight my guests saw me as the most beautiful Queen of Queens.

As I settled myself into place upon my cushions, I was greatly pleased with myself. For a heartbeat, I wondered what my grandmother Ishvari would think of me now—a thought I hastily pushed away.

It happened thusly, or it did not.

This is truth—or it is not.

The great king over all the lands between the river Sindhu and the Western Sea, from Cush to Colchis, invited all the empire to a feast worthy of his greatness. All the high princes attended this great feast, and all the governors of the one hundred and twenty-seven provinces. All the rich merchants came, and all the far-traveling traders. All the commanders of the army sat at the tables beside the noble lords of the land. All men were welcome at the king's feast.

A pleasant exaggeration, of course. It is true that during the feast, sweet cakes and wine and beer were handed out at the city gates to all who held out their hands for them. But only the nobles, and the wealthy, and the highest officers received invitations to the palace feast, to sit in the presence of the King of Kings.

Tyrian purple linen curtained the great courtyard; cords of purple and gold tied the curtains to silver rings set in marble columns. Each man reclined upon blue and yellow cushions on a couch of silver. Each man was given a goblet of pure heavy gold; each goblet different. And each man had a servant at his side to keep his vessel filled with as much wine as he cared to drink.

Each man kept his wine-goblet, too. Amestris was livid when she learned that; she counted costs. Still, the king created a magnificent setting, stinting on nothing. Including the wine.

And the great king smiled upon all his assembled guests, and commanded them to drink only as they willed. No man was to be constrained to drink as the king did.

Since a custom old when the land was young demanded that men drink each time the king did, this command was a thoughtful act. It was the last thoughtful act committed the seventh evening of the king's great feast.

The feast began at sunset, and continued for seven days and seven nights. Each man ate and drank as pleased him. And the assembled princes and nobles and commanders and merchants drank to the great king. Often and often they drank, and the great king smiled upon them. But the great king himself drank only sparingly of the royal wine.

And on the seventh night, as the moon rose high, the great king drank to his loyal guests.

A mistake; Ahasuerus had a poor head for wine. But the feast had been long and the night grew late, and he longed to rest. Weary, he drank deep of the royal wine each time his guests loudly praised the king's many virtues. And each time, one of the Seven Princes urged Ahasuerus to drink more, and more still.

The great king's guests vied to praise him most highly. The princes extolled his power, his sway over the wide world. The governors of the one hundred and twenty-seven provinces commended his justice. The commanders acclaimed his courage. The merchants applauded his riches. "Surely the great king is the sum of all virtues, and the possessor of all that is best in all the world."

"I possess everything worth possessing. I am King of Kings, owner of all the world desires." And King Ahasuerus raised his goblet, of the heaviest gold set all about with pure crystal and sapphires, and drank deep of the royal wine.

"The most precious gems," someone shouted. "Drink to the king!"

"The most learned mages. Drink to the king!"

"The most valiant soldiers. Drink to the king!"

Ahasuerus drank too, acknowledging their praise. "Great king," his chamberlain murmured, "the moon nears zenith. Perhaps my lord the king wishes to retire—" A sensible suggestion; one that Ahasuerus ignored. By this time he stood unsteady on his feet, wine and poppy raging in his blood.

"The most beautiful women! Drink to the king!"

A careless, drunken accolade. King Ahasuerus drank deep again, then held out his goblet as if it were the golden scepter of Death and Life. "I do. The most precious, most learned, most valiant. And the most beautiful. Anything that is mine you all may look upon, to know you have spoken truth, which is a Persian's honor."

All might still have passed safely until sunrise, when the feast ended. But the wine spoke now, rather than the men. Words escaped their lips, apparently unwary. Dangerous words.

"Drink to Queen Vashti!' cried Prince Shethar, the most ambitious of the Seven Princes.

And as men laughed and drank, another voice—no one after could truly say whose—soared above the noise of praise and laughter.

"Show us Queen Vashti!"

The King of Kings stopped with his wine-cup to his lips and stared out over the court-yard, seeking the face of the man who had made that outrageous demand. And as the king remained silent, so men fell silent in their turn; silence rippled back from the king's high table, flowed over the men gazing upon the king.

Then Prince Shethar said, "The great king promised to show us anything that is his. Show us Queen Vashti, the most beautiful in all the world."

The demand sobered Ahasuerus enough for him to realize what he had done. He remained drunk enough to be unable to free himself from the trap. Prince Memucan leaned close; spoke low and urgent. "It is forbidden for a woman to attend men's feasts. Would you bring your queen unveiled to the king's banquet hall?"

Prince Shethar laughed. "It's not as if she is a stranger to men's feasts." He said openly what until that night had only been whispered.

"O king, you cannot do this," Memucan said. "It is contrary to custom and to law."

"So is a king failing to do what he has promised." Shethar's words fell cold and heavy as stones.

The Seven Princes had Ahasuerus trapped. If he sent for me, he treated his queen like a dancing girl or a harlot. If he did not, he failed to keep the king's promise he had made.

The word of a king binds him. King Ahasuerus set down his golden goblet and sent his chamberlains to command Queen Vashti to come before him. And the chamberlains took the word of the king to Queen Vashti, where she sat feasting with the women, for Queen Vashti had given a feast also, vying with the king's glory.

"O queen," said the chiefest of the chamberlains, "the King of Kings summons you to come before him. Rise and walk with us, for the great king wishes to display your beauty to his guests, that they may see with their own eyes that the King of Kings possesses the most beautiful woman in all the world."

And when she heard this, Queen Vashti looked upon the chamberlain with scorn and said,

"Tell the King of Kings that the queen will not come."

That is how the tale fled from the palace of the King of Kings: That Vashti scorned the king's command. That Vashti's arrogance and pride goaded her to insult the King of Kings.

That Vashti thought herself above the king and above the law.

Well, I did disobey my husband. That much is truth.

When the king's chamberlains entered my banqueting hall, I was laughing at some jest. I laughed as I held out my hand to the newcomers and said, "Why see—the King of Kings has sent more guests to me! Come and sit. I am quite sure my feast will amuse you better than his!"

A harmless enough remark, and since it was mine, all my guests laughed. The king's chamberlains did not. After I stopped laughing—for like my guests, I had drunk a bit too much honey wine—I looked more closely, and thought it odd that Ahasuerus should have sent all seven of his highest-ranked chamberlains to me. A surprise? A gift? Then why did the seven eunuchs look so—I groped for the right word to describe their expressions, and at last settled on *uncertain.*

Uncertain, and embarrassed.

I set down my wine cup. "Well? What is it?"

Silence. The king's eunuch chamberlains looked at each other, and at the spangled silk panels draping the ceiling, and at the silent watching women, and at the Star Crown glittering in the lamplight. At everything in the banqueting hall, except at me.

"Tell me. The queen commands you."

"You," Carcas whispered to Harbona. "You are the most senior of us all." Clearly Harbona disliked hearing this, but not only had the king sent him here, but the queen had ordered him to speak.

Harbona coughed, and began. "O Queen of Queens, fairer than the morning star, most honored wife to Ahasuerus, king over—"

I held up my hand. "Yes, Harbona. I know who I am." Elegant laughter from my guests. "Now tell me the king's message."

"O queen—I beg of you, remember I only bear this command for the king. These are not my words."

"Yes, yes, the queen will remember. Now what does the king command?"

Harbona drew in a deep breath. "O queen, Ahasuerus, King of Kings, Lord of Half the World, commands this: that Queen Vashti come before his guests in the great hall. That Queen Vashti is to wear the queen's crown, and—and is to come before the king's guests unveiled, that all may look upon the queen's beauty and envy the king's happiness in possessing it."

The words echoed in the hall. Silence surrounded me.

Silence, and staring eyes. All the jeweled women waited to hear what I would say. To see what I would do.

Would I rise up, and go unveiled out of the Queen's Palace, into a courtyard filled with feasting men? The King of Kings himself had ordered me to do so—

—and would remember all the rest of our days that I had displayed myself for every man's eyes. *"It is not meet or proper that the queen attend men's banquets, or be seen by men"*—Ahasuerus's own words.

He will blame you. A silent whisper, in a voice not my own. Words from a past not my own. Queen Ishvari's voice, echoing down the years, refusing another king's drunken summons: *"My most precious jewels are my daughter and my honor, and I will not display either for the pleasure of drunken, impious fools."*

Anger kindled; an anger that belonged to me alone. Had not Ahasuerus himself forbidden me ever again to show my face at a men's banquet? How dare he ask this of me now? I was his wife; I was Queen of Queens. How dare Ahasuerus command me to come before all his wine-sodden guests? How dare he demean himself so, to cater shamelessly to men's whims? Well, if the king would stoop so low, the queen would not. *"Tell her she must behave like a queen."* Ahasuerus's own command. . . .

Slowly, I rose to my feet. And when I stood straight and tall, I looked at Harbona with calm, steady eyes. "My lord chamberlain, tell my husband, the King of Kings, the Ruler of the World . . ." I paused, waiting.

"Yes, O queen? Tell the king—?" Harbona prompted, and I smiled, and struck.

"Tell him that I will not come," I said, and sat down upon my silken cushions once more.

I learned what had happened from others who saw with their own eyes and heard with their own ears what passed in the king's banquet hall. And what happened was disaster.

Instead of returning to the king and whispering in his ear, Harbona stood and loudly proclaimed my words—just as Prince Shethar had paid well him to do. "The queen says this: tell the king I will not come."

After that public announcement of the insult to the king's power, even the king could not salvage the situation. Not after three of the Seven Princes told him how unforgivable my defiance was. I had rebelled against my husband, and against my king. Both crimes carried a penalty.

"You must repudiate her," Prince Shethar told Ahasuerus.

"Yes," Carshena agreed. "Set Vashti aside."

And even Memucan, who disliked any change to the world's order, said, "Yes, set her aside. She is not worthy of the crown you gave her."

All this spoken in the high, carrying voices used in the king's court so that even men who stood far from the throne might hear. All spoken to ensure every wine-addled man in the banquet hall heard every poisonous word.

So King Ahasuerus, drunk past sense, humiliated publicly by his insolent wife, and urged on by the Seven Princes, announced that Vashti was queen no longer.

And lest, sober, he change his mind on the morrow, Prince Shethar sent immediately for scribes to write the king's words into an imperial decree. Scribes came and wrote, and Ahasuerus sealed the words into law.

From that moment, I was no longer Queen of Queens. I was no longer Ahasuerus's wife.

I, too, had been feasting and drinking for seven nights. So, high-flown with honey wine, I laughed and preened, proud that I had not cravenly submitted to so mad a command. Then, in defiance of all law and custom, the Seven Princes walked into my banquet hall and my guests shrieked and squeaked and hastily veiled their faces. I did not scream, but I stared wide-eyed.

"How dare you?" I could not believe the Seven had violated the sanctity of the Queen's Palace, outraged the modesty of my high-born guests. "The king will—"

"Rebellious woman, we come here at the king's own command to tell you the king's decree." This from Prince Shethar, who spoke for them all whenever he could grab that privilege. "It is this: you are no longer queen. You are set aside and are to come no more before the king."

Cold words, sobering as winter water. "Set aside?" I said, unable to truly comprehend what I heard. "I don't believe Ahasuerus would do such a thing."

"Speak of him as the King of Kings. Did you think you could flout the king's summons? Laugh at him, make him a thing of mockery to all men?"

Anger kindled deep beneath my heart. "A summons to come to him at a public feast? He must have been mad to order me to do such a thing."

"It is the king's right to—" Prince Shethar began, and I cut off his words with my furious response.

"To display his queen to drunken men as if she were a slave for sale to the highest bidder? Is that a command a wife should obey, if she honors her husband?"

So cunning a trap. So impossible to escape.

"You acted like a child," Shethar told me. "A foolish, wayward child." The scorn in his voice should have flayed me, brought tears to my eyes.

But he was wrong. For the first time in my life, I had *chosen*.

I smiled. "No, my lord prince. I acted like a woman."

And then, in my last act as Queen of Queens, I put my hands to the Star Crown and lifted it from my head. Odd; I had not realized its weight before.

"Here is the queen's crown," I said. "Take it to the king."

I still sat upon purple cushions; Prince Shethar would have to bow low to take the crown from my hands, so he did not claim it from me. I smiled at the mortified anger in his eyes.

After the Seven Princes left, I rose and, carrying the Star Crown, I left the queen's feast and went through the Queen's Palace until I reached my bedchamber. There I sat upon my silver bed and stared, unseeing, at the crown I still held in my jeweled hands.

Set aside. No longer queen.

I was twenty years old. I had been queen for half my life.

No longer queen. What am I now?

BOOK FOUR

Star of Wisdom

ESTHER

I am quick-witted, I am clever, I can read and write Persian and Hebrew. I can speak Persian and Hebrew and half a dozen other tongues besides. I can tell to a daric how much a shipment of spices should cost. I can judge swiftly and fairly between two warring merchants.

If I had been born a boy, I would be a master merchant.

But I am a girl, and so none of my talents weighs so much as a swan's feather in the scale against my shapely body and my shining hair. Is a woman never to claim her will as her own?

It did not occur to anyone to ask if I wished to be paraded before the king like a prize mare. My cousin Mordecai never questioned that I would do my duty to him and to my people. In my cousin's mind, I was a good Jewish girl, and so he assumed my obedience. Never once did it occur to him to do otherwise.

Had he asked, I think I would have bowed my head and told him yes. *Yes, I will do as you ask, for your reasons are sound and the benefit if I succeed will be great.*

But he did not ask. He could not imagine that any girl would be less than delighted to compete for the queen's crown.

⁂

Until I was ten, I lived on a farm in the valley of the river Karoun, far beyond the walls of Shushan. My father Abihail raised horses—sturdy, surefooted beasts that could carry burdens long distances. My mother died when I was born, and my father, untutored in how to raise a girl, simply acted as if I were a boy. I was not confined to the house and its small courtyard. I had the freedom of all the valley.

I ran across the fields dressed in a boy's short tunic and trousers. Naked, I swam in the shallow river. My father, lonely after my mother died, talked to me as if I were his friend, rather than his daughter and a child. He taught me how to judge horses, and to judge the men who came to buy them, or to sell.

The men and boys who worked for my father treated me as he clearly wished me to be treated: as if I were his son, heir to all he owned. No one regarded me as the daughter of the house.

Do not think my father let me run wild; my father expected me to work hard. I learned not only to ride his horses, but to help train them. I not only ran across the fields, but also learned to judge whether the grasses were good for grazing, or whether we needed to plant new seeds next season. I had a knack for numbers, and so I kept the records, and could tell my father how well we would do from a sale.

No one spoke of my looks. I had no mirror except the river. I was praised for my ability to calm a frightened foal, not for my amber eyes; for my talent at reckoning the profit of a sale, not for my smooth skin. And if anyone spoke of the color of my hair, it was only to say that it must be true that fire-hair was a sure sign of cleverness.

Not that there was much of my hair to admire, for it did not flow down my back as a maiden's should. Nor was it even long enough to braid. My father had let me cut it off, so that it fell only to my shoulders, short as a boy's.

Yes, until I was ten, I was valued for myself. And I was truly happy.

My father's horses, and his skill at judging them, were far-famed, and many horse-merchants traveled long distances to buy his stock. My father trained me never to grow too fond of a horse, to think one too special to have a value beyond what the beast could bring in coin or in trade. "It's not wise to think any horse priceless. Remember that everything has its price."

This hard truth did not mean he cared nothing for the horses he bred and raised. It was known the length of the Royal Road that Abihail the horse-merchant treated his beasts better than many men did their sons, and that he would let his horses go only to men he trusted to care well for them. But my father did not want me breaking my heart over each horse sold; to love too greatly would bring me too much pain. And so while I might ride any of his horses, there was none of which I could say, "This horse is mine."

That changed the year before my father died. Just before the last snow melted, a caravan stopped near our house; a weary, road-worn group of men who had traveled through the winter. That in itself was odd, for no one risked the long passes in the winter. And the wares they offered were even odder: strange hides they swore came from dragons; beads of bone and cups of translucent stone, delicate as Egyptian glass.

They offered horses, too. Most of their beasts were small creatures, with roached manes and short necks; nothing my father deigned to examine. But they also had with them a pale, high-bred yearling whose elegantly curved ears flicked constantly back and forth and whose neat hooves seemed to dance in the heavy mud. I don't know how one of the Heavenly Horses of Nisea came to be with this caravan of oddities; my father said, later, that doubtless the men had stolen him.

The yearling drew my eyes, and I could not resist going to set my hands upon him. At first he shied away from my touch, and I saw he was unused to kindness. Then he gentled, leaned his head against me as I stroked the graceful arch of his neck. He was beautiful; even so young, I could see what he would one day be. Now he was a dark gray, like tarnished silver. That dark coat would lighten as he grew. One day he would shine like moonlight, or like pearls.

Like any decent man, my father granted the caravan hospitality, and its men set up round tents and rested on our land for a day. I took charge of the gray colt, for I could not bear to see him tied out by the tents with the rest of the weary beasts.

I led him into one of the horse sheds. There I held a bucket of water for him to drink and brushed dirt from his winter-thick coat. I fed him sweet grain from my hand.

I pretended he was mine.

That evening I asked my father if he would buy the gray, and my father shook his head. I began to protest, pointing out the colt's virtues, until my father held up his hand. "Peace, Hadassah. I saw how he took your eye, and offered for him without success. Perhaps they hope to get a better price for him in Shushan. I am sorry, but now you see why I tell you never to set your heart upon a horse."

I spent that night in the horse shed, wrapped in a heavy blanket against the cold. The shed was as well made as a house, its walls trapping the heat of the yearling's body, and so I was warm enough. My father let me stay there, although he set two of his men to guard the shed, lest the strangers decide to take me, as doubtless they had once taken the gray colt.

When the caravan left the next day, the gray colt refused to be parted from me. None of the men could hold him, or force him to follow. At last they tied him to another horse. She stolidly dragged him along, no matter how much his temper flared. I knew I would never see him again.

Three dawns later, the silver yearling waited for me at the farmyard gate. Sweat had mingled with dust, muddying his coat, and his head sagged with weariness. But when he saw me, he lifted his head and whickered for me as if I were his mother. I longed to run to him, but knew better; horses do not like sudden movement.

Outwardly calm, I walked up to the gate, opened it, and waited for him to come through into the farmyard. Once he had, I carefully closed the gate again. Only then did I allow myself to put my arms about his muddy neck and weep for sheer joy.

My heart's delight had returned to me.

But although he had run long miles to come back to me, the yearling still did not belong here. As I led him to the stable, I thought of how and where I might conceal him. Even as I dreamed of keeping him hidden, of owning him in secret, I knew it was impossible. I must tell my father at once.

My father did not at first believe me, but he came out to the stable—and stared long at the dirty, weary colt. "I have been a horse-master for half my life, and never have I known a horse to do such a thing. You have won his heart, Hadassah." My father smiled at me, then shook his head. "But my dear child—"

"I know." I was proud of the steadiness of my voice. "He is not mine to keep. The men will come for him. But until they do, Father—may I pretend he is mine until then?"

"Very well, Hadassah. The colt is yours until they return to claim him. Now you had best groom him and feed him, and then let me cast my eyes over him and see that all is well with him."

Before turning to those happy tasks, I squeaked my thanks and hugged my father hard. He kissed the top of my head. "Just remember, you must give him up when they come. I only hope they do not think you enchanted him when they passed through here!"

I spent all that day grooming the colt's thundercloud coat, combing out his mane and tail, and testing names. *Cloud, Silver, Swift*—none seemed quite right. Then, as I rubbed his fetlocks clean, a flash of white gleamed against the dark gray. He had a star upon his left front heel. A good luck mark—or at least I took it as such.

I named him Star.

"Star," I said, and he arched his neck and nuzzled at my hair. "You are my Star."

The name was perfect.

The strange merchants never returned. Perhaps they thought their prize had run away and become lost. Perhaps—anything. All that mattered to me was that no one came to claim the gray colt. Star was mine.

And as months passed, I no longer worried that he would be taken from me.

⁜

Then my father died, and my happy life shattered as if it had been made of glass. I was my father's heir, but I was not only a child of ten, I was a girl, and this suddenly became a matter of great import. But when I gave our overseer a letter to carry the sad news to my father's family in Shushan, I did not know what I set in motion.

I was still weeping for the loss of my father when my cousin Mordecai came to claim me.

Mordecai was far older than I—the son of the eldest son, as I was the daughter of the youngest. The middle sons had returned to Israel when Darius the Great granted the Jews permission to return to their homeland if they so chose. Of all our family, only Mordecai and my father Abihail remained in Persia. And just as my father loved the freedom of the countryside, Mordecai loved that of the city. He dwelt in Shushan, the oldest and greatest city in all the empire. I had never met him, but my father had spoken of him fondly, calling Mordecai the wisest and kindest man he knew.

So when Mordecai stood at the courtyard gate and said, "Hadassah, I am your cousin Mordecai," and held out his arms to me, I ran to him and wept upon his chest. He did not tell me not to weep, but let me cry until I had no more tears left. Then he wiped my face with the hem of the soft shawl he wore over his shoulders.

"My poor little cousin, I grieve with you. Trust me when I tell you that one day the pain will pass, and you will remember only your father's love." Mordecai set me back and knelt before me, gazing intently into my eyes. "So you are my brother Abihail's daughter! He must have been very proud of you, Hadassah."

"Yes." My voice was still thick from weeping. "He was very proud of me." It was the truth, so I knew no reason I should not say so.

"Such a pretty girl—you are ten years old, are you not? I can see you will be a beauty soon!"

I stared at him, puzzled. Clearly Mordecai thought I should be pleased at his words; to please him, I managed to smile a little.

"And such a charming smile, too." Mordecai rose to his feet and held out his hand to me.

I hesitated, but only for the time it took my heart to beat twice. I put my hand in his; his grasp was warm, comforting, as my father's had been. It was many years before I truly understood how much the state in which I had lived with my father horrified Mordecai. My short hair and boy's clothing appalled him, my blunt speech astonished him. I seemed a wild creature, one that required cautious handling.

"I know we are cousins," Mordecai said, "but I am as old as your father was, and will be a father to you now."

A new father—one my own father had praised. I managed to smile again, and this time it was easier to speak. "I am glad," I said, so that he would feel welcome here. "And I can tell you anything you wish to know about the farm, and the horses, and how my father dealt with horse-merchants."

Mordecai smiled, and then spoke the words that altered me forever. "That is very kind of you, Hadassah, but I will leave those matters to the overseer. Tomorrow you will come to Shushan, to live there with me and my wife, who is longing to greet you as her daughter."

The next morning I rode out on Star. Had I known it was the last time I would race him, free as wind, across the valley, I never would have turned his head back toward the farm. When I cantered up to the outer gate, my cousin Mordecai stood waiting there.

"Get down from that horse, Hadassah. It is unseemly for a girl to . . ." Mordecai hesitated, then merely said, "It is not proper."

I stared down at him, and for a wild instant thought of turning Star and galloping away.

"Hadassah," Mordecai said, and I slowly dismounted.

"Star is my own horse," I said. "I trained him myself." Star leaned his head against me; his breath warmed my neck.

"I'm sure he's a very fine animal. Now let the groom take him." Mordecai barely glanced at Star. "Come into the house, Hadassah. There are many matters I must arrange before we return to Shushan."

Mordecai spoke for long hours that day to my father's chief groom, the man who had the running of the farm after my father and me. I tried to be of help, but Mordecai ordered me out. "This is men's business, Hadassah. Go tend to your own work."

So I did, but that did not please Mordecai either, for when at last he left the house and found me leading a yearling around the horse yard in gentle circles, accustoming the young horse to carrying the weight of a small sack filled with grain, he scolded me as if I had disobeyed him.

"Hadassah, what are you doing? I told you to stay in the house."

He had not, but already I had learned that Mordecai might be kind and wise, but he disliked being contradicted. I began to lead the yearling to the stable, but Mordecai called a stable boy over and bade him take the lead rope from me. "Now come into the house, Hadassah. You must tell me what you wish to bring with you to Shushan."

"Star," I said at once, and Mordecai looked down at me and sighed.

"Hadassah, I have no place for a horse in Shushan."

"Then I will stay here. The farm is mine now." I still did not wish to understand.

Mordecai stopped, and crouched down so that I did not have to tilt back my head to look into his eyes. "Of course the farm is yours, Hadassah. But you cannot manage the place yourself." Mordecai smiled, but I did not smile back.

"Why not?"

"Because you are only a child, and a girl, and running such a business is men's work. I know nothing of horses, but I will hire a man who does, and will keep close track of the accounts. This will be a fine dowry for you, when you marry." Mordecai regarded me hopefully.

I had to agree that I was only a child. And I knew many men would think me easy prey, rather than a fellow horse-master. So I nodded, and Mordecai seemed to relax; he drew in a deep breath.

"Good. Good. I knew you would be a sensible girl." Mordecai rose to his feet and patted my head, his hand gentle. "Now go and put on a decent gown—"

"A gown?" I said, baffled, and Mordecai sighed.

"Do you have no garb suitable for a such pretty girl?" he asked, and when I merely stared at him, he sighed again. "My poor little cousin—well, my wife will arrange proper clothing for you. Now let us go and pack your belongings, for I must return to Shushan tomorrow. I work in the King's Gate—did your father tell you I am one of the scribes serving the King of Kings?"

I rose long before dawn the next morning so that I might say farewell to Star alone. Star greeted me with sleepy whickering, and I slipped under the bar to his stall and climbed upon his back. I lay with my arms wrapped around his neck and wept. I cried harder than I had when my father died; cried until my eyes burned and my tears dripped from Star's mane.

"I will come back," I whispered to Star. "I will come back. I swear it." My misery sparked unease; Star shifted nervously and arched his neck so he might nuzzle my thigh. I slid down and laid my cheek against his.

We stood there, Star and I, until dawn light eased the darkness. Then I kissed him on his silk-soft nose and scrubbed my face dry and raw with the hem of my tunic. I left Star standing there gazing after me and walked out into the yard.

My cousin Mordecai stood there, just outside the stable door. His eyes looked as red and raw as mine; I remembered that my father had been his uncle, whom he had loved. Silent, Mordecai held out his hand. I took it, and we went back into the house.

The journey took ten days. The land stretched before us, endless and constant. Nothing changed. Mile after eternal mile. Shushan was worse. Flat, hot, and confined by thick walls—even the river flowed slow and sullen. The highest spot in Shushan was the palace. I stared up at the false hill crowned by a sprawl of shining white and gold. As I looked, I saw bright color move upon the vast steps leading upward. A column of yellow and blue and white; a flash of fire—soldiers escorting a litter so richly gilded it seemed to burn under the sun.

"What is that?" I asked, and my cousin smiled.

"That, Hadassah, is Princess Vashti of Babylon, come here to Shushan the Beautiful to marry the King of Kings. Be glad you are not a queen, Hadassah, for they are never truly free."

⁂

Mordecai led me through an endless series of narrow streets until we reached an area of the city close-packed with buildings that had an indefinable air of kinship, as if they housed brothers. "Most of our people in Shushan live here, in the Western Quarter," Mordecai told me. "Look, there is my house—your house, too, now."

I looked, and saw a house indistinguishable from the rest. Solid, plain, serviceable. Comfortable. But squeezed together with all the others.

Mordecai took me in through the gate to his house. In the small courtyard a woman waited, plump as a partridge, and as bright-eyed. "Deborah, my wife, here is my little cousin Hadassah, who is to be our daughter now."

Deborah stared at me; I saw her exchange a look with Mordecai. Then Deborah smiled and held out her arms. "My dear cousin Hadassah—come, be welcome!"

Mordecai shoved me gently toward her, and I found myself embraced by my cousin-by-marriage. I let myself be held close, relieved that I did not need to decide what expression to wear. Then Deborah stepped back, her hands on my shoulders.

"My poor Hadassah—you must be exhausted from such a journey."

"No," I said. "I am used to working on my father's farm. The journey didn't tire me at all."

A moment's silence; another look passed over my head between Deborah and Mordecai. "Well then," Deborah said, "even if you're not tired, you will still be glad of a bath, and of decent clothing."

And that was the end of my last link with my father's farm. Deborah's servant took away the offending garments. I suppose she burned them—or sold them. Certainly they were not cleaned and kept.

When I got out of the bath, the clothing that awaited me was an under-tunic of linen and over that a long gown. Garments considered suitable for a girl. A blue sash tied around my waist for no reason I could see, save that Deborah liked its color against the gown.

"There is nothing to be done about your hair, my dear, until it grows long again. Which it will, never fear." Deborah stroked my damp curls. "What a pity it had to be cut. Such a pretty color."

Pretty. I already suspected I would become very tired of that word. It seemed to sum up all I was expected to be now. Pretty. A pretty girl.

But one thing I had learned from my father was when it was wisest to keep silent during bargaining. My life in Mordecai's house would be one long bargain. The only price I would accept was my return to my father's farm—to my farm—in the Valley of Karoun. So I listened to Deborah mourn my shorn hair, and kept silent. Deborah thought me hungry and weary, so she combed out my hair, set bread and honey before me to eat, and then led me up the stairs to the housetop. A small room in the corner held a bed and an oil lamp.

"This is your room now, Hadassah. At night you can see the lights from the King's Palace. I know all this is strange to you, but we will try to make you happy here with us." Deborah kissed my forehead, and left me alone.

Deborah was right; if I looked up, I could see the lights burning throughout the King's Palace.

And if I looked higher, into the night sky, I could still see the stars.

Deborah was a woman of great worth, like the woman in the Proverbs. She set herself the duty of molding me from a rough, boyish creature into a smooth sweet maiden. Firm yet gentle, she trained me to walk with short neat paces instead of striding, to speak meekly instead of frankly, to keep my eyes downcast and my demeanor modest. To hide myself behind my pretty face.

Deborah taught me to cook and to spin, to sew and to bake. Soon I seemed no different from any other well-born Jewish girl in Shushan.

I liked Deborah, who was kind and good, and knew far better than Mordecai how to ease my path into this new life. She listened to me talk of the farm, and my father, and of my beloved Star. She neither laughed nor contradicted me when I told her that as soon as I was grown, I would go home to live in the shadow of the far mountains.

I often asked to go to the farm, only for a visit, to see that all was well, but somehow it never became possible. But in dreams Star and I raced the wind up the valley; in Shushan's fiery summers I remembered snow. . . .

Until the day that poisoned my memories; after that I woke from those dreams with tears burning my eyes. If I returned home, I would not see my Star. He had been sold.

This I learned by chance. I had been reading upon the housetop, and set aside the scroll because I was thirsty. I had dwelt two years in Shushan, but I still moved quietly, like a creature of the high wild valleys; Mordecai and Deborah did not hear me on the stair. When I heard their voices—Deborah's sharp with distress, Mordecai's low and unhappy—I stopped. I had keen ears, too. That day, I wished I did not.

"Sold him? Oh, Mordecai, how could you? She cherishes that horse!"

"Wife, what could I do? Deny the king's men? Apparently," Mordecai added, "that horse is a very fine stallion indeed. The king's agent paid a very high price; a fine addition to Hadassah's dowry." A pause. "And perhaps she will not care as much as you fear. Do you know, Deborah, I have not heard Hadassah so much as mention the beast—"

"Star," Deborah said. "She called him Star. Oh, what am I going to tell her?"

Another pause. "Nothing." Mordecai said. "Nothing unless she asks."

Slowly, I climbed back up the stairs. I did not weep. I could not. Pain beat within my heart; I pressed my hands to my breast, but the hurt only spread, until my whole body burned. Strange cold fire beneath my skin made me gasp for breath.

Star is gone. Home is gone. There is nothing for me now but this house, this city. This trap.

But I did not have to stand in front of my cousin and hear those words spoken. Unknowing, Mordecai had granted me that harsh mercy.

Nothing. Nothing unless she asks. Mordecai's words echoed; the misery in his voice echoed.

So I never asked.

That summer fever burned through Shushan. Deborah fell ill; the fever tortured her for only a day before it killed her. I wept for her, and for Mordecai, and for myself. Now all I had was my cousin Mordecai. A good man, a kind man, but a man with no more experience of raising a girl into womanhood than my father had possessed.

With Deborah gone, Mordecai took charge of my education—and so long as I behaved with maiden modesty, he did not care that I was clever. I think he took credit for my cleverness, choosing to forget all I had learned before I came to live in his house. I already spoke not only Hebrew and Persian, but also the Trade-tongue used by merchants along the Silk Road from Tyre to Cathay. I could read Hebrew. But now I learned to read Persian, Elamite, and Sumerian; to speak and read Babylonian; to speak Median, Nabatean, and Greek.

My skill at languages surprised Mordecai, who at first had thought only to teach me to read Persian. But I had been blessed with the gift for tongues, and it amused him to see how many I could learn. I eagerly studied all he would teach me. Learning, my father had always said, is never wasted. Who knew? Someday the ability to read Sumerian might prove useful.

I could compose poetry, too, in the styles of Egypt, Babylon, and Hind.

Sometimes I think my cousin Mordecai was either the wisest man I ever knew, or the greatest fool. For by the time I was fourteen, I was a better scholar than most men, and by the time I was sixteen, I knew it would be hard for Mordecai to find a husband for me. For I had grown not only learned, but—as Mordecai himself had predicted—beautiful. But beauty or not, my learning was too much for most men to willingly accept. Even my dowry could not persuade some men to overlook my extravagantly unsuitable education.

I should have been betrothed at fourteen and set to sewing garments for my marriage-chest, not sitting engrossed in annals of the law courts. At sixteen, I should have been speaking my wedding vows, not arguing with Mordecai over the correct pronunciation of some word in a language no one had truly spoken in a thousand years.

At least languages and literature were safe to argue with him. Mordecai loved me dearly in his own fashion, but he had small patience with what he called my "girlish follies." Despite the manner in which my father had raised me up, Mordecai expected me to act as humbly as if I had been strictly nurtured by the most old-fashioned Jewish parents in Shushan.

More important, at least to me, was my talent for understanding numbers, and how they added up—or did not. I respectfully petitioned Mordecai to let me handle the household accounts. After careful consideration, and to my hidden delight, he agreed. That skill I knew would be important to me. I had once again determined to return to my father's farm—my farm.

I hated the invisible chains that bound me, just as I hated Shushan.

Why the King of Kings, who could do whatsoever he wished, command whatever pleased him to be done, should choose to live in Shushan baffled me. If I were king—well, if I were queen—of half the world, I would live in the valleys between the high hills. I would live where the air blew cool and clean down the mountains, carrying the scents of pine and of cedar.

Yes, I hated Shushan. But Mordecai never dreamed I was other than content. Our life in Shushan pleased him; why should it not please me? But Mordecai left his house and went each day to his work in the King's Gate. He went to visit friends, and to the marketplace, and to the synagogue. I went only places my cousin considered proper for a woman, and those places were few indeed. Mordecai was good and pious, but strict in his views on a woman's proper place. And a woman's proper place was in her father's house, until it was in her husband's.

That Mordecai permitted me to study shocked the pious Jews. That Mordecai did not permit me to walk abroad freely angered me. I lacked Deborah's submissive skill at gaining her own way while convincing Mordecai that only his wishes counted. And as I grew from girl into woman, my life became ever more circumscribed, until the day I surrendered to my cousin's demand that I veil myself when I set my foot over the doorstep into the street.

I had fought against wearing the all-covering veil, but Mordecai insisted it was what was proper. And at last he found the right words to persuade me—that Deborah would have wished me to behave modestly, and wear the veil. Remembering all the kindness Deborah had shown me, I yielded. When I left the house, I wore a veil that hid me from the crown of my head to my knees. Like all of the Jewish women, I wore a veil of rich golden yellow.

At least, when I left my cousin's house, I wore such a veil. Beneath that, I often carried another veil—brown or green or blue—and changed veils once I was out of sight of Mordecai's house.

While I still loathed the veil, I also valued its one virtue: anonymity. Beneath the all-covering veil, who could tell one woman from another? This was the true reason only respectable women were permitted to veil, while women for sale and for hire could be flogged for daring to cover themselves. Some women wore veils richly embroidered with brilliant thread, or ornamented with spangles of copper, silver, or gold. My veils were bland as bread. No one could point at me on the street and say, "That is Mordecai's ward Hadassah; I know her by her veil."

So it came to pass that after four long years in Shushan it was womanly modesty that opened the city to me. After four years in Mordecai's house, even Shushan seemed a paradise.

Soon I knew Shushan—at least, those parts that were safe for a respectable girl to explore—as well as I had once known the Karoun Valley. The marketplaces, the gardens, the vast square at the foot of the Great Staircase; the constantly changing spectacle by the gates leading to the Royal Road.

Of all Shushan offered, I liked best to look out the northern gates opening on the Royal Road. That road stretched nearly two thousand miles across the empire, from Shushan to Sardis. I could stand by the gate and gaze upon the Royal Road, following its path with my eyes until the road disappeared into the horizon's haze. I rationed this bitter pleasure, for afterward I found it hard to walk back into the confines of Mordecai's house.

Once I even saw King Ahasuerus and Queen Vashti riding through the vast square at the foot of the Great Staircase. For the queen to ride out through the city was a shocking breach of court etiquette. A queen who wished to travel did so confined in a gilded litter. I was not too proud to stop and stare just as everyone else did. Queen Vashti was my age, too, she was just fifteen. She rode beside the king; I could not see King Ahasuerus's face, for he was turned away from me, his attention upon his laughing queen. I wondered what he had said, to amuse her so well. I wondered more that he indulged her so greatly.

True, a veil covered Queen Vashti's face, but the glittering fabric was so sheer I could see that her beauty was no mere courtly pretense. I had often doubted any woman could be as beautiful as Queen Vashti was reputed to be; now I saw I was wrong, for the queen truly was lovely as the stars. Her famously pale hair shone like snow on the high hills.

I watched as they rode away from me. My last thought of Queen Vashti was that she did not ride even half so well as she clearly thought she did.

She needs to balance her weight better. But I suppose the king does not notice, and no one else dares tell her—and that she would not listen if anyone dared.

The first time I saw the Lord Prince Haman, he was drowning a litter of puppies in the fountain by the Eastern Gate. He had tied the pup's mother, a beautiful sable-and-white gazehound, to his horse's reins; a groom held the restive horse as the bitch struggled frantically to free herself. She had no chance of saving her pups. Nor had anyone yet dared interfere with Lord Haman's deadly pastime—even though he polluted public water. Half a dozen small bodies already floated in the sullied fountain. Scowling, Haman dangled another squeaking pup by its neck and then shoved it underwater.

When I started forward, a woman caught my arm. "Let it be," she said in a low voice. "That's Lord Haman, the king's friend."

"My thanks for the warning," I said, and ran up behind Haman and pushed with all my strength, sending him facedown into the fountain. As he struggled up, swearing, I reached into the water, grabbing for the puppies. I could tell almost at once it was too late—all the pups save one fell cold and limp from my hands onto the stones paving the street.

But that last one still lived, and coughed up water as I rubbed its sides. I carried it over to Haman's horse and untied the desperate bitch; Haman's groom had dropped the reins to hurry over and help his master out of the fountain. Just as the gazehound bitch bounded free, a hand fell heavy on my shoulder. Haman pulled me around to face him.

"How dare you interfere?" He did not shout in anger, but seemed to growl, a low flat sound. "Who are you, to hinder a prince?" Before I could answer, he grabbed a handful of my blue veil and yanked it off, revealing my face. I heard gasps from those watching, and a few cries of outrage.

Doubtless Haman expected me to melt into the street from shame—and I admit his action shocked me.

"How dare you unveil a woman on a public street?" I held my head high, as if I were a queen and he a beggar. "And who are you, who dares kill dogs and pollute a public fountain?" Most of those watching would be appalled that he drowned puppies, and water is more precious than frankincense; no one corrupts a well or a fountain. The gazehound bitch pressed up against me, nuzzling for her pup; I tucked the puppy under my arm and stroked the bitch's lean elegant head.

"Here!" Haman snapped his fingers and gestured to the gazehound; I felt the bitch shrink back. "And you, girl, give me that mongrel—no, better, *you* drown the ill-bred creature."

Ah, so that's it—my lord prince's purebred bitch chose her own mate. I glanced down at the wet puppy I held, then looked back at Haman, who stood soaked and dripping.

"She will not come to you," I said, "nor will I obey commands from you."

"She will come or I will beat her until she learns obedience." Haman reached for the braided leather whip looped over his saddlebow.

"That will not teach obedience, but fear." Without taking my gaze from Haman, I stooped and gathered up my veil. "Let us pass, and I will not complain of this to my family."

"*You* will complain—do you know who I am, girl? I am Prince Haman." Clearly he expected me to gasp and grovel at this. When I did neither, he added, "The King of Kings calls me friend."

Even as I cautioned myself to prudent silence, I found myself saying, "Does the King of Kings know how you ill-use his subjects and his city?" Prince Haman seemed struck dumb by my defiance—but as I wrapped my veil around the puppy, Haman whirled and lashed out with the thick leather whip. He knew how to use that whip, and he meant to wound; meant to teach *me* obedience.

Had his blow landed, Haman's whip would have laid open my face from eye to chin. And if Haman's whip had marred me, many lives would have changed forever.

But Haman's whip never touched my flesh, for I knew better than ever to take my eyes from an enemy. I heard the creak of leather and the swish of the lash, and I did the one thing no man would ever expect: I swiftly stepped toward Haman.

Instead of slashing my face, Haman's whip cracked in the spot I had been only a heartbeat ago. And as the whip sagged and slithered onto the paving stones, I grabbed the lash and pulled, using all my weight. His balance lost, Haman stumbled forward, and I tugged again and wrenched the whip out of Haman's hand.

He did not expect me to be strong, and he did not expect me to do anything but cower weeping before him. Nor did he expect those gawking and looking on to laugh. Prince Haman, the king's friend, pulled to his knees by a girl? A girl who already had pushed him into a fountain?

Laughter—a thing men like Haman cannot endure. Haman lurched to his feet; he slipped on the damp paving stones, which angered him further. He reached for me, thinking perhaps to grasp back his whip; I stepped back as the gazehound bitch growled. Haman stopped, and demanded,

"Who are you? In the name of Ahura Mazda and the name of the King of Kings, I command you to tell me the truth!" Blood had rushed to Haman's face; crimson flared across his cheeks.

I was sorely tempted to tell him he should command by Ahriman the Dark and not by Ahura Mazda the Good, but I said only, "I am Hadassah."

"Don't play games with me, girl, or I'll have you taken up as a common harlot. Whose daughter are you? Whose wife?"

"I am Hadassah, daughter of Abihail. I am no man's wife yet." I coiled Haman's whip and tucked it into my girdle. "Since you took my veil, I will take your whip in exchange."

For a moment I thought Prince Haman's blood would burst through his skin; never before had I seen such fury. "That is *mine*."

"It is mine now." I do not know how I kept my voice steady. "But I will give the whip to you if you give me the bitch. I can promise you will never lay eyes on either her or her pup again."

I knew I was risking much—but I hoped that Haman, already mocked by onlookers, would wish only to swiftly end this clash of wills. If he did not, I would lose, for I was neither a prince nor the king's friend. At first it seemed that anger would rule him, but as Haman looked from me to those looking on, the furious crimson faded from his cheeks.

"If you want that worthless bitch, she is yours if she follows you." Haman laughed, a harsh, almost cruel sound. He turned and spread his hands wide, as if offering his false contrition to the crowd. "Is that fair and just?"

A low murmur from the people surrounding us; a few, braver than the others, called out that Prince Haman was both just and fair.

I looked at the fountain, which would have to be drained and cleansed, and at the wet bodies of the dead puppies. I pulled the coiled whip from my girdle, tested its weight in my hand. I felt the sun burn hot on my uncovered hair.

Fair and just.

I let the whip fall from my hand and walked away from Haman with my head high, a wet shivering puppy wrapped in my ruined veil and a thin nervous bitch trotting along with me, pressing close to my side and making soft whimpering noises. All I could think, as I led her home, was that Mordecai would be furious at me for being unveiled on the public street.

Once I returned home and settled the bitch with her puppy, I went to wash the dust of the street off my face. It was only then that fear fled through my blood, faster and ever faster, until my hands shook so I could hold nothing. I still sat pale and trembling until Mordecai returned home. When he questioned me, I told him all that had passed that day.

"And I am sorry I was in the street unveiled, but truly, cousin, it was not my fault. The bitch and pup are in the garden. I couldn't think where else to put them."

To my utter astonishment, Mordecai put his arm around me. "Better the garden than the kitchen," was all he said. I waited for him to forbid me to set even the shadow of my foot beyond our doorstep henceforth, but he did not.

I don't know whether the dogs or my actions appalled Mordecai more. Persians cherish the creatures. Good Jews keep neither cats nor dogs.

But Mordecai found the bitch and her pup a good home with a Persian who owned farms far from Shushan.

And he warned me that I must never let Haman set eyes on me again. "For Haman hates Jews, and you have given him reason to hate *you* twice over," Mordecai said.

"I think Haman hates everyone," I said.

"Perhaps—but he is an Agagite, and hates Jews more than all others."

Of course, thanks to Mordecai's teachings, I knew the story. Long ago, King Saul of Israel had defeated King Agag in battle, and disobeyed the Lord's command to slaughter all those he and his army had taken captive. The Prophet Samuel seized King Saul's sword and himself slew King Agag. All Agag's men were put to the sword. Not even their beasts were left alive.

I agreed with Mordecai that I must never again face Haman—but I did not believe he hated a whole race because of a battle that took place five hundred years before he was born. That ancient battle was merely Haman's excuse.

The great feast given by King Ahasuerus entertained all the world, and the bazaars of Shushan flowed over with fine goods to tempt the king's guests and their retinues. Like everyone else in Shushan, I had watched seemingly endless processions of noble and royal guests glitter their way through the streets to the palace. Both the Great Staircase and the King's Gate had been gilded in honor of the feast. At night, when a thousand torches burned, a river of fire seemed to flow up from the city to the palace above us.

But even wonders, too often seen, become familiar. By the seventh day of the feast, I only glanced at the dazzling spectacle high on the hill before I went early to my bed. Late in the night I heard someone banging upon our door. But it was not my place to run and answer such a summons, and a few moments later I heard Mordecai's voice. That made me sit up in my bed, for Mordecai rarely raised his voice, and if I could hear him now, he was amazed indeed.

The next morning I learned why Mordecai had been called in the night. The news whipped through Shushan like wildfire.

Queen Vashti had defied the king. Queen Vashti had insulted the king. Queen Vashti had been stripped of her robes and her jewels and her crown and was queen no longer.

"But what did Queen Vashti actually *do*?" I asked our servant Leah. Leah had been to the market early, to buy eggs while they were fresh, and had come running back out of breath and without eggs. And she hadn't stopped talking since, although as she repeated the same phrases over and over again, I had learned only enough to know that Mordecai must have been summoned to the palace to write upon the matter of the queen.

Leah gasped for air. "What did Queen Vashti do? I've been telling you, she defied him. The king, may he live forever, ordered her to come to his feast and—she refused!"

"Why?" I asked, and Leah gaped at me.

"What difference does that make? The King of Kings set her aside. There's a law, a decree. It says that *Vashti shall come no more before the king.* That's what it says. So she's not queen anymore."

For days, no one in Shushan seemed able to talk of anything but Queen Vashti's rebellion. I said very little on the matter, for I could not understand why the king would send for his wife when he must know she could not in decency obey him. Flaunt the queen unveiled before a hall full of drunken men? How could he? Doubtless he had been far too drunk to know better—

After seven days of feasting, I suppose they were all *too drunk to know better.* That was one of the many things I did not say. Mordecai, too, kept silent, saying only that the entire matter was most unfortunate. But he stared at me as he spoke; an odd, intent gaze.

Although a royal decree had been sent throughout the empire, north to south, east to west, proclaiming that Vashti was no longer queen, to everyone's amazement, she still dwelt in the palace. There was no talk of execution, or of exile. Slowly, as time passed, the gilt wore away from the Great Staircase. More slowly still, the gossip about Vashti died.

The king must take a new wife, of course. A new queen. Everyone assumed a proper princess would be found for him. Kings married princesses to ensure royal bloodlines and to seal political alliances. So it had always been; so it would be now.

When at last it was announced that a new queen was to be chosen, and how, all Shushan seemed to run mad.

Heralds strode through the streets, proclaiming loudly that all maidens might appear before the judges to vie for the queen's crown.

Whereas the King of Kings has set aside Queen Vashti for the crime of rebellion against him, and whereas the King of Kings is desirous of taking to himself a new queen better than she, the King of Kings decrees that any maiden who has reached the age of fourteen years but not yet that of twenty may come before the judges whom the King of Kings will appoint. And if these judges find her fair and worthy, she will be taken into the palace at Shushan. There the King of Kings will judge each maiden, and the maiden who best pleases him will become Queen of Queens.

There was a great deal more, of course. No woman who had been married might present herself to the judges. Many young fair widows wept over that restriction. No woman already betrothed might compete. Some girls I knew wept when they heard that. I do not think any woman wept to learn that the King of Kings would select a new queen not for politics, nor for wisdom, nor even for her sweet temper, but for her pretty face and shapely body.

Mothers assessed their daughters; girls demanded and got any oil or perfume they asked to beautify their skin and hair, any garments that would best display their form.

The madness spread as every jewel merchant, cloth merchant, perfume merchant, and wig merchant hastened to pull forward their most costly wares. Each hairdresser's and tailor's time was bespoken; each bathhouse devoted itself to special beauty treatments. Dancers were summoned to teach girls to move with supple grace. Elegant and expensive courtesans found themselves in demand by virtuous women who once would have spat in their painted faces—women who now urgently wanted their virgin daughters to learn a whore's tricks, hoping to enthrall the king.

Even I enjoyed the rush and swirl of excitement that swept us all along like a river in spring flood. I found myself gossiping with the other girls in the Jewish Quarter, something I rarely did. Seldom has it taken so long to fill pitchers and jars as we all stood around the well. And seldom has such arrant nonsense been spoken.

One offering was, "I heard the judges are to look upon the maidens naked, because Vashti had a tail and that is why she dared not show herself at the king's command."

I laughed outright at the one. "If the judges do examine the would-be-queens naked, it is not to search for tails!"

"Oh, and how would you know, Hadassah? You are very learned, but this is not a contest of learning. It is to find the fairest maiden in the empire."

"Is it?" I raised my eyebrows. "Where in the proclamation does it say that?"

The other girls regarded me pityingly. "It says 'the maiden who best pleases him.'" Rachel, who could never remember even two lines of the first book of Moses, could recite the entire text of the king's proclamation perfectly. And did, at least once each day.

"What else," Rachel continued, "can that mean but the one who is most beautiful? After all, Vashti was the most beautiful woman in the empire."

"And now is not?" I could not help teasing; I saw one or two of the girls smile.

"She's not queen anymore." This was enough for Rachel, and for most of the others, and led into the second most engrossing topic in all Shushan: Vashti's faults. Now that she was no longer Queen of Queens, Vashti's beauty had become sorcerous and her nature evil. Everyone had something to contribute to the tarring of Vashti's character as woman, wife, and queen.

"She slept with snakes." "She worshipped Ahriman the Dark." "She ordered her servants to work naked!"

"In a court ruled by protocol and its women ruled by modesty?" I said. "Nonsense."

No one liked this commonsense rebuke.

"Well, I heard it from —" Leah began, only to have Rachel ruthlessly interrupt.

"She did worse than that." Rachel lowered her voice with each word until even I found myself stretching my ears to hear what she would say. "She *refused* him."

"Refused him what?" asked Elishua; she was still a young girl, and sweet-minded, and even when Rachel hissed, "She *refused*—she denied him a son," Elishua clearly did not understand.

"Only the Lord can—" Elishua began, and the less kind girls laughed. Elishua's cheeks burned crimson, and I took her hand.

"You are quite right, Elishua," I said. "Only the Lord gives and takes. Blessed be the name of the Lord," I added, rather tartly, and some of the girls muttered the words after me. Where did modest, well-brought-up maidens hear such arrant, vulgar gossip? Who invented such ridiculous babble?

"Well, the king's well rid of her. A barren wife is worse than debt. Ten years wed, and no child!"

That sounded very bad for Vashti, until I remembered something, and quickly reckoned up years.

"True enough," I said, "but they were wed when she was ten. She's only twenty now. And how often do you think the king called for her, and went in to her? How many concubines does he possess who received his seed instead of Vashti?"

"Hadassah!"

"Rachel!" I echoed, mocking her shocked tone.

"Hadassah, you should not say such things."

"Everyone in Shushan—no, everyone in the empire—is talking of nothing else. Why should we be silent?" I was unsurprised when Rachel ignored this question, as did the other girls. The contest for the queen's crown held far more interest than did the king's concubines—at least today.

"Oh, who cares about Vashti now? Now that any girl in the empire—any one of us here—may become queen in her place!"

"Not *any* girl. Only the most beautiful one." Rachel—of course it was Rachel—made this statement.

The chatter ceased as all the girls fell silent; slowly, reluctantly, their eyes turned to me.

"You are beautiful, Hadassah. Very beautiful." Miriam sounded bitter, as if my beauty took away her own. "Perhaps you will win, at least here in Shushan."

I laughed. "I? I will not be chosen; I will not even be considered. Can you truly see my cousin Mordecai permitting me to enter such a contest? To be judged as if I were a heifer for market?" Everyone knew how strict Mordecai was, what a stern upholder of the law, and of tradition. The other girls seemed to settle back, comforted by my words.

Words I believed. Never, if I lived to be as old as Sarah the Laughing One, could I have imagined that Mordecai himself would insist I put my name forward.

But that is what he did. He came to me as I was reading *The Chronicle of Arslan,* and told me to set my book aside. I rolled up the scroll, placed it within its case, and then folded my hands and waited. And waited, as Mordecai stared at me, and then walked back and forth before me. At last I said, "What do you want of me, cousin?"

Mordecai stopped pacing. Without looking at me, he said, "Hadassah, put on your veil and go and drop your name into the queen's basket. There's one at the gate to this street."

I stared. "Are you mad, cousin?" I asked.

Still he did not face me. "You are my ward, Hadassah. You will do as I say."

Too stunned to yet feel anger, I rose to my feet. "No, I will not. If you think I will offer myself up to this slave auction, you're wrong. I won't do it."

Now Mordecai turned, and his face was stone. "You will, Hadassah. You will do it because I already have paid rubies to have your name written on the list of those who will go into the palace. And you will do it, Hadassah, because I order it. Now go and put on your veil."

Mordecai had *bought* my place among the queen-maidens, paid for me to enter the palace? The man who demanded I veil myself to my knees, walk with meek steps and downcast eyes, wished me to enter a royal slave market. No, not wished it—*ordered* it. I stared at him, unable to summon words.

"Rubies," I said at last. "You bought my place with rubies."

"Yes. Your mother owned a necklace of rubies, part of her own dower when she wed your father. They were to have been yours on your wedding day. But they are more valuable used to ensure you are seen by the king."

"Cousin, you are—"

"Hadassah, be silent and listen. You will go into the palace, and you will behave meekly and obediently. You have the chance to become Queen of Queens."

I would rather have had my mother's rubies. *Yes, and you would rather ride Star across the hills than bake bread in Shushan.* But I tried to discuss the matter calmly. "Very well, so you bought my place with my mother's rubies. *My* rubies." Rubies I had not even known I possessed. "Why?"

Mordecai looked uneasy. Guilty. "I will not be questioned," he said.

"And I will not be sold into the palace. Cousin, *why*?" There had to be a reason.

For long moments he said nothing. Just as I opened my mouth to ask again, Mordecai took my hands and stared into my eyes. His own eyes seemed oddly bright. Feverish.

"Because you will be queen, Hadassah."

I opened my mouth, then closed my lips firmly before I asked him if he had run mad. I managed to make my next words soft, as if I were a soft, biddable girl. "You cannot know that. Yes, I am fair to look upon, but there are many others as beautiful as I. Rubies may have bought my place in the contest, but they cannot buy the king's choice."

"The king has no more choice in this than you or I. The Most High decrees it, and so it will be."

And then, as if forgetting he was not to be questioned, Mordecai told me what he had done—and why he was so certain I must go into the palace and into the king's bed. "The Lord sent me a dream, Hadassah—and I dreamed it long before this contest was spoken of."

A dream. Mordecai wagered my future on a dream. My face must have revealed my dismay; Mordecai took my hand in his.

"You doubt, Hadassah. You must have faith, and trust in the Lord."

"Perhaps your interpretation of this dream is flawed." I had never known Mordecai to place any great credence in dreams before. What made this dream worth rubies?

Mordecai shook his head. "It is not mine. I knew the dream for a portent, and so I consulted Daniel, knowing he only could coax its meaning into the light."

"You went to *Daniel? You?*" Despite the high regard in which Daniel was held, I knew Mordecai's opinion of him was ambivalent at best. For Daniel was a Jew, brought as tribute to Babylon when Jerusalem fell. But not only had Daniel married a foreigner, the gift that had given him the name "Dream-Master" seemed, to Mordecai, perilously close to sorcery.

"Yes, Hadassah. I." Mordecai regarded me steadily. "You remember the king's great feast?"

"Who in all the empire can forget it?" I said bitterly.

"The Lord our God sent me this dream the night before that feast began. It troubled me so greatly I knew I must discover its meaning." Mordecai drew in a deep breath before continuing. "Listen, and you will understand why you must enter the palace. I dreamed, and I went to beg Daniel to unfold its meaning . . .

"In my dream, it was deep night. I stood upon the city wall and gazed into the heavens. I saw the stars gleaming bright as the queen's jewels. The most brilliant star blazed up and then fell, and as that star fell all the stars whirled about me as if they sought to climb the heavens. Then another star rose, burring hot as the sun."

Mordecai looked at me; his eyes hot and bright as the stars he spoke of. "And this is what Daniel told me: Queen Vashti's star falls. Another queen rises.

"Esther." Mordecai's eyes looked past me, into the future he had dreamed. "Your Persian name is Esther."

A name I had chosen myself. A name chosen so that I would never forget my past. A name that now sealed my future, for Esther meant—

Star.

Even after hearing Mordecai's dream and Daniel's words, I still thought Mordecai mad. I said many things about the selection to Mordecai—everything except, in the end, a final *"No."* I wondered, for a time, why I seemed unable to utter so small, so simple, a word. All I had to say was *"No. No, Mordecai, I will not do this. I have yielded in everything else, but I will not yield in this. No."*

At last I knew why I did not say it. I could not endure refusing, and having my refusal ignored.

I was Hadassah, daughter of Abihail; I read half a dozen languages and spoke half a dozen more. I studied the great books of Babylon and Sumer, could recite the epics of Homer. I could add a hundred numbers and reach a true tally. I could play the harp and the flute. I could cook and weave, sew and bake.

All that I was weighed as a feather on the scales against my beautiful face and shapely body.

The only skill demanded of me now was obedience. I put on my long yellow veil and walked with Mordecai to the gate to the Jewish Quarter. A palace guard stood there, beside a tall narrow-necked basket of gilded willow. Mordecai reached out his hand to the basket, and the guard held out his hand. "No. The rules are that the girl herself must do it."

I saw the guard trying to peer past my veil, perhaps to see if I were willing or not. Silently, Mordecai held out the square of papyrus with my name written upon it. I put my hand out through the slit in the veil and Mordecai laid the papyrus on my palm. For a breath I stared at my name on the creamy surface—the name by which the palace would know me.

I felt Mordecai's eyes upon me, the silent pressure to obey. *I need not. The rules are that I myself must put my name into the contest. I could stop this here, now—*

I turned my hand and dropped my Persian name into the gilded basket.

Esther.

BOOK FIVE

Palace of Dreams

VASHTI

No one seemed to know what would happen to me now that I was no longer queen. My handmaidens and queen's ladies wept and mourned as if I had died. Tajet wailed, "What will become of you? What will become of you?" until I held up my hand and demanded they all be silent.

"I am not dead, and your wailing gives me a headache. Leave me, all of you."

They obeyed, slinking out, eyeing me speculatively. If I were no longer queen, was I still to be obeyed? Were my wishes still commands?

Then I was alone. And to say truth, I didn't know what I was supposed to do with my days, with my life. There was no law setting down those things that a queen whose crown had been taken from her must do, or not do. There were no rules she must obey.

For the first time since I was born, I had no rule to follow. In taking my crown, the princes had set me outside the traditions that governed every other man and woman of the court.

I did not sit long alone, for Queen Mother Amestris summoned me.

⁂

For the first time, I walked through the palaces without all my attendants clamoring for the great privilege of escorting me. Most of them slipped away as I passed, fearful lest my disgrace taint them.

Others, as I would learn, remained constant. One whom I never lost, even for a heartbeat, was Hegai. Now he strode ahead of me with as much dignity as if he still conducted the Queen of Queens. I had often dashed off without waiting for him, but today his presence comforted me.

When I reached the Queen Mother's Palace, I found Amestris awaiting me in her own small throne room. And even she seemed uncertain what to do now. For the first time since I had been brought to be the king's wife, I saw weariness in her eyes, and doubt. Even the Queen Mother could not undo what the King of Kings had sealed into law.

"Vashti, how could you have been so foolish?" she demanded. "You know the king's lightest word is a command. Have you no sense at all? To openly defy the king! Now—"

"But what was I to do? If I obeyed—"

"You should have sent to me."

I was about to complain that she had been lying deathly ill, when Amestris went on without giving me the chance.

"You should have sent to *me*, Vashti. I would have told you what to do."

As you have since the day I wed your son. For a breath I thought I had spoken those words of fire aloud, that they hung upon the air between us like winged serpents. "You were ill, Queen Mother. And a woman may not appear at a men's feast. What was I supposed to do?"

"You should have delayed. Yes, delayed until you could get word to me. I would have arranged matters."

You have arranged too much. Another thought that slid unbidden into my mind. "Well, it is too late now."

"Yes, too late. And you need not look so complacent, Vashti. You are not a clever girl, but surely even you must realize you are no longer Queen of Queens?"

As she always had, Amestris derided any claim I had to being able to think for myself. She had ensured I was taught only to play, and now chided me for learning my lesson well.

Sudden anger burned my skin. "Yes, I do realize that. That fact has been made very clear to me. I have only one question for you, Queen Mother Amestris."

"And what is that?"

"What am I to do now?"

For the first time since I had met her, on the day I was ten years old, Queen Mother Amestris could think of nothing whatsoever to say. I did not wait for her to regain her sharp command over words. I bowed, most properly, and turned and walked away, out of her presence.

"I'm not sure that was wise, little queen," Hegai said, as I stepped out of the Queen Mother's Palace into the rising day. I paused, and looked up at him, and found myself smiling.

"Probably not," I said. "But may I tell you something, Hegai?"

"Of course, my queen. Anything."

"I don't care." As I began the long walk back to my own palace—or was it still mine?—I kept my head high and my back straight. Behind me, I thought I heard Hegai laugh softly. But my blood beat so against my ears I could not be sure.

After I had faced Queen Mother Amestris, and had walked back to my palace like the queen I no longer was, I dismissed my servants. I even ordered Hegai to leave me. But once I stood alone, the silence pressed upon me, the very air rasped against my skin.

At first I curled upon my bed, my marmoset burrowed against my neck and my silver foxes cuddled in my arms. But even my pets failed to soothe my restless thoughts. I was grateful to Suri and the fox twins—my wolves and cheetah and little deer had fled from me when I tried to grasp them in my arms.

Will even beasts not come to me because I am no longer queen? Hegai left me alone without one word of protest. Is he no longer mine? Mocking, Amestris's words echoed in my mind: *"You are not a clever girl, but surely even you must realize you are no longer Queen of Queens?"*

Tears spilled down my cheeks; one of the foxes licked them away, its tongue soft and swift. I looked down into its bright eyes, and to my surprise, my despair vanished. "I am no longer Queen of Queens." A burden I had not even known I carried slid away, leaving me feeling light enough to dance upon clouds. Free. *I am no longer queen. I am free.*

I kissed the fox's gleaming black nose and gently set my pets onto the cushions beside me. *It was foolish of me to send Hegai away, to tell him I no longer needed him. Of course I need him!*

Well, I would remedy that error now. I would go to Hegai, and I would beg his pardon and ask his advice. And if ever Amestris learned I had so greatly demeaned myself—

I do not care. I do not care! Perhaps she will turn to stone in outrage!

His famed silver mirror, taller and wider than a large man, dominated Hegai's reception hall. A silver Vashti regarded me gravely from its gleaming surface.

"My queen." Hegai would have bowed, but I held out my hands and without hesitation he clasped them in his. "You should have summoned me."

"And you would have come." My voice sounded thin and weak; uncertain. Not at all the firm voice of the mature woman I wished to sound.

"And I would have come. What troubles you—other than having lost your crown and the good opinion of the Queen Mother?" He smiled, squeezed my hands, and I laughed.

"I know now I never had her good opinion." All I had been to Amestris was a malleable game piece. "And I don't care about my crown. I came to ask your pardon, and your advice."

"You need never ask for the first, and you may always have the second. How may I help you, my—" The slightest of pauses, as if he had been about to speak a different word. "—my queen?"

HEGAI

When I learned that Vashti stood waiting in my own reception hall, for one joyous moment I thought her heart had opened to me. That she had come to me as my beloved. Such a thing was not impossible; eunuchs often married, although not often for love. *She is fond of me; she will grow to love me; we will marry and I will make her happy. She shall be truly loved and happy . . .*

Vain dreams, swiftly dead. One look at Vashti before my silver mirror, and I knew my hope was no more than fruitless folly. Still, when she saw me she reached out to me—better than nothing, although so much less than I desired. Drawing upon long years of control over my thoughts and passions, I asked why she had come, rather than sending for me to go to her.

To my astonishment, she solemnly begged my pardon—for what, I did not ask, for she also begged for my advice. And when I asked, she raised her eyes to mine and said,

"What do I do now, Hegai?" Her voice held steady; no tears blurred her eyes. "I am no longer queen, but what am I?"

"You are Vashti," I said. "You are always Vashti. And you know already what we must do now."

She smiled and flung her arms tight around me. "Go to Daniel Dream-Master?"

"Yes." I kissed her forehead, her skin warm under my lips. "Go to Daniel."

As always, to enter the gate into Daniel's garden was to walk into soothing peace. Nor was I surprised to find Daniel waiting on the blue bench. "Does nothing surprise you, Dream-Master?" I asked. Beside me, Vashti laughed softly.

"Many things, Hegai," Daniel said, even as Samamat came out of the house carrying a bowl full of cherries.

"That's because you never learn that people aren't sensible, Daniel." Samamat set the bowl down and sank to her knees beside it; looked up at Vashti. "So what do we call you now? Have some cherries; they're particularly sweet this summer."

"So you heard?" The most foolish of questions; who had *not* heard what happened at the king's great banquet—and the queen's? Samamat's son Dariel must have told them almost at once.

"My dear Hegai, of course we've heard all about it. The entire empire will know by the end of the week." Samamat smiled at Vashti. "Well done, Ishvari's granddaughter."

Vashti's pale skin flushed warm pink; Samamat's praise pleased her greatly. She knelt gracefully beside Samamat, who silently handed her a handful of cherries. "So," Samamat added, "what do we call you now?"

For a few breaths, Vashti stared down at the shining fruit in her cupped hands. Then she looked at Samamat and smiled. "Vashti," she said. "Call me Vashti."

Samamat laughed, Daniel smiled, and Vashti glared. Queens are not accustomed to being laughed at. I bit the inside of my lip to keep silent until I could speak in a steady voice. "That is not proper. Even if you are no longer queen, you are still a princess."

"Princess of Babylon." Spoken by Daniel, the words seemed to summon a faraway time and place. Then he shook off whatever waking dream had claimed him. "Well, I don't suppose the two of you came just to inform Sama and me what happened at the royal banquets. After all, I have a reputation to uphold, so ask your question, Vashti."

Not "queen." Not even "princess." But kings had bowed to Daniel Dream-Master. He spoke as his god directed. Never, since the day he had saved me from my owner beating me to death, had he said one word he did not mean.

Vashti glanced swiftly at me, then gazed into Daniel's eyes. "My world has fallen into shards around me. I am no longer Queen of Queens. What am I now? What do I do now?"

"What do you want to be?" Daniel asked. "It's your life, Vashti. How do you wish to live it?"

VASHTI

"What do you want to be? How do you wish to live . . . ?"

Once again I did not know the answer. Once again I knew nothing.

After I had spoken with Daniel, I paced my rooms like a restless cat. Nothing I caught up pleased me. At last I stood quiet and weighed an ivory dagger in my palm. An odd gift, I had thought the day Hegai had placed it in my hand, although the dagger was very beautiful. Upon its moon-pale hilt, leopards of gold leapt at invisible prey. A leopard's head of solid gold crowned the pommel. The beast's eyes glinted fire and blood; rubies. *What do you like to do?* A question asked of me long ago, one to which I thought I had learned the answer. Now I knew that I had not.

I let myself dream, trying futures as if they were jewels.

Perhaps I will become an Amazon. After all, I could ride and shoot, even if Ahasuerus did laugh at my lack of true skill—if only the Amazons had not passed into the Land of Shadows a dozen dozen lifetimes ago.

A soft scratching upon my door; I turned and saw one of my maidservants hesitating there. "O queen," she began, and then stopped, her cheeks burning redder than the paint upon her skin.

No one knew how to address me now. As the maid struggled to find the right words to begin, I said, "What is it, Elea?"

Grateful that I had eased the path, she bowed and said, "The King of Kings awaits—awaits—"

"Me," I finished for her. "Thank you, Elea. Where is he?"

Ahasuerus awaited me in my reception room; although he did not wear his royal robes, he carried the gold scepter. An official visit, then.

"So you are here as the King of Kings." The words escaped unbidden, surprising me more, I think, than they did Ahasuerus. It is for the King of Kings to speak first. I could be killed for such an offense.

"I am the King of Kings," he said, and his voice sounded both sad and sullen.

"Is there any doubt of that?" I sounded more bitter than I intended.

He set aside the scepter; what he spoke now would be his words, not a king's. "I am sorry, my queen—"

"I am no longer your queen, Ahasuerus." I would not dare interrupt a king's words; a man's, yes, that I would dare. "By your own seal, I am set aside."

"But not by my wish."

He looked so miserable I longed to clasp him in my arms, smooth his hair, comfort him as if he were a small unhappy child. "I know. They have tricked you, my—" Suddenly I realized he was not my love; I could not say the word truly. I drew in a deep breath. "My dearest friend, now it is our turn to trick them." The words came from nowhere, but Ahasuerus promptly looked more cheerful; puzzles always amused him.

"How? You know the law cannot be revoked once sealed."

"No. But—but another law can always be made, and sealed, can it not?"

"I suppose it can. But to what purpose? I cannot decree that you be my queen again."

I do not wish to be your queen again. The words came unbidden; rang so clear in my mind that for a horrible moment I thought I had spoken them aloud. Shaken, I merely shook my head, which Ahasuerus took for abject grief and assent. He put his arm around me and said,

"Don't cry, Vashti. You won't suffer for this."

I stared at him, and saw that he truly believed what he said. Well, why should he not? He was King of Kings, Lord of Half the World. And he was a man; given even the breath of a chance, he would convince himself that I was better off set aside than I had been as his indulged wife. Suddenly I felt much older than he, and very tired. I sighed and rested my head upon his shoulder, as I had so often done before.

"I will not suffer if you will seal into the laws that I shall still dwell here, in the Queen's Palace, and that I shall keep all that belongs to Vashti, and not to the Queen of Queens. Let it be written and sealed that—"

Then I paused. That what? Desperation summoned my next words. "The edict says that Queen Vashti shall come no more before King Ahasuerus. But if you come here to me . . ."

"Then you are not coming before the king!" He smiled at last. "Yes, that is what shall be written and sealed. That Vashti shall dwell within the palace and the king may go to her as he wishes," Ahasuerus finished. He put his arm around me; kissed my forehead. "Vashti, I don't—"

"Write the decree now," I said. "Please, for me?"

"Anything you ask." He sounded happier, now that he could grant me favors, mitigate the harsh command that had severed me from him. "Send one of your pages to fetch Mordecai the chief scribe—he will know how to word it properly. This law must be perfect before I set my seal upon it."

The scribe came and bowed to Ahasuerus and then to me, and listened to Ahasuerus describe what he desired. Mordecai had bowed to me with respect; he looked upon me with neither avid interest nor pity. I decided I liked Mordecai the scribe.

Mordecai sat and wrote, and then read the decree aloud. "By the will of Ahasuerus, Lord of Half the World, King of Kings, Emperor over the Medes and the Persians and all the lands from the Western Sea to the Eastern Mountains, the royal lady Vashti shall dwell in the Queen's Palace in Shushan with all that is hers, and the King of Kings will enter the Queen's Palace as pleases him."

Mordecai looked up from the decree. "Does that wording please the king?"

Ahasuerus took the decree and read it for himself. Then he handed it to me. "Should anything be added, Vashti? I want nothing left out."

I read the decree; so simple. Surely there should be more? Then I remembered what Ahasuerus had said: that the scribe Mordecai would know best how to write it. I looked at Mordecai and raised my eyebrows in silent question. Without hesitation, Mordecai nodded. I handed the decree back to Ahasuerus.

"Add nothing," I said, and Ahasuerus took the decree and set his seal upon it. Now it was law; now I was protected, honored. My heart warmed with love for Ahasuerus—but I loved him as a sister loves her brother. I did not love him as a woman loves the man she desires most in all the world.

Amestris had ensured that I did not. She had denied us passion, knowing its power.

But a friend's love is great, too. Amestris, friendless, did not know that truth.

I had thought myself well-loved. Now that I was no longer Queen of Queens, I swiftly learned that I had only been well-liked. Liking that vanished swiftly as swallows the moment the Star Crown no longer circled my brow.

Oh, some, cautious, still bowed and flattered. I still dwelt within the Queen's Palace; I still was treated well by the king. These vacillating courtiers saw that while Vashti came no more before the king, the king still came to Vashti.

Others, more fickle, sought to avoid me. They would not look upon me, and would hastily slide away if I chanced to stroll through a corridor or a garden in which they stood. I will not pretend it did not hurt. Some had been, I thought, my friends.

And some remained unchanged—and only now did I know them for true friends. Hegai was one. My scribe Nikole was another; she and her husband Doud, one of the court singers, remained, as Nikole assured me, my humble servants.

"I don't need humble servants, Nikole," I told her. "I need friends. I have learned that, if nothing else."

"Then you have learned a great lesson." Nikole hesitated until I held out my arms to her. Some boundaries are too great to cross without a sign that the risk is worth taking. When I reached out first, Nikole dared put her arms around me.

"It will all come right, my queen," she said as I buried my face against her neck.

"How?" My voice was muffled by Nikole's hair; she stroked my back as if soothing an infant. "Nothing is the same now, nothing."

"Nothing ever stays the same," Nikole said, "not even what is written in the laws of the Medes and the Persians."

So I still had friends. And I still saw Ahasuerus, my dear friend and brother. For despite the iron rule of the law, we had seen the loophole through which our own wishes could slip.

But it was a strange, half-lived life.

HEGAI

Vashti's fall from grace opened the door wide for Haman . . . always lurking about the court, always ready to do any man a favor, he now became the king's friend—his dearest friend. This was Amestris's doing, for now that Vashti was queen no longer, she needed someone to guide Ahasuerus in the ways she wished him to go. She needed a new tool, another toy to distract and amuse her son.

Haman seemed perfect for the role. Still young enough to ride and hunt and race with the king; old enough to know how to defer without seeming to do so. Wellborn enough to be at court, lowborn enough to seem harmless to the Seven Princes.

And so Amestris made her greatest mistake.

She introduced Ahasuerus to Haman.

In his new role as the king's greatest friend, I saw Haman more often. Ahasuerus thought nothing of bringing his dear friend Haman into the Women's Palace; into the Queen's Palace. Of course Ahasuerus might grant entry to the harem to any man he chose to honor. I should have been mad with rage—for years I had longed for Haman's disgrace and death.

Death was easy to achieve. Disgrace—I had not yet conjured up a way to achieve that. Every plan I concocted proved inadequate or impossible.

But oddly, the more I saw Haman, the more tranquil I became.

Do not mistake me; I never lost my hate, but the raging blaze became a banked fire. *Patience, have patience, my son. Wait.* I do not know whether the command was truly my mother's ghost guiding me, or simply my own good sense. For soon or late, Haman would overreach himself. Make a mistake. Haman climbed high—and the higher Haman climbed, the greater would be his fall.

So, obedient to that silent voice, I waited, serene.

Save for my dreams.

In dreams, Haman groveled at my feet. Felt the gelding knife on his flesh. Screamed and begged for mercy as I thrust a blade deep into his greedy, cruel heart.

I did not need Daniel Dream-Master to interpret *those* dreams. And someday . . .

Someday they would come true.

VASHTI

Happier than he had been since he had been forced to cast me aside, Ahasuerus wished Haman to be my friend as well as his. I was glad to hear the joy back in Ahasuerus's voice, the light once more shining in his eyes. I was less delighted to have him bring Haman to visit me as a matter of course—or that Haman seemed suddenly to have become Ahasuerus's closest friend and advisor.

I had seen Haman on the occasions when I had played the king's page—and although I had heard him described as tactful, thoughtful, and talented, I could not quite like Haman. I knew Hegai distrusted Haman, although when pressed for a reason, Hegai said only,

"I do not like his eyes, my lady Vashti."

But Ahasuerus loved Haman dearly, and that delighted Amestris, who had chosen him for her son's companion. A companion whom she could use to sway Ahasuerus's decisions. A clever, circumspect tool.

Time proved Haman all that Queen Mother Amestris thought him—and more. Haman was as ambitious as Amestris herself. He was even more ruthless. And unlike Amestris, Haman was reckless as well.

Who else would have envisioned choosing a new queen with a contest open to all the empire's maidens?

The contest began as a jest—at least I think that is how it all began, for Haman's jests always seemed labored. Ahasuerus had come to dine with me and, for the first time, brought Haman with him. I did not like Haman, but I could hardly refuse hospitality to the king's dearest friend. And to give Haman his due, he treated me with as much reverence as if I were still queen. Haman's courtesy to me pleased Ahasuerus, and I was glad to see Ahasuerus happy. So the dinner progressed well. My cooks had created a new dish of apricots and honey that sweetened all our moods, and Ahasuerus had sent a gift of rich Shiraz wine that my clever cooks had fashioned into an icy drink that soothed throat and tempers.

So content, we spoke idly of nothing—or rather, Ahasuerus and I spoke without great thought, amusing ourselves between bites of melon and sips of wine sherbet by discussing the new fashion for topaz rather than turquoise. Ahasuerus had drunk the last of the wine sherbet; I noticed and beckoned to the steward.

"Bring more of the wine sherbet," I told him. "If we have not already drunk it all, that is." I laughed, knowing it important to make such an order an easy thing. My servants and slaves never feared telling me truth.

My steward smiled. "There is more wine, princess. Ice, however—of that we have only one more block. Does my lady wish us to make more of the sherbet?"

I glanced at my guests. Ahasuerus shook his head, very slightly, and Haman remained silent, understanding that Ahasuerus did not wish to trouble the kitchen for more of the drink. "No," I said. "But please tell the kitchen staff how greatly their work pleased the King of Kings."

"As my lady princess commands. Shall I return with the dish my lady princess created for the king?"

"Yes," I said. "Bring it and set it before the king."

"My lady princess honors me." My steward bowed and left us, and I turned to Ahasuerus, who smiled.

"You created a new dish for me, Vashti? I am flattered—and amazed."

"Flattered the king may be, but there is no need for amazement. I did nothing but suggest certain fruits be combined with certain spices in a honey-cake. The cooks did all the work."

Ahasuerus reached out and took my hand. "See what a treasure I possess, Haman?" Ahasuerus kissed my palm; I found myself pulling my hand away. Haman stared at me, his eyes dark wells, revealing nothing.

"The king is most fortunate," Haman said, and Ahasuerus sighed.

"Fortunate and foolish. If only . . ."

No. Do not say it, Ahasuerus. I sensed that freeing the words would give Haman a power he longed for but did not yet possess. I should have spoken, even though it meant interrupting the king. But I waited too long, and Ahasuerus revealed what many had guessed, but that only he and I had known as truth.

"If only Vashti were still my wife—still my queen. I was a fool, Haman." Ahasuerus turned away from me, gazed at Haman. "You're a clever man. Surely you can tell me how I may once more rejoice in my queen?"

Haman lowered his gaze; stared into his wine-cup. He must think hard and fast, for what Ahasuerus had asked of him could not be answered with any words that it would please the king to hear. An act sealed into the Great Laws could never be revoked. And even if the laws of the Medes and Persians could be swept aside—

I do not want to go back.

Haman kept his head bowed, as if deep in thought. And when he spoke, he ignored Ahasuerus's plaintive demand to do the impossible. Instead, Haman offered up the wildly improbable for the king's approval.

"If my lord the King of Kings languishes for lack of a queen"—Haman cleverly transmuted the king's wish to defy the law into a perfectly reasonable desire to wed again—"is there not a simple remedy?"

"Is there?" Ahasuerus glanced up swiftly, as if gauging my reaction; I smiled, hoping to reassure him of my support for whatever plan he had devised—that I would not be jealous if he chose a new queen. Abruptly, he tossed the lion-cup to Haman, who shied away from the gold missile, but managed to catch the cup just before it crashed to the floor.

Ahasuerus laughed. "Keep it, Haman. A sign of the king's favor. Now tell me this simple remedy."

To give Haman the credit due him, he was ready with an answer. "O king, does not your empire stretch from the Western Sea to the Eastern Mountains? And does not such an empire possess the rarest, the finest of living gems? Let the best of the empire's most beautiful, most accomplished maidens be selected and brought here to the palace."

Ahasuerus leaned forward, his interest caught. "A clever notion, Haman. But how would such maidens be chosen, and brought to Shushan?"

Haman paused as if to draw a breath; I saw it for what it was—Haman stalling for time. "Oh, all that can easily be arranged, great king."

He has no more notion than I how this may be achieved.

"The important thing is that no worthy maiden be overlooked." Haman's voice gained confidence as he spoke. "Then my lord king will have his choice of the sweetest fruits of the empire."

Haman need only present this grand and glorious scheme to King Ahasuerus—and then bow himself away, leaving others to try to fulfill the king's command. So Haman began to speak, sounding more certain that he spoke rightly each time Ahasuerus nodded approval. As for me—I sat astonished. Who would dare even dream such a thing, save Haman?

"O king, may you live forever, nothing could be simpler." Haman smiled; I knew he plotted something—but what?

"So you say, Haman, but I can think of a dozen dozen difficulties."

"Then I humbly petition and request that the king permit me to assume this burden. Or better still . . ." Haman's gaze slid round to me.

Oh, no. But I did not speak swiftly enough.

"Better still, permit me to lay the matter in the hands of one who knows you better than you know yourself." Haman bowed, nicely managing to seem to honor both Ahasuerus and me. "Who better to choose a queen than one who has been a queen herself?"

Almost anyone else! I thought I shouted the words, but they did not pass my lips. I stared as if struck dumb. *Choose the new queen? Me? Is Haman mad?* I turned to Ahasuerus, who smiled at me as if he'd just been given the finest gift in all the world.

"How clever!" Ahasuerus laid his hand on Haman's shoulder. "Is he not the best of friends and advisors, Vashti?"

I could think of nothing at all to say—at least, nothing that would have been acceptable. Taking my silence as assent, Ahasuerus continued happily, "We all know I must choose a new queen—"

"And it cannot be me. There can be no trickery, no setting the crown back on my head." I spoke in more haste than was flattering, but fortunately Ahasuerus, caught up in Haman's grand design, didn't notice.

"You're right, Vashti. I am sorry, but you can never again be my queen."

"Of course not, and of course I understand. But my lord Haman's idea—"

"If I may speak?" Haman bowed again, glanced up at me through his lashes, a beast seeking prey. "If my idea finds some small merit in the eyes of the King of Kings, I am content. Of course I know nothing of choosing women fit for a king's palace, but I know that Princess Vashti was chosen by the Queen Mother herself. And so I ask again: who better to undertake the task of selecting a new queen to delight the king?"

About to decline this dubious honor, I hesitated. *Chosen by the Queen Mother*—What would Amestris think of Haman's plan? *Doubtless she thinks to once again pick out a queen for her son, another girl she can train up as a biddable puppet.*

I heard again Amestris castigating me for acting without consulting her. The words *foolish girl* echoed, silent, in my mind. Such small words, to invoke so great a decision.

"If it please the king," I said, "give me the right to command this in your name, and I will undertake the task my lord Haman has set before you."

And that is how it came to pass that Vashti, queen no longer, was charged with selecting the next Queen of Queens.

Fearing the Queen Mother's talent for getting her own way, I suggested that the edict decreeing an empire-wide search for a new queen be drawn up at once. "Surely the three of us can write up such an edict?" I made myself sound doubtful, and added cunningly, "Perhaps we should ask the advice of the Queen Mother and the Seven Princes before embarking upon this venture?"

I could see Ahasuerus's distaste for the idea of asking the Seven—the men who had made him look so foolish before all the empire—for any advice whatsoever. And I had coupled Amestris's name with the Seven, so Ahasuerus rejected her counsel as well.

"I am quite capable of making a decision without my mother's approval," he said. I could only wish he'd been as firm of purpose before I had been stripped of my crown. "What do you think, Haman? Shall we draft the edict now?"

Haman stroked his beard; I could almost hear his thoughts. Agree with the king? Always politic. But if the king later doubted the rightness of his acts? Perhaps it would be wiser to equivocate . . .

"Oh, come, Haman—Vashti, who is only a woman, answered at once. Surely you're a man who can make up his own mind?" Ahasuerus sounded half amused—and half angry.

Forced to answer, Haman began by flattering me. "To say that my lady Vashti is only a woman is to do her less than justice. And may I suggest, my king, that some special rank or title be given her? For no one—"

"No one knows what to call me, and so they all mumble gibberish with my name the only clear word!" I smiled at Haman, for once approving of him. And this digression on my proper station would give Haman a few moments' grace to think of a good answer to Ahasuerus's demand for an instant edict.

"A special rank, a special title—yes, that is an excellent notion." Ahasuerus nodded, gravely approving. "But what? She cannot be a queen."

"I am still a princess of Babylon," I pointed out. "And—and your dearest sister. Will that suffice?"

Ahasuerus considered this, then smiled. "Princess Vashti, the King's Sister. It sounds fitting and pleasing. We must set that down in the edicts."

"It shall be done, my king." But if Haman hoped to elude further questioning on the contest for the queen's crown, he was disappointed. Ahasuerus had been only briefly distracted by the question of my new title.

"I can always rely on you, Haman—and on you, Vashti." Ahasuerus rose to his feet, so Haman and I must also stand. "And so I lay the matter of a new queen in your hands. Do as seems good to you."

With that casual command given, Ahasuerus picked up a slice of the spiced honey-cake and bit into it. "This is excellent, Vashti. Now I will walk in your garden so my beloved sister and my good counselor may freely discuss my next wife."

Haman and I were left staring at each other as the servants waited for another command. Beyond the archway into my garden, Ahasuerus bent to inspect a rose.

"I lay this matter at your feet, my lady princess." Haman's black eyes glinted with anger—whether at himself or at the king, or even at me, I could not tell.

"I take it up into my hands, for the king has asked it of me. And do not glare at me like that, my lord prince. This contest for queen was your idea, not mine."

He bowed, a little too low, a little too obsequious. "As my lady princess says. And if my lady princess requires any aid—any assistance whatsoever—in this delicate matter, may I suggest my wife might be of assistance?"

"My thanks, Prince Haman, but I chose his concubines before. Why not his next queen?"

I had the pleasure of seeing Haman, for once, at a loss for a tactful reply.

⸸

Hegai didn't bother with tact when I revealed the plan to him. "Haman suggests an outrageous notion, and the king nods, and then—chaos!" Hegai shook his head. "Every maiden in the kingdom will be standing at the palace gate before the next new moon!"

"Every heart-free maiden." I sighed. "Well, it is done now, and we shall have to organize this—this virgin market."

"Who else?" For once, Hegai permitted himself to sound both resigned and bitter.

Who else? I put my arms around him and rested my head against his chest. *And how?*

"We can start with the provinces," I said, unsure what next to say. Never before had I actually organized anything, not even so much as a meal. All I had had to do was say, "Prepare a feast," and it was done. Never once had I thought of all the work that went into creating anything—let alone a new Queen of Persia.

"One hundred and twenty-seven maidens for the king to chose from?" Hegai sounded as doubtful as I felt.

"Too many. But each girl must have her fair chance." For a moment I stared past Hegai, into the Queen's Courtyard. A new queen meant the Queen's Palace, the Queen's Courtyard, would no longer be mine . . . I shivered; Hegai stroked my hair.

"My princess? Are you unwell?"

I shook my head. "No. No. I was just thinking . . ." Should I tell Hegai my true thoughts? No, I would not burden him with my foolishness. "I was just thinking you are right. Who else but you and I can do this task?"

"This outrageous task," Hegai corrected, and I looked up at him and smiled, as I knew he'd hoped I would.

"Come," I said, and slid my arm through his.

"Where are we going?" he asked, and I smiled again.

"Where else? To Daniel."

Daniel and his wife were among those who treated me no differently now than they had when I was queen. They seemed unsurprised that I should come to them asking their aid.

"I have no idea how to even begin to find a new queen." I sat cross-legged at Daniel's feet; I gazed hopefully up at him. "Tell me what to do, Dream-Master."

"Well," said Daniel, "first you tell me what you think you need to do, Vashti."

I stared at my hands, thinking hard. "I must find one maiden from each of the provinces and bring her here to Shushan and present her to the king and—"

"Where will they stay, these maidens?" Samamat asked. "And who will judge them?"

The answer to the first question was easy. "They will stay in the Women's Palace," I said, relieved at being able to answer without hesitation.

"And how will they be selected, and who will judge them?" Samamat said, and these questions closed my mouth again. Ahasuerus ruled over one hundred and twenty-seven provinces, so there must be one hundred and twenty-seven candidates for the queen's crown. It seemed a vast number—but there were thousands of beautiful maidens in the empire. How to choose only one hundred and twenty-seven of them?

I remembered how I had been chosen: a woman I had never seen had come and ordered that I should be queen. My wishes, my dreams, had possessed no weight, no value. *This time it will be different.*

"The girls themselves with choose whether they wish to enter the contest," I said, and Samamat smiled.

"Others may force them to enter," she pointed out, and Daniel laid his hand over hers.

"You can't control everything, Sama," he said, and then he, too, smiled at me. "It's like Vashti to consider the wishes of the candidates themselves."

Exhilaration burned beneath my skin. I had pleased both Daniel Dream-Master and Samamat. Encouraged, I went on, "And the girls from the farthest provinces will have the longest journeys to Shushan. They should be chosen first, so that all the maidens arrive within the same month."

"An excellent idea," Daniel said. "So each province will send a candidate for queen?"

"That is only fair," I said, and then realized I had overlooked a vital point. "But there is something more important than the number of candidates."

"And what is that?" Daniel asked.

"That," I said grimly, "is how we are to chose the judges who will select the girls."

"All one hundred and twenty-seven of them," Samamat added helpfully.

"That is indeed a problem." Daniel seemed to consider the matter, then said, "Do you think each province should also choose its own judges?"

That sounded only just and fair—but I hesitated. "If each province chooses its own judges, perhaps they will not be impartial?"

"Only perhaps?" Samamat said, sounding so incredulous that I laughed.

"Hegai knows what pleases the king," I said. "Hegai can select the judges."

"Fortunate Hegai," Daniel said, and smiled.

"The king will choose a queen from among all the maidens of the empire. All the virgins who dwell in the lands of Persia are entitled to pass before the king, that he may make his choice."

Haman had sent out the proclamation without consulting me—more drastically, with consulting Queen Mother Amestris. When we learned of it, Hegai warned me to say nothing, as if I had expected Haman to do so. I did as Hegai advised and held my tongue. Amestris said enough for both of us, and only Ahasuerus telling his mother that he had granted Haman permission for such a proclamation silenced her.

I think Ahasuerus was as surprised as I by the proclamation, but it no longer mattered. For the proclamation engendered wild excitement—and a wave of ambition flowed like poisoned honey over the lands Ahasuerus ruled.

I knew it would take many weeks before all the chosen maidens entered the Women's Palace. I only hoped that would be time enough to arrange the palace to accommodate them. Usually only one or two new women entered the palace at a time, and that not often. Ahasuerus did not keep a large harem—not for a King of Kings.

"So we must decide where the girls will live, and what they will wear. A hundred and twenty-seven maidens, Hegai! What are we going to do?"

Hegai smiled, calm as a cat. "We will manage beautifully, my clever one. I always do."

He was so confident that I laughed. "If you say so, Ruler of the Harem, then I must believe. But where do we start?"

"By walking through every corridor and chamber in the Women's Palace, and seeing for ourselves what must be done. There is enough space for three times the women who now dwell here."

So that is what we did. Hegai and I explored every courtyard and garden, every sleeping chamber and balcony. We studied the baths, examined the kitchens and the storerooms. I found myself listening to lists of how much bread would need to be baked, how many fish caught, how many sheep and goats and pigeons butchered. I looked at bolts of cloth high-piled in storage rooms. Never before had I truly understood that a palace required more than gold and silks and polished marble halls.

Never before had I understood how much work was required to make so vast an undertaking as the search for a new queen run smooth.

"I suppose this is what it is like to organize an army on the march," I said to Hegai, after we had spent an hour discussing how many girls could share a bedchamber, and whether each girl truly needed a eunuch devoted to her needs alone. "This is a nightmare, Hegai."

He smiled. "Yes, my lady princess, it is. But it is a nightmare from which we will someday awake." He paused, as if carefully weighing his next words. "My lady princess—you do realize that the new queen will owe you a great deal?"

I set down the list of names I had been studying. The palace employed a great many eunuchs; I was amazed to learn just *how* many. "Yes, Hegai, I realize that. But will *she*?"

"Make sure that she does," Hegai advised. "Now, what are we to do with the girls whom the King of Kings, may he live forever, does not choose?"

"All one hundred and twenty-six of them." I sighed and rubbed my temples. "Well, they will not go home disgraced. Not if they may take whatever they choose of their ornaments, and the king's favor for their families."

"Not all will wish to leave, even if they are not chosen as queen," Hegai said.

"Well, then they may remain as—as concubines." I knew those who did so might only see the king one night a year. But if it pleased them better to remain in the King's Palace than to return home, why should they not? "Ahasuerus is King of Half the World," I said. "Surely his palace can support a hundred new concubines."

The wave of enthusiasm for this manner of selecting a new queen astonished me—but even I found the contest for queen exciting, for it was *mine*. Never before had a serious task been set into my hands. The more I labored at this incredible, bewildering responsibility, the more I delighted in the work. I sat long hours with Hegai, poring over maps of Ahasuerus's empire, making lists of the peoples who lived within the empire's borders, estimating the time it would take for each province to select its candidate and for her to reach Shushan.

"They cannot all arrive at once." I stared at the map, trying to make all the routes to Shushan miraculously become of equal length.

"Perhaps that is just as well," Hegai said.

I waited, but he merely looked back at me. I knew this gambit; Hegai wished me to find the answer myself. A surge of warmth swept through me, pleasure at his faith in me. Hegai never laughed at my attempts to be more than a pretty, silly girl.

"If all the candidates arrive at the same time—with all their attendants—it will be chaos." I tried to think like a maiden from Issus, come a month's journey to the King's Palace. *Only one can become queen. What will the others have?* "And the girls should have their chance to be carried through Shushan in triumph," I said, and Hegai smiled.

"It will be a great honor simply to be one of those chosen to come to the king," he agreed.

"So," I said, leaning past him and setting my finger upon Issus, and wondering what it would be like to live in a palace that looked out upon the sea, "the farther away the satrapy is from Shushan, the earlier they should select their candidate and set her upon her journey."

"That course has much to recommend it," he said. I felt his fingers upon my hair, leaned into his touch. For a heartbeat we stood there, close; suddenly I wondered what I would do, if I did not have Hegai. I could not even imagine such a loss.

Then I remembered I was supposed to be organizing the search for Ahasuerus's next queen, not worrying over impossibilities. I straightened and continued my attempt to ensure the contest ran smoothly. If some girls arrived many weeks before the others . . .

"What will the maidens do during the time we await those coming from the farther satrapies?" I asked, and this time Hegai answered me.

"Prepare to meet the king," he said. "What else?"

By the end of a month, the judges had been selected and sent out from Shushan to all the provinces of the empire. Hegai had decided that he would be one of the judges in Shushan itself. I thought this wise; who knew better than Hegai what would please Ahasuerus in a woman?

The rules for the contest were mine, and I had struggled long hours creating them. In the end, I abandoned lengthy, elaborate protocols in favor of seven simple, clear sentences. Each of the judges carried a written set of these rules that anyone might read, or have read to them.

> Any maiden in the empire between the ages of fourteen and twenty may put her name into the contest. She must do so herself. No one else may set her name into the contest. No one may force her to enter her name, or prevent her from doing so. The judges will consider each maiden who wishes to come before the king and decide upon she who will represent each province.
>
> King Ahasuerus will choose his queen from the candidates sent to the palace at Shushan. The maidens he does not choose may themselves choose to remain in the King's Palace or return to their homes in all honor.

I had done my best to ensure no girl would be forced either into or out of the competition, but I soon learned how easily my rules could be evaded. Hegai came into my garden where I sat reading, my lazy cheetah lying across my feet. I looked up; Hegai's face seemed shadowed. I set the scroll aside. "What is it, Hegai? What troubles you?"

"There is a new maiden you must see." Hegai sounded almost worried.

"Why? Who is she?"

"Because she is Prince Shethar's daughter," Hegai said.

"Surely that will count against her, rather than in her favor?" I thought Shethar far too ambitious, and I knew Ahasuerus also regarded him cautiously.

"Perhaps." Hegai conveyed his doubt with that one word. I rose to my feet and called for Ajashea to take the cheetah to her cage, and told Hegai to take me to see the paragon who so troubled him.

When I saw the prince's daughter, my heady confidence vanished in a breath. In a garden of beautiful girls, she simply was, beyond any doubt, the most beautiful. Night-black hair and skin like new ivory; night-dark eyes and lips red as pomegranate seeds . . .

"Yes," Hegai murmured, answering my question before I asked it. "Her name is Tandis."

"She is very beautiful."

"She is." Hegai's tone seemed to dismiss Tandis's perfect beauty; I looked up and saw him smiling.

"She's more beautiful than I am," I said.

"She is," Hegai agreed.

I stared at him, mock-indignant—at least, I told myself I jested. "But no woman is more beautiful than I—everyone has always said so."

"That was when you were Queen of Queens."

"So I lost my beauty when I lost the queen's crown?"

"Some of it, my princess." Hegai regarded me steadily. "And she is younger than you."

"How much younger?"

"She must be fourteen at least, if she is here."

"You think she is not?" I studied Tandis more carefully, noting the round curves of her cheeks, the way her clothing fell away from her body rather than displaying its shape. *Younger.* Then Prince Shethar had violated at least one of the contest rules. *How many others has he ignored?*

"Is it worth accusing Shethar? By the time all the rest arrive, she will doubtless be fourteen in truth." I wondered if it would matter—perhaps Tandis's sheer beauty would dazzle Ahasuerus into setting the crown upon her midnight hair.

"Perhaps the nobly-born lady Tandis does not desire to become queen," Hegai suggested.

"I wonder you can say those words without laughing! Prince Shethar's daughter not wish to become Queen of Queens? After all he has done to place her where the crown will tumble onto her head?"

"Perhaps she is a willful child, ungrateful for all her father has done."

I considered Hegai's words. "What do you know of her?" I asked at last.

"Less than I should, save that she has a twin sister; Shethar keeps a strict household. But the mere fact that she is here—"

"—means her father intends her to be Ahasuerus's choice," I finished. "Yes, that much seems clear." I studied the nobly-born lady Tandis, wondering if she obeyed her father eagerly, or merely dutifully.

She held herself stiffly, her chin lifted; she seemed proud, even haughty, which did not surprise me in Prince Shethar's daughter. Her shining black hair hung in a thick threefold braid down her back—

Just as my hair had been braided, the day Queen Mother Amestris had come to look upon me when I was ten years old. Three braids woven with strings of pearls, then twined into one braid so heavy it had tilted my head back and made my neck ache. . . .

"I wish to speak with her," I told Hegai, and instead of summoning a servant, he went over and brought Tandis to me himself.

"My lady the Princess Vashti, beloved sister of King Ahasuerus, behold the nobly-born lady Tandis, daughter of Prince Shethar. She is the candidate from Daskyleion."

Hegai's stiffly formal introduction made me smile as Tandis bowed.

"It is an honor to meet Princess Vashti, beloved sister of the King of Kings." Tandis's voice was soft, pleasing to the ear. But when she straightened again and looked at me, she did not smile.

"It pleases me to meet you. Are you well and happy here?" I made my voice sympathetic, coaxing.

"Oh, yes, princess." Tandis tried valiantly to sound happy.

"No, you are not," I said. "Tell me what troubles you—I will have the matter corrected at once."

Her eyes glinted bright with unshed tears. "I miss my sister," she said.

"I understand. I wish I had a sister." Only a small untruth; seeing Tandis's longing created envy of such affection. I already knew the answer to my next question, but I wished to draw Tandis into conversation, learn what I could of her and her wishes. Was she as nakedly ambitious as her father? "Is your sister older than you, or younger?"

Tandis hesitated, and I smiled. "Your father is not here," I pointed out, "and I will not reveal anything you tell me."

She looked intently at me for a moment, clearly weighing her father's power against mine. "We are the same age," Tandis said at last.

"Fourteen?" I said, raising my eyebrows.

Another pause; Tandis chose to consider my word a statement rather than a question. "She is my twin. I have never spent even an hour away from her. And now—now I will never see her again."

"Of course you will."

Tandis shook her head. "Our father the nobly-born Prince Shethar said he will keep Barsine to ensure I obey him always. I swore I would always do just as he ordered me."

Her perfectly curved lips quivered; she pressed them together hard and stared at the ground. I reached out and lifted her chin so I could look into her eyes.

"Was Barsine permitted to put her name into the contest?" I asked, and Tandis shook her head. *Another rule broken.*

"I see." I put my arm around the girl. "Don't cry, Tandis, or your servants will be in despair at the ruin of all their hard work." I turned to Hegai. "Send for Prince Shethar's daughter the nobly-born lady Barsine. Tell the prince that because he denied Barsine the right to place her name in the contest, he must send her as well. If her twin sister is worthy of the notice of the King of Kings, so is she."

Tandis flung herself to her knees and grasped my hands. "O princess, I will serve you always! I will do whatsoever you wish! So will Barsine, I swear we will—"

About to assure Tandis I had no need of such effusive gratitude, I changed my mind as she kissed my hands. "Thank you, Tandis. I think you and your sister will be valuable friends to have."

"You do realize," Hegai said, "that raises the number of candidates to one hundred and twenty-eight?"

"No," I said, "it means we now have only one hundred and twenty-six—for both of Prince Shethar's daughters are too young to be considered at all and so I am taking them into my care. Prince Shethar not only forced a daughter to enter the contest, but sent one who is not yet fourteen. That is two rules broken, so I will take two daughters from him. And," I added, "the satrapy of Daskyleion does *not* have permission to try again with yet another candidate!"

"A wise decision," Hegai said, and I smiled at him. For a moment I thought he would say more, but he merely smiled back.

As soon as Prince Shethar's daughter Barsine was brought to the palace, I knew why it was Tandis who had been forced to enter the contest. The nobly-born lady Barsine looked exactly like her twin; Barsine, too, was physical perfection. But Barsine lacked Tandis's quick wit and clever mind. Barsine was sweet and soft as a kitten, and as heedless. I greeted Barsine kindly, and ordered both Tandis and Barsine to be given rooms near mine.

No one sought to object, and Tandis and Barsine kissed my hands and thanked me ecstatically. They regarded their father with fear, and gladly gave me their allegiance.

"That was well done, Vashti," Hegai told me later, as we stood on an upper balcony and watched the two girls playing with a gilded leather ball in the garden below.

His praise warmed me; I slid my arm through his. "It cost me nothing, and gained me two devoted attendants—one clever and quick as a mongoose, and one who will do what she is told. And," I added, smiling, "Prince Shethar is *furious*."

Furious, yet powerless to interfere once I had invoked the king's privilege to have any woman he chose sent to the imperial palace. My scribe Nikole had written an elegantly stern demand that I had sealed with the king's own seal, which Ahasuerus had gladly lent to me. Such an order could not be ignored or disobeyed; Shethar had perforce sent me his daughter Barsine.

"Yes, he is very angry. You have made an enemy there, Vashti." Hegai seemed undisturbed by this.

"Prince Shethar was always my enemy." I knew that now. "The only difference is that now everyone knows it. And," I added, "Shethar knows his own scheming lost the queen's crown. Do you think that punishment enough?"

"Punishment enough," Hegai said, and we both smiled as Tandis and Barsine tossed each other a golden ball in the garden below.

BOOK SIX

One Night with the King

ESTHER

On the first day of Tishri, all the Shushan girls who had flung their names into the contest baskets were summoned to judgment. The vast square at the foot of the Great Staircase had been turned into a series of pavilions. The king's Immortals guarded the pavilions, and kept out of the square itself everyone save girls who had entered the contest and their guardians. Most of the girls were escorted by their mothers; I had Mordecai.

We waited an hour to reach the table where all our names had been set out on a list. Mordecai said my name, and the man in charge of the list ran his finger carefully down the names. "Esther," he said. "Esther, ward of Mordecai the king's scribe. Oh, yes." I thought he exchanged a swift glance with Mordecai, but it can be hard to discern subtleties through a veil. "You go into that pavilion, Esther—the blue and white one."

Just before I left him, Mordecai touched my shoulder. I stopped, waiting.

"Now remember, all is arranged." Mordecai sounded as if he tried to convince himself, rather than me. "You have only to smile and do as you are told, and you will be taken to the palace."

That is unfair! The other girls have no chance at all! But I knew the protest useless.

Silent, I walked into the pavilion as I had been bidden. The moment I was within, a woman lifted away my veil. To my intense relief, I faced only two eunuchs and a half-dozen handmaidens. I had been afraid all the girls would be judged at once—*As if we were yearling mares charging about a paddock.* I smiled at the thought, and the taller of the eunuchs suddenly looked at me with more interest.

"Well, this one may be worth looking at," he said.

Ah, he sees promise in me—but does not wish to pay too dearly! I had seen such cautious judging on the faces of many men who had come to my father's farm.

"Who is this maiden?" the tall eunuch asked. He was a beautiful creature, elegant of bone. Kohl lined his long dark eyes; ruddy gold ornaments and a robe of peacock silk enhanced the dark amber of his skin. A jeweled net confined his pitch-black hair; the myriad tiny gems seemed like stars scattered across the night sky. Unlike many eunuchs, he had not run to excess flesh, nor did he seem either indolent or careless.

The other consulted his list. "Esther, my lord."

At a sign from the eunuch who had asked my name, the handmaidens came forward and began stripping my garments from me. Although I had been warned this would be done, I burned with embarrassment. How could my cousin, my strict, pious cousin, a man who praised modesty as a woman's chief virtue—how could he have urged me on to this? *They are not men,* I reminded myself. *They are eunuchs. And the maids are women. I have nothing to blush for.*

"Why bother?" I heard one of the maids whisper to another, "this one's name is already written—"

I turned my head, and looked into the eyes of the handmaiden who silently listened to the first's unwary words. She smiled, and I saw her swiftly pinch the other, who ceased talking. *So, another who can see beyond the next turn of the sands.*

"What is your name?" I asked, and saw the girl glance sidelong at the tall eunuch, who lifted his hand—only a little, so that only one watching closely would see that he had moved at all.

"Kylah," said the clever handmaiden, and I repeated the name to myself. I would remember her, and the tall eunuch as well. Command rested upon his shoulders as easily as the elaborate robe he wore. He clearly was someone of greater importance than he wished to reveal. *Now, who—? Of course. Hegai. The Chief Eunuch of the Queen's Palace.*

The answer came easily, once I had asked myself the question. Who had a greater stake in the search for a new queen than the Chief Eunuch? And I had heard my cousin Mordecai speak of Hegai often enough. Hegai ruled the Queen's Palace; one of the chief officials of the imperial court, whose word could be countermanded only by the king—or the queen.

I was being judged by the Chief Eunuch himself; a sign of great favor—*and of the great price Mordecai paid to place me here, before Hegai's eyes.*

"Well, maiden," Hegai said, his voice gentle, soothing, "let me look upon you."

"Is there any need?" I asked, and Hegai suddenly regarded me with far more interest.

"Do you think so little of yourself?" Hegai continued to eye me keenly.

My skin burned under his gaze, but I kept my head high. "I think so truthfully of myself. My hair is a much-praised color. My skin is without blemish. My body is without flaw. You have eyes. You do not need me to tell you I am beautiful."

I said these words with neither pride nor arrogance. I stated facts, no more than that. I tried to stand placidly; it was hard to be serene, bared to so many eyes. A long-ago memory: *I swam naked in cold pure river water, and above me hawks wheeled in a turquoise sky—*

"You are very blunt. Are you so confident you will be chosen?" Hegai walked slowly around me, returned to gaze upon my face once more.

"I am already chosen, my place bought and paid for." I decided to risk my future on the truth. He knew it already. Why lie?

"And you think that settles the matter?"

"I think it a bargain sealed only if you form a good opinion of me, my lord." I did not say his name, as he had not offered it.

"Should I form a good opinion of a maiden with a clever mind and a strong will?"

"That depends," I said, and paused, waiting.

"Consider the question asked," he said at last, and I smiled at him.

"On what virtues you seek in the next Queen of Queens," I said.

He gazed upon me for long moments; I stood quiet, kept my breathing calm. *Do not think about the fact that you stand naked for him to judge you. Think only of what he needs, and what you can offer. Remember how your father dealt with those who wished to buy his horses, or to sell him theirs.* Then, shocked, I realized I sought Hegai's favor. *Why do I care? Do I wish to be queen, like all those other foolish girls?*

As I waited, the hot air heavy upon my skin, I looked boldly at Hegai's face. I did not expect his next question, which seemed almost random, as if honor demanded he ask me something.

"Do you wash your hair with henna?" He lifted a handful of my hair, rubbed his fingers over its strands.

"Is there a woman in all Shushan who does not?" I answered, and saw him smile.

"I know of two. You are one of them." He waited, but I did not ask who the other was, for she could only be Vashti, the queen infamous for her disobedience and famous for her ivory hair. After a few moments he released my hair; I let it fall and did not attempt to arrange the strands prettily.

Hegai regarded me steadily; I studied him in turn, seeking hints to his character. *He is clever, of course, and I think he may be kind. He is dark, but comely . . .* I smiled, and Hegai promptly said,

"The world holds many beautiful women. Do you truly think yourself worthy of being presented to the Lord of Half the World, the King of Kings?"

"Yes," I said instantly. I expected Hegai to order me out at once, but he did not.

"Why?" There was no emotion whatsoever in his voice.

Why? I had not expected so many questions, or such intense ones. I hesitated; Hegai waited unmoving, and the other eunuch and the six handmaidens in the pavilion seemed turned to statues. *Why was I beautiful enough—? No. No, not that. He said "worthy." That is what he wants to know—and he wants a real answer, not "because you took the rubies; because you are bought and I am paid for."* I could think of only one reason the Chief Eunuch would ask that.

Like my cousin Mordecai, Hegai, too, saw a crown when he looked upon me. Ice flowed through my veins as my dreams of once more living in freedom faded and reformed into the jeweled prison of the Queen's Palace. A cold weight pressed upon my brow, tightened about my temples. . . .

Terrified, I summoned all the most maddening gestures I had ever scorned in other girls. I tossed my head and shifted my weight so my body curved and twined a lock of my hair through my fingers. I slanted a flirtatious glance through my lashes at Hegai and forced my voice to become honey-sweet, my words coy. "Why, because I am so beautiful. That is what the king, may he live forever, seeks, is it not?" I laughed, the teasing ripple of sound I had often heard other maidens use when they sought to seem falsely modest.

Still Hegai watched me and said nothing.

"Even you called me lovely, and surely you would know!" I managed to giggle, and tossed my head again. "But I suppose you think me vain," I prompted, praying he would dismiss me.

"No, I think you a good judge of your face and figure. So few are." After a moment's silence, he said, "The bargain is sealed," he said—softly, so that only I could hear. To the waiting eunuch, Hegai announced, "This one goes to the palace. Put down the name of . . ."

So I had failed to win free and now must accept my fate with either grace and courage, or wailing and weeping. *I refuse to snivel,* I told myself, and felt the uncanny terror fade. I stood straight and spoke calmly. "Esther," I said, and saw amusement light Hegai's eyes. *Did you expect me to forget the name I have been forced to give you? Well, Hegai, you are no fool—but neither am I.*

"Write down the name Esther of Shushan," Hegai said. "Now, Esther, you may ask for three things to take with you to the palace. Anything you wish."

"Anything?"

"Anything in all the kingdom."

"Then I ask for a gown to cover myself, and Kylah for my handmaiden." *I wonder what most of the chosen maidens demand?*

"And the third thing you ask to take with you to the palace?"

"Your friendship." *Ah, that took the bland composure from your face, Hegai!* "You said 'anything in the kingdom,'" I added.

"If those are the three things you ask for, those are what you shall receive." Hegai made no sign that I could see, yet Kylah moved toward me and bowed.

"Come with me, mistress." Kylah led me out of the large pavilion through a tunnel of crimson cloth into a shadowed, smaller tent. There I stood and waited as she opened a long chest and lifted out garments. "What will you have, mistress?" she asked, and I smiled; I knew this game.

"You choose what I should wear now." *That will show Kylah that I trust her judgment—and that I am not fool enough to think I know what is proper in the palace simply because I now compete for the queen's crown.*

I thought I saw her smile; we both openly studied each other, judging the value of our new alliance. "Do not be too trusting, mistress."

"Hegai gave you to me," I said, "and it is to your advantage that my garments make me pleasing to the eye. Once you've chosen your horse, it is best to stay on its back until the race ends."

Kylah stared at me, apparently baffled by such plain words. Then she laughed, softly, and began the task of garbing me for my short journey to the palace. She chose well: a green silk gown heavy as cream, a long vest of cloth-of-silver sewn with silver pomegranates. She combed my hair into a neatness I never quite achieved myself. Against the cloth-of-silver, my hair burned like dark fire.

"Very nice," I said, and Kylah smiled.

"Thank you, my lady Esther." Not for her the vainly humble protest; clearly Kylah knew her own talents. I noted, too, that I had become "my lady Esther" rather than "mistress."

Yes, I thought she and I would work well together.

I was carried to the palace in a gilded litter, hidden behind curtains of blue-and-white-striped silk. I had hoped to watch as I was carried up the Great Staircase to the King's Gate, but that was not permitted.

"You are the king's now," Kylah told me. My new-won handmaiden sat curled at the other end of the litter, looking pleased with herself. "No man may set eyes upon you, save the king."

"Is that why he summoned Queen Vashti to come before him at a men's banquet?" I asked, and heard a small gasp.

"No one—" Kylah began, and I smiled.

"No one will say what everyone knows? Why not?"

"Because it is not—safe. You are going where you may trust very few, and it is never wise to speak too freely."

"But you are my handmaiden, Kylah. May I not trust you?" I saw she knew there was no good answer to this.

"I will not willingly betray you," she said, "but how can you know I am speaking truth to you?"

"If you are not, and I cannot trust you," I said, "I would rather know it at first—than at last."

For long moments Kylah stared at me. Then she smiled. "I am glad you asked for me as your handmaiden, O Star of Wisdom. Truly, you are worthy to be queen."

"Perhaps I am. But truly—I would rather I were thought worthy to decide my own future."

Even clever Kylah did not know what to say in answer to that. Neither of us said another word, but our silence lay peacefully between us. We waited as we were carried up and up, the bearers climbing the long flights of the Great Staircase steadily, smoothly, so that the litter only rocked gently from time to time until we reached the top, and the palace of the King of Kings.

I knew when we passed between the huge winged bulls that guarded the entrance to the palace, for I heard a man ask what business this litter had within the courts of the King of Kings, and the reply of the eunuch who escorted me. "These curtains veil a gem for the king's delight." The eunuch sounded rather smug, as if my beauty were somehow his achievement.

"Enter, and may Ahura Mazda smile upon what you bring to the king." The guard's words were solemn, measured; as the litter moved forward my keen ears overheard the man mutter, "Another—how long until . . ."

Then the gate and guard were behind me, and I considered his exasperated comment. *"Another—how long until . . ." How long until this contest ends? How long until the king chooses the new queen? Yes, that fits. If the king truly is to judge among as many maidens as he rules provinces, it could take months.*

And just how was the king to make his choice? Would we all stand in a line, and he walk along, gazing upon us? Would he sit in state as we all paraded before his throne? Would he call for us one by one, night after night, until he at last found a woman who made his heart happy?

"My lady?" Kylah's soft voice interrupted my consideration of the logistics of this grand scheme. "We are within the Women's Palace now."

Now it begins—no, it began when I let my name fall into the basket. I chose my horse; now I must ride it.

I stepped out into my new world.

The palace was a maze; a labyrinth of gardens and dwellings; columned halls and bright balconies. Pillars of sardonyx, pillars of marble in every color of earth and sky. Statues of winged beasts with men's faces. Ceilings set with silver and gold stars mapping the heavens. Walls inlaid with turquoise and ivory, mother-of-pearl and malachite. Later I learned the palace held darkness, too, but at first all seemed brilliance and light. Some never saw past the veil of bright illusion to the shadows beyond.

I was shown into rooms so luxurious that for a moment I thought I had been given the queen's apartments by mistake. A bed wide enough for three people; silver tables; bright silk rugs blossoming beneath my feet. I went to a tall narrow window; I looked out and could see rooftops, and sky.

Later, I learned that Hegai had given me rooms far beyond anything I was entitled to as one of the candidates for queen. But that first day, I knew only that I now played an exhilarating game. I turned away from the window and went to stretch out upon the wide bed. I ran my hand over the embroidered rug covering the bed. My fingers touched hard beads; when I looked, I saw that the covering was stitched with pearls.

Pearls were all very well, but I hoped I would be permitted books. I could not read pearls. And all I had to do—all I could do—was wait.

Wait until the moment I would learn if I pleased the king.

HEGAI

I knew she was the new queen the moment she smiled. She walked calmly into the pavilion and stood quietly as the maids removed her garments. She blushed, but neither protested nor flaunted herself. She was beautiful, of course, but I barely noticed her body, for when she smiled light seemed to halo her, its radiance brilliant as winter stars.

After considering the matter, examining her words and reactions, I knew what had so impressed me—and it was not her astonishing beauty. No, it was her calm assessment of her own worth. She knew she was beautiful, and she knew, too, that she could not take credit for her perfection of face and form.

Light—she must be sent by the Good God, a light to triumph over darkness.

The examination was a formality only, for even had her place in the contest not already been bought, Esther would have been chosen as Shushan's candidate. She was beautiful as a goddess is beautiful, a perfect balance of the carnal and the pure. I sought a word to describe her . . .

. . . and at last, to my surprise, I settled upon "judgment."

VASHTI

"My lady Vashti?" Hegai interrupted me as I was trailing a peacock feather in the fountain pond, enticing the golden fish to dart at the brilliant blue-green lure. At Hegai's words, I paused and turned my head.

"Yes, Hegai?"

"I do not wish to interrupt my lady's pleasures . . ."

I laughed. "You are the most dreadful liar, Hegai; you interrupt my pleasures any time you deem fit. And as you see, I am engaged in the most important matter of my day." I laid the peacock feather on the fountain's rim. "Tell me you require me to do something more interesting than teasing fish!"

"I do, my lady. The harem gate has closed behind the last of the king's maidens. The girl from Shushan."

I jumped to my feet. "They're all here? At last? Well, we had best go inspect them. Come on."

Hegai caught my arm. "Wait. I will send word and have them all—"

"Overdressed and overpainted and overawed because they know the Chief Eunuch and Vashti the Wicked come to judge them? No, let's go see them as they are. Where are they?"

"They all walk in the Garden of Roses. That and the queen's banquet hall are the only places in the Women's Palace that will hold all of them at one time."

"Then you and I shall go up to the balcony that looks upon that garden and watch them all. One hundred and twenty-six maidens!" Of course there were several hundred inhabitants of the Women's Palace, but most of them were slaves and servants. Only a hundred concubines dwelt there, and they had not all arrived in one large group.

Time had pressed hard. Beautiful maidens to parade before the king meant servants to tend upon them: handmaidens, yes, at least three for each girl. And that was not all, for I discovered the Women's Palace would need more cooks, more bath slaves, more, in fact, of every kind of servant that kept the palace in order and its inhabitants happy.

Once we set the search in motion, it had taken surprisingly few months to select the maidens and transport them to the great palace of Shushan. Obstacles I thought nearly insurmountable had been tossed aside like chaff by everyone from governors of provinces to slave girls in the kitchen.

Oddly, this mass offering of helpfulness did not depend upon a city, or a family, having a girl fit to send for the king's choice. The contest had kindled the empire's imagination. Everyone wished, even in some small way, to be a part of so grand a scheme.

And now, at last, it was time to look upon the prizes we would set before the king—and see the next queen.

I rarely concealed my hair, but before Hegai and I went to the Garden of Roses, I chose a dark veil and arranged it so that my hair was hidden. I could not learn anything useful about the girls if they knew who I was. Hegai and I had spent long hours talking over what qualities the next queen should have. The ability to flatter the influential was not among them.

I do not know why, out of all the girls gathered in the Garden of Roses, it was the maiden Esther who caught my eye. She was not the most vivid, nor the most vivacious. There was no maiden here who was anything less than exquisite. Perhaps the color of her hair set her apart—the color of banked coals; fire in darkness, slow burning under the warm sun.

Then I realized her pride drew my eyes to her. The amber-eyed girl carried herself like a warrior. . . .

For a breath I wondered why I thought of her as a warrior, rather than a queen. Then I decided it didn't matter.

"Ah, you, too, see the future in her." Hegai leaned forward, his shoulder brushing mine. "That one holds much promise, my lady princess."

"You like her." I turned to look at Hegai. "Tell me."

"You tell me," he said, and I studied the girl with the dark-fire hair, seeking Hegai's answer.

She spoke to her rivals as if they were her friends. She took the time to smile at the servants, and to seem to ask, rather than command. Although a stranger to the palace, she seemed at ease, without seeming foolishly overconfident.

And she troubled herself to come over to me, and to speak to me. She must have thought I, too, had been brought here to compete for the queen's crown; that I was only another girl like herself, hopeful and uncertain of the future.

She walked up to me, her movement graceful and deliberate; she glanced at Hegai before smiling at me. "Welcome to our garden. You see how we are treated here—all of us pampered like queens."

Dark hair, tranquil voice, clever eyes. Totally unlike me; good. The last thing a man with a guilt-ridden heart needed was a new bride who resembled the one he had cast aside.

"I am glad to hear that," I said. "And I am glad you chose to come here."

She gazed back at me, her amber eyes cool as river water. "I was chosen to come here; I did not choose to come."

"How often in her life does a woman truly have the power to choose? What is your name?"

For less the time it takes to draw in breath, she hesitated. No one not palace-born and bred would have noticed. I did. Whatever the girl was about to say would be a lie.

"Esther. Esther of Shushan." Her gaze flickered to the left as she spoke. Esther was not her true name, then. The question I must answer now was whether the lie mattered.

"And tell me, Esther of Shushan, how you were chosen to grace the king's harem? It is not an easy thing, to get a maiden's name upon the Queen's List."

For a long moment she gazed into my eyes. Then she shrugged, a movement supple as a dancer's. "Rubies. My place upon the Queen's List was bought with a dozen rubies, each as large as a dove's heart and red as that heart's blood. How do you think most girls had their names inscribed upon that list? For their golden hair?"

"Apparently," I said, "it was for their golden coins."

Startled, she stared at me again, and then laughed. "You speak truth. Who are you? My guardian—he who paid to have me brought here for the chance to wear the queen's crown—ordered me to make friends of everyone. So tell me your name, and I will be your friend if you will be mine."

Laughter danced beneath her solemn words; gleamed in her eyes like sun-spangles upon water. I smiled, and pushed back the veil hiding my hair.

"My name is Vashti, and until I refused to obey my husband's command, I wore the crown King Ahasuerus will offer to one of those upon the Queen's List. Do you still wish to be my friend—Esther?"

She looked at Hegai again, then glanced down, veiling her clever eyes with her thick lashes. "You are still here, Queen Vashti. That tells me much."

Yes, clever as well as pretty. Now to test her courage. "And if I say I shall have you taken from this court and set outside the palace gate? That you shall be sent home to your father untouched by the king?"

She raised her head, lifted her chin. "I have no father," she said.

"That is not what I asked."

"No, it is not. But what you asked needs no answer, for you will not do it, even if you have the power to command it." Clear amber eyes gazed into mine. "For I think the next queen will be chosen by you."

"And why do you say that, you whose name is not truly Esther?" I noted that she did not ask how I knew that. "How were you called by your mother?"

"My mother died bearing me. My father called me Hadassah. But—"

"But your guardian thought it too Jewish a name, and so now you are called star, for your bright eyes. Oh, don't look so surprised—Mordecai is one of the palace's chief scribes. Do you think a queen does not know all that passes within palace walls?" Even if she were too foolish to pay much attention to the knowledge that flowed past her, as I had once been.

"I think—too much, I am now told." Her voice held bitterness; clearly once her learning had been prized and now was scorned.

"Shall we then call you Hadassah?" I asked, hoping to please her. Already I liked seeing her smile; I soon learned most people wished to enjoy Esther's smiles.

She shook her head. "No. My guardian commanded me to forget that name, and of course I must obey him. Esther will do." Then she answered a question I had almost forgotten I had asked as we talked of her names.

"As for why I say you will choose the next queen—well, that is a guess. But why else should you come among all of us who vie for the crown, asking questions and judging our quality? And who else knows so well as you what will please the king?" She paused, added, "So I will tell you at once that I have unmaidenly talents. I can read Sumerian and Aramaic. I was raised on a horse farm in the Karoun Valley and could ride better than any man who worked for my father, and I can keep accounts as well as any clerk. I can play the harp and write poems in the style of Hiralal of Hind. I can also weave and bake, although I do neither well."

I stared at her, then laughed. "Well, those are far more than I have. I can—" Suddenly I stopped, for I could not think of one talent I could claim. *I can sit and look beautiful. I can display my ivory hair.* That was all I had; hot blood burned my cheeks.

I thought I saw understanding and compassion in Esther's eyes. Perhaps that is why I heard myself saying, "I cannot do anything, Esther. I can't do anything at all."

ESTHER

I never expected to feel sorry for Queen Vashti—but as I heard her confess herself ignorant of any useful—or even useless—skill, I found myself longing to put my arms around her and comfort her. I did not quite dare, so I tried to make her smile.

"Perhaps you are wiser than I, then. It might be better if I could not do anything at all."

"But you can read Sumerian and Aramaic and—"

"And who," I asked, "will wish to wed a maiden who can read Sumerian and Aramaic, and write poems in the style of Hind?"

To my surprise—although why I should be surprised at anything a woman who had refused a king's command might say, I do not know—Vashti spoke words I remembered always.

"A man who cares more for the woman within, whom he alone may know, than for the beauty that belongs to any who lays eyes upon it."

"And does such a man breathe upon this earth?" I asked.

"I do not know. I hope; even I am allowed hope." Then the brooding look vanished. "I am sorry, Esther—I have no wish to distress you. This is your home now; be welcome here. And since you are clever, will you please tell me if there is anything that should be provided to make the maidens happy as they wait for their chance with the king?"

The question astonished me. That one who had been a queen since she was ten years old should think of the happiness of girls who were not only strangers to her, but who vied for the man who had been her husband, told more about her than a thousand songs of fulsome praise.

"You say you have no skills, no talents," I said. "But you are wrong, for you have one great talent. You are kind, Vashti."

"Is kindness a talent?"

"Yes, it is."

Vashti smiled. It was true that she was beautiful, as any exotic creature is beautiful. But it was not a comfortable sort of beauty; her eyes and her famed pearl-pale hair insisted on attention. It was impossible to imagine Vashti as anything but the ornament of a palace. But her smile made her seem somehow less perfect, more—loveable.

As I smiled back, I wondered if all her life Vashti had been bound with chains woven by her long ivory hair. Perhaps, someday, I might ask her, and she might tell me.

"Hegai—the Chief Eunuch—speaks well of you," Vashti said. "And now I understand why. You are not only beautiful, but wise and good."

"My lady princess, you cannot possibly know anything of me yet but that I am indeed beautiful. Every word I have spoken to you thus far may be a lie. I have my own future to consider, you know."

Vashti laughed—I don't know why she thought my words amusing, for I had spoken only truth. I could easily mislead her; she knew nothing of me or my nature.

"And you have a clever wit, too!" Vashti slanted a glance back at the Chief Eunuch Hegai, who had retreated to the shadows of the colonnaded walkway that led to the Garden of Roses. The Chief Eunuch smiled at her and came forward again into the sunlight.

"Has my lady princess satisfied her curiosity?" Hegai spoke lightly, as if of a minor matter.

Vashti tilted her head, as if thinking deeply upon his words. "Yes, I have. As always, your advice has proven sound."

Perhaps she thought her words innocuous enough, but I knew better. Already it was clear to me that both the Chief Eunuch and the deposed queen had looked upon me and found me good. *They think to make me queen.* I tried to feel some emotion at the thought, and could not. Just as well, for what Vashti and Hegai believed they desired might change with the next wind that blew. I knew nothing of either of them, after all, save what I had gleaned from common gossip.

They think to make me queen—at this moment.

"You think deep thoughts, Esther." Hegai's voice reined my attention back; I gained a moment by bowing.

"I think only that it is wonderful that so great a lady as Princess Vashti, and so highly placed an official as the Chief Eunuch, should spend so much time upon so humble a maiden as Esther of Shushan," I said, and was rewarded by hearing both Vashti and Hegai laugh.

I watched the two of them walk out of the Garden of Roses. Vashti curled her arm through Hegai's and he bent his head, speaking words to her that I was too far away to hear. As soon as they vanished into the palace, a flock of the other girls hastened up to me.

"That was Queen Vashti!" one of them said, breathless with delighted shock.

"And the Chief Eunuch," added another. "What—"

What did they want of you? The question was asked in a dozen different ways by a dozen different girls. They all stared at me, expecting some outrageous answer—or rather, hoping. I considered carefully before I answered.

"I do not think they wanted anything of me that they may not also want of you. Did not Princess Vashti, the King's Sister—" I laid stress on Vashti's proper title now, "—speak with many of you before me? And have not you all spoken with the Chief Eunuch, who has us in his care now?"

I gave them time to think this over and to murmur assents before I added, "My sisters, they wanted to look upon the next queen. For she stands here now, in this garden. And only the King of Kings himself will know who she is."

The most surprising thing to me was the queen's innocence—yes, and the king's, too, when at last I met him. They reminded me of Egyptian kittens, pampered and petted and fed upon cream and fresh-caught fish. Never had they had a hand raised against them, never had they known a moment's pain.

Now I understood why Hegai gave me such extravagantly fine rooms; my apartments lay very close to the garden between the Women's Palace and the Queen's Palace. I could easily come and go between the two palaces to visit Vashti and play with her many pets, and obey her pleas for endless stories of my life both on my father's farm and in my cousin's house here in Shushan. I had always thought my life rather dull, especially under Mordecai's care—but in Vashti's eyes, I had lived great adventures. Odd, to think that one who had been Queen of Queens envied me.

Hegai also assigned to me seven handmaidens who tended me alone. None of my servants attended upon any of the other girls. I set Kylah over the others, making her chief among my female servants. For my household also included half a dozen eunuchs, and they were ruled only by their own kind.

I studied my eunuchs, judging their character and abilities, before I chose one named Hatach to hold pride of place as chief. I also, of course, consulted with Hegai before making such a decision.

"And why do you wish to set Hatach over your eunuchs, Esther?" Hegai asked. "He is not the oldest, nor is he bold, and he perhaps worries overmuch about trivialities."

"The oldest is fat and self-satisfied, and wishes only to live out his days in comfort. The others are all too young. And Hatach may not be a lion for courage, but I do not need a warrior. And the position of head eunuch will keep him too busy to worry over any trivialities but those that affect my household."

Hegai smiled. "Very well, if it is your desire that Hatach be chief over your eunuchs, let it be so."

"I know very well it is your desire," I told him, "or Hatach would not be in my household at all. None of the others is at all suitable for the post and both of us know it."

"Star of the Palace, do you never tire of speaking blunt truth that is much better veiled in tactful hints?"

"Chief Eunuch, if you did not find me amusing, I would not have the chance to speak to you at all, truthfully or no." I bowed. "I thank you for your approval of my choice of Hatach. He really is very sweet, you know."

Hegai merely shook his head and gave me leave to go. But as I walked away from his room, I heard him laugh, and I smiled.

Life as one of the Chosen Maidens passed dreamlike; each day brought the same rituals as we were prepared to meet the King of Kings. No maiden here was less than beautiful. Now the eunuchs and handmaidens strove to make us perfect. We spent long hours in the bathhouse, where our skin was scrubbed with sea salt. When at last they stopped, we slid into the vast pool, savoring the water soft against our bodies. Still more servants helped us out again, and handed us into the care of women whose task it was to smooth oil of myrrh into our tingling skin.

Three women attended me. Two massaged rose-scented oil over my body, while the third combed out my wet hair and spread it over a rack created from Indian sandalwood. If nothing else, I would be sweet-smelling when I at last met the king.

Beauty treatments seemed to be the only preparation we were to receive. After all, what else could a man possibly desire of a woman except beauty?

⁜

If Hegai and Vashti had their way, I would be Queen of Queens, just as Mordecai's dream had foretold. Of course, they might change their minds—but I sealed my fate in Vashti's mind the day one of her pets wandered out of the gate to the Queen's Palace and, timid and confused, slunk into the Garden of Roses. I was inhaling the spice-rich fragrance of some newly opened roses when screams from the other girls startled me so much I stabbed my fingers on the rose's thorns. I turned as girls ran past, jostling me—I do not think they even noticed I stood there. Across the garden half a dozen others clung to each other, shrieking for help. I looked around for the cause of so much distress, and spotted a gray shadow crouched beneath a lilac bush.

One of Vashti's wolves had wandered into our garden and now pressed shaking against the ground, terrified by the girls' screams. I walked slowly forward, wishing I had some food to tempt the beast with. I heard one of the girls call out to me, urging me to run.

"Be silent," I said, "you're frightening him." I had reached the lilac; I crouched down and held out my hand. "Come, Vayu," I crooned, "come, you know me. Come to me and be safe."

Fortunately the girls had obeyed me, and now clustered silent as I continued to coax Vayu. Now that there was no shrieking, the wolf hesitantly sniffed at my fingers, but just as he seemed about to crawl forward to me, the clamor began anew as a dozen eunuchs armed with ironbound canes ran into the garden. Vayu withdrew, trembling harder than before. I stood up and rounded upon the eunuchs.

"Stop that noise at once, and stop making such great fools of yourselves. You all know perfectly well that this is no demon and no wild beast, but one of Princess Vashti's cherished pets. If any harm comes to him, you all will be . . ." I didn't know precisely what fate would be meted out in such a case, so I settled for ". . . punished severely. Now all of you please *go away* and stop frightening the poor creature."

To my great relief, they did as I had commanded. Silently thanking the Lord for His aid, I finally succeeded in coaxing Vayu to me and slipped my veil through his collar for a makeshift leash. I led the wolf back to the Queen's Palace, where he lunged out of my grasp and ran into her gardens as soon as he saw the open gate.

Vashti's gratitude was touching, if overwrought. "Oh, Esther, *thank you,* thank you a thousand times! Tell me what you desire of me and you shall have it, whatsoever you ask for, it is yours. Oh, I was right, you are meant to be queen—"

"What, because I managed to catch a frightened animal?" I reached up and unclasped Vashti's arms from around my neck. "Calm yourself, Vashti, your pet is unharmed."

"Yes, and but for you he would have been *killed.* Everyone hates wolves, you know that. They would have been glad to kill him."

"Nonsense," I said firmly. In fact, Vashti was right, for Persians believe wolves are creatures ruled by the Dark, and even if they are not, no man with herds or flocks is very fond of the beasts.

Vashti shook her head. "You saved Vayu, Esther, and we both know it. If ever I can repay you, you have only to ask."

"I will." Even if I did not become queen, someday it might prove useful to be owed a favor by the king's most beloved sister. Who knew what the future would bring?

Although I heard much about her, I did not set eyes on Queen Mother Amestris until I had already lived in the palace for a month. One morning, Hatach came rushing in to my bedchamber, and told me I must come at once to the baths—

"For the Queen Mother wishes to look upon you today—you and all the other girls who have arrived for the king—and you must be bathed and perfumed with myrrh, and—"

Hatach seemed so anxious that I meekly followed him to the baths, and let him garb and jewel me as pleased him. I thought myself overdressed and overjeweled, but perhaps that was not, that day, a bad thing.

At noon, I and the other girls followed the Chief Eunuch Hegai, who led us through two small gardens and a long corridor that opened into a courtyard large enough to hold all 126 of us. At the far end of the courtyard a tiny, elegant woman sat upon a tall chair. The Queen Mother.

Hegai bowed. "The king's maidens, O queen."

We all bowed; I studied Queen Mother Amestris through my lashes.

Beautiful still, but growing old; ambitious still, but growing weary. I had seen that same look of stubborn pride and refusal to yield to time in the eyes of our herd's aging lead mare . . . Swiftly, I summoned my mind back from the past. I must watch Amestris carefully, for she still held great power.

For long minutes, we all stood waiting, and Amestris studied us without speaking. "Very pretty," she said at last, and I heard the girl to my left stifle a sob. I lifted my chin, and smiled. Each girl here was beautiful as a pagan goddess, and the Queen Mother, not being blind, knew that full well.

"Very pretty" indeed! Now I know what to think of you, Queen Mother Amestris. If you ever seem to offer kindness, I'll know it for a lie.

My wry smile drew the Queen Mother's attention to me. Silent, she stared at me. I looked back steadily. For an instant, she seemed almost to smile back. Then she lifted her hand again.

"Very well, Hegai. Take the girls away."

And that was all. After all the hours of bathing and grooming, that was all. A steady glance, and dismissal.

Well, it could have been worse. But I could not convince the other girls of that. Some of them wept for hours, convinced they would be sent home without ever seeing the king, since his mother had not smiled upon them. I knew better. Vashti and Hegai, not Amestris, ruled this race. But I did not make the mistake of discounting the Queen Mother's power. Amestris would challenge them, if she found a candidate to her own liking.

So I suppose I had better hope she likes me—at least better than she likes any of the others.

HEGAI

Of course Esther delighted the eye—she was one of the most beautiful women in the empire, after all; beauty worth a queen's ransom in rubies—but her wit and grace gave that beauty life. Any woman might possess beauty of face and form. Without a lovely mind and spirit to inhabit that body—

Only look upon Tandis and Barsine to see the outcome of that! No, that is not fair or just. Barsine is brainless as a butterfly, but she is sweet-tempered and biddable. . . .

"Hegai?" Vashti tugged the ribbons braided through my hair. "Stop *thinking*, Hegai! We are here to choose a perfume for Esther—"

"Which is hardly so earthshaking a task that it requires a dozen people to accomplish it," Esther said. "If the Chief Eunuch has other duties, surely Hatach can help me select a scent."

Appalled by Esther's lighthearted words, Hatach began hastily to explain that surely she hadn't meant any such thing. "Your perfume is of the *utmost* importance, my lady Esther! And while it is true I have some small knowledge of fragrances, the Chief Eunuch"—here Hatach bowed to me—"is a master of the art, and even were he not, it is his privilege to supervise all that passes in the Women's Palace, most particularly when it concerns the maidens awaiting their night with the King of Kings, Lord of Half the World, Lord over the Medes and the Persians and—"

Esther reached out to clasp Hatach's hands to stop the flow of titles. "Peace, Hatach. I will do just as seems best to you. Please don't fret so." She then looked rather severely at Vashti and added, "I know it is a very *serious* task to prepare me to meet the king, Hatach, and I am deeply grateful for your efforts on my behalf."

Vashti stopped laughing—or at least, she pressed her face against my shoulder. I could feel her body shudder with hidden mirth.

"My thanks, for I know that *you*, my most gracious lady Esther, truly appreciate the labor involved in my task." Hatach would have expanded upon this, but I thought it time to intervene.

"Very true," I said. "Now, Hatach, what have you to show us?" For all his fretting and fussing, Hatach did indeed have a keen sense of what would suit his charge.

Hatach waved his hand over the vials awaiting our judgment. "I have selected half a dozen from the perfumers' stock, and compounded another half a dozen myself."

The glass vials glittered in the sunlight; Esther regarded them speculatively. "I am not accustomed to wearing perfume, so I depend on you to guide my choice. Although I do like the scent Princess Vashti favors."

"Oh, no, no, no." Hatach shook his head. "No, my lady Esther, that would not do for you at all." He looked to me for confirmation of this, and I inclined my head, striving not to laugh myself. Beside me, Vashti, too, trembled on the brink of laughter; I squeezed her hand admonishingly.

Esther managed to look completely serene. "No? Well, what then do you advise?" And then, because she always found joy in knowledge, she asked, "And why will Princess Vashti's perfume not do for me?"

"Among the reasons are these," Hatach began. "Princess Vashti's perfume is composed primarily of amber, and amber is a warm scent, which would not suit you. And also—" He paused, and I knew he had realized that to tell the chief reason would be excessively tactless. Rather than let him flounder in a morass of explanation, I took over the task.

"In addition," I said, "it is important that your fragrance be *yours,* and not—"

"My predecessor's," Esther finished, her voice flat. "Yes, I understand that is most important."

Vashti reached out and grasped Esther's hand. "Truly, Hegai and Hatach know best what will suit you—"

"—and please the king?" Esther's eyes glittered; I saw she was on the verge of tears. I caught Hatach's eye and subtly indicated first Esther and then the waiting perfumes. Hatach promptly moved over to the table and beckoned to Esther.

"Come, my lady Esther—come see if any of my efforts are pleasing to you." Hatach seemed to study the vials, then picked up one shaped like a teardrop. "Will you not at least take one breath of the perfume?" He managed to sound both coaxing and mournful. Esther closed her eyes for a moment; when she opened them again, she smiled and, still holding Vashti's hand, walked over to Hatach.

"Of course I will, Hatach." Esther's voice was steady, her face calm. "Now, show me your fragrant magic."

She has control over herself. She is kind and she is clever in both deed and word. We have chosen well, Vashti and I. I watched as Esther and Vashti awaited Hatach's revelations.

Clearly delighted with his audience, Hatach lifted the stopper from the iridescent teardrop-shaped vial. "O Star of Women, this perfume is like you—"

"High-smelling?" Esther interrupted, and Vashti put a hand up to her mouth, pressing back laughter.

Frowning, Hatach began again. "O most beautiful of women—"

"O most flattering of eunuchs, I am no such thing."

"You *are!*" Hatach stamped his foot to emphasize his words. "Of course you are. Who is a better judge of that, you or I?"

I thought it time to intervene before Hatach persuaded himself to throw a tantrum. "Or I?" I said, and they all looked at me: Hatach sulky, Esther amused, and Vashti falsely solemn. "Hatach, don't let the women tease you. And you, Esther, remember you were chosen as the most beautiful woman in Shushan."

"You see?" Hatach told Esther. "Why deny what is plain to all our eyes?"

"Very well, I will not deny that I was chosen as the most beautiful woman in Shushan—" Esther slanted a glance at me and added, "—or at least as beautiful as rubies. But Hatach, you cannot say I am the most beautiful of *all* women, for you have not seen all the women in the world."

"But Esther, of course he can say that. In fact, he just did." Pleased with this devastating logic, Vashti linked her arm in mine. I saw Esther prepare to respond, so I firmly steered the conversation back to the original point at issue.

"The perfume?" I said.

Hatach held out the vial to Esther. She took it and held it under her nose—and promptly handed it back.

"If I am like that perfume, my hopes of becoming queen are doomed," Esther said, adding, when Vashti raised her eyebrows in silent question, "Too much musk."

"Of course you are right, that one *is* quite hopeless," Hatach promptly agreed. "Try this instead."

Again Esther refused to try the perfume on her skin once she inhaled its aroma. "Too sweet. You of all people, Hatach, should know that I am not sweet."

"You are," Hatach said firmly. "You are sweet as spring honey. And truly, that scent is far too simple to suit you." Hatach studied the vials and at last selected one of pale green glass. "This one. This one is perfect. The most wise and beauteous Queen of Sheba herself might have worn such a fragrance."

"I know that one, and I think you're right." I remembered Vashti trying that perfume. A subtle mixture of sandalwood and spikenard, cedar and clove and frankincense, it had proved far too lush to suit Vashti at all. No, my darling Vashti remained faithful to the scent I myself had crafted for her; even now the warm bite of amber drifted in the air about her.

Pleased by my agreement, Hatach cradled the green glass vial in his hand. "Yes, this one might have been compounded for you alone. Like you, it is complex, sophisticated, elegant."

"Oh, no," said Esther, glancing down demurely. "I'm only a simple country girl."

"Esther," said Vashti, "I don't know how you can utter such an outrageous untruth without bursting out laughing! Do you, Hegai?"

Ignoring both girls, I nodded to Hatach, who told Esther to stand still. Outwardly meek, Esther obeyed; Hatach stroked the perfume over her throat and wrists. "Now wait," he told her. "Let the perfume decide."

Esther smiled at him. "I will, and I promise to say nothing witty about it."

"Good. It is utterly unnecessary for a woman to be witty *all the time*." Hatach regarded her sternly; obedient, Esther waited until Hatach nodded. Then she lifted her hand, breathed in the fragrance, and smiled. "Sandalwood," she said, "and . . . cedar?"

Hatach nodded, and I smiled, too. "Yes, and spikenard, frankincense, and clove—and other essences as well."

"And," said Hatach, "they all combine to create the scent of Esther."

He had done well, and was so pleased with himself and his charge, that I decided to let him have the final word on the subject. Everyone with eyes can see the result of their labors, but palace eunuchs themselves get little enough praise for all their hard work.

ESTHER

Time flowed, a slow yet steady river. Each day the same rituals, each night the same quiet determination and despair.

I remember that time as if it were all one endless day and night. Only a few hours spring into bright focus, when I look back upon my waiting time.

One was the moment I realized that Hegai loved Vashti. Not as a brother loves a younger sister, or a eunuch cherishes a valued concubine in his charge—but as a man loves a woman.

I saw how his eyes followed Vashti, how when he touched her, his fingertips lingered on her skin or her hair. . . .

And I saw that Vashti accepted Hegai and his eternal perfect care of her without question, and without noticing his deep and abiding love. Oh, she was never unkind, and she clearly held him in great affection. But mere fondness was not what Hegai longed for from her. Fondness, I knew, was not what he dreamed of in the dark.

Another was the day I saw how clever Vashti really was—how fine her mind would have been, had she ever been encouraged to use it. I already knew that Vashti was determined that she—and Hegai—would set the rules and control all that was done in this bizarre quest for a new Queen of Queens. She begrudged all attempts by Queen Mother Amestris to advise her to favor one candidate over another.

So Vashti set out to ensure that the very mention of the contest wearied the Queen Mother. The nobly-born ladies Tandis and Barsine had been given Vashti's twin handmaids Ajashea and Bolour as their servants. And the four girls, quick and clever as mongooses, were given the task of carrying messages to the Queen Mother. Lengthy messages requiring an equally lengthy answer. Frivolous queries—should Vashti give all the candidates new names? Should she require they all dress alike when they went to the king?

Messages a dozen times a day, until Amestris at last told her servants not to admit Vashti's couriers.

The morning they were turned away at the Queen Mother's gate, Tandis and Ajashea dashed back giggling so hard Hegai reproved them for unseemly behavior, while Vashti and I laughed. In that laughing moment, I saw that Vashti had skillfully created a brace of spies—the four girls were all nearly the same age, and most people could not tell whether two girls running to do Vashti's bidding were Tandis and Ajashea or Barsine and Bolour. By now, no one questioned the four girls' right to be anywhere in the women's palaces.

But the memory that shines brightest was the golden afternoon I roamed alone through the Queen's Palace, and came upon a living reminder of long-vanished glory.

I walked slowly through the bars of light and shadow until I came to a gate. The gate seemed ancient, the planks that formed it worn smooth, as if it were older than the palace itself. Gold traced images upon the time-darkened wood; djinn dancing in flames. For a moment I hesitated, then put my hand to the latch. *It will be locked,* I told myself, but when I lifted the bar, it rose lightly, easily, and the gate swung open when I pushed upon its polished and gilded wood.

I stepped through the gate into a small garden. Walls covered in tiles blue as the sky above me rose high, twice as high as my head. The small rich roses of Damascus spilled over marble pots, perfumed the warm air.

The garden was very quiet, and at first I thought I was alone within it. Then I saw the old man.

At first I could not imagine what man would dare enter here, into a private garden within the walls of the women's world. Then he looked at me, and as I gazed into his serene blue eyes I knew who he must be.

Daniel, called the Dream-Master. Daniel, who had given peace to madness-ravaged Nebuchadnezzar. Daniel, who had vainly warned worthless Belshazzar. Only so great and so old a man would be permitted to wander where he pleased in the Queen's Palace.

"Dream-Master," I said, and bowed before him.

"Oh, dear," Daniel said. "Not another one." And as I stared at him, puzzled, he smiled. Dreams did not cloud his eyes; they were bright as the sun-gilded sky far above us. "You are as bad as the Beautiful One, O Star of Shushan. Neither of you satisfied with mere rank and riches."

"You know who I am."

"Of course. And not"—he lifted a minatory hand—"*not* because I can read dreams. Everyone in the palace knows precisely who the girls who battle for a crown are. There is no privacy in a palace; remember that."

"I will. May I ask—"

"Oh, sit. You are so full of life it tires me to watch you trying to stand still. Yes, you may ask."

I sat at his feet; it seemed only proper. "Can you see my future, Dream-Master?"

"Yes. Your future here will be harder for you than for the others."

"Why should it be? I am as beautiful as they, and more learned."

"Because," Daniel said, "you are a Jew."

And then, as I stared, he added, "Don't bother to deny it, Star of the Palace. I know because your stiff-necked cousin came to me so I could tell him what he could have told himself. Did he tell you that?"

"Yes," I said.

Daniel shook his head ruefully. "Remember that I, too, am a Jew. Once my pride was to keep all our laws, even in the court of the King of this world's Kings. That didn't last long."

I did not catch at this bait. I let the silence between us grow heavy, as if truth fell to the ground between us, unspoken.

Daniel smiled. "Yes, you are clever, my lady Esther. Stay that way; it is the only safe path for those trapped as we are. And remember, while you have friends within these gilded walls, they weave their own futures as they do yours."

Now it was I who smiled. "Queens have no friends," I quoted.

"No, I suppose they don't. But remember that your foe's foe may aid you for a time."

"*May*—or may not." Daniel's foreign wife stood in the doorway to the blue-tiled house; she regarded me critically.

"Come again if you wish, or if Samamat or I can help you." Daniel hesitated, glanced at his wife. "If you dwell in a palace, it is good to have friends."

"It is good to have friends you can trust," Samamat amended.

"Yes, it is." I rose and bowed to them both. "Thank you. I will remember your words."

"You go to listen to the Dream-Master?" Vashti smiled, and slid her arm through mine. "Is he not wonderful? He is always so clever, and knows so many stories—yes, let us go to Daniel's garden."

As easily as that, she claimed my privilege as her own. I was not sure I liked having Vashti come with me to listen to Daniel, but I could think of no good reason to say *no* to her.

Vashti more than repaid me for my loss of solitude with Daniel Dream-Master, for she took me to gaze upon the king. One afternoon, she came and grasped my hand and drew me through the labyrinth of the palace until we reached a window covered by an ivory screen carved in intricate lattice-work. "Look, Esther!" Vashti sounded greatly pleased with herself; I stepped forward, cautiously.

I looked through the ivory lattice and for the first time looked upon the face of the King of Kings. Slow fire kindled in my blood. I had not expected that; never thought I would desire him. When I saw him riding through Shushan beside a laughing Queen Vashti, I had not seen his face—but I had remembered ever since how he had sat easily upon his restless horse.

Did I desire him now because he was pleasing to look upon? For Ahasuerus truly was what all kings were called: handsome. He was tall and well-formed, broad-shouldered and lithe. His hair curled night-dark over his shoulders; his skin gleamed rich as amber. The King of Kings plainly spent many hours in the sunlight, and he shone with health and moved with supple vigor. His strides as he paced before Prince Haman were long, each sweep of his legs kicking his heavy gold-embroidered robes aside.

Now I know why I am here. He is the man destined for me before our mothers were born.

Below us, Ahasuerus reached the end of the balcony, turned back so that the sunlight fell upon his face. His eyes were the rich brown of good fertile earth. . . .

"Well, now you have seen the King of Kings," Vashti said to me, and I drew in a deep breath, willing my blood to calmness.

"Yes," I said, "I have seen him."

"Now that you have seen him, do you think you would like to be Queen of Queens?" she asked.

"I do not know if I would like to be queen," I said, speaking each word slowly and with care, as I did with any language new to my tongue, "but I do know that I would like to be the king's wife."

Again I looked down, found myself staring at Haman. As he smiled and gestured, and the king smiled back, I realized that not only Queen Mother Amestris stood between me and the king. Another obstacle was Prince Haman.

I did not like Haman even before he revealed his evil heart to all the world. When I looked upon Haman, I saw a man who drowned half-breed pups and fouled water with their small bodies. A man who tore away a woman's veil on a public street. Lord Prince Haman, the king's friend—so sleek, so attentive, so obsequious. Even had I not encountered him before, I think I would have disliked what I saw. And what I most disliked was seeing my king smiling upon this man.

"That is Prince Haman, is it not?" I asked Vashti. "How did he become the king's favorite?"

Vashti looked and shrugged; light flowed over her pale hair. Haman, she told me, had always lurked about the court—

"But he became the king's good friend only after I was queen no longer. The Queen Mother always favored Haman, and I think she set him in Ahasuerus's path. She wanted Haman to be his friend—and Haman knew how to make Ahasuerus like him. Ahasuerus needs friends," Vashti finished, rather wistfully.

So Queen Mother Amestris has her own pawn in play. But I think she misjudges, this time, with this man. I guessed that Amestris thought to rule Haman. Amestris had not learned that soon or late, a blade grows too heavy for an aging hand to command. That Haman was a weapon that would turn upon its wielder.

"Why do you call him the favorite?" Vashti possessed a disconcerting ability to remember what had been said many words ago. She clearly wished to understand my thoughts. I answered as seriously as she had asked.

"Because he so clearly is. See how he stands, his body curving toward the king? And how the king reaches out to him, permits him near?" I distrusted Haman's fulsome devotion to the king. I saw Haman's loyalty for what it was: a sham.

"Everyone turns to the king, Esther."

"Not as Haman does. Not so . . ." I hesitated, trying to choose the right word to describe Haman. Images slid through my mind. *Serpent. Wolf.* But they did not fit; the serpent, the wolf, were merely animals, innocent. *Haman is truly evil.*

"Esther?" Vashti's voice, questioning, concerned. "Are you all right? Suddenly you looked—ill."

I managed to smile and shake my head. "No. Perhaps I am a little tired, that is all."

Vashti's worried eyes brightened. "Of course you are. We will go to the baths. That will soothe and rest you."

Vashti led me to the Queen's Bath—she no longer held the title of queen, but all that had been hers remained hers save that title and the crown. All the world knew Ahasuerus still went to her. A dart of jealousy stung; I forced myself to ignore it. No matter how my heart burned for him, the king did not yet know I existed. *He might never know, if he chooses another. If he does, I will die—or wish to. How can I ensure I am the first maiden to go to him?*

All such pains and questions vanished in the Queen's Bath. Of course I had been bathed and perfumed in the palace baths, and thought myself pampered like a princess, but compared to the Queen's Bath, the palace baths were as a bucket in a shed.

I seemed to walk into an underwater world where maidservants bathed me in water that smelled of roses and washed my long heavy hair. After I had been bathed and rinsed until I thought I must melt if one more drop of water touched my skin, I was permitted to lie upon one of the marble slabs so the maids might rub sweet oils into my skin. The women were so skilled in their art I fell asleep as one combed out my hair and another rubbed myrrh into my feet.

I awoke refreshed as if I were once again a child on my father's farm, when each awakening was to joy. I stared up at the high-arched ceiling, admiring sunlight glinting through little stars. Stars; a good omen. I was Star, now.

Omens! What would Mordecai say? Sunlit stars, water and warm oil. My body naked to perfumed air and expert hands. No place, no position, for a good Jewish girl. *But by my cousin's own order, I am no longer a good Jewish girl. I am not Hadassah bas Abihail. I am Esther, one girl among many in the palace of the king.* I stretched, supple as a cat, or as a courtier's back—or as my cousin Mordecai's scruples had proven to be. As I stared up at the sunlight stars, I found myself thinking of Vashti. She had no true place in the palace anymore, and nowhere else to go.

I asked her whether she could not return to her father's house. The question startled her.

"I never thought of it, Esther."

"Think of it now. Would you be happier there?"

"No." Her answer came swiftly, without pause for the briefest thought. Then, more carefully, "No, I would not. I have not dwelt beneath that roof for so long I think I have forgotten even the scents and sounds there. And I don't think my mother would welcome back a daughter so disgraced and dishonored as I."

VASHTI

"I would like to be his wife," Esther said, and I stared at her. Ahasuerus was king, and he was kind and generous, and I loved him as a sister loves her dearest brother—but what I saw in Esther's eyes was a pure hunger, a longing I had never felt for him.

Can she love him? So swiftly, so easily? And if she did, was that good or bad?

I put the question to Hegai later, when all the queen-maidens walked about the gardens, enjoying the warm evening air. I explained what we had done, and what Esther had said, and how her eyes had looked as she gazed upon the king.

"My lady Vashti, will you never learn caution?" was Hegai's first response. And when I pointed out that he himself had suggested it might be wise to learn how Esther would regard the king, Hegai sighed.

"Yes, and I—that is, you and I would have arranged something together. Something safe and secret."

"It was safe and secret," I said. "And—oh, Hegai, her face glowed like a star, and her voice sounded like—like poured honey."

"Sticky," Hegai said, and I laughed.

"Oh, Hegai, you know I have no gift for clever words. Esther does. But do you think it will please Ahasuerus, that she already loves him so greatly? He never liked me clinging to him, you know."

Hegai frowned, considering. "Let us examine this matter. The maiden Esther is beautiful and virtuous, learned and witty—and she has fallen into love with the man, and not the king, as a pearl falls into a pure well." The thick black lines of kohl stretching past his dark eyes curled up as his face creased in a wide smile. "I believe it just possible, my lady Vashti, that the King of Kings will like *her* to cling to him."

For a heartbeat anger bit sharp; I shoved the unworthy emotion away, scolding myself. *No envy, no sighing over the past. There was never love like that between us. Free him and yourself. All that matters now is the future, and Ahasuerus's happiness.*

I had chosen Esther, and now it seemed Esther herself had chosen as well. Now it was time to unfold her future before her.

Yet somehow the moment never seemed quite right. At last, one day when the two of us walked together in my garden, I simply said, "Esther, you are going to be queen."

Esther stopped walking. "Vashti, you cannot know that."

"Yes," I said, "I can. Because it is what I want, and what Hegai wants, and—"

"But is it what King Ahasuerus will want?" Esther looked—angry.

"Oh, Esther, of course it is! You are perfect. You—"

"I will not trick him into choosing me." Esther's mouth set in a firm line.

She does love him—loves him as I never did. I regarded her rather wistfully. "Of course not, Esther. But he will choose you."

"Because you will arrange it?"

"Yes. Because it is what is best for him. And while I do not love him as you do, Esther, I want him to be happy."

"And you think I will make him happy?" Esther asked. I noticed she did not deny loving Ahasuerus.

"I think you will make each other happy."

"And you, Vashti?"

"Esther, I came to this palace when I was only ten years old. I was called queen for another ten years. And yet only now, when I no longer wear a crown, am I a queen in deed instead of merely in name." I wore a circlet of golden flowers; I lifted it from my hair and held it out to Esther. "Set this upon your head, O Most Beautiful, and may you learn more swiftly than I what it truly means to bear its weight."

A grand gesture, but life is not a necklace strung with grand gestures as its gems. I was still Vashti; still a young woman who had been raised for half her life with every whim treated as iron law.

That night I cried myself to sleep, and my dreams were not pleasant things.

ESTHER

At last all the maidens had finished the months of preparation; it was time for the king to choose his new queen. Each maiden was to be allotted one night with the king—one night to decide her future and his. To make the allocation of the nights fair and equitable, all the maidens were to draw ivory tokens. Each token had a number written upon it in gold. We would go to the king in the order of the number we had drawn. We were to choose our tokens tomorrow.

"I've never heard of anything so outrageous." I stared at Vashti, and saw nothing in her eyes but a faint, wistful amusement.

"The court is outrageous," Vashti said. "And Amestris is the most outrageous creature in the court. This is her plan."

"And it's absurd. How can the King of Kings make an intelligent choice in one night?"

"You think two would be better?"

"I think it's the way one chooses a concubine, not a queen. Surely the King of Kings desires a Queen of Queens, not merely someone—"

"Beautiful, supple, and compliant?" Vashti rested her chin upon her knees, wrapped her arms around her legs, hugging herself into a tight ball. "I think that Ahasuerus desires what his mother wishes him to desire. And if I had learned that earlier, I would still be queen today."

"I am sorry," I said, and she glanced up at me, and smiled.

"Don't be. If I'm a fool, you clearly are not. You are what the Seven Princes demanded—a maiden wiser and more worthy to be queen than I."

Vashti uncoiled and rose to her feet, leaned upon the wall beside me. "This is war, Esther—and I intend to triumph over Amestris."

"By making me queen?"

"Yes, by making you queen. We must ensure that Ahasuerus chooses you, Esther—and no one else."

I remained in the tiny balcony long after Vashti had gone, watching the sky burn from turquoise into red and gold. Queen of Persia—I, Hadassah, jewel of learning, must win the crown by competing in a contest to satisfy a king's lust.

And if I did? If King Ahasuerus chose me, what would that mean for me?

Somehow I suspected that being queen would not mean I could sit in my study and read all day—although if I became queen, Queen Mother Amestris would undoubtedly encourage me to do just that. I knew how she had controlled Vashti's life, and she would seek to do so with the new queen. And I would not allow her to control me.

Then I must ensure that Queen Mother Amestris is rendered powerless to interfere in the queen's life.

I had no idea how I could achieve that goal, but I refused to worry myself over the matter now. I would only need to draw Amestris's fangs if I became queen. If I did not—

If I do not, I shall ask Vashti to send me back to my father's farm. I shall raise horses there, and be happy.

So I told myself—and knew that I lied.

To draw the lots that would determine our fate—or at least, our night with the king—we all gathered in the Garden of Roses, under the watchful eyes of Vashti and Hegai. Hatach called out our names to come and pull an ivory token from a deep-necked jar. There was a number written upon each token; we would go to the king in the order of our numbers. Hatach called my name first; I saw despair and anger in the eyes of many of the other girls.

I walked slowly up to the jar and put my hand down into the darkness. Vashti had told me how to choose: one token would have a small imperfection marring its smooth surface. That was the token I was to grasp as my own.

I felt carefully through the cool smooth ivory disks. All alike—except one. One of the disks was chipped; rough at the edge. I closed my fingers around that one and withdrew my hand from the jar. As all the other girls waited, staring, I opened my hand.

When I looked at the number upon the ivory disk, it seemed to waver. *Forty.* Not *one.* "Forty," I said, and saw smiles as my rivals realized they still had a chance to outdo me.

I looked at the number upon the ivory disk and swiftly calculated the date that would be mine. The last night of Adar. Spring. Far too long to wait before I went in to the king. He might choose any of the girls who went to him before me.

I may never look upon his face. I may never feel the touch of his skin against mine. If he chooses another . . .

Too long to wait. Why had Vashti not arranged for me to draw the first night? *Forty nights until my chance with the king. Why so long? Does Vashti play some cruel game with me?*

"My lady Esther?" Kylah bowed and spoke soft-voiced, a sound that did not carry as a whisper did. "You are summoned." She slanted her eyes; I followed her gaze and saw she looked to where Hegai and Vashti sat. I followed Kylah to the alcove and bowed before the Chief Eunuch.

"I am here," I said.

"Here and unsmiling," Hegai said.

I held out my hand. The ivory disk lay warm upon my palm; the golden number glinted in the sunlight. "Forty. That means I do not go to the king until the last night of Adar."

Vashti regarded me placidly; she seemed half-dreaming, as if she had been eating lotus. Hegai's face was a mask of paint, he a player. "Have you no faith, Esther?"

"Shall I squander my faith upon your games?" I kept my voice low, my tone cheerful. The watching, waiting girls must not know my thoughts or feelings.

"The date was well-chosen. All the stars smiled upon it. Come to me later." Vashti's words slid through the air between us, softer than dawn breeze.

"And trust us, O doubting one." Hegai waved his hand, dismissing me, and I bowed and backed away.

As she had commanded, I later went to see Vashti. She received me in her garden, beside a fountain that poured water into a star-shaped pool. An old trick; watersong foiled eavesdroppers. Hegai, too, sat there. They both smiled at me.

"Clearly you both are well-pleased with your cunning plan," I said. "Now will you reveal it to me? I have only to carry out the scheme, after all." I reined my voice hard; refused to let bitterness enter my tone. Vashti was not like Mordecai, stiff-lipped and silent; she would chatter everything to me if I asked it. Well, now I asked.

Vashti rose and hugged me hard. "Don't worry, Esther. We thought long and hard on this—well, Hegai thought long and hard, and—"

"Vashti," I said, "stop speaking of yourself as if you're a fool. You are quite capable of thinking long and hard."

Color flamed over her cheeks; this faint praise delighted her. "Very well, Hegai and I. Oh, I know you thought to be the first girl the king would see, and that was my first thought as well. But Esther, it would not answer."

She was right, and I saw that once I stopped thinking only of those forty nights when the king would look upon other girls, and not upon me.

"The palace is a place of beauty and of riches," Hegai said, "and also of plots. You are not the only girl who has those who wish to see you queen. Had you drawn the token numbered one, I doubt even I could have kept you safe. You are too much favored, Esther."

"So—forty. And what is to keep the king from choosing one of the thirty-nine maidens who will go to him before I do?"

"Me," Vashti said. "By the king's own decree, I set the laws for this choice of queen. I speak to the king to tell him about the girl he will see, and will speak to him again after her night with him. I can easily persuade him the others are not worthy to take my place."

This plan sounded unreliable, but I had to admit at the moment I could think of nothing else myself. I looked at Hegai, knowing he would see my doubt; Hegai shrugged.

"The king is not overeager to choose a new queen," Hegai said. "He still comes to Vashti for comfort, after all. He still listens to her. It is the best we can do."

Vashti looked at me intently. "You don't like it? You're so clever, Esther—surely you'll think of something better. When you do, tell us at once."

Vashti had more faith in my mind than I myself possessed. Still, perhaps I *would* think of something better. That night I sat quiet in my room, trying to invent a plan without flaw. I could think only that if Ahasuerus chose another to be his wife, I would die of grief.

At last I grew irritated with my own misery. If Ahasuerus chose another, I would *not* die. I would live with pain in my heart all my life, but I would not die. *I do not want to live my life weeping for what I cannot have. So I must think of a way to gain my heart's desire. And I have forty days to do so.*

No, less than that. I must ensure my future before the first girl was summoned for her night with the king, for he might choose her simply to end this mad contest. For that, I must find someone wiser than I. Even as I thought that, I knew I must again ask advice of Daniel.

Daniel seemed unsurprised to see me at his gate. Well, by now all the world knew the numbers each of the Chosen Maidens had drawn. *Forty.*

"Esther," he said. "Come in and sit. Be welcome—although I'm not sure I can do anything for you this time."

"You can listen," I said, and Daniel smiled.

"Yes, that I can do. Speak, then, and I will listen."

And he did, sitting quiet as I told him everything. Vashti's plan, Hegai's doubts, my fears—all poured out before him like water from a broken jar. "And so I will be the fortieth girl the king sees. It is so long to wait, there are so many chances for all to turn to dust in my hands."

Daniel waited, but I suddenly had no more words to offer.

"Would it be so bad a thing, if you are not chosen queen?" he asked.

"I don't care about being queen. I—" I drew a deep breath. "I love

Ahasuerus. I don't care about the rest, save that I cannot have him if I do not win the crown."

"You are sure?"

I laughed, shakily. "I think I am sure. How do you know your own heart?"

"That is indeed a hard thing to know, Esther. I didn't know my own until—well, not *too* late. But—"

"But you have her, your Samamat." I liked Daniel's wife, foreign though she might be. Samamat was clever and kind; I wished she were my mother.

"Yes, I have Samamat now. But I nearly lost her, and Arioch too, because I was afraid."

Arioch—? Oh, yes, the captain of Nebuchadnezzar's guard, the man who had helped Daniel save himself from the wrath of mad kings. "Now it is my turn to listen," I said, and Daniel laughed softly.

"That is *not* a tale for your maiden ears, child. And it was all a long time ago. A very long time." Daniel sighed, and gazed into the fountain, as if he saw dreams in the bright falling water. "Arioch—" Daniel turned his face to me, and I saw the past shadowing his sky-eyes. "He won Samamat, for I was too slow to speak first. And too afraid of what the other Jews would say, if I married her."

Daniel turned his head and came back to me. "If you love Ahasuerus, you must cast out fear. And always remember that small fears are more killing than the great. '*What will others say? Will I look foolish? Will he say no?*' Those things don't matter. Dare and win."

"Or dare and lose?"

"Yes. But even if you fail, at least you will have tried. You will not spend all your days reproaching yourself because you let small fears rule you."

Sound advice, as I only truly understood later. Now I yearned for more tangible guidance. "But what am I to do? How can I ensure the King of Kings chooses me?"

Daniel stared past me, as if he saw my future in the soft hot air. At last he said, "Did you not say that Vashti wishes you to be chosen?"

"Yes," I said.

"And did you not say that Hegai looks upon you with favor?"

"Yes. Yes, he does."

"Then," said Daniel Dream-Master, "I suggest you ask them, and not me. If the banished queen and the keeper of the king's women both want the king to chose you, I'm sure they have some plan in mind—probably something so exquisitely devious it would give the Sphinx a headache. Go and ask them what their cunning plan is, and then come up with a plan of your own. Something simple."

I looked at him closely, to see if he jested. His eyes smiled, but his mouth remained solemn. "Something simple," I echoed.

"Yes," said Daniel Dream-Master, who had counseled kings. "Something simple, Esther. There are far too many clever deceptions coiling through the palaces like invisible serpents."

For a breath I felt the cool malice of such serpents slide over my skin. I shuddered, chilled. "I will avoid them."

"That would be wise. It may not be possible. Remember that nothing is secret in a palace. Nothing. May the Lord Our God protect you, Hadassah. No one else will."

Something simple. The words repeated themselves in my mind, like a song that will not be forgotten. *Something simple.* The king must chose me, he *must.* Vashti wished it; Hegai wished it. And I—I desired it with all my heart. My blood burned for Ahasuerus.

Something simple—a simple plan to ensure he chooses me—

"If only I could just tell him!" I cried aloud, and as the words faded into the air, I knew what I had to do.

"You want me to tell him now to choose you?" Vashti stared at me with her huge silver-green eyes. "Just tell him?"

"Yes," I said. "It's what we all want. So tell him. Why gamble when the stakes are so high? He will listen to you, I think."

She looked thoughtful, twirled a lock of her ivory hair about her fingers. "Yes, he will listen. And—oh, Esther, I think it may work."

"It will work better than scheming and hoping. I think you should tell him plainly what you wish for him, and for me. Too many have played with him as if he were a puppet rather than a man and a king."

Vashti regarded me wide-eyed, then nodded. "You are right. But—what if he says no?"

"If he says no—well, that will at least end the suspense." If the king refused me sight unseen, I would weep for a day. If he refused me after I had spent my one night with him, I would weep until I had no tears left. I would walk dry-eyed and stone-hearted for the rest of my days.

"You're crying." Vashti put her arm around me. "What's wrong, Esther?"

What is wrong is that I burn for a man who has never set eyes upon me. I am so afraid he will not choose me that my heart hurts with each beat.

I longed to say these words aloud, to unburden myself. I knew Vashti would be kind, would soothe and cosset me and try to make me smile again. I nearly did say them—but then I remembered Daniel's words.

Nothing is secret in a palace. Nothing.

I drew a deep breath and pressed my fingers to my eyes, wiping away the betraying tears. I smiled. "What's wrong is that I am tired, and that I think too much on the forty long days and nights I must wait to see the king. That is all."

That was quite enough to set Vashti calling for my handmaidens and giving Kylah a dozen orders for my care. I said nothing, but sent Kylah a look that the clever girl rightly interpreted as meaning, *Listen and nod and say, "Yes, my Lady Vashti." As soon as she leaves, we can forget it all.*

I smiled at Kylah. I closed my hand over the ivory disk I had tied in my sash. *Forty.* Mine, mine to keep always.

Much later I had a palace jeweler carve a small hole in the disk, and for many years I wore it on a silk cord about my neck. Whenever life grew hard to bear—even palaces hold sorrow—I would touch my fingers to the ivory token, and take comfort from its smooth warmth.

VASHTI

When I chose Esther to be Ahasuerus's next queen, I did not realize I also chose a friend for myself. Not since Ahasuerus and I had been playmates together had I known so close a bond. Esther's mind ran swift and clever, and she was so learned I could only shake my head and profess myself unequal to her.

"Nonsense," Esther said. "You are just as clever as I. You simply never have learned to use your mind for anything but play."

"How would I learn to—not play?" I asked, and Esther smiled.

"By hard work and perseverance, Vashti. And by practice."

"And if I work hard, and persevere, and practice . . . ?"

"You will learn to think your own thoughts, rather than those of others. It's a useful skill to have."

"I wish I could change places with you—oh, not in the contest, but I think—I think it would be wonderful to live outside palace walls."

"Most would change places with you, and not with me, Vashti. May I ask a question of you?" For the first time, Esther sounded uncertain.

"Yes, and I will even answer. What would you ask?" I waited with interest; I never knew what Esther might say, what she wished to know.

"You have been Queen of Queens. If it were possible, would you wish to be queen again?"

And I thought carefully before I answered. Did I want to be queen again? If I could trick the king into choosing me, as if we all lived in a tale of *peris* and phoenixes, where hearts were worth more than crowns, would I do it? *No. No, I do not want to be his queen. I do not know what I do want, but I do not want that.*

Esther waited; I could read nothing in her eyes. When I did not speak, she said, "Some would commit any act, if it would ensure even a chance at a crown. One girl rubbed tar into her twin sister's golden hair so that it had to all be cut off. No one would choose a girl with a shaven head for the king to look upon. Another washed her face and found her smooth pale skin blotched and red. Yet another—"

"Stop," I said. *How terrible, how cruel the choice of beauty.*

But Esther possessed more than a keen mind, more than a vibrant beauty. She owned that most rare, most elusive, charm: she was likeable.

Everyone liked her—even maidens who competed against her for the crown liked Esther. Hegai liked her, and Hegai liked few people. Sometimes I wondered if he truly liked me, but I never quite dared ask.

It was good to have a friend—and twice good that friend was Esther. A girl my own age, one who understood what I longed for. And Esther knew much that I had not yet learned. I listened avidly to her tales of growing up wild in the mountain valley, and of slipping unnoticed through the city below the palace. I could not go to the valley—

"But you can take me down into the city, Esther. Yes, we will go and you will show me how men and women who are not kings and queens live."

"No, we will not," Esther said flatly.

That was the beginning of an argument that lasted from one end of my garden to the other and back again—for Esther liked to move about, as if she were a restless mare, and I had learned to walk with her. It was also an excellent way of ensuring no one eavesdropped upon our words. Esther steadfastly refused to do my bidding in this, and I begged and cajoled, promised her whatsoever she desired. At last I said,

"If you will not come with me, I will go alone." I held my head high and proud, waiting.

Esther regarded me critically—no, resignedly. "You have been a queen too long, and have forgotten there are things women may not do."

"No, there are things a great queen may not do. I am Vashti; I do what pleases me. And it pleases me to go out into the city—well, into the upper city at least," I amended, seeing the expression on her face. I had seen such a look on the face of a waiting-woman when her little daughter had tried to balance upon the edge of a deep lotus-pond.

Esther drew in a deep breath, and nodded. "The upper city. Yes, that we can do—if walking the palace beyond the Women's Gate will not content you."

"That I have done already." That I had done beside Ahasuerus, playing at being his page. And when his mother had scolded us, Ahasuerus had only laughed, and then Amestris had smiled . . .

"Vashti?" Esther put her arms around me. "Why do you weep?"

"I don't," I said, and blinked hard. "I was remembering . . ." I told her how I had dressed as a boy, followed the king about, and how Amestris had not been truly angry at us. "I remember how she smiled," I finished.

"How did she smile?" Esther asked.

I hesitated. With—satisfaction? Pleasure? "I do not know, I only know that—"

"That Queen Mother Amestris rules here, and intends to do so until she draws her last breath. And if there is one thing I have learned with all my reading and study, it is that those like her live long, long lives." Esther pushed me back, regarded me again, and then wiped my eyes with her own veil. "I think, you know, that it is at the Queen Mother we should look, Vashti. We should look long and carefully."

A thought slashed unbidden into my head. "Do you think Haman is her creature?"

"Is there anyone in the palace who is not? Save you and I and Hegai?"

I noticed she did not add Ahasuerus's name to that short list. "I do not like Haman overmuch," I said, and Esther laughed softly.

"What, after all his pains to cozen you into friendship? Unkind, Vashti!" After a moment's pause, Esther added, "I do not like Haman at all."

When I asked her why, Esther only shook her head. "Why doesn't matter. I am unlikely ever to meet him ag—in the Women's Palace."

"Oh, let us forget about Prince Haman and Queen Amestris! You promised to show me the upper city."

"No, you demanded I take you there. Never lie to yourself, Vashti, even if you lie to others."

My unruly thoughts gave me an idea I thought very clever: I dressed as a young man, and so Esther would be a well-born lady walking with her brother. She wore the full veil, covering herself to her knees. I need only line my eyes as a man would and hide my too-bright hair beneath a turban. No one beyond the palace knew my face, after all.

I commanded Varkha to wear flowing robes and let his hair fall loose down his back. Varkha would play with my wolves at the far end of my garden; anyone who looked for me would think they saw me with my beloved pets—for very few people would dare approach close enough to see the deception.

As I had promised Esther, it was not hard to walk out of the Women's

Palace, a place all longed to enter and few to leave. Then it was only a matter of leading Esther through the courtyards until we reached the King's Gate, and then to walk out through the King's Gate to the Great Staircase.

For a moment we stood there at the top of the vast expanse of smooth-polished marble, gazing out across the bright city to the mountains far to the east.

"Look." Esther tilted her head back, staring up at the endless sky. "A falcon."

I glanced at the soaring bird, then looked down the long hill of stairs, a staircase wide enough for a dozen horsemen to ride up abreast. "Come on, sister. I want to see the city." I thought I heard her sigh, but it might have been the wind that swirled about the palace.

It took us almost an hour to make our way down the Great Staircase. We walked down and down, past the bazaars selling all the world's wares, past merchants and soldiers and courtiers. Past heavily-veiled women accompanied by eunuch guards, and past heavily-curtained litters carrying ladies too high-born to be looked upon at all. But as we walked lower, I began to see women who were not hidden from the world. Their faces, free for all to see, had been painted yellow as saffron, and although the thin silk of their garments clung to their bodies, the cloth was always a dull green. Necklaces of coins hung heavy upon their breasts.

"Harlots," said Esther. "Don't look upon them—dear brother."

Odd that so honey-voiced a girl could speak sharp as lemon. Honeyed lemon, to be sure. I never learned the trick of it.

"A man may always *look*, dear sister." Brash, arrogant words that I thought a boy might wish to speak in such a moment.

"When you are a man, then you, too, may look. Until then, guard your eyes." Nothing Esther said would sound in the least odd to any who listened, even did they hear her soft words. Any sister might gently chide a younger brother so.

At last we reached the bottom of the Great Staircase, and there we stopped to rest. To descend those stairs took almost as much effort as it did to ascend. We moved aside, beneath a rose tree in a green-tiled pot. "Are you content yet?" Esther asked, and I shook my head.

"Very well." Her voice was placid; I sometimes wondered if anything ever troubled her. "An hour then, and do not say, 'No, I want more.' It will take us until midafternoon to climb those stairs again, and if we are missed—"

"It will not matter," I assured her.

She leaned close, and when she spoke I felt her breath upon my ear through the sheer cotton veil. "You are no longer the Queen of Queens, and I am no one at all. It will matter." She straightened again, and adjusted her veil. "Come, brother. You promised to show me the Sunrise Street, and to buy me a bangle there."

All went smooth as butter until we turned back, and thought to find a shorter path to the palace than that we had taken to the Sunrise Street. A man began to follow us; a man who had walked past us, and stared intently at my face. He turned and his footfalls paced ours. At first, I thought he must know who I was, but I could not have been more wrong. My disguise proved too convincing.

Soon, instead of following, our shadow came up to walk beside me. "Greetings, pretty one," he said. "You look too fine a boy to be shackled still to your mother."

For a moment I was too astonished to answer; then wicked delight filled me. He thought me a real boy! I nearly laughed—but then he stepped ahead of me and I had to stop. The man looked me up and down, as if I were a horse he thought he just might bargain for.

I drew myself up, about to speak in arrogance and outraged pride, when I heard Esther's sharp indrawn breath. A gasp of fear, half-muffled by her silvered veil.

I think wisdom began for me that day, in that moment, summoned by that breath. For I remembered that I was not Vashti, Queen of Queens. Here, now, I was not even a girl. I was a young man, a very young man. And I must curb my tongue and speak as what I seemed to be would speak.

But I was still Vashti, and so what I said was, "My sister would not like it, sir."

"What a pity. And do you always do as your sister says?"

"I try to be a good brother," I said, and as Esther grabbed my arm and pulled me away, I glanced back over my shoulder. The man smiled at me, and winked. My face burned hot and I willingly went where Esther guided me.

"Are you quite mad?" Esther demanded, as we fled back down the narrow street. There we stopped, sucking in air in great breaths, and I began to laugh. "Be quiet," she hissed. "Be quiet—*brother*—or I will slap you."

"You dare not," I gasped. "Oh, Esther, he thought—"

"I know what he thought. He thought you a boy and me only a woman, and so he could do as he liked with us both. *That* is what he thought, and it is not in the least funny. Oh, do stop laughing!"

"I wonder what he would have given me?" I managed to ask, and despite her scolding, Esther answered,

"And I wonder what he would have done, when he found himself fondling a woman and not a boy!" Then she, too, began to laugh.

But once we had returned safely to the Women's Palace, Esther turned to me and said, "Never again, Vashti. I should never have let you persuade me to such folly. Think on what would have happened had we been discovered."

I started to protest, but Esther held up her hand. "No, Vashti. Think, not of yourself, for you would not suffer more than a tongue-lashing for this. Think of what would have happened to Varkha for his part in this escapade. And think of what would have happened to me. I would have lost all chance of even seeing the king. I would have been lucky if I had been relegated to the concubines' palace."

I stared at the bright tiles beneath my feet. Esther was right. Of course she was right. But—"Why did you come with me, then?"

Esther sighed. "Because I am tired of being trapped behind walls. Because it is very hard to deny you what you ask. And because I am very, very tired of waiting to see the king. So you see, Vashti, I have no more sense than any other girl."

I hugged her and kissed her cheek. "I am sorry, Esther, truly. Be patient for a little longer. Ahasuerus will choose you. I know it."

Esther sighed. "I am number forty, Vashti. I know you and Hegai believe the king will choose me, but—"

"He will. I myself will speak to him before the first maiden goes to him. You are the perfect queen for him, and I will tell him so."

For a long moment, Esther said nothing. She pressed her lips together hard and closed her eyes tight against tears. At last she looked at me and said, "I would rather be the perfect wife for him. Remember that, when you speak with the king. Now come and change out of those boy's garments before Hegai sees you dressed like that."

Since I could not go to Ahasuerus—for the edict forbidding me ever again to come before the king remained forever sealed into the laws—I must summon him. And since I must speak to him on an important and delicate matter, I must make sure I set my request before him at an auspicious moment. I asked Hegai if he thought I should go to Daniel Dream-Master for advice.

"You have no dream for the Dream-Master to interpret for you," Hegai pointed out.

"You are right—do you think I should ask a priest to throw the *pur* for me? To tell me what day I should ask the king to come to me?"

Hegai sighed. "My lady Vashti, the day to ask the king is this day. To wait is risky. Ask him now."

I knew Hegai was right; I must act at once. I sent for Nikole, who came prepared with her box of pens and her clay tablet and papyrus, and sat cross-legged by my chair, writing-board across her thighs, waiting as I dithered over the words of my message. At last Nikole said,

"May I ask a boon, my lady princess?"

I stopped twisting bracelets around my wrist and looked at Nikole. She regarded me calmly over her writing-board. "Yes, of course," I said.

"If my lady princess will permit me, I will write a draft of the message, which you then may approve or alter, as pleases you."

"An excellent idea," Hegai said, before I could answer.

I looked from Nikole to Hegai, and realized my inability to decide even upon the first words of a simple request would keep us bound here until nightfall.

"Yes," I said to Nikole, "it would please me greatly if you would write what I should say."

"Thank you, my lady princess." Nikole bent over her writing-board and began putting neat, swift words upon the papyrus. A few moments later, she held out the message, and I took it without waiting for a maid to hand it to me.

If it please my lord the king, his loving sister the Princess Vashti begs him to come to her when it best suits him so that she may speak to him upon a matter of the utmost importance.

I read the short missive, and began to laugh. So simple, so direct—and so different from the long, convoluted attempts I had made to compose my message. I rose and walked over to Hegai.

"Nikole has written precisely what I would have said, were my head not filled with clouds instead of thoughts." I handed the message to Hegai. "Please send this to the king at once. And tell the page who delivers it to wait for a reply."

Ahasuerus's answer sent me into another panic, for he would come to me that very evening. Now I must decide how to receive him. With a splendid dinner of all his favorite dishes? With wine and fruit? Or should I await him in my courtyard, a suppliant?

And what should I wear? My finest robes? A simple gown? Or . . .

"Vashti, you are chattering like your brainless marmoset." Hegai's statement stopped me in mid-dither. I barely noticed that he had used my name alone, unadorned. "You've known the king since you both were children. Do you really think you need to await him as either queen or supplicant?"

"But what I must say to him is so important. I must find the right words, the *perfect* words. I must—"

To my surprise, Hegai put his arm around me, as he had when I was a small girl new-come to the palace. His embrace comforted me; I leaned my head on his shoulder.

"You must speak to the king as you always have. Fairly and plainly. Yes, what you must say is important, but it is not difficult. Tell him the truth. That is all you can do. What happens then is in his hands."

Hegai's advice calmed me, for I knew he was right. I remembered Esther saying too many had played the king as if he were a puppet. I would not treat Ahasuerus as if he were a mere chessboard king, moving by my whim.

"Thank you, Hegai." I kissed his cheek, an impulsive intimacy. He stiffened, and withdrew his arm, leaving me standing alone again. Feeling oddly bereft, I asked him to arrange matters as he saw fit for the king's visit that evening. "And choose what garments you think I should wear. I will be guided by your good judgment in all things."

Thanks to Hegai's good counsel, I greeted Ahasuerus as I always did—fondly, respectfully, and dressed in a gown I had worn twice a dozen times and knew he thought pretty. When Ahasuerus entered my courtyard, I was glad I had not garbed myself in elaborate robes and garlanded myself with jewels, for Ahasuerus had come to me from a day's hunting, and had not wasted time changing.

"Because your message said the matter was of the greatest importance." Ahasuerus sat down and beckoned me to sit beside him; when I did, he took my hands in his. "What is this urgent affair, Vashti?"

Now I must speak plainly and truthfully. And hope he will listen and heed. I had practiced a well-reasoned argument while I waited for the day to pass, but all the well-chosen words vanished.

"I want you to choose Esther of Shushan as your queen." Well, that had been plain and truthful. Had it been wise?

Ahasuerus stared at me, then laughed—laughter that rang unpleasant; mocking. "That is your urgent matter? You have chosen a queen for me? And what makes Esther of Shushan any different from the other greedy girls awaiting their chance with me?"

"I'm sorry, my lord king. I—oh, Ahasuerus, I spent all day composing the most beautiful argument to lay before you, and I forgot every word. I only meant to speak plain truth."

"A little too plain, perhaps." Ahasuerus smiled and squeezed my hands, then released them and sat back. "Still, I know you mean me only good, Vashti, so tell me why you want me to choose this Esther of yours."

"Not only I," I hastened to assure him. "Hegai regards her with great favor as well. And so does—"

"This isn't Athens," Ahasuerus said. "I'm not selecting my next queen by vote."

"If you did, Esther would win the crown. Everyone likes her. Even the other chosen girls like her."

"And so I must like her as well?" He sounded—hard. Cold, as I never before had heard him.

Esther is right. He is tired of being a chessboard king.

Ahasuerus answered his own question. "Like your Esther? Oh, doubtless I shall like her well enough—all the maidens will strive hard to please me. And I am a man, Vashti. I will enjoy them. But I will not enjoy their vain attempts to convince me they are more than a night's amusement."

"Esther is different," I said.

"How is she any different from the thirty-nine maidens I will embrace before she comes to my bed?"

I looked into Ahasuerus's eyes and saw pain there, and confusion. *He is so unhappy. He must choose Esther. She will bring him joy.* I knew my next words would seal all our fates; I risked all on the toss of a *pur.*

"Esther is different because she loves you, Ahasuerus."

He began to laugh, a harsh, cutting sound. I spoke swiftly, ignoring his unlovely laughter.

"I speak the truth, Ahasuerus. Esther saw you walking with Haman on the lower terrace—"

"She did, did she? And just how did she happen to be roaming through the great palace?"

"I brought her out of the House of Women. I wanted her to see you."

"Of course. Clever, helpful Vashti."

His mocking words sparked my anger. "I do only as I have been taught, my lord king. Most *carefully* taught." Who had trained me in the ways to travel unseen the labyrinth of the great palace? Who had tutored me in reckless daring?

He had the grace to look away. I refused to abandon my purpose. "And how or why Esther came into the great palace is not the point. What matters—to all of us—is that Esther looked upon you and she—"

"And she what?" Ahasuerus asked as I paused for breath.

Now, or never. "And she fell in love with you."

The unadorned words seemed to tremble in the air between us.

"She fell in love with the king?" Ahasuerus at least listened now.

"No," I said, carefully patient. "Esther fell in love with *you.* With Ahasuerus." I remembered Esther's radiant eyes, her passionate voice as she said—"She said she didn't know if she wanted to be queen, but she knew she wanted to be your wife."

There was nothing more I could say. Now all rested with Ahasuerus. He stared at me for long moments, and I could read nothing in his troubled eyes. At last he said,

"This is your petition and request?" The timeworn words drew as formal a response from me. I stood, then sank to my knees before him.

"If it please the king, and if I have found favor in his sight, my petition and my request is that the King of Kings choose Esther of Shushan to be his wife." I bowed my head and waited.

"That is all? Nothing for yourself?" There was an undertone of sadness in his voice.

"If it pleases the king to choose Esther, and to set the crown upon her head, it will be all that I desire."

He rose from the bench and looked down at me. "A most interesting plea, Vashti." He hesitated, as if he would say more, then turned and strode away toward the garden gate.

"Will you choose Esther?" I asked, and he turned.

"I don't know," Ahasuerus said, and went out the garden gate, leaving me convinced I had ruined Esther's chance with my painfully inadequate appeal.

I sighed and rose from my knees. Now I must go and tell Esther and Hegai how matters stood. And we all must pray to our gods that Ahasuerus would choose Esther of Shushan for his wife and queen.

HEGAI

Vashti stood before the silver mirror; tilted her head as she studied the gleaming metal. "I have a favor I wish to ask of you, Hegai." She turned away from the mirror, for she was not one who found pleasure in her own reflection. "May I borrow your mirror?"

For you, anything. But I said only, "Of course, my princess. For how long—and why?"

She laughed and put her hand on my arm. "Not for any trick or jest, I promise you. Truly, I swear it, so do not look so wary!"

I looked down into her laughing eyes. "Truly, I believe you. But what do you plan?"

"Nothing outrageous." She leaned her head against my shoulder; rubbed her cheek against my arm. "*Dear* Hegai, *please* give me your mirror. I need it only for forty nights."

"Ah, I see." I could not resist turning so that she slid into the curve of my arm. For a moment I closed my eyes and savored the feel of her body against mine; delighted in the scent of amber and roses freed into the air by the warmth of her skin. *If I only dared*—If I only dared take her into my arms, would she soften to my touch? Would she give her lips to be kissed? Or would my advances repulse her? *I could not bear that—could not endure seeing revulsion in her eyes. . . .*

"Hegai?" Vashti tapped my chest. "Where have you gone? Come back to me."

I took her hand in mine—she would think nothing of that, for since she was a child, she had held my hand for guidance, for comfort. "I am sorry, my princess. I was thinking."

"Unhappy thoughts?" Vashti gently squeezed my hand.

I shook my head. "Only unworthy thoughts. Now tell me why you think our candidates for queen deserve my mirror."

"Your *famous* mirror." Vashti tucked her arm through mine and looked up at me slantwise. Her eyes reflected the mirror's silver light. "Now you understand why—"

"—you want my famous mirror. Yes, and it is a clever thought." The girls would be dazzled—this would be the only time in all their life when they would see their whole body reflected. It would be a moment they would cherish; one never to be repeated.

Vashti smiled; she treasured compliments to her mind. Very few people knew her well enough to offer such praise. Half a dozen people who valued Vashti, rather than Vashti's ravishing beauty.

"I thought that we could put your mirror in the main courtyard. Then each candidate can look upon herself before she goes to Ahasuerus. I think that will help." Vashti's voice lilted the words into a question; sought my approval.

I tilted my head, as if considering long and hard. At last I said gravely, "Yes. I think that will help."

And seeing themselves in all their beauty of face and form and fine garments would give them, if not confidence, then at least something else to think of as they walked to their meeting with the King of Kings other than their own nervousness. Depending on the girl, such anxiety could be mere unease or utter terror. I knew which girls would suffer most from anticipation and which would face their night with confidence.

I was rewarded by Vashti's pleasure at my words. *I suppose that Esther will not wish to bother looking into the mirror at all! Sometimes I think she is far too much like Daniel Dream-Master for her or anyone else's good.*

BOOK SEVEN

For Such a Time as This

ESTHER

For all that I had longed for this night, had dreamt of it by both night and day, when Hegai came to tell me that it was at last my night to go to the King of Kings, panic gripped me. My blood beat cold beneath my skin; I struggled to breathe.

"Esther, be calm," Hegai said gently. "You have known this day was coming since the tokens were drawn."

"I know. I know. But—"

"But now you have only to put yourself in the capable hands of your handmaidens and your eunuchs. They, too, have long awaited this day—and night. Come, let them do what must be done."

Hegai's calm, sensible words soothed me, gave me strength. "Yes," I said. "You are right. Thank you." Then I confessed, "I always thought myself brave. I had not thought that when this moment came I would be—afraid."

Hegai laughed. "If you were not afraid when facing so great a moment, I would have chosen wrongly. Only fools rush to their fate without fear or thought. You are not a fool."

"I'm afraid that I am. Oh, Hegai, if Ahasuerus—if the king—" I despaired of finding the right words. "What if he does not *see* me?"

Hegai smiled and laid his hand upon my cheek. "He will see you. You will shine bright, Star of the Palace. Now let your servants take you to the baths."

By day's end, I had been transformed from Esther of Shushan into a creature of ice and fire. My skin gleamed from oil of myrrh and had been painted with silver. Silver lines swirled over my arms and legs. Upon the palms of my hands gleamed silver stars.

My hair had been washed with lemon-water and dried over a brazier burning amber and frankincense. It had been combed out to ripple down my back, gleaming so that its dark fire burned hot.

My body had been perfumed: the soles of my feet, behind my knees, between my thighs, between my breasts. My hands, the tender curve of my inner elbow, beneath my arms. The hollow beneath my throat. The sandalwood and clove, spikenard, cedar and frankincense, of the perfume Hatach had so carefully chosen for me caressed me as I walked.

Purified, perfumed, and light-headed, I returned to my chamber to be adorned. Vashti awaited me there, clearly eager to see what I would choose to wear on this night of all nights. Apparently none of my clothing had been deemed suitable for this occasion and the apparel laid out upon every surface, offered up by every handmaiden and eunuch, all was strange to me.

"What will it please my lady Esther to wear?" Hatach asked, and I looked into his anxious eyes and realized I simply did not know.

I stared at the garments strewn about the room, at the gems glittering upon swathes of silk bright as those jewels. So many, and all so rich, so ornate. *How am I to choose? What will please Ahasuerus?* In the privacy of my thoughts, he was always "Ahasuerus" to me, never "the king."

"My lady Esther?" Hatach began to sound worried; I saw Kylah move forward.

"Perhaps my lady Esther requires a few moments to decide?" Kylah suggested, and I shook my head.

"No, what my lady Esther requires is advice." I ran my hand over a veil thin as morning mist. "Tell me," I said to Vashti, "tell me what the king likes."

I might have asked her to calculate the distance from Shushan to the Sun. "I—truly, Esther, I don't know." Vashti's brilliant opalescent eyes held only bafflement. "My garments were always laid out for me; I had only to don them."

You were his wife for half your life, and you don't even know what most pleases his eyes. Poor Vashti. And poor Ahasuerus.

I managed to smile, and ask quietly, "Well then, who chose what was laid out for you?"

"Hegai, of course." Vashti sounded surprised that I need ask. "He is Chief Eunuch, in charge of all pertaining to the queen's care."

Relief flowed through my blood like warm honey. "Then I will ask Hegai to choose for me. Please tell him that Esther begs him to come to her, for she wishes to ask his advice."

Vashti herself ran to take Hegai my message. She was not with him when he came to me, and he offered no false astonishment at my summons. "I wondered how long it would take you to send for me, O Bright Star."

I spoke as plainly as he. "Hegai, I don't know what to wear tonight. And Vashti was no help whatsoever."

"Did you think she would be?"

"I thought she at least might know what the king liked to see on a woman. What pleases his eyes."

"Esther, our dear lady Vashti knows nothing about what a man likes to see. She never needed to learn, for she was queen since she was a child."

"Does she know what pleases a man—the king—in—in love?"

Hegai smiled. "It pleases a man to be liked, admired." He slid around my question, seeming to answer without actually doing so. "You will please the king; never doubt that."

"Will I please him more than Vashti?"

For a breath I thought he would evade this question, too. Then he took my face between his hands and looked long into my eyes. "Yes, you will please him more than Queen Vashti did."

"Why?" If I knew that, perhaps it would help me win Ahasuerus's love.

"Vashti sees him as the friend of her childhood." Hegai hesitated, then said, "She sees him as a sister sees a brother. But you, Esther—you see him as a man, a man whose touch your body yearns to receive. Now come, we must prepare you to meet the man your heart burns for."

It became instantly clear to me that Hegai had chosen what I should wear long before this hour had arrived. He did not even glance around at the waiting robes, but pointed to what looked like a swirl of cloud lying upon my bed.

Kylah lifted up the gown while Hatach slipped the shawl from my body. With his own hands, Hegai draped the chosen garment upon me, spent long minutes assuring himself the cloth was draped and pinned to perfection. He spent longer assuring himself that the only gem I wore lay as it should.

And when he nodded and stepped back, finished, I might have been wearing nothing at all.

My gown had been crafted of cloth sheer as morning mist—a simplicity far more extravagant than decking my body with gold and gems. A chain of ruddy gold hung to my waist; from the chain dangled a black pearl the size of a pigeon's egg. That was all.

Once I would have been ashamed to wear so wanton a garment even alone in my own bedchamber. A year separated me from that learned, pious girl . . . .

"All the others chose queenly robes, and a royal ransom in jewels." Hegai studied me; smiled.

"So I shall be a woman going to see the man she desires, and not a candidate seeking a crown. Wise Hegai!"

"My wisdom is useless unless the one I counsel is wise enough to follow my advice."

"I will do everything as you order it," I said. I knew Vashti had told Ahasuerus that he should choose me—and I also knew that he might not. If I did not please him, if he did not like my eyes, or my voice . . . in the end, the king alone would decide if Esther would be queen.

⁂

Before I began the journey that would take me to the king's bedchamber, I thanked each of my servants and kissed their cheeks. If the king refused me, I had no future here.

In the main courtyard of the Women's Palace, I did as thirty-nine maidens had done before me: I stopped and looked upon myself in the silver mirror that Vashti had ordered placed beside the gate into the King's Palace. The tapestry that covered it had been pulled aside so that I, this night's choice, might gaze upon myself. Polished until it shone like glass, taller than I by at least a cubit, the mirror displayed my body, from the top of my head down to my henna-rose feet. Never before had I looked upon myself fully, seen myself as others saw me.

It is true. I am beautiful. I had seen the other girls who battled for the queen's crown; lovely, all of them. I had seen Princesses Tandis and Barsine. I had seen Queen Vashti. And now, at last, I saw Esther.

A tremor ran through me as my image gazed back from the mirror's silver depths. For I knew that if only beauty counted with the king, then I need have no fear that any other girl who waited for him was more beautiful than I.

But is that enough? If beauty alone drew the king, would his love vanish when time summoned my beauty from me?

Before I could worry myself into tears, Vashti came up to me to wish me good fortune. "Oh, Esther! You are beautiful as Ishtar! You are more beautiful than I. You are more beautiful than stars."

Her extravagant praise touched me; I held out my hands and she clasped hers around mine. Her hands burned like fire against my cold skin. "Thank you," I said. "I may never see you again—but I wanted to tell you—"

Vashti squeezed my hands hard. "Don't," she said. "A crown of stars awaits you. And it will look far more beautiful against your hair than mine."

That freed laughter. "Oh, Vashti—only you could think of such a thing at such a moment!" I tried to free my hands to embrace her, thank her as a sister, but she backed away.

"Don't, Esther. You'll spoil all the work on your hair and gown and—"

"I don't care." Reckless urgency flared; my blood beat hot now, not cold.

"You'll care when your paint's smeared and there's no time to re-do all the designs." Vashti's prosaic, practical tone sounded oddly familiar. Vashti leaned forward and carefully kissed my cheek. "Go with good fortune and your god's favor, Hadassah," she whispered.

It was only when I had passed through the gate and was walking down the corridor that led to the golden doors that I realized who Vashti had sounded like.

She'd sounded like me.

I lived now in dreamtime, flowing and elusive. Torchlight flared; shadows fled as I passed. I walked forward, steadily, until I stood at last before the entrance to the king's chamber.

Guards barred my path; I waited, and they pulled open the great golden doors. Beyond lay lamplight and darkness.

I walked through the doorway, making myself move without haste. My blood beat so hard that the wild rush of it echoed in my ears. As the doors closed behind me, I bowed, and waited.

"Approach, Esther." The king's voice, at last.

I don't know why the fact that he knew my name surprised me. Of course he would know. The true surprise was that he chose to use it.

I lifted my head and paced toward him; slow, deliberate strides, like a hunting cat's. When I was an arm's length away from him, I stopped, and bowed again.

"So you are my next queen." Ahasuerus regarded me almost angrily; a proud, wary lion. I bowed my head.

"Only if the King of Kings wishes it."

He raised his eyebrows. "Truly? How odd—I have been told by she who was once my queen that I must choose Esther."

He sought to shock me; I found myself smiling. "I hope Vashti was more tactful than that."

"You know?" The subtle anger vanished; he regarded me with a kinder interest.

"Yes." I hoped he liked plain speaking as much as Vashti had assured me he did. "And I told Vashti she should simply tell you. She had a great many very convoluted schemes for my success—"

To my surprise, Ahasuerus laughed. "Oh, I have no doubt she did! Vashti never did have any sense at all."

"But she was never taught to have any sense, my lord king. It must be learned, like any other skill." Not the conversation I had dreamt of having with my heart's delight, but I sensed only truth would serve—and I yearned to hear Ahasuerus laugh again.

"And I suppose you have many skills, Esther?" Now he sounded sullen, almost as if he expected a rebuke. Although who would dare rebuke the King of Kings—

Amestris. The Queen Mother; of course. Well, I have no intention of becoming Ahasuerus's mother!

Again I answered plainly, keeping my voice serene. "I do, my lord king." I then counted my heartbeats, waiting for him to speak first.

"Well, name them." Ahasuerus sounded both intrigued and impatient.

Poor man. This contest must be hard on him. Obedient to his command, I began to number my talents, using my fingers as counters.

"I can speak Median, Persian, and Aramaic. I read Persian, Aramaic, Sumerian, and Elamite. I add sums, and call the stars by name. I play the small harp and the flute. Those I do well. I can weave and bake, not so well. I can order a household. I write poems. And I can ride a horse—although I have not done so in many years. That I did best of all."

"An impressive list. And if I call in my chief scribe and ask you to speak to him in Median?"

"I will do so, my lord king—although it seems a sad waste of what may be our only night together."

Startled into laughter, Ahasuerus beckoned me closer. I wondered if he even noticed my sandalwood-scented body through the cloud-drift gown, or admired my nightfire hair. "Come," he said, "sit by me."

He sat upon the edge of the massive bed, so I sank down to sit by his feet. There I could lean against his thigh, look up into his face. If he objected, he had only to order me away. He did not.

"Vashti says," he began, then stopped. After a breath, he said, "Does it trouble you, that I speak of—"

"Of Vashti? Why should it trouble me? I love her dearly; she is as a sister to me. A rather sweetly overenthusiastic sister at times, I grant. But a sister nonetheless."

"Vashti tells me I should choose you as my next queen."

As your wife. Choose me as your wife, my love.

"She tells me also that you love me. It is easy to love the king. Every maiden who has come to this chamber has loved the king."

I looked up into his earth-brown eyes and thought that every other maiden had been a fool. *I wish you were not the king, Ahasuerus. I wish—I wish you were a horse-farmer in the Vale of Karoun.* But I said only,

"We all love the king, my lord. I love the king most dutifully."

I saw understanding spark in his eyes. He doubted; wished to believe, yet feared lest what I promised prove false.

Ahasuerus reached down and put two fingers under my chin, tilted my head back. Coals of fire scorched my skin where he touched me.

"And do you think I believe this tale that you looked upon me and loved me at once with all your heart?"

"I think you are King of Kings, and so must be very tired of being told—oh so subtly—what you must do, or not do. I think you are weary of being manipulated. So I told Vashti to tell you the truth. I will always tell you the truth."

"Always?" he said.

"Yes."

"The truth then—what would you do if I said to you now, 'Esther, I do not choose you. You are free. Go and do whatsoever you wish.' "

If he did not choose me, if he ordered me to go. *To be free—*

"I have a farm," I said. "A horse farm in the Vale of Karoun. I would go there and raise horses, as my father did."

"A horse farm?" This seemed to intrigue him. "Why then are you here, in Shushan?"

I sighed, and dared press my cheek against his thigh. When he neither shifted away nor ordered me back, I allowed myself to savor the warmth of his skin beneath the heavy fluid silk he wore. "I am here in Shushan because my father died, and my cousin, who is my guardian, thought horse-farming not a suitable occupation for a woman. Nothing," I added, "is a suitable occupation for a woman, save to marry and bear children."

"Is that what you truly wish, then? Shall I let you go?"

I hesitated, and he said, "You promised me the truth, Esther."

"No," I said. I could barely hear my own voice. "Do not let me go. I loved you as soon as I saw you. If you deny me, it will rip the heart from my breast."

He looked at me with those night-dark eyes; slowly, he leaned down toward me. *Oh, yes,* I thought. *Yes.* And I swayed upward, drawn to him by his eyes—and his hands, firm and gentle on my arms.

My lips touched his. And then I stopped thinking about anything at all.

VASHTI

The moment Ahasuerus walked into my garden the morning after Esther's night, I knew my plan had succeeded far beyond my hopeful dreams. His heart, as well as his mind, had chosen Esther. He looked—different. I tried to see what had changed. His eyes, his smile? The way he moved?

I bowed as he came toward me.

"Rise, Vashti." He took my hands as I rose and gazed into his eyes. Happiness, bright and clear. "I came to tell you—"

"That you have chosen wisely?" I teased, testing his mood.

He laughed. "That *you* have chosen wisely. As has Hegai. And Esther—" He stopped, clearly unsure what he should say now.

I knew he feared to wound my heart, but he could do that only if he no longer had any fondness for me. For that was what we had, Ahasuerus and I: the fond love of a brother and sister who were dear to one another. But that was all.

"Esther loved you the moment she set her eyes upon you," I said. "And you? Tell me what you thought when you first looked upon her."

When I asked that, he seemed to glow radiant as the sun. "It was not when I looked upon her, Vashti—although she is very beautiful. Like a dark flame. It was when she spoke. She is wise, and kind, and clever. Do you know her father raised horses?"

I bit my lip to keep from laughing. "Yes, Ahasuerus, I know that. Come, sit with me and tell me all about it." I had heard Esther's shy, joyful tale of her night with the king, and now it was the king's turn to unveil the story to me.

So we sat upon the alabaster bench in my garden, warmed by the pale clear sun, surrounded by the scent of lilacs, and Ahasuerus eagerly told over the story of his night with Esther. Fortunately, I already had the story of that night of nights from Esther herself, for Ahasuerus revealed very little, save that his heart and Esther's beat as one, and that no woman in all the wide world compared with Esther for wisdom and warmth.

"And she agreed to be my wife," Ahasuerus finished, marveling at so great a wonder.

He looked so happy my heart ached; a wistful longing for what he and I never had known together. Smiling, I took his hands and kissed them. "Oh, my lion-hearted brother, I am so happy for you and for her. When is the wedding to take place?"

"This very hour, if that were possible. As it is, it will be as soon as my mother can arrange the ceremony."

I longed to order the wedding myself, but held my tongue. To arrange his wedding ceremonies truly was his mother's duty and right.

"I have a boon to ask of you, Vashti."

"Anything, of course."

Ahasuerus put his hands on my shoulders and kissed my forehead. "No man could ask for a better, dearer sister! You are the first I have told, no one yet knows save Esther, and me."

I do not know how I kept from laughing. All anyone need do was look at him to know that last night had changed his heart and his life. And Esther had told only me, and Hegai, but she glowed like sunlight on the mountains. I think every person in the Women's Palace and the Queen's Palace knew by now that the queen's crown would rest on Esther's head.

"I am grateful for the king's kindness. What does my lord king desire of me? You know I will do anything I can to aid you."

Ahasuerus smiled. "Will you tell my mother I have chosen Esther of Shushan as my queen and my wife? And ask her to begin preparations for the wedding at once?"

⁂

I took unworthy delight in begging an audience with Queen Mother Amestris, and I drove my handmaidens half-mad as I decided on and then discarded garments. At last Hegai took charge, and so I went before Amestris clad in a gown of gold-woven cloth and a vest of Cathay silk dyed with true Tyrian purple—the color permitted only to those of royal blood and rank.

I might no longer be queen, but I remained a daughter of the royal house of Babylon. *And I am Ishvari's granddaughter.*

"My lady princess might consider a less gleeful smile before she goes to the Queen Mother," Hegai suggested, "for at the moment my lady princess looks like a marmoset stuck in a honey-pot."

I laughed and stretched upward to kiss his cheek. "The Keeper of the King's Women is most wondrous wise! Oh, and send for Tandis and Barsine—I wish them to attend me when I visit the Queen Mother."

Hegai sighed, but I saw him struggle against his own laughter. "You wish them dressed alike, I suppose?"

"Yes—now you may help me decide what they should wear. I must impress the Queen Mother properly, you know."

"Yes, my princess." Hegai abandoned his effort and smiled back at me; light seemed to dance in his dark amber eyes. "I know."

So, dressed like a queen and attended by two princesses gowned in gold and silver, I presented myself at the gate to the Queen Mother's garden. I wished Hegai had also escorted me, but he had deemed it wiser to remain out of Amestris's sight. "I am known for cleverness, and you are not," Hegai had said.

I agreed; Amestris had raised me to be a frivolous, foolish girl, a pawn easily manipulated. But I now struggled to become more. *It's my turn to play, not be played.*

Of course Amestris knew already that Ahasuerus had made his choice. I had never doubted that; she had doubtless known before Ahasuerus left his bedchamber that morning. And the knowledge infuriated her.

"Vashti, how fortunate that you chose this time to visit me. Come and sit by me now and tell me what Ahasuerus said to you this morning."

Amestris waved me closer. "Well, make haste. I must know how bad the matter is."

Tell you what my dear brother Ahasuerus confided to me? No. I drew my brows together, as if puzzling out her order. "Bad? But it's wonderful! Again the king has a queen. After forty nights—I thought he never would choose!"

Amestris stared at me; thin lines radiated from the corners of her mouth. "Vashti, you always were a fool. Do you not realize—no, of course you don't. There's nothing in your head but clouds and air."

Once her harsh words would have whipped tears to my eyes. Now I wanted to laugh—but I did not. I think I managed to look quite as foolishly baffled as she thought me. "But my lady queen, the maidens came to the palace so that my lord brother the king might judge them. What is wrong? Do you not like Queen Esther?"

For one delightful heartbeat, it seemed Amestris might melt from fury. "*Queen Esther?* Queen of one night! Who *is* this conniving girl? Who are her people? Where does she come from?"

I answered as if Amestris truly wished to gain this knowledge from me. "Her name is Esther, and she comes from here, from Shushan itself. She is—"

Amestris turned on me, her eyes fiery as a basilisk's. "I know her name is Esther, you silly girl. From Shushan itself. And I know she is the ward of Mordecai the Scribe, and anything else there is to know about her I will know before nightfall. As for her becoming queen—" Amestris shook her head. "A nameless thing with nothing but beauty? For all your faults, you at least are Belshazzar's granddaughter!"

"Ishvari's," I said.

"What?" For once, Amestris seemed taken aback.

"I am Queen Ishvari's granddaughter, too."

"Queen Ishvari? What does she matter? She's been dead these forty years! You are too foolish, girl." Amestris looked past me, at Tandis and Barsine standing quiet by the gate. I saw the corner of Tandis's mouth quiver, and shook my head very slightly; Tandis bit her lower lip and gazed modestly at the ground. Amestris raised her hands as if supplicating the gods. "Oh, *why* could that silly boy not choose one of Prince Shethar's daughters? Now, what am I to do about this appalling wedding?"

For even Amestris could do nothing, now that the king's choice had been proclaimed, save follow the rules laid down for royal rites. The king had decreed a wedding; a wedding there would be.

I stared at my feet; counted the poppies embroidered upon my golden slippers. When I thought I could keep my face smooth and my voice meek, I said, "I could help, perhaps." A timid offering, as if I expected a rebuff. "You know I planned the search for the new queen." Now I made my voice earnest, while searching my mind for the words that would ensure Amestris gave me the task of planning Ahasuerus and Esther's wedding. I found them. "And—and I would do just as well at this task!"

Amestris stared at me, clearly appalled. Then, slowly, she smiled. "Why, yes, Vashti. Perhaps you would."

Now I produced a delighted smile, as if Amestris had just granted me the world to rule as I saw fit. "Oh, I will, I will! And I vow to consult you on everything needful."

Amestris waved this aside. "I am quite certain that your decisions will prove everything I could desire, my dear. Do just as you think best."

And that is how it came to pass that I, Vashti, the set-aside and disgraced queen, managed the wedding of Ahasuerus, Lord of Media and Persia, King of Kings, to Esther, a Jewish maiden of the ancient city of Shushan.

ESTHER

After my night with the king, the next seven days seemed to rush past like a stream in spring flood. I did not see Ahasuerus again until our wedding day, but he never vanished from my thoughts and dreams.

To my surprise, it was Vashti who managed to have me standing with my hands in Ahasuerus's, vowing I would honor and obey him always as my husband, within a week's time. When she put her mind to it, Vashti could ignore obstacles with the single-mindedness of a monkey set upon obtaining the moon from the bottom of a well. And although the monkey might fall and drown while reaching for that illusory image, Vashti succeeded in her determination that Ahasuerus and I have a lavish royal wedding—

"One to make the entire empire forget his and mine," she said. "You need do nothing, Esther, save look beautiful and say a few words before the Sacred Flame. Here, I wrote them down for you." She shoved a scrap of papyrus into my hand and then ran off again.

Not a monkey, I remember thinking on that occasion, *a mongoose.* . . .

I was glad for someone else to take on the work of organizing my wedding, for I had enough and more to do. The moment my name was announced as the new Queen of Persia, the rooms, the garments, the gems that had been riches beyond my imagining became unworthy of me. No longer did I live in the best apartments in the Women's Palace; I was led back from my night with the king to the Queen's Palace.

For the Queen's Palace now was mine.

And a dozen dozen new servants were now mine, although I demanded, and got, my own servants to serve me closest. "I know I will have many others," I said, "but those who have cared for me lovingly and loyally this past year shall always hold the highest rank in my affections."

Then I demanded, and received, a promise that Vashti would not be forced to leave the Queen's Palace. That she would continue to live in the apartments that had been her home since she was ten years old.

"There is room enough for a dozen queens in this palace," I told Hegai, "and I will not evict Vashti from her own rooms. Tell everyone I turned my nose up at them and called them second-rate and second-hand, and that I demanded apartments of my own decorated to please myself."

"Extravagantly?" Hegai suggested, and I raised my eyebrows and replied, "Of course. Beyond dreams."

I meant it for a jest, but the jest became truth. I was Queen of Queens; anything I could even dream to wish for was mine for the asking. The trouble was that I could think of little I wished for, save to hold Ahasuerus in my arms. When I confessed this to my eunuch Hatach, he shook his head, appalled at my folly.

"Well for the sake of peace, don't tell him *that,* O queen!" Hatach fussed over my hair himself, proud of the fact that he was now chief chamberlain to the Queen of Queens, ruler of the Queen's Palace. This elevation pleased Hatach immensely, and made him thrice as fretful.

"But it's true, Hatach. Yes, pearls will do very well."

"It may be true—" Hatach snapped his fingers and a maidservant knelt, held out a tray on which ropes of ruddy pearls lay coiled; their rosy fire would glow like sunset against my hair. "—but it is completely unnecessary to tell the *entire* truth *every single moment.*"

"What should I say, then?"

"Say you wish whatever he wishes to bestow upon you. Or better yet," Hatach finished, "say nothing whatsoever. Just smile, and let the man think what he will."

So I, Hadassah bas Abihail, wed Ahasuerus, King of Kings, Lord of Half the World, before Ahura Mazda's Sacred Flame, by rites laid down so long ago no man living knew when or how. No woman, either.

I scarcely noticed the ceremony, or the flame, or that I spoke pagan vows. All I saw was Ahasuerus, and the love in his eyes. Then we were married, and walked together through the gate into the Queen's Palace to begin our new life together.

It was not so simple as that, of course. But for a month of sun-bright days and honey-sweet nights, I could pretend that it was.

All unwitting, Ahasuerus made it easy for me to lie to myself, for he proved a most loving and generous husband. Too generous, I told him—

"—truly, it is not necessary to bestow a gift upon me every hour of the day." The outpouring of gold and gems, slaves and silks, made me uneasy.

"Not necessary, but delightful," Ahasuerus said. "It gives me pleasure to bestow gifts upon you, beloved. Surely they give you joy?"

"It pleases me to give you pleasure, my lord and husband."

Ahasuerus smiled. "Then you will be very pleased indeed with this." He motioned Hatach forward; Hatach came forward, and bowed, and, with a smug look at me, placed an ivory casket in Ahasuerus's hands. Ahasuerus dismissed Hatach, then turned and set the ivory casket in my hands.

The precious box was old, the ivory deepened to the color of wild honey. Dragons coiled over the panels; whoever had carved them had been a master of the craft.

"It's beautiful," I said. "Thank you, my—Ahasuerus." Hot blood rushed to my cheeks; I had not yet become accustomed to such intimacy.

He leaned closer and kissed my cheek, his lips cool against my skin. "You are too easily pleased, Esther. That is not your gift. Open it."

Even more flushed, I obeyed, and found myself staring at a coiled necklace of rubies red as heart's blood. I looked up into Ahasuerus's eyes. "These are mine?"

He knew what I meant. "Yes, these are yours. Hegai presented them to me as a suitable morning gift for you. Apparently I am the only one in all Shushan who did not know you would be my queen."

There was a rueful amusement in his voice; better far than anger, but I did not want him ever to think what he had said half in jest was truth. I closed the casket's lid over the jewels that had bought my place in his palace, in his bed.

"No," I said, "there was one other who did not know it. I wept myself to sleep for forty nights fearing you would find your bride among those who came before me. And then I feared you would look upon me and—"

"Not see your beauty?"

"Not see your wife," I said.

"I will always see you, my wife," Ahasuerus said, and kissed my forehead. "Never forget that. Always."

Yes, even a king is entitled to his marriage month, when he and his bride seek only each other's company. But while a common man may enjoy as much longer as he wishes, a king must answer to duty. We claimed our days and nights full moon to full moon as husband and wife. And then Ahasuerus became King of Kings once more, and I—merely his queen.

It was hard, after the honey-sweetness of that month, to return to the strict routines of the women's world. Being queen did not bring me more freedom than most women possessed, but less. Oh, I will not pretend I did not enjoy many aspects of my royal and pampered life. Or that I did not stare into Hegai's famous silver mirror amazed at how I looked with the queen's diadem shining against my hair.

But I missed my husband. Being king, he had much he *must* do. I reminded myself of this daily, schooling myself to greet him only with fond words and open arms. That he was king was hardly his fault—nor could I claim I had no notion before I wed him what that would entail. Ahasuerus did all he could to make life weigh light upon me—and he remembered every word I had spoken to him during our halcyon time together.

I learned much more about my husband once we no longer dwelt on love alone. He liked to give gifts, and he liked to surprise me. I suspected he had at least one dedicated spy reporting to him, and that her name was Vashti. That was how he knew I liked singing birds, and why he sent me a nightingale in a golden cage. It would not sing in the cage, so I released the unhappy creature into my garden. The bird's wing-feathers had been clipped, so it could not fly free—and by the time its feathers had grown long again and it could fly away if it chose, it had become accustomed to the food I provided and to the safety of the garden's trees, and so it remained. I listened to the nightingale sing every night until the sweet melody ceased, or I fell asleep.

That, too, was how he knew that I, like Vashti, loved animals—Vashti had a veritable zoo of pets both exotic and commonplace, and she was pleased that I did not shrink away from them as many did. Truly, there was no need to fear any of them, for her animals had been reared as gently as highborn children, and had the soft nature such rearing engenders in animals.

For the past ten years I had missed the comforting presence of animals about me, but as I have said before, good Jews kept neither dogs nor cats, let alone wolves, cheetahs, and foxes.

So the day I opened a gilded basket set into my hands by Ahasuerus and looked down into a small fluffy face and very round dark eyes, I was so astonished I could only stare. The amber-furred puppy stared back, then began to crawl determinedly out of the basket. Regaining my composure, I scooped up the puppy before it fell; it promptly snuggled under my chin, apparently content.

"Do you like her?" Ahasuerus asked. "She comes from Cathay, and no other woman has such a dog."

"Of course I like her! Oh, Ahasuerus, *thank you.*" The only dogs I had touched since my father died and I came to live in Shushan had been the gazehound bitch and the pup I had saved when Haman drowned all the rest of her litter in a public fountain. *When Haman pulled off my veil, and tried to slash my face open with his whip.* But I knew better than to accuse Haman, the king's good friend and the Queen Mother's tool—just as I knew better than to say that Vashti, too, cherished such a small imperial dog, although hers was old, its golden fur woven now with silver. And Vashti's, too, had been given by a man who loved her. . . .

Ahasuerus leaned forward and kissed my forehead; the puppy yipped in outrage. "Yes, guard your mistress—who values you more than any gem I have given her." He stroked the puppy's chin. "What will you call her, my love?"

The name came unbidden to my tongue. "Ishtar. Ishtar, if you think the goddess will not object."

Ahasuerus laughed, and gently tapped the puppy's nose. "As this dog is far more royal even than I, and her ancestors belonged to gods—no, my heart, I do not think the goddess of love will take the name amiss."

That Ahasuerus put great thought into his gifts delighted me. But no gift pleased me so much as the one that granted a wish I had not even dared to dream. Hatach came seeking me as I sat reading on my favorite balcony, the one looking eastward to the sunrise hills, and announced that it was the pleasure of the King of Kings that his queen attend upon him. I rolled up my book, a history of the endless wars of the Greeks against Troy, and followed Hatach back to my chambers, smiling as the puppy Ishtar indignantly followed; I had disturbed her nap.

"O queen, the King of Half the World wishes you to come to him, and to wear this to please him." Hatach spread his hands, indicating the clothing spread upon a sandalwood chest.

I stared at the garb Hatach had laid out for me. A tunic of heavy amber silk; leather trousers sewn with golden leopard heads. Boots to lace up over my calves. "You are certain the king said I was to wear these garments? You heard him with your own ears?" I would not put it past a malicious rival to slip such a command into the chain of servants that ran between me and my husband. I would not accept hearsay.

"Yes, O queen, may you live forever. The King of Kings set them into my arms himself."

That surprised me more than the garments. Well, then Ahasuerus had some surprise planned for me. Something that required me to wear trousers—I remembered that when Vashti was queen, she had ridden out with him. And I remembered I had told him I was raised on a horse farm in the Karoun Valley.

So he wishes to surprise me by letting me ride with him—and I shall be as astonished as he wishes.

Ahasuerus still managed to amaze me. For when he led me through the stable courtyards, he stopped in the largest—a vast open space as large as some men's palaces—and gestured toward a line of horses, each held firmly by two grooms. Beautiful animals, well-muscled and strong-boned, the sunlight throwing a sheen of gold over their sleek hides. Nisean stallions, restive and powerful, hard even for two strong men to hold. Puzzled, I slanted a glance up at Ahasuerus.

"Fine stallions," I said, question in my tone.

"Ah, you have not guessed all my surprise, for all your wisdom, my love. Look closer—is there not one above all the others that takes your eye?"

I studied the stallions again. At first I saw only that any of these horses was worth a prince's crown. Then, as I turned my eyes down the line, my gaze stopped, caught by a heavy-muscled gray. I looked, and looked, and then I forgot I was Queen of Persia and stood by the side of the King of Kings. I pulled my hand from his and ran three paces forward. Then I put my fingers to my mouth and whistled.

The sound cut the air, piercing as a hawk's cry. The gray flung his head up, then half-reared and bounded forward off his haunches. The grooms could not hold him; he cantered across the smooth stones of the courtyard and stopped, pawing the ground, a few feet from me.

"Star," I said, and held out my hand.

He bowed his head and delicately stepped the last short distance between us. I set my hands upon the sides of his beautiful head, and he leaned his forehead against me. "Oh, my Star." I began to cry, and felt Ahasuerus's hand upon my shoulder.

"You are pleased, my heart?" he asked, and I managed to nod. When I stopped crying against Star's neck, I stepped back and examined him. I had not seen my hot-spirited darling for a decade; time had changed him. Age had paled his coat to moon-silver and added heavy muscle to his neck and shoulders. The pure white star still shone upon his left front fetlock, but I did not need that mark to know him.

The Master of Horse approached, bowed. "O queen, this is indeed a fine animal, but he is used only to set to the mares. No one can ride him, and did he not sire such fine offspring, he would long ago have been gelded."

"That still would not have reconciled him to a man upon his back," I said. "But I can ride him." I grasped a handful of Star's mane—and then I remembered, not that I was queen, but that it had been ten years since I had swung myself up onto a horse. I turned to Ahasuerus.

"If it please the king," I said, "and if it is permitted, will he assist me up?"

Ahasuerus smiled. "It pleases the king," he said and then, to the utter horror of the Master of Horse, bent and linked his hands together. I set my foot upon his hands and sprang onto Star's back.

Star danced sideways; my body swayed with the motion, remembering. I bent to kiss the crest of Star's neck, and to hide more tears.

"He was in my own stables all along," Ahasuerus said. "Is that not wondrous?"

"Oh, yes—almost as wondrous as you—I mean, my lord king—"

Ahasuerus laughed. "I'm your husband, Esther. You may call me by my name, or by any other name that pleases you."

"I am honored." I also had no intention of doing so, save in our most private moments. I knew what was due the king's dignity. Ahasuerus might wear that dignity easily—I liked him for it—but his queen should not seem to hold his honor lightly.

Nor should the king's dearest friend. It seemed to me that Haman acted too freely in the presence of the king—and not only in private, when a king could choose to set aside his exalted rank and remove his crown for a few brief hours. Ahasuerus had raised Haman high, and Haman took immoderate advantage of that favor.

Ahasuerus took great delight in presenting me to Haman, who was now the king's vizier; second only to the king in honor and power. I had no warning, no chance to don a veil. I could only pray that Haman had long ago forgotten my face.

But that hope did the moment Ahasuerus took my hand and said, "Dearest Esther, behold the man I love above all others. I hope Haman will prove as good a friend to you as he is to me."

For once I could think of no words to say. I clasped Ahasuerus's hand tightly and inclined my head. Haman stared at me, and I saw recognition flare in his angry eyes. He had no choice but to bow before me; I could see how he hated that.

"Haman, my good friend, you see that I am the most fortunate man in all the world—and I owe my happiness to you." Ahasuerus smiled upon us both.

I found my voice. "How so, my lord and my king?"

Ahasuerus seemed surprised. "Did not Vashti tell you that the reason you are here is because of Haman? The search for my queen sprang from his mind—I never would have thought of such a thing."

"Then I am in Prince Haman's debt." Since I knew it would please Ahasuerus, I managed to smile. I prayed I would never lay eyes upon Haman again, but that prayer was not answered—or say, rather, that the answer to my prayer was "no."

For since Ahasuerus regarded Haman as a brother, he brought Haman with him when he came to visit me in the Queen's Palace. I always made them both welcome; ordered Haman's favorite dishes prepared to set before him. My courtesy to his friend pleased Ahasuerus, and that pleased me. But I loathed Haman; my judgment of him could never be impartial.

I could never forget the image of Haman in a rage, drowning still-blind puppies in a public fountain. When forced to endure his presence, I retreated behind my veil, no matter that it was sheer as smoke, and spoke as few words to him as possible. Ahasuerus attributed this withdrawal to my innate modesty, but I do not think my chaste reserve deceived Haman. Just as when I looked upon Haman, I saw the man who had ripped away my concealing veil on the public street, when Haman looked upon me, he saw the woman who had wrenched his own whip from his hands. Only Ahasuerus kept us from engaging in open battle. I loved Ahasuerus too much to distress him by behaving cruelly to his dearest friend—

—and Haman loved being the king's friend too much to risk losing the riches and power it bestowed upon him.

So on days that Ahasuerus brought Haman into my garden, I greeted him with a low murmur of words that barely passed beyond the delicate fabric of my veil. And while Ahasuerus and Haman played chess, or Twenty Squares, or discussed the affairs of empire, I studied them both. I knew Haman was my enemy, for he both hated and feared me. Each time he accompanied Ahasuerus and was forced to laugh and talk, Haman watched me with keen eyes.

I feared that someday Haman would force Ahasuerus to choose between his friend and his wife. I knew I must never allow that day to come.

What I did not know was that I was already too late to prevent it.

VASHTI

I had liked Esther from the hour we first met in the Garden of Roses, and had admired her through the long year that had followed. But only now that Esther had become our queen did I understand how truly she deserved her crown. Its weight did not alter her, nor did the power that was now hers change her.

Queen Esther did not forget those who had befriended her, or those she had befriended. Generous with both coin and kindness, she even seemed to win Queen Mother Amestris's friendship—at least after Amestris's first anger faded. Esther dealt with her easily, softly, without apparent effort.

"It is simple," Esther said, when I expressed my admiration for her skill at managing the Queen Mother. "Amestris loves only one thing, power, and wishes only one thing, to be queen forever. I bow before her, and beg her to advise me, and I listen carefully as she speaks."

"But Esther—" I stopped, realizing that I was merely a princess of the House of Babylon—and Esther wore the diadem of the Queen of Queens. I had schemed to put that diadem on Esther's midnight-fire hair, and now must bow before the queen I had created.

Not an easy lesson, but a vital one. Ahasuerus must never be forced to choose between his beloved wife and his dearest sister.

And I knew I had much to learn from Esther. Esther's nature was a generous one, her heart a kind one. She was as clever at lessons and gifts as she was at languages and numbers.

My favorite gift from her was intangible—but most useful. I thought I rode well; I was wrong. Once I saw Queen Esther upon her Star, I knew I only sat upon a horse without falling off. Esther—she and the horse became one creature. I watched, entranced, as that creature danced across the earth. So swift, so fast.

So free.

"I would like to ride your Star," I said, when Esther rode back to me, and was astonished to hear her answer,

"No."

How dare she deny me! Swift anger kindled in my blood. Then, as I stared at Esther, the anger receded. *I am not queen. She is.*

"No one rides Star but me." Esther smiled; she did not know that her simple "No" had changed the way I looked upon the world.

That it had changed *me.*

I still dwelt in the palace as if I were a queen, but that was illusion only. I could dwell here all the rest of my days—as the king's sister, as the queen's friend, as—

What? The crown no longer bound me. But I was not yet free.

For a time, Esther's gift released me from my troubled thoughts. Soon after she had refused to allow me on Star's back, she came to me and said,

"I have a gift for you, my sister."

"A gift?"

"Yes, Vashti, a gift. Surely you have been given one before?" Esther smiled, and beckoned. "Come and see."

Esther's gift stood in the stable court, stamping her shining hooves impatiently. A mare, her coat the rich gold of honey, her mane and tail shimmering like jet. Dark sunshine dancing in the hot light . . .

"Mine?" I spoke as if never before had I set eyes upon a horse. The mare saw me and her restless hooves paused, then she sidled sideways, her small curved ears flicking back and forth.

"Yours." Esther, kind, did not laugh.

I had owned horses aplenty—or rather, the Queen of Queens had possessed a stable full of fine steeds, many of them as pale as my hair. But this mare was different. She had been chosen for Vashti. *For me.* Esther had taken great care, had chosen a horse matched to my temper and my skill.

After that, I rode almost every day upon Sunrise—for so I named the mare. Esther rode with me as often as she could. Under her tutelage, I became—not as fine a horsewoman as she—but at least a much better rider than I had been before.

I loved Esther's gift, and I loved Esther for her care for my happiness. Everyone loved Esther. Ahasuerus could have made no better choice for queen than she.

ESTHER

I was surprised when Daniel sent a message asking me to come to him; he had never done so before. When I arrived at his house, Daniel and Samamat sat waiting and neither smiled, so I knew something was very wrong. I sat at their feet and Daniel said, "Your cousin Mordecai came to see me again."

"Did he have another dream?" I asked, and Daniel shook his head.

"No, this time Mordecai came because he overheard a plot against the king. He was working in the King's Gate . . ."

Mordecai had missed the beginning of the ridiculous, deadly conversation, for the two eunuchs did not whisper. They spoke softly, but openly. Apparently it did not occur to them that they were not the only ones in the empire who understood Akkadian.

Of course, few men spoke that ancient tongue now, and of those who did, fewer still dwelt in Shushan. Mordecai, however, was one of them.

He had continued writing, creating neat, precise copies of the palace receipts, as the two eunuchs stopped conversing and began quarreling. It was that change in rhythm that had caught Mordecai's ear.

"The two of them argued the respective virtues of wolf's-bane and viper's venom." Daniel paused; Samamat added, "To use on the king. To make him ill, you understand, so they could cure him and gain his favor."

Ridiculous, and deadly. "What a preposterous notion. It's laughable. Who are these eunuchs?"

"Bigthan and Teresh," Daniel said. "Apparently they talk far too much. Perhaps that's why they're no longer servants in the king's chambers, but keepers of the doors."

Servants in the king's chambers until recently, now doorkeepers to the king's chambers. Unhappy with the change, hoping to re-enter the king's presence by poisoning him—and then curing him. Earning the king's eternal gratitude and favor—

Idiots. How can such fools be so dangerous?

Daniel handed me a letter. "This is from Mordecai."

I had not heard from my cousin Mordecai since the day I walked into the blue-and-white pavilion where my future awaited me. Now I looked once more upon words written in Hebrew in his neat scribe's hand.

> *Two palace eunuchs, Bigthan and Teresh, plot to poison the king. They wish to make him ill, that they may cure him with a miraculous antidote and earn his undying gratitude and reinstatement as servants in his chambers. Warn the king.*

I folded the message and tucked it into the emerald-set girdle about my waist. I knew better than to rush through the palace crying out that the king's life lay in danger. I would arouse panic, and Ahasuerus's guards would lash out in deadly reaction, seeing traitors where none existed.

No, this was a fool's plot by two fools. They alone should pay for their folly. My skin grew cold as I envisioned the two eunuchs pouring poison into Ahasuerus's wine. *Don't they know one can never be sure, with any poison? A drop too much, and no antidote under heaven can save him.*

Now I must warn Ahasuerus, but quietly. I allowed myself to think acidly that only Mordecai would deem it necessary to order me to warn my husband that he was in danger of being poisoned.

I returned to my own rooms and told Hatach to ready my riding clothes.

Then I sent a message to Ahasuerus, saying that it would please me greatly if it would please him to ride out with me before the sun set today.

Fortune favored me; it pleased Ahasuerus to honor my request. In the dying light, we rode beside the Choaspes, savoring the scent of the sweet water. I reined Star to a halt, and turned to Ahasuerus. "If it please my lord husband, there is something I must unfold to you."

Ahasuerus drew his horse to a halt beside Star; curbed his mount's attempt to snap at mine. "Well, my love? What is it?"

From the glint of laughter in his eyes, I knew he expected to be amused. The laughter swiftly died as I told him of the danger Mordecai had revealed to me. "So I beg of you, neither eat nor drink anything until the two have been taken. Do not put your hand into a chest, or into a pile of cushions. Do not touch—"

Ahasuerus held up his hand. "Stop, Esther. I am here, and safe. Now, how did you learn of this plot? Who told you?"

I laid my hand on Star's neck, calming, for my agitation had distressed him. "Mordecai the Jew—he's one of your best scribes, my lord king."

"And how do you know him?"

He is my cousin. I, too, am a Jew. You must know this, heart of my heart. How could Ahasuerus *not* know? Had he not regained my Star for me? Surely he must have learned that Abihail the horse-trader had been a Jew?

Or perhaps not. Perhaps Ahasuerus had merely said, "Find me such-and-such a horse," and thought no more upon the matter. For all that he had a keen enough mind, I had to admit that never had my beloved husband been encouraged to think for himself. Thinking, like any other skill, takes practice.

Why must the fire of my heart and the light of my eyes be—well, not a fool, but not very wise? Why does only this man of all men in the world delight my soul?

"My queen?"

I realized I had been staring at Ahasuerus instead of answering his question. "When he learned of the plot against you, Mordecai sent word to me, my lord king."

"And why not to me?"

My lord king chooses a fine time to ask clever questions! I touched my heels to Star's sides, a movement invisible to Ahasuerus; Star danced sideways, shaking his head. Soothing my apparently restive stallion gave me time to think how to answer.

"Perhaps Mordecai thought it safer to warn your queen, knowing she would at once inform you. And since all the world knows I cannot live out of your sight"—I slanted my eyes at him, and Ahasuerus grinned back at me—"my urgent request to ride out with you seemed only . . . commonplace. I'm sure Mordecai wished to avoid warning the traitors inadvertently, causing them to advance their plans and act in haste."

"Very wise." Ahasuerus stared down at his hands, and sighed. "Now I suppose I must attend to this matter. And those two fools will die for folly."

"And for plotting poison, my lord." I thought it wise to remind Ahasuerus of this. Still . . . "But I know you have a just and a merciful heart, my lord, so I suppose you'll merely hang them."

The empire meted out many far harsher deaths.

"I suppose so. I won't think about it right now. Remind me later to have it all written into the Court Record. Come, my queen and my love—I'll race you to that outcrop of rock. Now!" Ahasuerus urged his horse forward into a gallop.

Smiling, I held Star back, although only for so long as it took me to count to three. I knew Star would easily outstrip the king's mount—but I did not wish him to seem to win too easily.

Later, I carefully reminded Ahasuerus to have the entire incident written into the Court Record, that endless book of everything that passed in the palace and in the king's days. Sometimes, when Ahasuerus found it hard to sleep, I sat curled beside him, reading to him the minutiae that filled the scrolls. For the most part, the record was exceedingly dull; half an hour's reading in my quietest, softest voice, and my beloved husband found sleep easy to summon. I loved to see him so, peaceful and quiet in his mind as he seldom was during his over-full days.

I waited until we shared his bed, Ahasuerus curled about me like a great, fond cat. I leaned my back against the high-piled pillows and selected a scroll of the Court Record at random. "Before I read, may I remind you of a duty as yet undone?

"My love?" In the intimacy of his bedchamber, we were not king and queen, but husband and wife. I reveled in speaking without every other utterance being "my lord king."

Ahasuerus looked up at me through his dark thick lashes. "What duty would you have me perform, Esther? Whatever you desire is yours, to the half of my kingdom. What would please you?"

"Would you truly please me, my heart?"

"Of course. You are my beloved; all I possess is yours for the asking."

"Then if you would please me, cease offering me half your kingdom. I am your wife—your wife who dearly loves you. That love came freely, poured into me by the grace of the All-Wise God. You cannot buy me, Ahasuerus. I am already yours." I bent and kissed his brow. "I was yours the moment I set my eyes upon you, as you walked with your friend Haman on the western balcony."

He reached up, coiled his fingers about my wrist. "Would you deny me the pleasure of bestowing gifts upon you?"

"No, of course not. But such extravagant, meaningless vows have no place in our private world. Ask me plainly what I desire, and I will tell you. And I promise I shall never ask for the half of your kingdom."

"Why not?"

"Because that is not enough."

"What will satisfy you, then, my star?"

"Not half your kingdom"—I kissed him upon his mouth, my lips lingering, coaxing—"but your whole heart."

"That you have already." He pulled me down beside him, tossed the scroll of the Court Record onto the floor. "Forget that tedious recitation. I no longer desire sleep."

I put my hands on his chest and held him off. "Nor do I, but neither have I forgotten that I was to remind you to cause the affair of the treacherous eunuchs written into the royal record. You remember? Your loyal scribe Mordecai foiled the plot to poison you?"

"Of course I remember—it's not every day I am the target of such utter folly." Ahasuerus touched his fingers across my lips; frowned. "I suppose I should send for a scribe before the entire matter is lost to memory."

A scribe, and the scribe's apprentice carrying the tools of the writer's trade. And a guard watching from the doorway, and a eunuch to watch the guard—and farewell to our private, loving night together. I looked down into Ahasuerus's eyes, enthralling as night sky. "I have a better idea," I said. "Tell me what you wish the chronicle to say, and I will write your words into the Court Record myself."

He raised his brows. "You?"

"Yes, I. Do you not remember that among my other talents, I read and write half a dozen languages?" I sat up and shoved my hair back. "I am at your service, my lord king and my husband—unless you truly would rather spend half the night summoning scribes..." I shrugged; the robe I wore, translucent as black water, slid off my shoulders and down my arms, baring my breasts. Lamplight glinted on the gold dust powdered over my skin.

"Get the newest scroll," Ahasuerus said, his voice thick against the warm soft air, "and write as I will tell you. Write swiftly."

I laughed and did as he ordered. I think that was the most concise entry ever written into the Court Record of Ahasuerus, King of Kings. And the moment I drew the final stroke of the last word, Ahasuerus wound his hands through my tumbled hair and pulled me down until we lay breast to breast, skin to skin. The scroll and the pen fell away. Neither of us missed them.

Unmarked time later, we both fell into the heavy sleep of sated pleasure. And we both forgot the scroll of the Court Record in which I had written of how Mordecai had saved the king's life.

VASHTI

While Ahasuerus delighted in his wife, Haman savored the bloodshed to come. The death of all the Jews would rid the empire of Queen Esther, and King Ahasuerus would be no match for Haman, who would catch the crown as it fell. Haman saw himself seated on the throne, saw all the court bow down to Haman, King of Kings....

How do I know what Haman thought? Very simply: Zeresh told me, once she was safely Haman's widow. Haman's death freed her from a marriage worse than slavery, and Queen Esther offered her a place among the queen's ladies, a home in the palace. Zeresh accepted both eagerly—and revealed what had been behind Haman's plot to eliminate the empire's Jews.

Treason.

For Haman came to believe that he owned a better right to rule than did Ahasuerus. Oh, Haman wished the Jews dead, but the Adar Law was a means, rather than an end in itself. Haman desired the crown, and me as his queen. The slaughter of an entire people would send shockwaves through the empire, and in the fear and outrage that would follow, Haman would rise as savior of peace and safety. Since many Jews worked in the empire's service, after the thirteenth of Adar there would be many empty positions in King Haman's gift.

Zeresh knew Haman's devious plans because Haman himself told her. She feared him too much to betray even so much as one word—and she had been kept close-confined as a prisoner. Haman could not resist gloating over his cleverness, over the assured success of his wicked schemes.

And now that his plans lay in ruins and he as food for crows, Zeresh spilled forth all the words she had never before been permitted to utter.

So when I say "Haman thought such-and-so," I tell truth as Zeresh told it to me. . . .

When Ahasuerus divorced me, Haman considered that I was now . . . nothing. Surely I must spend my days weeping until my eyes reddened and my head ached. Haman thought me a soft, silly little fool. But fools can be useful—especially a beautiful fool who must miss the weight of a crown upon her head. Haman decided he must court me, entice me into friendship. Women, to Haman, existed only as vain, frivolous creatures, easily persuaded. They could be bribed with a few glittering baubles, or, if they were stubborn, convinced by a few well-placed blows. A woman did as she was told. Haman never tolerated a woman's whims.

Haman was certain I must bitterly regret my folly. A little sympathy, a little guidance from Haman—and I would become his ally within the palace. I was no longer Queen of Queens, but I remained a princess of Babylon. I remained King Belshazzar's granddaughter—

And Haman was a king's son.

Few knew this, for Haman's mother had been neither wife nor concubine to King Darius. She had been the too-beautiful wife of one of Darius's most devotedly obsequious princes. Prince Memucan denied his king nothing—not even his wife. The child King Darius had sired upon her had been claimed as Memucan's and given to another, far less exalted, family to rear. Until the Queen Mother had looked with favor upon Haman and he had become Ahasuerus's friend, Prince Memucan had ignored him utterly.

Now Memucan treated Haman with the utmost propriety—but he never met Haman's eyes.

I was unsurprised to hear Zeresh say that it was Queen Mother Amestris who had revealed his true parentage to Haman. Amestris had needed a new playing-piece, and a grateful and ambitious Haman suited her perfectly. And she disliked Prince Memucan, who made no secret of his opinion that the Seven Princes should have controlled the young king, rather than his mother.

Haman vowed that someday Memucan would kneel to him. Memucan would crawl to kiss Haman's feet. Haman vowed a great many things, Zeresh said.

So Haman had vowed and plotted—and then Haman's suggestion that Ahasuerus choose a new wife transmuted into an empire-wide contest to select a new queen. Haman had unwittingly handed me power when he abandoned management of the contest to me. That act meant I, and not Haman, influenced the king's choice. Haman had not succeeded in ingratiating himself with me, a failure he blamed upon Zeresh, by the time the king had made that choice.

When messengers rode out from Shushan carrying the news across the empire that the king had found his queen, Haman found new reasons for anger. Chief among them should have been his own folly, but it was easier to blame his troubles on someone other than himself.

In Shushan, the proclamation had been shouted out in all the squares and streets, and Shushan had run mad with joy. Their maiden had triumphed; the new Queen of Queens was their offering. Even this harmless delight infuriated Haman, but he showed only smiles to Ahasuerus; said only words of good wishes and ardent congratulations.

To Zeresh, Haman snarled that any real king—any real *man*—would have wedded and bedded his new woman within a month of banishing that foolish girl Vashti.

And Haman wondered just how pleased Ahasuerus thought his cast-off wife would be to hear him extol the virtues of the woman who would take her place. Certain that I must burn with anger and hurt, Haman confidently expected me to be grateful for an ally. He could not imagine that I did not secretly long to once again be queen.

Surely, Haman thought, I needed a strong friend now, one who dared risk all to gain the prize. A man who could set a crown upon my head once more.

A man such as Haman himself.

Once that thought slipped into Haman's mind, it coiled deadly as a waiting viper. As time passed, Haman's ambition reminded him that he, too, was King Darius's son. That he could have been king . . . that he *should* be king.

King Haman—why not? His blood was as royal as Ahasuerus's. They were half-brothers, after all.

And King Haman would need a queen; who better for him to marry than the daughter of Babylon's kings? Who better than Vashti? Haman saw himself reigning as King of Kings, with me as his adoring queen. Haman vowed he would not be a weakling swayed by a woman's soft voice and pretty face. A king should be stone and iron; strong and feared. . . .

The image of himself enthroned and crowned, with me kneeling before him kissing his feet and vowing eternal love and gratitude to my husband King Haman, brought a smile to his face.

Then, of course, said Zeresh in a flat, dead voice, Haman realized that to achieve his desires, both Ahasuerus and Esther must die.

This caused Haman no distress. He did not love Ahasuerus. And he hated Esther.

Haman had hated Esther since the day she had stopped him as he drowned mongrel puppies. To find her elevated to Queen of Queens shocked him, and discovering how greatly Ahasuerus relied upon her infuriated him. To

Haman, Esther was everything he loathed in women: educated, talented, strong-minded.

Jewish. Haman hated the Jews, too—sometimes it seemed, Zeresh added, that before he died, Haman had hated everyone. Why did Haman single out the Jews for his hate? Oh, because five hundred years ago a Jewish prophet had slain an Agagite king, even though the Jewish king had spared him, and Haman himself was descended from that slain king.

Not even Haman himself seemed to believe this a sufficient reason even for so uncritical an audience as his wife. More important, and more plausibly, a large number of vital posts in the imperial bureaucracy were held by Jews—a people notoriously loyal to the royal house. As Haman's plans transmuted from securing a place as the king's favored friend to claiming the crown for himself, the massacre of the Jews became vital to his plans. Such a bloodbath would create chaos; in such madness, the murder of the king and queen could easily be blamed on whomever Haman wished to name.

So Haman always intended the Jews within the civil service to die.

When the new queen turned out to be an old enemy, Haman expanded his plan still further.

All the Jews in the empire would die. And the Jewish queen would know she had brought about the death of her entire people. She and her cousin Mordecai.

Both of whom had committed the same crime.

They had told Haman "no."

Esther had refused to let Haman murder dogs and befoul water. Mordecai refused to let Haman trample people and law. Mordecai's encounter with Haman had occurred at the foot of the Great Staircase a few months after Ahasuerus married Esther. Haman's temper had grown even more vicious than it usually was, and he had ridden through the city with his usual brutal carelessness. But at the Great Staircase even Haman had to rein in, unable to see a clear path.

"Make way!" his servant called out. "Make way for Prince Haman, the king's friend!"

Few heard or heeded; the noise of hundreds of voices swept over the Great Staircase, rhythmic and unstoppable as the sea. Haman's servant shouted again, waiting for a path to open before moving upward. Being thwarted even in so small a matter set Haman's temper past anger into fury.

"Out of my way!" Haman spurred his horse, iron thorns drawing blood. The stallion bounded forward, thrusting Haman's servant aside and fleeing across the first stair at a gallop, in defiance of every rule governing use of the Great Staircase. A half-dozen strides, and the stallion shied, half-reared. A man barred Haman's path.

He stood straight and tall, and regarded Haman with stern reproach. "Such riding is a danger to you and to others, and it is against the law besides."

Haman glared at the man, recognized him as one of the king's favored scribes. A scribe—how dare the man accost and accuse him? "I am Prince Haman. Bow before me and get out of my way."

"No," said the scribe. "You are in the wrong, not I."

Rage burned; Haman slammed his spurs into the stallion's sides again. The stallion sprang onward—but Haman's hope of seeing the scribe knocked to the ground and trampled was thwarted by the man's simply stepping aside. Haman looked back and saw the man still standing, watching him.

By the time Haman reached the top of the Great Staircase, hot fury had cooled to steady anger. And he had remembered the scribe's name.

Mordecai.

Haman already knew all about Mordecai the chief scribe. The man lived a life of almost unbelievable virtue. His work was praised, his character extolled, his wisdom lauded. A Jew, Mordecai had little family in Shushan, for most his kin journeyed to Jerusalem when the king granted the Jews the right to return to their homeland. Mordecai's only family now was a cousin, his uncle's daughter, Hadassah.

Queen Esther.

⁜

Easy to declare that all the Jews in the empire must be destroyed—harder to put such a plan into action. The mere execution would not, Haman thought, be difficult; most of the Jews dwelt in the empire's cities. Trapped within city walls, they would be easy to catch and kill.

But such a slaughter required legal backing . . . that would be difficult to arrange. Not impossible, but difficult . . . Haman once again calculated paths to his goal. When he settled upon one, he assessed it carefully, mentally tested each facet until he saw no flaw. Then he waited until the time was ripe for him to set his scheme in motion.

That time came when King Ahasuerus had left Shushan on a royal visit to Babylon and did not asked Haman to accompany him. Haman took this as the sign he had waited for.

And then, Zeresh said, Haman requested an audience with Queen Mother Amestris.

ESTHER

When Haman begged the Queen Mother to receive him, deep satisfaction warmed Amestris. She knew Haman intended to use her to forward his own schemes—but he was *her* weapon, and must be taught his proper place. Once she no longer needed him, Haman would fall as swiftly as he had risen. . . .

How do I know Amestris's very thoughts? I did not—then. Only much later, when Amestris surrendered the power she had stolen, did she reveal her mind during those murderous days. Once she had fallen, I found myself—not her friend, but her confidant. I rarely had to ask a question, for Amestris longed to talk. To display her long clever schemes, her plots intricate as silk knotwork. And that was when I realized that for all her power, Amestris had been lonely, even if she herself did not understand that.

For she had kept too many secrets, and had no one in all the empire who could know what she did, and marvel, and praise.

So here, then, is what Amestris did, and why she did it. . . .

When I first became queen, Amestris had been willing to be pleased with me once her first anger passed. A merchant-class Jew, well-educated and well-mannered—yes, Amestris had been prepared to shape me into a useful tool. She had done it before, with Queen Vashti.

But I was no pliable, obedient child, as Vashti was. It was too late for Amestris to mold me as she had Vashti. And even had I been meek and biddable, I was too in love with my husband to be of any use to Amestris.

If I had desired only to be queen, all would have been simple, but all the court saw how dearly I loved the king. Amestris saw far more; saw that I sought to open his eyes, to urge him to grow into his power. To Amestris, who had ruled as the Queen Mother for nearly twenty years, I posed a danger.

Amestris saw far too much of herself in me.

So she decided she must distract me from such meddling. She considered a number of ways to accomplish that delicate task: *Poppy,* had been Amestris's first thought. Common, easy, simple to insinuate into food and drink. Create in me a taste for poppy syrup and I would dream away my life.

But Amestris could not truly envision me captured by that vice—and feared I would notice the change in myself. What, then? Amestris considered inculcating in me a desire for voluptuous pleasures, for rich food and drink, for costly gems and garments. Even, perhaps, an over-fondness for my handmaidens—

Amestris chastised herself for sparing so palpably foolish a notion even a moment's thought. The most natural distraction would be a child, something outside Amestris's power to provide. Of course Ahasuerus and I most virtuously and often performed our marital duty, so surely soon I would announce I carried Ahasuerus's child. With the blessing of the Good God, I would bear Ahasuerus a son . . .

And then Amestris looked into the future, and what she saw there nearly doomed an entire people.

My son would be heir to the empire.

I would be Queen Mother if Ahasuerus should perish. Amestris knew she herself would be as nothing, with her son gone. Power would slip from her hands into mine. Amestris could not endure the thought.

So Amestris decided that I must be removed from her path. Once she reached this conclusion, she decided to set the question of my fate aside for a time. She was certain a solution would present itself.

Patience was one of the few virtues Amestris possessed.

The solution was presented to her by Haman, although when she granted his request for an audience, she had no idea her problem—me—was about to be solved. Amestris listened to only a few words of Haman's well-practiced flatteries before lifting her hand.

"Enough, Prince Haman. Tell me why you have come."

"O queen, I have learned of a people within the empire who threaten its peace—and its king."

"Really? And which race is that, Prince Haman?"

"The Jews. They keep their own laws, not ours. They are arrogant—"

"So are you, Haman . . . at times. So are the Seven Princes." Although she did not shift so much as her lashes, Amestris tensed, waiting; like a hunting cat, she sensed prey. Whatever Haman wished to say about the Jews would be very important to her.

"As my lady queen says." Haman smiled back and spread his hands wide.

"Yes, as I say. Now, Haman, what precisely is it that you want?"

Haman regarded Amestris steadily. "I want a decree ordering all the Jews killed. I will, of course, undertake the administration of the decree."

"Why?" Amestris asked, hoping to catch Haman off guard. He disappointed her.

"As for why I ask this—it's a simple thing, really. These people are . . ." Haman paused, as if selecting the word least likely to sully the Queen Mother's ears, ". . . a nuisance."

"A nuisance?" Amestris raised her perfectly arched brows. "So much trouble for you to take, my lord Haman, for a mere nuisance."

"No effort is too great when serving the King of Kings." Haman bowed and looked up through his lashes, silently implying his true service was to the Queen Mother herself.

"Of course." Amestris stroked her fingertips over the lion's head snarling beneath her hand. "And what would this so-great effort on your part cost the King of Kings?" She eyed Haman coldly. "To surrender an entire people into your hands—a people who pay tribute and taxes—the empire will lose much if you gain this boon."

Haman smiled. "There are not so very many of them—a few thousand at most. And the empire will lose nothing. I myself will pay for them."

"I see. Shall we say—ten thousand talents of silver?" Now she would see just how greatly Haman desired this favor.

"A most fair price," Haman said, and Amestris laughed, low and scornful.

"You would pay ten thousand talents of silver to rid the empire of a nuisance? Do you think me a fool? Tell me your true reason or the Jews will live long and prosperous lives."

Haman sighed, and seemed to yield. He claimed long-smoldering anger at the Jews, that he was heir to a feud dating back to King Agag's defeat by King Saul, and Agag's execution by the Prophet Samuel. "I am descended from kings—from King Agag. It is my duty to avenge him."

Here, Amestris told me, she nearly laughed—a joy she denied herself. Amestris did not believe for even a breath that this was Haman's motive. "Vengeance for a battle lost five hundred years before Haman was born? What nonsense!" she told me, and I had to agree. *"Men,"* she said, and for a moment I felt sorry for her. . . .

However, Amestris allowed herself to smile at Haman. "I see. Well, that will do for a reason, I suppose. Well, since you think the Jews worth ten thousand talents of silver to you, you may have them."

Haman had bowed very low, perhaps to conceal his expression; he had, after all, apparently won the encounter. "But there is one slight difficulty—oh, not with the silver; that is a trifle. There must be a decree written, and it must be sealed into the Laws of the Medes and the Persians with the king's own seal."

"That should not be even a slight difficulty." Amestris tilted her head to the side, regarding him slantwise. "Write an edict against the Jews using the words you think best. And my lord Haman?"

He paused in mid-bow, looked up. Amestris kept her face still and cold as mountain stone.

"There is no need to trouble the King of Kings over so trifling a matter."

"But the seal? The edict must be sealed into law by the king."

Amestris knew this for the most dangerous, delicate part of Haman's murderous plan. *My softhearted son will never knowingly seal such a decree into Median and Persian Law. Even if his own queen were not condemned by it—which she is.*

Amestris smiled. "Sealed by the king's seal. Bring me the edict, when you have written it as you would have all done, and the king's seal will turn your edict into law."

She watched as Haman realized she possessed a copy of the king's seal—but that Amestris had not actually admitted as much.

Once Haman bowed himself out, all sly reverence and cunning evil, Amestris put her hand between her breasts, reassuring herself that her copy of the king's seal still lay there, as it had since the hour the infinitely precious object had been delivered into her hands. Ahasuerus had been a child of seven then.

No one but she herself knew of its existence. The jeweler who had created it had died suddenly—a pity, for he had been very skilled, but Amestris trusted no one. Whoever held the king's seal owned the empire. Ahasuerus had never suspected—why should he? What great king can know every edict governing an empire stretching from Hind to Tyre?

And Amestris had been very, very clever. She had not had two seals made, but three. Two she had, with all due ceremony and honor, placed in Ahasuerus's hands when he came of age. Half the court had whispered that she had a copy of the king's seal; that never would she give it up—whispers that ceased when she gave those two seals into Ahasuerus's keeping. Ahasuerus kept one seal; the second had been ground into dust.

The third remained her most cherished secret; her ultimate weapon.

Now that seal would once again serve her well. Of course Ahasuerus would, in time, know of this law concerning the Jews—but not until the edict had already been sealed into a law bought and paid for by Haman's silver. Even the king could not alter a sealed law. And why should Ahasuerus care about the Jews?

But Amestris knew he would care about me. This edict would condemn even the Queen of Queens to death—and even the King of Kings could not save her.

Amestris decided to ensure that Ahasuerus was far from the heart of the empire when Haman's law was carried out. That would be wisest—the king far away from Shushan, hunting in the Zagros Mountains. By the time he returned, it would be too late for the Jews.

More important to Amestris, it would be too late for me. Amestris decided to tell Haman he must kill me himself, and first. Yes, Ahasuerus must be far away . . .

And then it would be necessary to find her son still a third queen. Briefly, Amestris considered trying to reinstate Vashti, rejected the idea. Vashti no longer seemed as malleable, as oblivious to all but her own childish pleasures, as she had been before she had defiantly refused to obey a royal command.

No, Amestris must find yet another queen. She strove to regard this as a challenge. Oddly, she could not summon any emotion other than a flat distaste. For a heart-freezing moment, she found herself thinking, *I am growing old and tired. . . .*

Silent words that frightened her into fierce anger, a fury she released on the slaves who had the misfortune to enter her presence bearing bowls of grapes and peaches and tall pitchers of wine. Their fear helped reassure her that she was not old.

Not powerless.

Not yet.

VASHTI

I heard of the edict against the Jews before any other, for Haman himself hastened to reveal it to me. He had his reasons, which I soon learned. I have said Haman cherished ambition greater even than that of Queen Mother Amestris, who merely sought to cling to power she considered her own. Amestris preferred others to be happy—happy men and women did not think too hard or long.

Haman could be comforted in his heart only when all around him were less than he in all things. For Haman, it was all for him—or it was nothing.

Unaware that I did not like him, Haman sent a message to me. I thought this strange, so I took the folded and sealed parchment to Esther before I broke the seal.

"Esther—Haman has just sent this to me." I held out the small triangle of parchment on the palm of my hand as if it were an offering to a goddess.

She smiled. "Perhaps you have an admirer, Vashti?" As I made a disgusted face, Esther laughed. "Well, it looks like a message. Why don't you read it?"

"I don't want to. I don't know why, but I just don't. I thought of burning it."

"A waste of papyrus. You want me to open and read it, don't you?"

"The queen is, as always, wise," I said in the honeyed tones of an importunate courtier, and she laughed again.

"Oh, very well—but you're as lazy as that cat, Vashti." Esther gestured at the long-haired white kitten sleeping on the window ledge; the small creature radiated warm peace. I set Haman's message in Esther's hand, and she gazed down upon the black wax, sealed with the sharp-beaked bird that was Haman's sigil. She slid her gilded thumbnail under the seal, prying it off unbroken, a knack I was always too impatient to employ.

"Ah," she said a breath later.

"Well? What does Haman want of me?"

Esther slanted her hawk's eyes at me. "He wants you to grant him an audience, Vashti. Privately. I told you—an admirer." She did not sound as if she thought Haman had suddenly discovered strong lust for me in his heart.

"Privately?" That sounded odd, and unseemly. "Well, I will not see him, privately or no."

"Hmm. Actually, Vashti . . ." Esther folded the message back into the tight triangle, pressed the seal back down. She tossed the message back to me. "I think you should grant Haman's request."

"You do? Why?"

"Oh, I am *so* tempted to say, 'Because the Queen of Queens commands it'—but I won't. It is because, my dearest Vashti, I very much want to know what it is that Haman wishes to say."

⁂

That is how I, who had been a queen, became a queen's spy. Once Esther had explained, I delightedly undertook my part in the affair. Excited, I wrote out an answer to Haman, copying down words Esther gave me. Haman was to meet me on the Great Staircase, on the western side of the third step down from the King's Gate.

"You may disguise yourself as my beloved brother again," Esther said, as I folded my message. "No, don't seal that. If it falls into anyone else's hands, it will not bear your seal."

I nodded, delighted at this chance to act on Esther's behalf. Odd—since I had lost my crown, I had done far more than I ever had while I had worn it. I had ruled the search for the new queen. I had *chosen* the new queen.

And now I played the spy for the queen I had chosen. For a moment I understood why Amestris would not release the reins of power.

Meddling was delightful.

To undertake Esther's task, I was forced to take Hegai into my confidence, and then forced to listen to his extremely long list of reasons why I should not, could not, must not do this thing. At last I put my hands on his arm and said,

"Dear Hegai, can you truly be saying I should disobey the queen's command?"

"The two of you," Hegai snapped, "should have been soundly whipped as children. Perhaps you would not now be striving to drive your devoted servants mad."

But Hegai, too, had been charmed by Esther—and he knew she did not ask great favors lightly. She would not ask such a thing of me at all did she not think it urgent to know what Haman desired. So Hegai brought me the saffron-dyed tunic and blue-and-white trousers the king's pages wore, helped me bind up my hair and hide it beneath a crimson turban. As a final touch, Hegai pinned a gold star set with a blood-red stone upon the turban and pronounced me ready.

"And I will accompany you. Close your lips, Vashti, for either I go with you or I go to the king and lay the entire matter in his hands."

"But Hegai, everyone knows you!"

He smiled. "Of course they do. Everyone knows me very well."

I sighed. "Too well. Now, how do we disguise you?"

"We do not. Hegai the Chief Eunuch chooses to walk abroad to savor the last of the spring air, accompanied by a page. A pretty boy, with a look of She-Who-Is-No-Longer-Queen about him. By Varkha, in fact. But you would know nothing of that resemblance, of course."

Hegai always had been able to make me laugh—and I admitted it a clever scheme. It would seem far less odd that Hegai sent his page to speak to Haman on the Great Staircase than that Haman should stop to engage a pageboy in intent conversation.

And that was how the Chief Eunuch of the Queen's Palace came to be walking upon the Great Staircase, carrying a white horsehair flywhisk and followed by a tall, pale-faced king's page.

Haman waited for me on the third step down from the King's Gate, as he had promised. As we reached that step, Hegai stopped and beckoned me forward, then nodded toward Haman, who paced impatiently along the edge of the step. I bowed, and ran over to Haman.

"Prince Haman. I am here." I could not imagine what Haman had to say to me. "Speak quickly; I cannot remain here long."

"Of course not, O queen." Haman managed to incline his head without, quite, bowing.

Already his manner irritated me, but I kept my voice low and calm. "I'm not queen now."

"*Now.* But *now* is not *forever.* You can be Queen of Queens again."

So that was it: treachery aimed at Esther. Proud of my cool tone, I said, "Can I indeed? And how is that possible?"

Haman smiled, and at that sight of the look of triumph in his eyes, my heart seemed to beat cold and slow. Whatever he would say was going to be bad indeed. But I could not guess *how* bad—who could, who was not as mad as my great-grandfather King Nebuchadnezzar?

"It is possible because soon Queen Esther will not exist. For all the Jews in the empire are condemned. *All,*" he repeated, as if he relished the word. "All of them—no matter what their rank or riches. Since Queen Esther is a Jew, she, too, will die." Haman smiled again. "I think I shall reserve the privilege of slaying her for myself. With Esther gone, the gate will be open for you to return to King Ahasuerus."

As I stared, unable to believe such evil words, Haman stepped closer. "You were set aside by one decree, but another can be written. I will write it myself and it shall be sealed into the Laws of the Medes and Persians that you shall again be queen. You see how good a friend I am to you? I know you will be grateful to so good a friend. Grateful, and generous, and kind."

I kept my eyes wide, gazing at Haman as if astounded—which I was—and admiring—which I was not. Even with the summer sun pouring its light upon me, ice seemed to press upon my skin. "Kill all the Jews?" I repeated. I hoped I sounded only slow-witted, and not horrified.

Haman bowed his head. "Indeed."

"But—how?" How had Ahasuerus been persuaded or tricked into sealing this slaughter into law?

"Ah, now that was not an easy task to achieve." Haman puffed himself up, a man who has labored hard and virtuously for no reward but his own good opinion. I called upon every god and goddess I had ever heard mentioned, begging them all for aid, for I knew I must keep all my wits about me now. I opened my eyes even wider.

"Surely it cannot have been! Will you tell me how you accomplished so great a labor?"

Haman lunged at the bait—Haman loved to boast—and once he began to speak, I quickly feared he never would stop.

"This evil race deals in treachery and witchcraft, but I have arranged to destroy them before they wreak disaster upon the King of Kings and all he possesses. I have worked long and hard, and now they will be destroyed utterly. A decree has been written, and sealed into the Law of the Medes and Persians with the king's own seal. The law says that all of them shall be slain."

"All?" *All the Jews in the empire? All, because he hates Esther? He is truly evil, or mad—or both.*

"Yes. All." Haman savored the words.

"I could warn the queen of this," I said, and Haman smiled.

"You could." His tone clearly said he knew I would do no such thing.

"Queen Esther is my friend." I lowered my gaze, as if I could not meet his eyes.

Haman laughed, the sound mocking, vicious—and I looked up and saw a smug certainty on his face. A certainty that Queen Esther was only a woman.

Now I strove to be Haman's image of me: a deposed queen longing to regain her royal title, a scorned princess striving to hide her angry envy of the current queen. A foolish, jealous woman—

"Queen Esther thinks she is my friend," I amended.

"That I believe," Haman said. "So long as she believes it until—"

"Until when?" I marveled at how calm I sounded. I did not permit myself to think of how or why Ahasuerus could possibly have set his seal to such a decree.

"The day is set and sealed. The thirteenth of Adar."

"Why then?"

Haman smiled. "Because that is the day the *pur* decreed." He opened his hand; within it lay a *pur* carved from bone. He held the gambling piece out to me.

I pretended to hesitate. "When she learns of this decree, the queen will plead with Ahasuerus, and he will—"

"He will do nothing." Pleasure thickened Haman's voice. "He will do nothing because he will not call for Esther to come to him. I have seen to that."

"How? Ahasuerus returns from Babylon tomorrow. We all know he is besotted with her, and cannot bear to be without her for long."

"But he must endure without her until the next new moon. Before the king left Shushan, we played at lots—I used this very *pur,* for luck—and the king lost. The stakes were a month without the woman dearest to our hearts. The king's month begins on his return. Esther will await his summons in vain." Haman gloated over his own cunning.

One of the oldest decrees in the law tablets forbid anyone to come before the king except at the king's command. Guards flanked the king's golden throne, their sword blades honed to razor keenness. Even the queen could not approach the king's throne unless summoned. Even the queen would be cut down by the guards. . . .

"Princess?" Haman's sharp voice jolted me back, reminded me of the role I played.

I frowned, as if trying to think. "But my lord prince, surely the king will learn of this decree? Surely someone will show him the Adar Law?"

"What if they do? I shall tell the king the law is a forgery, that no one will believe its order, still less carry out murder on its command. I shall tell him the proclamation has been removed wherever it was posted." Haman smiled, showing too many teeth. "But who can know how many copies of the law were given out?"

I frowned, as if thinking hard. "But suppose—suppose *I* told him?"

Haman shook his head. "Ahasuerus cannot make you queen again. Only I can do that. And," he added, "even if you *are* foolish enough to warn Ahasuerus, I am not fool enough to let him believe you."

I opened my eyes very wide. "Oh, no, I am not so foolish as that!"

The *pur* still gleamed bone-white upon his hand. "Pretend to take this for the Chief Eunuch. Remember how a king's page would act."

Haman's assumption I could not retain my role without his prompting goaded me, but I proved him wrong to my own satisfaction by remaining smooth-faced, and bowing just as a king's page would do. "As my lord prince Haman says."

I held out my hand. The bone lot slid from Haman's hand into mine.

"To remind the true queen of what awaits her," Haman said. "A crown again—after Adar."

ESTHER

When I was told that Mordecai knelt at the foot of the Great Staircase in sackcloth and ash, that he wept and moaned and tore his poor garments, I am ashamed to say that my first thought was *Oh, what does he want of me* now?

And to prove no ill thought goes unrebuked by the Lord of All, no sooner had I thought those churlish words than Vashti came hastening into my room unannounced.

"Oh, Esther, I have spoken to Haman. And I've never heard anything so wicked in my life. There could be nothing more evil under the sun and the moon." She gasped her words, her breath catching as if she had run long and hard. Her hair had been pinned up in an untidy mass; as she spoke, it slid free, tumbling down her back. A voluminous robe swathed her, and as she reached out to me, the robe fell open. Beneath it Vashti wore the garb of a king's page.

This is going to be very bad. I knew in my bones that whatever Vashti had to tell me about Haman, it had something to do with Mordecai's sackcloth and mourning. Nevertheless, I remained calm—at least outwardly.

"Vashti, come and sit, and breathe slowly. I can hardly understand a word you say." I put my hands on her shoulders and guided her to a pile of cushions, gently pushed her onto them. She sat and stared up at me, her moon-shadow eyes a swirl of pale colors. I saw a fearful excitement there, and a deep horror.

"Hush," I said, as she opened her mouth to speak again. "Wait."

With Vashti resting silent, I turned to my servants. "Leave us, every one of you save Hatach and Kylah." Looking back down at Vashti, I asked, "Where is Hegai?"

"He—he has gone to ask who knew of—oh, Esther, there is a decree, a decree sealed with the king's seal, that the Jews are to be killed. All of them, *all.* On the thirteenth day of Adar—and Haman told me he will kill you himself and raise me up again as queen and expects me to be grateful to him! *Grateful!* And—"

"Stop," I said. "Vashti, this is madness."

"Yes, because Haman is mad. Mad and evil and—"

"Have you seen this decree? Did Haman show it to you?"

Vashti shook her head. "Hegai will bring a copy. I told him you must see it for yourself."

"And Haman said this evil decree is sealed into law? With the king's seal?" I shook my head. "No. Never. Ahasuerus would not—" I stopped. No, Ahasuerus, kind and just, would never seal into law the slaughter of an entire people. So if Haman's decree had indeed been sealed with the king's seal . . .

Then there is another seal.

It was the only answer. And who would possess such a seal, and wield it, save the Queen Mother? Queen Mother Amestris, who had ruled in her son's name since he was seven years old; who lived for power. I closed my eyes; swayed, dizzy. *Ahasuerus's mother—will he believe such evil of his own mother?*

I opened my eyes; the world remained. *I am not dead yet.* And now I knew why Mordecai had clothed himself in rags and ash. He mourned his death, and mine, and that of all our people.

"No," I said. "*No.* Ahasuerus will not permit this. When he learns—"

"Haman will ensure that he doesn't. And it's sealed with the king's seal, Esther!"

I saw that Vashti was too distressed to think at all. "Go to your own rooms," I told her, "and wait. I must send a message to my cousin Mordecai. When he has answered me, I will come to you. I want to speak to Hegai as well."

"Haman will not touch you. I will hide you in my rooms. We will take Star and Sunrise and ride away to the mountains." Vashti's fierce desire to protect me made her voice unsteady. "I will kill Haman myself! Esther—"

"Vashti, stop." I put my arms around her and held her close, her cheek pressed to mine; her body trembled and her skin was cold. "Be calm, or you will make yourself ill. Send your girls to find Hegai, and go to your own apartments and *wait.* Be patient. No one will kill me today. The thirteenth of Adar is still a month away."

VASHTI

I sent Tandis and Ajashea to bring Hegai to me, and together we waited. With Hegai's aid, I summoned patience, a hard thing for me. I did not pace, nor constantly ask Hegai when he thought Esther would bring news. Instead, I sat beside Hegai and held his hand.

To pass the time, I talked to Hegai. I knew he would listen quietly to my words, however far my thoughts might wander. I spoke of journeys we might undertake; of far horizons we might seek. Hegai agreed it would be a wonder to travel and to see with our own eyes the glories the empire possessed. *Mountain valleys rich with flowers. Burning deserts with heat rippling over endless sand. Ruined cities as old as time. Shining waters of the Western Sea. . . .*

"I want to see everything, Hegai. I want to ride the Royal Road from Shushan to Sardis. I want to see the land silk comes from. I want—"

"You want to *live,* my princess. Palaces and precious gems are not enough to make you happy."

"And what do you want, Hegai? What would make you happy?" Never before had I thought to ask him such a thing.

At first I thought he would not answer, for he neither moved nor spoke. Then he leaned to me and kissed my forehead; his lips warm against my skin. "It would make me happy to see you happy."

Once I would have thought he jested, and cajoled and teased him until he gave me a true answer. Today I looked into his eyes, and saw that he, too, feared the future Haman planned. So, weary from the day's events, I leaned my head upon his shoulder; I trusted Hegai as I did not even trust myself. For a moment I closed my eyes; savored the comfort of Hegai's arm around me, strong and sure as a wall at my back.

At last I heard sounds at my door. I darted toward the archway, only to be pulled back by Hegai's hand on my arm.

"Patience, Vashti. The Queen of Queens approaches. Remember that."

"No, today Esther approaches." But I let Hegai put his hand on my shoulder, and I waited for Esther to come in to me. When I saw her, I was glad I had not run to her, for Esther stood very straight, and her face might have been an ivory mask.

I waited, but she said nothing, so I spoke first. "Esther? What happened? Tell me!"

"My cousin Mordecai sent me a message." Esther's lips closed again; set in a firm line, as if they never again would open.

"Yes, yes, you heard from your cousin. What did he say?" I knew Mordecai, wise and good and just, would have found a way out of this trap.

For too long a pause, Esther said nothing. Then, "That I need not think I shall escape, merely because I am queen. That I must go to the king and beg for the lives of my people. And he also said, 'Who knows but that you were set upon the throne for such a time as this?' "

"Was that all?"

"Yes. That was all." Esther managed to smile at me. "Well, I'll have a fine tale to spin for Ahasuerus—strange pillow-talk for a reunion of man and wife, but I think my husband will find it of some interest."

She expected Ahasuerus to call for her as soon as he returned. But I knew what Esther did not: that the king would not send for her again until it was too late. "Esther," I said, "there is something else I must tell you. Haman has—has—" Tears burned my eyes; I found I could not find breath to finish.

Esther sat down beside me and took my hands. "Softly, Vashti." She bowed her head, staring down at our clasped hands. "I think I can guess what Haman has done. He has ensured that the king will not send for me. Am I right?"

I nodded. "He must spend a month without the woman dearest to his heart. Haman said a wager at dice—"

"The cause does not matter. All that matters is that Ahasuerus thinks he cannot, in honor, call for me, or come to me." Esther sighed. "Well, then, I must go to him—no matter what he wagered with that venomous Haman."

"But you cannot go to the king unsummoned, Esther!"

"Do you think I do not know that? How odd—you lost your crown for not coming when called by the king, and I shall lose mine for going to him when not called."

I looked at Esther standing there, and realized that she had grown into a woman, and a queen. Suddenly I realized that I—I, foolish, brainless Vashti—I had taught her—but it was Esther who had learned. Now she was the one who must think, and choose. I bowed, low, and spoke softly.

"O queen, live forever." And then I went and curled up like a cat upon the cushions, waiting. She would know I was hers to command, but that I would not interfere. This was her test, not mine.

Hours flowed past, slow as poured honey. Whenever a servant crept in, I shook my head, sending them away again. Sunlight faded; shadows led into darkness. The last hint of day vanished. I could only see Esther because starlight called answering fire from the jewels in her hair.

"Vashti?" She sounded as if she woke from deep sleep.

"Yes, Esther. I am here."

"Still? You are a good friend." A pause. "It's dark." She sounded baffled.

I rose slowly to my feet, stiff from my vigil. "Esther, it's night."

"It is?"

"You've been sitting there still as stone since you told me you must think what to do. Esther . . ." I almost hesitated to ask, but I knew I must. "Have you—"

"Thought what I must do?" A sigh; she sounded as weary as if she'd labored hard through the slow hours. "Yes, Vashti, I have."

I waited, but she said nothing more. "Well, what? Tell me. We must act swiftly." I did not know if it would be possible to act at all, but we could not just sit in the Queen's Palace drinking pomegranate wine while an entire people was slain in the king's name. I could not even imagine the chaos and terror that would follow such a massacre. Would the empire even survive such an evil deed?

"I must go to the king and petition him before all the court," Esther said, and for a breath I thought she had run mad, or I had. Surely I had not heard those deadly words?

"Esther, you—wait. We need light." As I padded across the balcony to the room beyond, I thought I heard Esther whisper, "Yes, we do." But it might have been the night wind.

I called for lamps and torches to be brought, and food and drink. Esther said nothing until I came back and tried to lead her inside. "You are kind, Vashti, but I know what I must do. And so do you. You just cannot yet admit that this is the only way."

"It isn't," I said. "You cannot just walk into the king's throne room."

"Why not?"

Because if Ahasuerus does not hold out the scepter of Death and Life to you, you will die. But Esther knew that already. I said, "Suppose—suppose Amestris learns your plan? She will never let you do this thing."

"If she discovers what I plan to do, then you and Hegai must foil whatever plot she comes up with to prevent me. I must see the king. And since he will not come to me, I must go to him. Now there is one more thing we must do."

"What?" I stared at her, baffled.

"What both of us would have done at once, had we not been numbed by shock and horror. Come," Esther said, and grasped my hand.

"Where are we going?"

Esther laced her fingers through mine as she pulled me toward the high doors to her garden. "To see Daniel Dream-Master."

I stopped, and Esther swung around to face me. "Of course, Esther! But it's the middle of the night—"

"—and this cannot wait for a morning that may never come. Now. And I want Hegai to be there as well. Wake one of your little spies and send her to fetch Hegai to us."

ESTHER

Although it was past midnight, neither Daniel nor Samamat seemed surprised to see Hegai, Vashti, and me at their gate. They welcomed us in as if this were the most commonplace of times for a visit. But they wasted no time on pleasantries. They knew nothing less than disaster would bring us here at this hour.

It took only a few words to lay out Haman's plan and hand Daniel a copy of the Adar Law. "Here is the decree, sealed into immutable law. The proclamation is to be posted across the empire tomorrow."

Hegai, Vashti, and I waited in silence as Daniel and Samamat swiftly read the law. All color fled Samamat's face.

"A decree ordering the destruction of an entire race?" Samamat gasped; the horror in her voice echoed against the blue tile walls. "Are all kings mad?"

Daniel laid his hand over hers. "I doubt this king had anything to do with drawing up the law. Note how carefully the proclamation was timed. While the king was away, and giving less than a month to find a way out of this disaster."

Samamat turned her gaze upon him. "Daniel, you do realize this law means they'll kill you, too?"

"Well," said Daniel, in a tone of the utmost reasonableness, "they've been trying to kill me for sixty years. Maybe this time they'll manage to do it."

"I don't think that's in the least amusing, Dream-Master." Even as I said the words, I found myself laughing, and then we all laughed, even Hegai. My laughter turned to tears; Vashti put her arms around me. We looked at Daniel.

"Daniel," I said, "I have come to beg your help."

"My dear child, I don't see what help I can be. I'm only an old man."

"You're the wisest man in all the empire. If you cannot help me . . ." Tears burned my eyes again.

Samamat asked a question that, oddly enough, gave me time to recover my composure. "O queen, exactly what is it that you need from us?"

I closed my eyes, commanded myself to be calm. Serene. No good came from panic. "What I need from you and Daniel, my lady Samamat, is advice."

Queen or no, I sat at Daniel's and Samamat's feet, with Vashti sitting cross-legged beside me and Hegai standing grimly quiet behind us. I told Daniel and Samamat everything that had happened since the moment Haman's summons had been laid in Vashti's hand. "So you see," I finished, "I must ask the king for help. But since his return, he has not sent for me, and I may not go to him unsummoned. Not," I added, "without breaking the law."

"And being cut down by the guards before you can utter a word," Hegai pointed out.

"And have you thought of any way to accomplish this?" Samamat asked. Daniel merely watched, and listened.

"No," I said. "So I will go to him unsummoned and beg his aid. He is the King of Kings. There must be something he can do." I stared down at my hands; hands heavy-laded with gold and precious stones. So much treasure; so useless.

"O queen, I suppose you're planning on going to the king in his bedchamber?" Samamat asked, and I shook my head.

"I don't think that's a good idea. This is a matter of imperial law, of the good of the empire, not just of the lives of the Jews."

"Although it certainly is that," Daniel said, and Samamat shot him a sharp look.

"This cannot be done in darkness, and in secret, as so much in this court is done. This must be seen in the light, so that light may triumph." I sounded more confident than I felt.

"For light to triumph, Ahasuerus must forgive your defiance," Samamat said. "Are you truly willing to trust your life to that?"

I did not pretend to misunderstand. "I love him." Words both loving and rueful.

"Why?" Samamat asked, and I struggled to answer truthfully.

"Why? Who knows? 'Why' is not a word love understands."

"Do you think he loves you?"

"Yes, I think he does—as much as he can. And he will love me more if I teach him to open his heart. He can be a good man."

"Just as he can be a good king," Hegai said, "once he's no longer under his mother's paw."

"A matter of imperial law . . . So you need to act"—Samamat shrugged—"imperially, I suppose."

"What do you suggest, Sama?" Daniel asked. "That Queen Esther march into the throne room and confront the King of Kings before the entire court?"

"Why not?" Samamat asked. "It's not as if things can get any worse."

"My lady Samamat," I said, "I couldn't think of anything else either. So yes, I will march into the throne room and confront the King of Kings before the entire court. You're right—it's not as if things can get any worse."

"Oh, trust me," said Daniel, "things can always get worse." He sounded as if he quoted some oracle of wisdom; Samamat glared at him.

"I must. This is one decision our king must make for himself. No one else can make it for him." I stared into the lamplight as if it could reveal my future, but saw only dancing flames. "I will go before the king. And if I die—then I die."

Slowly, as if speaking with a child, Vashti said, "Esther, he—the king—Ahasuerus—"

I managed to smile. "You need not speak words you think disloyal, Vashti. I know he is as a brother to you. But he is a husband to me. Do you think I do not know my own husband?"

"And if you are wrong?"

"To fear death too much is to fear life." I took her hand, laced her fingers through mine. "And Vashti—I refuse to live in fear."

"Well said." Daniel smiled, but he looked pale and bone-weary. "I don't know why you needed me—you already knew what must be done, and are brave enough to do it. Now how can we help, Hadassah?"

The sound of my true name shattered the unnatural stillness that had frozen the air. Yes, I was still Hadassah. Hadassah owned the courage Esther lacked, and Esther possessed the wisdom Hadassah had not learned. This time my smile was not feigned.

"I have a great favor to ask of you. Daniel, will you and Samamat come to a banquet I shall prepare for Haman and the king? I think we will need your wise counsel at that table."

"A *banquet*? O queen, have you run mad?" For once Hegai's beautiful, practiced control vanished. "Haman plans to murder an entire people—and you wish to ask this monster to a *banquet*?"

"Yes," I said. I could not explain, for I hardly understood myself. I only knew this was the path I must follow.

Hegai drew a shuddering sigh. "A banquet fit for a king and a monster. Very well. When?"

"Tomorrow." I thrust my hands under my crossed legs to stop their trembling.

"I think you mean today," Daniel said. "It will be morning soon—and the Adar Law is being posted even as we speak."

But the Most High had one more jest to play before I must risk all to save thousands of lives. Even I laughed when I heard the tale, and I had the story from a dozen mouths before I even left my bedchamber. But it was Hatach's account that made events I had neither seen nor heard spring to life, thus:

The King of Kings, Ahasuerus, who ruled over all the lands from the Western Sea to the Eastern Mountains, could not sleep . . .

Ahasuerus stared at the ceiling. Deep night, and sleep eluded him. The soft snores of his chamber servants grew infinitely annoying. Why should they sleep when the king could not? Irritated by a particularly loud snore, Ahasuerus flung back the violet silk that covered him and got out of bed.

"I cannot sleep. Read me something."

"What would it please the king to hear?"

"Anything. One of the chronicles of the reign." That should be dull enough to send him to sleep.

"Which chronicle would it please the king—"

"Man, just go and get one. I don't care which."

When the flustered servant returned, Ahasuerus lay back on his bed and bid the man read. And the very first words read to the sleepless king were,

"On the third day of Tammuz, two eunuchs evilly plotted the death of the King of Kings by means of arcane poison. The two eunuchs were named Bigthan and Teresh. The plot was overturned by the virtue of one Mordecai, a king's scribe, who discovered the treachery and told of it, and so the honor and life of the King of Kings was saved."

Ahasuerus waited, but the servant rolled up that section of the scroll and began a new section, concerning the billeting of the Immortal Ten Thousand.

Puzzled, Ahasuerus said, "Stop. What honor did I bestow upon the scribe Mordecai for saving my life?"

The man rolled back the scroll, shook his head. "There is nothing written upon that matter. The record ends with the words 'the honor and life of the King of Kings was saved.'"

"The life, but not the honor if I did not reward the man who saved me from poison." Ahasuerus nodded, and the man continued to read, but Ahasuerus paid no more attention. He was trying to decide how he could have forgotten so important a matter, and how best to now reward a man who should have had honors heaped upon him the very moment the plot was revealed.

And as the sun rose and the king rose from his bed, in which he had not slept, the Grand Prince Haman strode into the king's chamber, for he had the right to help the king greet the day. Seeing his great friend, Ahasuerus smiled, and said,

"Haman, my friend, you'll know—how best may a king reward a man he particularly wishes to honor? Something very special to show his delight in this man."

Now Haman, being proud, and the king's great friend, and the king's vizier besides, thought to himself,

Who can the king mean to honor in such a fashion but me?

"Hatach," I said, trying to sound stern, "You cannot possibly know what that evil wretch Haman *thought.*"

"O queen live forever, I can. For when the Grand Prince Haman at last went home again, he told the tale to his sow-faced wife the lady Zeresh, and she told it to her handmaiden, who told it to the kitchen slaves, who told it to—"

"Yes, yes, I understand. Very well, Haman thought Ahasuerus meant to honor him. Haman would think that, wouldn't he?"

"As my queen says," Hatach agreed, prim-mouthed, and continued.

"Well, my dear Haman?" Ahasuerus asked. "What do you suggest? I know your idea will be good and clever."

And proud Haman, convinced the king wished to honor Haman himself, spoke these prideful words:

"For a man whom the king delights in and wishes to honor, bring a royal robe that the king has worn, and bring a horse the king has ridden. And bring also a crown that has been set upon the king's head. Give these to a great prince of the empire, who will take them to the man the king delights to honor.

"And the great prince shall array the man in the king's robe and the king's crown, and set him upon the king's horse, and lead him through the city, calling out, 'This is how the king delights to honor this man!' "

Ahasuerus smiled. "Thank you, Haman. You're the best of friends, and the best of my great princes. Go and do all, exactly as you said it to me, to Mordecai the Jew. He's one of my scribes, so you should find him working in the King's Gate."

Hatach paused for a much-needed breath as I laughed. I knew nothing had altered: the Adar Law still doomed the Jews. But when I thought of Haman trying to look flattered at the king's trust in him, when surely all Haman wished to do at that moment was shove the King of Kings into the nearest sewer-pit—

"And did Haman do as the king commanded him?" I finally was able to ask, and Hatach nodded. Hatach managed to cough, rather than laugh. I admired his tact.

"Yes, Star of the Palace, the Great Prince Haman obeyed the King of Kings. He took the king's robe and the king's crown, and arrayed Mordecai the Jew in them and set him up on the king's horse and led him through all the streets of the city, calling out, 'This is how the king delights to honor this man!' over and over and over.

"And then," Hatach went on, and the prim laughter vanished from his voice, "Haman went to his palace, looking black-visaged as Ahriman. And Mordecai the Jew put back on his sackcloth and ashes, and once more sits waiting just outside the King's Gate."

"Esther, your Mordecai has been honored by the king! All must be well. Now you're safe, you need not defy the law—" Vashti came dashing in to my room; she burned so bright with happiness I hated to quench it.

I shook my head. "No, Vashti. This is not salvation. This is a jest. A mad, ill-timed jest."

Her brightness faded. "A jest. Whose?"

"I don't know. Perhaps Fate's. The Greeks worship Fate as a god."

"Is Fate stronger than your god?"

I sighed. "No one is stronger than the Most High. But I confess to you, Vashti, that I can't see His hand in this. I must be blind."

Vashti rushed over and flung her arms around me; hugged me hard. Her extravagant hair fell over us both. "You see more clearly than anyone else I know. Except Daniel Dream-Master, of course. And—"

"—and I have also learned that Haman has built a gallows so tall it can be seen over the walls of his house, and plans to hang Mordecai upon it," I said. "So you see, Vashti, nothing has changed. Well, by noon I shall have all my answers. If I do not return, please be kind to my servants."

"You mean to go to the king today? Now?"

"Today. Now. There is no time left, Vashti. Now come and help me dress. I promise not to ask you what I should wear."

VASHTI

I longed with all my heart to accompany Esther to the throne room, but she would not allow it. She argued, rightly, that seeing me would only remind Ahasuerus of what a fool he had been—never a good thing to summon into a man's mind, as Hegai added. Then it was Hegai's turn to demand that he should walk with Esther, and his to be refused.

"No." Esther's voice was gentle, but firm. "I and I alone will risk my life in this. And my life is already forfeit to the Adar Law."

"Do you think we would let anyone harm you?" I demanded, and Esther answered,

"I do not think you would have a choice. I do this alone. But thank you. It is good to have such friends."

"But you cannot go alone." As we all turned to stare, Hatach lifted his head. "I shall escort you to the throne room, O queen." His voice trembled. But he said the words.

"Hatach. Thank you." Esther put her hands on his shoulders, swiftly kissed his cheeks. "No."

Tears shone in Hatach's eyes—whether from sadness at Esther's refusal or relief, perhaps even he did not know. "You can't. All that way . . ."

She smiled. "All the way to the throne? It's not so far, Hatach. All will be over soon. Now I must go—and you must do as I asked."

"Prepare a banquet. Esther, why a banquet? I thought you wanted to ask the king's mercy before all the court."

"There I ask his mercy for me, that I may approach him unsummoned, and live. But that is not the time to ask him to revoke a law that we all know cannot be undone. So I beg him to come to a banquet prepared for him. Everyone will know I have some great boon to beg—and that it is not that he come to a banquet! But until the Adar Law is thwarted and my people are safe, no one must know what it is I ask. So prepare the feast and invite those I have told you. Please, Vashti—or should I say, the queen commands it?"

Esther turned to go; I knew I might never see her again. "Wait," I said. I lifted my hands, carefully, for what I carried remained oddly heavy. Once I had thought I cherished this object above all else that was mine. I looked at the circle of gems glittering in my hands, and then I set the Star Crown upon Esther's head. The crown burned bright against her burning hair.

"This crown belongs to you now, O Queen of Stars. You are the queen I could never have been."

⁂

I did not see Esther walk out of the Queen's Palace and through the courtyards to the King's. Nor did I see what happened when Esther walked into the throne room and between the long lines of men until she reached the steps to Ahasuerus's throne.

So I will tell the tale as it was told to me, and as it still is told from one end of the Royal Road to the other.

Knowing her people's lives hung in fate's balance, Queen Esther fasted and prayed, and then robed herself in a single garment sewn from silk white as the full moon. Wearing her royal crown as her only adornment, Queen Esther went to the king, knowing that if she approached and he did not hold out his golden scepter of Death and Life to her, the king's guards would cut her down at his feet.

And when she set her foot upon the floor of the throne room, all gathered there fell silent as they saw her, until silence filled the vast chamber. For no one might come before the king unsummoned and live.

Queen Esther looked nowhere but at the king, and as she drew near the throne, she smiled at him. And the great king held out his scepter, and Queen Esther touched the tip of the royal scepter, and knew she had won her own life. Then the king said, for he could think of no other reason she had come to him in so extraordinary a manner, against all law and custom,

"What is your request of us, Queen Esther? What is your petition? Whatsoever you ask will be granted."

And Esther the Beautiful replied, "If it please the king, let him come to a banquet I have prepared for him. And let the king bring with him the king's friend Haman."

ESTHER

For many years after, I woke crying out from dreams in which I walked that endless path to the throne. Sometimes Ahasuerus raised his scepter to me too late. Sometimes he turned away and refused to save me. And sometimes he stared and did not see me at all.

But at least I lived to suffer the bad dreams.

Once I had made my request that Ahasuerus bring Haman to a banquet at my palace, I expected to retrace my steps. No longer borne up by fear and hope strong as wine, I dreaded the long walk back through the throne room. But that ordeal I was spared; as I hesitated, Ahasuerus lifted his hand, and the captain of his guards came forward.

"Escort the queen back to her proper place," Ahasuerus said, and the captain led me to a doorway in the wall behind the throne, through private corridors until we reached my palace. I thanked him fervently before we parted, and then ran to my own rooms. I longed to weep for sheer relief, but dared not permit myself such indulgence. I had told Ahasuerus to come at midday, and it was midmorning now.

My instructions had been faithfully carried out, and the banquet I had promised Ahasuerus was being prepared: simple, elegant dishes, cooling sherbets, fresh fruits, the most delicate of wines. Hegai and Hatach would serve us. My other guests already waited: Vashti. Daniel and Samamat.

And Queen Mother Amestris.

I had not been sure Amestris would accept my invitation. I had hoped the lure of so intimate a banquet, the other guests so carefully—so oddly—assorted, would draw her in. I had been right. Queen Mother Amestris could not endure ignorance of anything that passed in the palace; she came to see what I was plotting.

I bowed to her; she inclined her head.

"Do you really," Amestris asked, "propose to entertain the king dressed like that?"

"Why not?" I said. "I walked the length of the throne room dressed like this. Apparently my attire and demeanor pleased the king, for as you see, I still live."

Amestris glared at me; I smiled.

The banquet pleased Ahasuerus; the fact that Daniel Dream-Master and Samamat, Lady of Stars, had come at my asking delighted him. The banquet pleased Haman; that I, his intended victim, so honored him elated him. The rest of us sat tense, waiting—I for the right moment to strike. Amestris watched us all, wary. She sensed something wrong, but did not yet know what it might be.

Ahasuerus smiled at me a great deal.

At last, when Hegai came to the table to pour the king wine from a silver pitcher, Ahasuerus said, "Now tell me, Esther, what is your petition of me, and what is your request? It will be granted, to half my kingdom."

Now. Now the true test begins. Slowly, I rose to my feet. "If it please the king—if it please the king—"

"Yes, queen of my heart? What do you desire?"

I looked around the banquet table; drew strength from Vashti's passionate anger, from Daniel's quiet wisdom and Samamat's calm assurance. Daniel nodded encouragement, and I turned back to face Ahasuerus.

"If I have found favor in the king's sight, and if it please the king, let my life be given me at my petition, and my people's at my request. For we have been sold to be destroyed—"

"What?" Ahasuerus slammed his wine-cup down so hard the wine splashed scarlet over the table. "Esther, is this some ill-thought jest?"

"Ill-thought, yes. But it is no jest, my lord king. I am condemned, as is Daniel Dream-Master—"

Horror flared in Haman's eyes; Amestris seemed turned to stone.

"—and every other Jew dwelling in your empire. On the thirteenth day of Adar, all Jews—from babes to elders—are ordered slain. It is law, written and sealed."

Ahasuerus stared at me, and relief softened his night-dark eyes. "Esther, that's impossible. Only the king could write and seal such a law. And I am the king, and I would never do so evil a thing."

"I know," I said. "It is Haman who wrote the law."

Slowly, Ahasuerus looked to Haman. Haman's face so clearly proclaimed his guilt I had no need to say more. I nodded to Hegai, who summoned the king's guards. Ahasuerus did not trouble to ask how the guards came to be there; he ordered Haman bound and gagged and tossed at my feet.

Then Ahasuerus said, "What is the text of this wicked decree?"

I signaled to Hatach, who went and brought in my cousin Mordecai. I had ordered Mordecai to come to my palace, and to bring a copy of the Adar Law. Now he bowed and handed the law-scroll to Ahasuerus. "This is the text of the Adar Law, O king."

Ahasuerus read the decree Haman had written; in cold anger, he said,

"And who sealed this murderous decree into law?" Only silence answered him. At last, slowly, he turned his gaze upon Queen Mother Amestris.

"Mother," he said, "do you have a copy of the king's seal?"

"I ruled as regent!" Amestris cried.

"When I was a child. Answer my question." Ahasuerus gazed steadily at her.

Amestris tried to stare him down. "I am your mother, Ahasuerus."

"And I am your king, Mother." Ahasuerus held out his hand to Amestris. "Give me the king's seal."

Queen Mother Amestris stared at her son the king, and the rich honey of her skin slowly darkened, then paled, until she looked gray as death. As I looked upon her, I felt sorry for her—until I reminded myself that this woman had sealed the death warrant for an entire people. Time and past time power left her hands.

"Mother. The seal. Now."

Slowly, Amestris reached up to her throat; slowly, she drew a chain up from beneath her gown. A seal of jasper bound with gold dangled from the chain. Amestris lifted the chain over her head, weighed the seal in her hand. Her fingers clutched the seal and she closed her eyes for a long moment. Then, as we all watched, the Queen Mother bent her knee before the king and let the jasper seal slide into his waiting hand.

Ahasuerus closed his fingers over the seal. "I shall have a new Great Seal made. There shall be only one, and no law shall be sealed except by my new cipher." Ahasuerus looked down at his mother, and added, "And I think I shall have a new royal ring created—to match my new seal."

"That is wise, O king," Mordecai said. "But there remains the problem of the order Prince Haman wrote and Queen Mother Amestris sealed into law. I have studied every scroll, read each text in the royal records. There is no way a sealed law can be undone. There is no precedent for revoking such a law."

For long moments, no one spoke. Vashti broke the silence. "Then make such a precedent. Write a new law that states laws sealed with the king's Great Seal may be altered."

"That is unwise—" Mordecai stopped, then said, "O princess, that may seem wise, but it is not. It would invite chaos if sealed laws could be altered at a whim."

For a dozen heartbeats, cold silence surrounded us. Every one of us remembered that it had been a drunken whim that had set into motion events that led inexorably to this moment. Had the king not called for Vashti, had she not refused to obey, had the king not sealed her banishment into law—

Had those things not come to pass, I would not now be Queen of Queens.

And if I had not been chosen queen, there would be no one in all the great palace who would have cared what Haman planned for the empire's Jews.

My voice, clear and calm, broke that silent ice. "True, law should not be subject to whim—but every law in the royal records, every single law the Medes and the Persians now hold sacred, was once new and without precedent."

"My beloved wife is right, and so is her cousin." Ahasuerus glanced at Haman, shackled and silent. "But I have done too many deeds upon the bidding of others, and in haste. Let me think on this. The thirteenth of Adar is still a month in the future."

I bowed; Mordecai looked as if he wished to speak, but did not. Ahasuerus turned to Daniel, who had remained seated, as had his wife.

"My lord Daniel, have you any advice for me? Speak freely."

"Not just at this moment, great king. You seem to be doing well without anyone's aid." Daniel smiled, and moved slightly; when I looked closely, I saw that Daniel Dream-Master's hand leaned heavily upon the lady Samamat's knee. The lady Samamat was biting her lower lip. I wondered what she wanted to say, but decided this was not the time to ask. "Or interference," Daniel added.

"Your good opinion of me means much," Ahasuerus said. "I decree the following now: Haman is no longer prince, no longer entitled to look upon the face of the King of Kings. He is no longer vizier. All his ranks and honors, his lands and riches, are now the property of Mordecai the King's Scribe, who is now the King's Vizier in Haman's place."

Haman made a strangled noise; I thought he would burst like a rotten egg. With that decree Ahasuerus had all but killed Haman. Ahasuerus's next words completed Haman's fate. "And since Haman so thoughtfully built a gallows—hang him on it."

The Immortals began to haul Haman away; I stepped forward. "My lord king?"

Ahasuerus's face softened. "Yes, my queen? Would you have him flayed first?"

I swallowed hard. "No, my lord king. Death is punishment enough."

Death, and the loss of all his ranks and fortune to the Jew he hates most in all this world and the next.

"Then what would my queen have of me?"

I would have been justified had I asked that all Haman's sons be slain and his wife thrown naked into the street. But I could not ask for such evil and remain the woman my husband loved. "I would have Haman's wife, and his children, taken under the king's protection," I said. I did not look at Haman. Whatever Haman's eyes held, I did not want to know or to see.

HEGAI

I looked upon Haman lying bound and gagged at Esther's feet. Two strides would take me to him. And I could at last reveal myself to him. *Yes, "Father," it is I, the son of your first wife, whom you murdered before my eyes. It is I, the boy you tormented for seven years, the boy you gelded and sold into slavery and prostitution. Look upon me and see how utterly you failed to ruin me and my life. Think of me as you die upon your own gallows.*

I had yearned for this moment since I was seven years old; since Haman slit my mother's throat. I had dreamed of vengeance upon him. Now Haman had fallen into a pit of his own digging. Revealing myself to him would add salt to his wounds. *A last torment for him, and still it will not be enough . . .*

As I stared at Haman struggling against his bonds, Vashti grasped my hand; laced her fingers through mine. I looked down into Vashti's face, and knew I would not take those few steps to Haman's side. *For years I have dreamed of making him suffer as I did. But I cannot.* Nothing could make Haman suffer as I had, for he cared for no one and nothing but himself.

And my suffering had led me to love. To Vashti.

With Vashti's hand warm in mine, I turned away from Haman. And as I did, a burden I had not even known I carried slipped from me and vanished. For a moment, I seemed to feel soft, smiling lips against my cheek, and I knew who it was.

Thank you, Mother. And good-bye.

VASHTI

A week later, after Ahasuerus had considered carefully, and asked advice from the wisest men in Shushan—and the wisest women, too, for he asked counsel of both Esther and Samamat—he had a new decree sealed into Median and Persian Law. Once each year, it would now be the right of the King of Kings to revoke or to alter one of the decrees he had sealed into law. The moment he pressed his seal to that decree, he revoked Haman's death-sentence on the Jews. As an added incentive to his subjects to keep peace with their Jewish neighbors, Ahasuerus created a second Adar Law: if any man took up weapons against the Jews, the Jews had the right to defend themselves. If they killed while defending their own lives, it would not be counted murder.

"And the Jews have the right to the property of any who raise weapons up against them," Esther finished reading me the new decree, and smiled. "That's one of the lady Samamat's suggestions. She said the threat of loss of property would restrain more men from violence than the threat of loss of life."

"Do you think she's right?" I asked, and Esther laughed.

"Oh, yes, she's right. I forget you've lived all your life in palaces, Princess Vashti."

"So it's all over now?"

"Yes, I think so. I hope so. I want only to live in peace with my husband." Such love shone in Esther's eyes my own heart ached. She seemed to glow; she laid her hand over her belly, and then I knew. Esther carried Ahasuerus's child.

"I wish I knew what I wanted." I should have been as joyous as Esther; instead, I felt dull and weary. Life in the palace as Esther's friend stretched before me. "I wish . . ."

"What, Vashti?" Esther asked, her voice gentle.

"I wish—oh, not that Ahasuerus loved me as he loves you. But that *someone* did. I look upon Daniel and Samamat, and upon you and Ahasuerus, and—"

I stopped, for Esther was laughing.

"I am glad I amuse the queen," I said stiffly, and rose to my feet. "May I have the queen's permission to leave her presence?"

"Oh, sit down." Esther reached out and caught my hand. "Vashti, you already have what you desire. How can you not know it?"

I stared. "Know what?"

"That Hegai loves you, Vashti. He loves you as a man loves the woman of his heart. Don't you know that?"

I stared at her. "But—"

"But he is a eunuch? They cut off a piece of flesh, Vashti. They did not cut out his mind or his heart."

"He has known me since I was a little girl. How can he love me so? Ahasuerus did not."

"Ahasuerus has always been as a brother to you. Hegai watched you grow up, and he saw what Ahasuerus did not. That you became a woman. A woman he loved."

I tried to stretch my mind to hold this revelation. Since the first day I entered the great palace, Hegai had always been there. Guarding me, caring for me. Loving me.

"Hegai loves me?"

"Deeply. Passionately. Can you love him, Vashti? If you cannot, you should release him."

"But—if I take Hegai from you, you will have no Chief Eunuch." I realized even as I spoke the words were nonsense; that I sought to not think of what Esther had said.

She laughed. "I think Hatach will do in that office. I would rather have a Chief Eunuch who thinks most highly of *me,* not one who's madly in love with my predecessor! Now go, Vashti, and look into your own heart. And think well on what you do next."

⸸

I did as Esther commanded. I looked deep into my own heart, and when I had, I knew that I could no longer stay in the palace, or in Shushan. If ever I were to claim life for myself, I must leave. If I did not, nothing ever would change for me.

I would live and die as nothing more than Princess Vashti, who once had been Queen of Queens.

That is not enough. I did not know the voice that whispered behind my ears. Perhaps it was my grandmother, Ishvari of the Black Horse People. Perhaps it was my own heart. It did not matter. What mattered was that I heeded the warning.

I gathered up the ivory dagger Hegai had given me long ago and sought him in his own chambers. I walked in and stood gazing at him, trying to pretend I looked upon him for the first time. I could not; I had known Hegai too long and too well. But when he looked up at me, startled that I should come to his rooms, I saw the light in his eyes, and his smile, and I thought that perhaps Esther was right. And even if she were not—I owed too much to Hegai to abandon him now.

He had never abandoned me.

"Vashti," Hegai said, "what are you doing here? Is something wrong?"

I shook my head. "No. I came to tell you that I am leaving, Hegai. And to ask if you will come with me."

My words brought him to his feet. "And you say nothing is wrong? Do not tell me you have quarreled with Queen Esther!"

"No, I have not. Nor have I yet told her what I tell you now. I am nothing here, Hegai. I must go."

"Go and do what?" Hegai scowled at me, as if I were again the little girl new-come into Shushan's palace. "You are a princess; you are not meant for harsh roads and hard ground. Now listen to me, little queen, and—"

"Stay here and rot slowly, like overripe fruit that no lips will ever taste?" I shook my head. "No. I am leaving. Come with me."

"I? I am Chief of the King of Kings' Eunuchs. I rule the Women's Palace." His eyes darkened; old and sad. "What is there for me beyond these walls and gates?"

"What is there for me? I will never know if I remain here. Come."

Again Hegai shook his head. I drew in a deep breath and lifted my hands to my hair. Slowly, I pulled out the golden pins that had held up the heavy mass. My ivory hair tumbled down my back; it reached my knees.

From my sash, I pulled the leopard-headed dagger and held it out. "Cut off my hair, Hegai."

That shocked him out of grief. "Little queen, you can't be serious! Your beautiful hair!"

"I'm not little, I'm not a queen, and I am not my hair, Hegai. Cut it off. It's too heavy anyway."

"No. You'll be sorry tomorrow. You always are."

"Not this time." I walked forward and laid the dagger in Hegai's lap. I put my hands on his shoulders and slowly, giving us both time to withdraw, I leaned forward and put my lips to his. The moment our mouths touched, I knew Esther was right. Hegai loved me—and not as a brother did his sister.

More than that, the caress of his lips awoke something within me that until now had slept.

Passion.

Shaken, I pulled back. "You have always loved me better than I deserved, and I was too blind to know that until now. And I love you." I slid my hands up to his cheeks. "How could I *not* love you? You have protected me, taught me, guided me safely through the court's dark shadows.

"I do not know if I can love you as you love me, but I am willing to try. I am leaving this place. I beg you to come with me."

For long moments he said nothing, as I counted my heartbeats and slowly the warm strength that had brought me here ebbed. Then, just as I was about to beg his pardon and walk away, Hegai stood up.

"How short do you want your hair, my love?" he asked, smiling.

On the thirteenth of Adar, we stood at the palace gate, Hegai and I, with our horses awaiting us and all that we would carry with us loaded upon three pack camels. That was Esther's doing; I had first thought to ride off and leave all behind. Gently, Esther had pointed out that I would need food and clothing, money and supplies. And she had firmly ensured that I had them.

She had insisted I take servants, too; strong men to tend the camels and guard us upon the road. "Freedom is strong wine, Vashti, and its taste is new to you. But you cannot simply gallop off with only the clothes on your back and no one to protect you."

So: a small caravan. A woman, a man. Servants and pack animals. Waiting to say farewell, and depart as the sun rose to light our path.

Queen Esther had come to the gate to watch me ride away. Hatach stood beside her, pride in his rank as Chief Eunuch giving him new distinction. "So this is good-bye," Esther said. "Vashti, you are certain this is what you wish to do? I cannot persuade you to remain?"

I glanced over at Hegai, who smiled at me. I shook my head.

I stood there beside Sunrise, feeling the mare's breath warm against my neck. I looked at Esther, and heard myself say, "Come with me. Ride with me as my sister."

For an instant she looked—wistful, I thought later. Then she smiled, and shook her head, and the tiny gems chained into her dark-fire hair glinted like hungry eyes.

"I can't. Even if I could bear to leave Ahasuerus, there is—"

"The child. Yes, I know. You'll be a good queen."

"Perhaps. I can only try. It will be easier once the scandal Haman caused is forgotten. That will not take many moons. This is the court of Persia; memories last only so long as they are convenient."

She would make a better queen than I had done. Perhaps all queens should be reared first by horse-traders and then by scholars. Just as I no longer needed the shelter of a palace, the false protection of a crown, she no longer needed either Hegai or me. Sunrise blew upon my neck; a soft warm reminder that she waited.

"This is farewell, then." I set my hand upon Sunrise's muzzle. Soft as velvet. I smoothed my hand down her proudly arched neck. Strong as steel. So would I be; strong and gentle both. And more, I would be free. Free to be hungry, to be tired, to be dead if I could not keep myself alive.

I can. I can live. And I can die. I can be Vashti. I thought of embracing Esther, of kissing her, but already she seemed to withdraw, shielded by the silk and jewels glowing in the dawn light. So I did neither. I merely said, "O queen, live forever," and turned and vaulted up onto Sunrise's waiting back.

And so we rode out the palace gate, Hegai and I, as the sun rose and the palace turned to burning gold behind us. I looked back, once, but the gate was shut and the Immortals stood before it once more, faceless and silent.

"Which way, my heart?" Hegai asked, and I laughed.

"Does it matter?" I reached into my belt and pulled out the *pur*—the lot—that I had taken from Haman. As Hegai watched, I closed my eyes and flung the small carved bit of bone into the air. I opened my eyes again, looked down into the dust beneath my horse's feet.

"That way," I said. Hegai would have dismounted, to retrieve the *pur* and set it once more into my hand, but I shook my head. It was morning, and I had no more need of anything from the palace. The *pur* had told me all I needed to know. Men and women hastened past us through Shushan's great gates into the city, seeking the center of the world. Hegai and I rode out through those gates, to the west, following the rays of the rising sun.

HEGAI

Delighting in Vashti's joy, I rode after her. I had known my beloved since she was ten years old; I knew her thoughts. Well, she had divulged them to me eagerly enough, between eager kisses. Vashti yearned to be free, to ride beyond the horizon. She craved passion and adventure. She desired to chase the sun into the west.

And so she will . . . for a time. I saw no reason Vashti should not indulge these yearnings. *I, too, will savor this time of freedom.*

But Vashti had been born a princess of Babylon; she had been wife of the King of Kings. She could not run wild into the world—not forever. She would not be safe, and if I knew nothing else about Vashti, I knew that never again would she consent to be a pawn in the games of power. Never again would she endure being a weapon in someone's hand. She could not be free and unguarded both.

My poor queen, you cannot live as the wind's darling. Oh, she might pretend for a span of time—but soon or late, we must return to our proper place.

That place was a palace. A palace at the foot of the mountains awaited us, given with goodwill by Ahasuerus. There Vashti's servants and her pets waited for us. Yes, a palace of our own—and within its walls Vashti would rule my heart.

But for now—for now, let us follow the lot she has cast. I do not care where we ride, so long as we ride there together. I smiled and touched the flowers I had tucked carefully into my sash. Blooms plucked from the garden I had planted for her, when I thought dreams were all I would ever possess.

I looked back at the palace gate, gleaming panels closed upon the merciless years I had spent behind walls and hate. *Hegai dwelt there. I do not.*

The palace of the King of Kings lay behind us. Ahead lay our future. Smiling, I reined in my horse. "Wait, my love," I called to Vashti. "I have something I wish to tell you at last." She slowed her mare and turned back to me, smiling. "What is it, Hegai?"

"My name is Jasper," I told her, and handed her the nosegay of scarlet poppies.

ESTHER

After Vashti and Hegai rode away, I climbed the stairs to the roof of my palace. There I gazed out into the west, as if I could watch their journey into tomorrow. But by the time I reached my post, even the dust of their passing no longer hung in the warming air. I remembered the days when I had ridden with the wind, and for how many years I had longed for nothing more than to reclaim that childhood freedom. *Now I am only a queen, and never again will I run where I wish.* I sighed; footsteps came up soft behind me. I sensed my beloved's presence, and reached out to him. Ahasuerus grasped my hand.

"What troubles your heart, beloved?"

I owed him too much, loved him too well, to fob him off with *Nothing, O great king. Nothing can trouble me while you are with me. He deserves truth, as well as love.*

"I envy Vashti. She is free to ride where she wills now. Truthfully, my love, I did not think you would let her go." I had even doubted Ahasuerus would permit her to marry Hegai. The King of Kings does not easily open his hand and free what he holds—even if he does not desire what he possesses.

To my surprise, Ahasuerus laughed. "She's wild as a falcon, but she rides with Hegai, and he drives a harder bargain than any merchant. Yes, I let her go. I trust Hegai to take care of her—and when he thinks the time is right, he will hood his ivory falcon and teach her the joys of—"

"Chains?" I asked, and Ahasuerus released his hold on my hand and put his hands on my shoulders, turning me until I faced him.

"Have I chained you, Esther?"

I searched his face, seeking truth. Neither anger nor sorrow marred him now. He waited for my answer, waited until I choose to give it. "Of course, my lord." I reached up and laid my hands against his cheeks. "For I love you, and that is a stronger chain than iron or fear. And Vashti loves Hegai. And because that is so, for him she will be tame—"

Ahasuerus raised his eyebrows. "Willingly? *Vashti?*"

I laughed. "Yes, my king and my love. Vashti."

"And you, my queen? Have I tamed you? The danger you fought has passed. If I take my hands from you, and say that you may go free and with all honor if you desire—would you choose to walk away from the palace, Esther? From the crown? From me?"

I smiled and slid my hands down over his shoulders, his arms, his hands; I wove my fingers through his.

"From the palace and from the crown, yes, easily. From you? Never. How many times must I tell you that I love you, Ahasuerus?" I lifted his hands and kissed them; looked up smiling. "Let me tell you one thing more."

"One thing more?"

"Yes. My last secret." I lifted his hands and kissed them; looked up smiling into his cloudless eyes. "My name is Hadassah."

To my surprise, he bent over my hands and kissed them as I had his. "Yes, my queen, my last and best and only love. I know."

EPILOGUE

Dreams

DANIEL

Sunset; in the small courtyard the day's heat pooled, a comfort to old bones. Daniel and Samamat sat watching as shadows darkened. In the endless sky above them, the first stars burned. "The brightest stars," Samamat said. "The strongest stars. They appear first each night."

"The brightest and the strongest." Daniel gazed up at the faraway stars. "Bright and strong. Like our two queens."

"The fiery star and the fixed star. What do you suppose she'll do? Vashti, I mean." For Samamat, there were no light questions, and so Daniel considered the matter thoroughly before answering.

"In truth, Samamat, I don't know. She might do anything or nothing. Perhaps she and Hegai will settle down and farm. Perhaps she'll lead an army. Who knows?"

"I hope she'll be happy. I hope they'll both be happy. We'll never know, will we?"

"Not unless you see them in the stars."

"Or you in dreams."

They both knew neither the stars nor dreams revealed truth so easily.

For a while they sat silent; savored the comfortable, easy quiet of long intimacy. Just the two of them now, where for so many years it had been three. . . .

"At least we're still here to see what happens," Daniel said, and Samamat smiled.

"With a new queen and a king who might as well be new, considering the change in his conduct? Yes, that will be amusing to watch. Sometimes, Daniel, I think it's good to be old. Whatever happens, good or bad, it won't affect us for long."

"You know, I'm not sure that's actually a lot of comfort, Sama."

"It should be. Think about it: suppose we were the young king and queen, waiting to see if Haman's plot would succeed—it so easily might have. And if it did, imagine how many years we'd have to hear screams and weeping in our dreams."

"Samamat, do you remember Susannah?"

"Of course, Daniel." Samamat hesitated, took his hand before she went on, "You haven't mentioned her name in years. Why now?"

"Do you realize that if I hadn't saved Susannah's life, I might never have come to Shushan? And if I hadn't . . ." *If I had not been here, would Vashti have refused the king's command? Would Esther have become queen? If I hadn't been here to advise two queens—*

"If you hadn't—?" Samamat prompted, and Daniel lifted their clasped hands and kissed her fingertips.

"If I hadn't, I'd probably be lying dead now, along with all the other Jews in the empire. Without Vashti and Esther standing in his way, Haman's plot probably would have succeeded."

"Well, Haman's plot *was* foiled, and Haman's dead. One man instead of many. That's a good come out of evil." A breeze sighed through the olive leaves. Samamat paused, listening. "Do you know, for a breath there I thought I heard Arioch."

"Oh? And what did he say?"

"That 'it would have saved everyone a lot of trouble if Grand Prince Haman had accidentally fallen off his horse riding down the Great Staircase and accidentally broken his damn neck. My lord king.'" Samamat mimicked Arioch's dry, matter-of-fact tone so closely it made Daniel smile.

"Yes, I can just hear him saying it. If he'd only still been alive . . ."

"Haman would have met an unfortunate accident?"

"I think so. Yes. You know what Arioch was like."

"Practical," she said.

"Yes," said Daniel. "Very practical."

Samamat sighed and laid her head on Daniel's shoulder. "Oh, Daniel—I do miss him. You know I love you, but—"

"You loved him, too. I know. So did I, Sama."

"We still love him, Daniel. You don't stop loving someone just because he's no longer in this world."

"No, I suppose not."

"But I do wonder where he is now, and what he's doing."

Unbidden, dreamless, a vision rose before Daniel: Arioch, garbed in his warrior's armor, arguing with a dark gatekeeper. . . .

"I'm sure that wherever he is, he's being Arioch. You're the astrologer, Sama. What do the stars tell you?"

"The same thing your dreams tell you, Daniel." Samamat kissed his cheek, and smiled. "That he'll be waiting."

ACKNOWLEDGMENTS

First and foremost, thanks to my sisters: Rosemary Edghill, whose advice about using music has gotten me through days of no "inspiration" or even "desperation," and Bonnie Edghill, who thinks I'm a great writer, even though she's read all my books and should know better. Rosemary—Arioch, Samamat, and Daniel are for you, with love. Bonnie—Star is for you, ditto.

Heartfelt thanks to:

Nichole Argyres, my wonderful and perceptive editor.

Michelle Ayala—you were right, Michelle; moving the computer *did* help!

Rebecca Bridge, whose magic touch brought my characters to pictorial life.

Laura Chasen, for helpful comments—and for making me get things done on time.

Ginger Garrett, for encouragement, inspiration, and her terrific Biblical novels.

Anna Ghosh, my perceptive and wonderful agent.

Nicole Jordan, for advice, cheerleading, and her spicy romance novels.

Michael Kourtoulou, for perceptive comments, music, and (you guessed it) encouragement.

Cynthia Ripley Miller, for support and comments, and "Sunrise"!

Kylah O'Neill, who provided an organized character.

Ajashea Perez (and her cousin Crystal) who kindly allowed me to use their names, and who provided me with two intelligent, enthusiastic characters who really deserve their own book.

Laura Pilkington, who, when I was positive I would *never* finish this story, reminded me that "You say that *every* book. You'll get it done—you always do."

Diane and Buddy Rawlings for supportive comments and for sending me *One Night With the King* (which I spent lots of time rewatching when I suppose I should have been writing . . .).

Jill Eileen Smith, for inspiration, encouragement, and her terrific Biblical novels.

Lauren Hougen, for her keen eyes.

NaNá Stoelzle, my copy editor, who made sure cousins stayed cousins and the Great Staircase wasn't built twice.

And a very special "thank you" to J. O'N., S. C., and D. J. I couldn't have done it without you!